"Each of us has a vision of good and of evil. We have to encourage people to move towards what is good. Follow the good and fight evil as we perceive it. That will be enough to make the world a better place."

Acknowledgements

First and foremost I would like to thank my grandmother who never gave up on me. We did it! I would not be where I am today if it weren't for her love and effort. My lovely wife (Feedie) for giving me the daily inspiration to follow my dream of becoming a published author. She is the perfect woman for me, and I would be lost without her. My sister for putting the finishing touch on everything. And lastly, I'd like to thank the Creator for protecting me as I experienced the brutalities of life; which I now share with the world. To all the foster children, abused women, and forgotten souls I've met during this journey; help is on the way. God willing, this fiction book will spur real-life change.

Pierced

By

A

Rose

Harrison Charles

Buttress Publishing Company

2448 Broad Creek Dr.

Lilburn, Ga. 30087

All Buttress titles, imprints and distributed lines are available at special quality discounts for bulk purposes, for sales promotion, premiums, fundraising, educational or institutional use.

Buttress Publishing and the Buttress Publishing logo Reg. U.S. Pat. & TM Office.

ISBN 978-0-9903079-2-1

Pierced

By

A

Rose

Harrison Charles

Prologue

"Excuse me sir.........."
"Sir!................"
"*SIR!!!!!*"
"What do you want?" mumbled the man.
"You can't sleep here. You'll have to find somewhere else to go."
"Yeah?.........Go to hell," he spat, rolling back over chasing sleep.
The sound of screeching tires, blaring horns, and a woman's scream yanks his attention away from the trespasser. Adding to his bewilderment, engines rev and shouts of profanity begin. Assuming there's been an accident, the suited man runs from the awning covered entrance, and dashes across the parking lot. The second he makes it to the street, he sees him. Known around

town as "Doc", he was once a highly respected surgeon, but alcohol has beaten him out of everything he owned. Stripped of his medical license, he wanders the streets of Atlanta in an intoxicated daydream wearing his old lab coat telling stories of how his shaking hands used to save lives. Being nine in the morning, he's already so inebriated, he's collapsed on the side of the road with his feet hanging in the street. The group of people at the bus stop gasp laugh and gawk—out come the camera phones. The city bus operator stops and throws the

hazard lights on; packed with commuters rubbernecking and pointing.

"He was stumbling in the street yesterday when I saw him," the driver begins. "I thought he was going to get hit for sure today. Remember when he used to be in the papers? Messed up how life did 'em. Let me see if can get nine one-one on the line," said the suit.

The club bouncer lifts him with care. Working this strip for the past twenty years, he's encountered Pearl on multiple occasions. Being the city's premier district for seedy entertainment; nightclubs, new-age speakeasies, hotels, and lounges sit buddied like beetles and dung balls.

Pearl has a deteriorated stethoscope around his neck with a flask in his back pocket. Soaked in his own urine, he smells like a liquor haul. The tragedy of him losing his family to a drunk driver the night he was to accept an award from the American Medical Association plunged him into an abyss of heavy drinking and deep depression, and before he knows, he's sleeping behind a laundromat without a penny to his name.

"Instead of taking pictures, why don't y'all help!" he yells to the people huddled around.

A gentlemen gets off the bus and runs to assist. After pulling him to the sidewalk, he stands to his feet and shakes his hand. "Thanks brother. People suck nowadays."

Thirty minutes later an ambulance arrives to take the former surgeon to the hospital.

The bouncer returns to his post, irritated the homeless man has the audacity to still be sleeping there. He hurries his stride, reaches down, and pulls the wool blanket off, exposing his frail body to the mid-fall chill.

"Why don't you get out of here? How many times do I have to tell you these people don't want you sleeping in front of their business?"

"They ain't even open. Do whatever you want. I don't have anywhere else to go. So like I said, go to hell," and uses a section of the tattered cardboard he's lying on to fling over himself.

A folded blue tarp masquerades as a pillow, the backpack tucked between him and the brick holds his scant possessions.

The brute in the suit promptly grabs the makeshift bed and begins dragging.

"HEEEEEY!"

He's rolled off, the bed thrown aside.

"Why don't you go find yourself a shelter or something? This is private property, act like a human being. I don't want to physically remove you from the premises, but you're leaving me no choice."

"Go to hell I said," pushing himself off the ground.

Reluctantly he begins gathering his possessions.

"What's your name?"

"Vagabond."

The bouncer snickers.

"Say,…I've got a couple warrants. Go on and call the cops so I can get a few hot meals and a cot before the winter sets in," holding out his wrists.

The doorman looks at the fresh slashes and responds:

"…Go to hell," and prepares to leave.

As he unlocks the door and ambles back inside he turns.

"If you really wanna die, quit playing with yourself and run out into traffic. If not, you should find a way to get in touch with your higher power, find something to lift yourself out of this hole you're in. I'm sure something gives you a reason to live; go find a purpose or something," and slams the door.

The adult entertainment megaplex doesn't open until two o'clock, and it's barely nine twenty. The man with no destination heads off the property. A stray dog locked in a zigzagging pattern sniffs the ground for edibles, a putrid mound of decomposing squirrel flesh merits a slight wag of the tail, but deemed ineligible for a meal.

The iridescent morning sun warms the side of his face, a breeze sneaks coolly up his leg. He feels the greasy film encapsulating his sock-less feet, and can only imagine how bad they'll smell once he takes them off.

A series of buses-planes-trains-and-automobiles drive, fly, rumble, and speed by in-route to deliver occupants to the un-known. Meanwhile he traverses the busy thoroughfare seemly oblivious to the reckless abandon of the frenzied morning rush, equally oblivious a wanted fugitive is brazenly walking down the street in broad daylight. The dusty duffle bag hangs lazily over his shoulder while his wrinkled trousers are falling down. Up ahead, the intersection offers a bench riddled with three unsanc-tioned advertisements, two traffic control devices, and one path to obscurity; regardless of which way he wanders.

A rush of blood to courses through his veins! Something resem-bling a crumpled green back seesaws precariously on the edge of the bench. Excitement quickens his pace, and much to his sur-prise it *is* a green back, and a twenty dollar one at that! The day seems to be turning for the better! He's fallen a long way since his days of blowing money on strippers and owning a successful restaurant. There was a time when he would've turned his nose up at someone chasing a dollar, but now he's being sneered at. Only a second ago he found the money and it's already burning a hole in his pocket.

Some old habits never die.

His stomach is telling his brain it needs some filler, his brain is telling his stomach to shut the hell up; this twenty dollars is going on his habit.

"Fucking prick talking about finding God, finding a purpose. Screw him! He don't know anything about me. He don't know what I've been through, he don't know why I'm out here."

The Waffle House diner across the street is pumping out aromas of things being scattered, smothered, covered, and chunked.
His stomach growls.
Hopefully the owner won't throw him out this time, considering he'll be a paying customer instead of a restroom sleeper.
Preparing to commit the petty crime of jaywalking, he steps off the curb and onto the boulevard, and is almost hit by a vehicle rounding the corner at high speed!
Looking through the windshield, he thought he recognized the female in the passenger seat of the fast moving Chrysler® 300. The notion he saw the infamous person from his past only pushes him further into remembrance of his former life, the one of a little boy who grew into the adopted brother of one of the nation's most prolific villains. There's not a second that goes by where he doesn't think the authorities are about to arrest him. That's the reason he's been condemned to the life of a homeless drifter. It's the only way he can afford to hide.

Occasionally, the thought to go to the precinct and spill his guts crosses his mind, but is quickly discarded. Especially since they haven't proven anything yet. The warrant states: Sought for questioning. They have no hard evidence proving he's involved in anything, only hunches hearsay and suspicions. What they're really after is a mouth swab, or a lock of his hair. Since he's not a convicted felon, the state crime database has no profile of him. Broke, destitute, and ostracized from his family, hiding within the city's homeless community made sense on many levels. Alexander Zarbin and his *Fat Man's Bar and Barbecue,* are both shells of themselves; with the latter being sold and leveled to make way for the new *AMP Motor Sports Complex*. As Alex reaches the other side, he notices an outstretched arm hanging out the window of a burgundy '92 Camry. Telling from the look of the car, they're in no position to be giving away anything. But he bows his head and takes it anyway.

The elderly black woman offers a warm smile and grabs his hand. "Trouble don't last always baby…You just make sure you do something good for the world when the lord delivers you from this tribulation."

"Yes, ma'am. Thank you, and may God bless you too."

She pats his hand and drives away.

"Hell she talking about God, I believe in me."

The closer he gets to the entrance of the 24-hour eatery, the clearer the image of the passenger in the car becomes. Now on the property, he can see the people inside looking his way hoping he's not about to come in. Opening the swing-glass door he's mugged by the smell of fresh coffee, creamy grits, and sizzling meats being cooked to perfection. The woman at the register gives him a stale glance before reading of a long list of shorthand words from the yellow ticket she's holding. Somehow the burly cook understands every word, because the more she yells, the quicker he grabs items from the fridge and pantry. From the looks on the customer's faces, and the way their eyes burn into him, he isn't exactly a welcome sight. The man driving the 300 is sitting facing him, the woman has her back turned so he's yet to verify if she's indeed the woman from his past. He'll have to play it safe if he's going to find out, because if he doesn't produce some money fast, he'll be tossed out. Holding the twenty dollar bill in plain sight, he grabs a menu and sits the money on the counter. Taking a seat he can smell the odor hemorrhaging from his shoes and knows others can too. He'd caked a mound of baking soda under his armpits, but still, the stench has grown quite overpowering. Obviously the patron beside him thinks so too, because she grabs her plate and relocates to another booth. "Is this for here or to-go?" asked the clerk who appears out of nowhere. The tone of her voice tipping her hand to what she's hoping.

Despite the body odor and hard stares, he can't leave until he looks at the woman. But the guy she's with keeps glancing in his direction. He'll have to come up with a way to get close without getting ejected. The fact that he's a paying customer comes with certain legal protections. As long as he's spending money and isn't causing trouble, he can't be forced to leave. But he's a fugitive so he doesn't want to take any chances. Alex decides to make himself comfortable by taking of his jacket, his partially white shirt gives the impression it's clean, though he's been wearing it for the past four nights and three days. Sleeping with his clothes turned inside out hides the stains that come from lying on the ground. It also keeps people from seeing just how dirty he really is.

"It'll be for here," he answers with pride.

She rolls her eyes. "What?.....You ordering coffee?"

"*Yes!* For right now, that'll be all."

"Well you probably don't wanna' wait too long because we're real busy this morning. You sure you don't want it to-go?" hand on her hip.

Glancing over the top of the menu he hears the waiter's words, but he's focused on the woman who's preparing to get up.

"I'll take a waffle and a chicken breast *with* a coffee."

"Yeah? You sure about that?"

"Anything else?"

"Yes. Let me get a glass of water too please. Since you asked."

She sucks her teeth. "Sure," but not before seizing the money from the table.

The woman is now standing speaking to the guy. Judging from the rear, it seems like it could be the same lady, the wide hips and ample bottom are evident.

The moment she spins and starts walking his way, their eyes

meet.

Her strut is unmistakable! Her perfume is a rush of jasmine and juniper as she passes looking at him as if he's just another thirsty admirer.

Those hypnotizing brown eyes are unforgettable! *It's her!*

As she proceeds to the Jukebox to select a tune, her male companion keeps a close watch on him. A slick smirk appears on his face as he retrieves a cellphone from his pocket and answers. The waitress returns with his water.

He requested a glass, but before him sits a Styrofoam cup with a plastic lid.

"Maybe the glasses are reserved for the unsoiled customers," he smarts as she walks away.

Though it's been almost four years, he still remembers the night he and his late adopted brother Stockton decided to forgo the night's reconnaissance mission in favor of a more stimulating assignment.

Atlanta, GA, staked in 1837 by a Zero Mile Post, it marked the founding of its original name: Terminus. Though a beautiful and sought-after city, it also has an ugly and long standing history with strip clubs, prostitution, and government corruption. *Dream Kings* has some of the nation's preeminent female offerings, even people from abroad come to oblige them-selves to the plethora of beautiful women, many of whom are underage runaways trafficked from around the country. Atlanta, GA ranks as the world's #1 destination for human trafficking. A recent report commissioned by the Justice Department esti-mates that between 100-200 girls each day are sold into slavery in the city, far outpacing established heavyweights like Miami, Washington, D.C., Oakland, CA, and Queens, NY.

The plan was to have a few drinks and get a dance or two, but that was before he met this exquisite vixen who called herself *"Bailey Red"*. Ms. Red claimed to be twenty two years old, and a transplant from Toledo, OH. After hiring her for the normal run-of-the-mill partially nude teases, "Tim" elected to get up close and personal, and joined her in the secluded VIP room. Admission to this reserved area set him back two hundred and fifty dollars, and the cost of dances increased from ten to twenty five. Once there, she dazzled him with suggestive exhibitions of her anatomy, and after being fondled to near ejaculation, she proposed an erotic tryst off site. For thirteen hundred she offered to spend the night with him. He accepted, and subsequently had the most memorable night of his life. Fittingly, he wanted a replay and returned many nights thereafter, but it was like she vanished.

Now here she is, walking back past him after selecting a jam from the juke box. But she's looking nervous like something's wrong? It's obvious she's completely forgotten him and has no clue why this white man is staring so strangely at her.

The man she's with whispers something in her ear,

causing her to glance over her shoulder at him and shrug. A waiter stops at their table with two glasses of orange juice. The man says something to her and moments later she's heading his direction.

"Sir! Some of our customers are complaining about you looking them down."

Alex doesn't say anything.

"I'm not trying to be rude, but you have odor! Why don't you just wait outside and I'll bring your food?"

He smiles.

"Well I guess the sooner you get my food cooked, the sooner I'll eat and be out. But I won't be stepping outside. I think I'll just wait right here."

Agitated by his refusal, she sighs and spins away, before entering an office behind the kitchen. After about a minute a man sticks his head out, looks at him, and fans her away.

She shoots Alex another dirty look, and returns to refilling customer's glasses.

Seeing his message has been delivered, the man continues his conversation on the phone.

While Alex's brain works on a way to speak to her, his peripheral vision notices sun reflecting off the roof of a slow moving luxury vehicle. Black in color, and heavily tinted, it shines with waxed brilliance and doesn't seem to be your normal type of automobile; its gait is much too regal for this side of town. As the car continues past the building and around the side, the man with Bailey Red catches a glimpse of the car and his face changes.

In the seconds it takes for Alex to pick up something from his body language, the waitress returns with two steaming plates of food, places them on the table, and slides the condiments to the center.

BAM!

He slams the phone to the table, sending orange juice splashing in the woman's face, drenching her apron. She jumps from the sudden shock of the cold liquid against her skin! Spoons and plates drop, the startled cook scalds himself with hot grits!

For a second it looks as if she's about to lose her temper, but remembers her tip, and her $7.25 an hour, and her two children. With no support from the deadbeat father, she's on her own— swallows her pride, flashes a smile, and everything's okay.

"It happens all the time."

He on the other hand offers no apology, not even the recognition of what he just did, only scowls and whispers a quick word to the lady with him, takes a moment to situate himself, and heads for the exit without even looking her direction.

She blots the mess and heads to the office with her head hung and tears in her eyes.

A highly decorated war vet who flew with the Tuskegee Airmen, sits in the corner booth glaring with disgust at the sight of the rude young punk. The fact he's black just like him only further infuriates the honorable senior citizen. It's stupid thugs like this who make it hard for upstanding blacks, and to him, there's nothing worse than seeing a black man acting ignorant.

Alex watches the athletically-built dipshit head through the door and disappear around the side of the building.

He turns his attention to her. He'll have to think fast, but rationally. It's no telling what'll happen if an altercation ensues and the police are called. His adrenaline surges as he realizes this may be his only opportunity to make a move! But what's the move? What's he doing? What's he hoping to accomplish by speaking to a stripper he copulated with years ago? What can he possibly offer her?

But what can she possibly offer him is the question?

Being sure not to walk too fast as to seem overly submissive, but not too slow as to come across as nonchalant; he regains his composure as he prepares to meet the boss. The slime known as, "Troy Merciless" possesses the keys to Atlanta's shadowy under-world, one which consists of wealthy businessmen, mega-star athletes, an exploding film industry, and captive sex workers. Merciless guards the gate to this evil empire, but the being in-side the air conditioned vehicle is the one who rules the realm. As he makes his way around the curved alleyway, he locks eyes with the familiar 6' 8" behemoth holding the rear door. At four hundred pounds, he's one big S.O.B. Wearing a tailored suit, single-breasted, with size 23 Italian oxfords, he has the nerve to be fashionable. The twin Glock .40's holstered under each arm seem redundant. One would rather get shot twice than get hit once by him. With fists the size of bowling balls, they're sure to cause sudden death.

Once again making certain his cocky persona is in check, he definitely doesn't upset his superior. Taking a deep breath and a hard swallow, it's always a hairy situation when dealing with him. He's the headmost vulture in a self-eating world of rats maggots and roaches.

"Zeus," he greeted, before ducking inside.

He nods and shuts the door.

The confines of the limousine are dark and uninviting, the leather seats are comfortable and goose bumps prickle his skin; partly from the abnormally cold temperature, and partly from the extreme fear he has of the person he's sitting beside. The power he's emits is incapacitating.

Merciless keeps his head forward, it's against policy to walk ahead of him, or to initiate conversation without his permission. So he looks down at the long, gaunt, white fingers of the chairman, wondering why he popped on him like this. On his pinky is a ring said to allow the wearer intersection with the universe's dark forces, his hands are tightly interlaced with each nail neatly manicured. The mere sight of them, the way they seem to radiate terror spurs him to look away; he's well aware of the atrocities they command. To the outside world he's Troy Merciless, but now he's Terry Bostic, a two bit street chump who rose from crack head auto mechanic to an "esteemed" position. Despite being utterly reprehensible, the position affords him tremendous amounts of latitude and privilege. Fortunately, more than he knows what to do with. Getting there by proving his loyalty when he accepted a virtually impossible assignment no one else was willing to. No one knows how, but he proved victorious and claimed his prize. However, he as well as the other "help" know, they will never become fully vested members. It's no cleansing to be undertaken, no challenge to complete. To higher-ups they're only pawns, expendable tools used to protect and serve the ilk. In return for their loyalty, they're thrown a few scraps of sirloin, and a complementary seat at the table. But the prized filet, and the reins of power reside with *them.*

Only his breathing can be heard, and he wonders why it seems so forced. Though he's exhaling as softly as he can, it still seems loud.

"Why are you sweating archon?" asked the abominable figure. He didn't know there's perspiration dripping down the side of his face, and quickly uses his wrist to wipe it off, being sure not to make the fatal mistake of accidently elbowing him in the face. "I apologize my lord. I was unaware," he responds, still looking ahead.

Staring at the back of the driver's seat, and the side of Zeus' leg, he hears the rustle of movement and cuts his eyes to see him reach inside the center console. His heart begins racing! He tries to remember if he's done anything that can get him killed! But grew at ease when he notices a manila file folder has found its way on his lap.

"Do you recall our recent conversation and the instructions?"

"Yes my lord. I remember exactly."

"Inside are your new ones."

Without hesitation he opens the file and begins viewing the photographs and reading documents. Blueprints of a guarded shipping port, shift change times, banking information, medical histories, etc. Bostic has risen through the ranks of the minions by being fearless in his approach of managing the boss's minor affairs. But this latest assignment has him wondering if this is really a ploy for his assassination. He'll have to exhibit extreme caution if he's going to question his superior.

"My lord, if I may be so kind as to speak freely?"

The man-like being studies him.

"Proceed."

"Thank you my lord. To be sure I am following your exact order. The information you've provided are pictures of the objectives?" Pausing, he expects an explanation. But there's nothing but the low hum of the 8 cylinder engine, and the outside chatter of the a.m. commute.

He continues.

"I also don't see any in the instructions altering the method of extraction and termination. Are they still the same as follows?"

Nothing.

It's a widely understood that Mr. Denmark has never been witnessed engaging in smiles or laughter, and he almost never answers questions.

Denmark penetrates his soul with his piercing pupils. Within the silence is his answer.

Terry looks away.

"Yes lord."

The managing partner of 'Super Firm' *Denmark & Perminter*, the premier full-service practice in the Southeast, lightly thumbs his cufflink.

The door swings open! The instant rush of sunshine is both startling and delightful. Zeus stands to the side staring down at him with frost in his eyes.

"Good day my lord," and steps out without out saying another word. Without straightening his back, or popping his lapels, he clutches the envelope of new orders and starts walking like a puppy with his tail tucked.

By the time he rounds the side of the building and traverse the short alleyway, Zeus is already inside the flagship and driving away.

In ten more seconds, an insect as insignificant as a house fly can beat its wings up to two thousand times, twice the time it took for Terry Bostic to shape-shift from subservient finger puppet, to Troy Merciless, the murderous street king who wants to be feared by all.

In ten more seconds, his back stiffens and his chin returns to its arrogant form. The tough guy shtick is back as he pops his sport coat.

Another ten seconds and eighteen more people have died around the globe, the universe expanding ninety two more miles.

Drunk with ego, he snatches the door open and sneers at the homeless man. Moving with purpose and even more attitude, he treats the waiting customers to a wisp of his designer cologne as he speeds past their tables throwing looks of daggers. Bailey Red is scarfing down her food like she's on military time.

"Get up bitch! We gotta go!" he shot.

Having missed his grand re-entry, she looks up strangely. She's so hungry she didn't hear the bells clanging against the door when he entered.

Reaching in his pocket he extracts an obscene wad of cash, peels of a hundred, and palm-slams it on the table, bouncing the silverware like dominoes! Before she has the chance to savor another morsel, she's lifted out of the seat by her arm.

The old P-51 Mustang pilot boils with anger. Jerks like this are part of America's racial tensions. Cuffed inside his jacket is his Saturday night special on stand-by. He's waiting for him to make a false move so he can "stand his ground". Though it's Friday morning, he badly wants to bust a cap in his ass.

Merciless passes directing the lady by the arm, and is almost out of the door when he turns and looks at the homeless man. All twelve of the patrons, including the Waffle House staff are pissed. He pushes Bailey Red forward, rudely spins her around, and showcases her assets to the man.

"Now you have a close-up view," and grabs a hand full of her buttocks.

A woman gasps and covers her mouth!

"Everything in this world costs muthafucka!"

Extracts another crisp hundred, and tosses it on the floor.

"Go take a bath."

And walks out with his fingers dug into the woman's arm.

But he doesn't notice what she drops on the floor before he hurries her through. He was too busy mean-facing the dude who sleeps on the street.

But Alex saw it—it's laying on the inside of the doorway. The draft coming under the door is like angels breath, swooping the white tear of loose leaf paper up, skimming it across the floor where it comes to a rest somewhere under his table.

But he'll come back to it. For now he watches the man go to the passenger side of the car, shove the woman inside, go around the driver's seat and get inside. Seconds later he's gassing off, the high performance six liter Hemi blowing loud as he accelerates down grimy Stewart Ave.

For as much as his pride is hurt, so is his pocket. It infuriates him to have been subjected to that kind of treatment, but it burns even more that he's fighting the urge to bend down and take up money. Well if he's going to swallow his pride, he better get to swallowing fast! There's free money on the floor in plain view of needy people. He panhandles daily so he understands the hunger, but this is different—like bending over and taking a shaft of humiliation while everyone watches.

Obviously not different enough, because he leans over and snatches it, and stuffs it in his pocket.

Now he feels like shit, but glad he has the assuring weight of it in his possession.

A lady shakes her head in sympathy.

The fiery fighter pilot raises from his seat, and goes to the counter to inform the waitress he's footing the bill for the homeless gentleman.

The waitress wipes a tear from her eye and accepts; feeling the sting of how she too treated him.

The kind gesture is completed, and the kind-hearted man exits the restaurant with his appetite gone, and day thoroughly ruined. He wishes he was God so he could've struck that god-awful bastard down!

With the money on his mind he turns back to the note. Looking under the table, he becomes startled when a sense of deja-vu flashes over him like a Polaroid camera from his past life! The way the note is fluttering against his stinky shoe, is like a hitch-hiker flagging for a ride—it's begging to be noticed.

He reaches down and grabs it, and sees someone has used a torn piece of notebook paper to tally their work hours. But when he flips it over and reads the haphazardly scribbled message on the back, he knows the urgency in the misspelling is a message in itself.

Me an my cihild are n dagner, plesse help!!!!!!

Un.

$\mathcal{A}$ book claiming to be open may not be open at all. Perhaps, a curtain closed is not the end, but rather the precursor to the defining scene. There's an old wives' tale of a fisherman who every morning would travel to the same spot day after day with the anticipation of securing his bounty; the premier fishing point in the area, one that many other fishermen depend on as well. Being he has the luxury of owning the best equipment, and the nicest boat, he always secured the largest catch. But things take a turn for the worse, he starts bringing home less and less fish. He begins complaining to his wife that he doesn't understand why his most profitable location is no longer paying dividends. She explains the fish won't return until they've eaten the store they already have. After coming home with only one fish in his net, she suggested he take his lone catch of the day back, and maybe it'll birth new fish. But he disagrees with her assumption. Upset his wife is considering herself to be wiser than him, he waits until she's fast asleep, loads their entire stockpile onto the boat, and the following morning returns to his favorite cove.

Pretending to have fished all day, he prepares to return home, plump with pride he'll prove her theory wrong. But before he could, a giant wave turns the boat over and spills the fish into the sea, where they miraculously return to life. Fishermen from all around eager to finally have something to eat pour in. Sea gulls, pelicans, seals, and dolphins come to share in the feast. The reef transforms from barren wasteland to abundant oasis. He's mind-blown by the sheer scale and awe of activity, and understands the point his wife was trying to make. Feeling like a fool, he goes home empty-handed. Expecting to find his wife in an uproar, he arrives to find a huge sack of fish sitting on the kitchen counter. He asks where the fish came from? She says a friend dropped them off, saying there were so many fish available today that he had enough to give away. From that day on he understood the danger of continuing to eat once you've already had your fill.

Upon having his fill two days ago, Alex's stomach has long consumed the calories from earlier, and is now reduced back to hunger, and once again contemplating his next move. Had it not be almost two forty in the morning, he could make an attempt at visiting a church food or maybe work his cardboard sign. The hundred dollar bill is now three twenties, a five, a dime, and nine pennies. Every precaution is being taken to prevent losing his newly attained financial standing. He can always rent a cheap room at one of the many roach motels up and down Stewart, but can't afford the thirty five dollar charge. Instead, he broke into an aquatic center in a gated apartment community and took a free bath. Sitting four miles away his hair is still damp. The funk between his legs is gone and his feet are clean, but the chlorine from the pool has parched his skin. As time passes he becomes increasingly itchier, but despite all of his troubles he's in surprisingly good spirits. Lying atop the roof of an after-hours social club, looking at the sky, seeing the expanse of stars takes him back to science class and Galileo. Centuries later, here he is pondering about the accomplishments of a person he never met.

He thinks about all the horrible things he's done, and wonders are these the only type of contributions he can make to the universe? While the low hum of liquor, music, and sexual energy rumbles below him, his mind wades through a proverbial cesspool of past bad deeds. How did he go from easily intimidated son of an onion farmer, to wanted man? The one guy deserved it, he was scum and no one cared. But all the others are now starting to attack. They're in his dreams, they're in his reality, and still fresh on the minds of the investigators. He's wanted, and ten grand is nothing to flick your nose at. But if he keeps a low profile nobody will recognize him, he's found the perfect ghillie suit to keep him camouflaged within the undergrowth of Atlanta.

What was lost however, was his self. The one that got away when he accepted his role in the crimes. He's a coward who was ruled over so absolutely, he felt he had no choice but to submit to Stockton's will. Now he's gone, and he's left trying to pick up the pieces. It's no way to justify those things, they went overboard with evening the score. He learned long ago life isn't fair, and neither is fighting. In modern combat, the scarecrow sits far from the battlefield barking orders while the real heroes give their lives for a cause that lacks both merit, *and* justification. To him, the honor lies in each man's valiant effort to die for what he believes, not in the loss of life itself. That is a travesty.

But for the time being he'll have to keep his psyche in check, and his demons at bay. There's a meeting, and the *Coming of the Hour* is almost upon him.

When her handler left out of the Waffle House, he made the risky move of going to the table and explaining who he is. After making her privy to a few details regarding their one night together, she remembered him. At first she was nonchalant and standoffish, but after a minute or so her attitude took a drastic turn for the better, and she became very willing to talk. Out of desperation, he disclosed information about his current situation, and how he became homeless. She in turn explained she's a victim of human trafficking and in grave danger. The frantic look in her eyes spurred something in his soul. He's destitute, and she's talking life-changing sums of money. They outlined a scheme they believe will get him paid, and at the same time rescue a mother and child from the clutches of an international sex ring. She even gave him a cheap pre-pay phone and promised to be in touch. Contacting him later that next day, she offered him an update to the proposition. He accepted and began making preparations for the move.

Now fully prepped and partially rested, he awaits her late night call while talking to himself.

"If you had any courage you wouldn't be sitting on some freaking roof waiting on some stripper prostitute to throw you a life preserver, you wimp! Why couldn't you have told him to go fuck himself? Now you've let this lady sweet talk you into getting in some more mess. You're one pansy-ass guy Alex. I see why your wife left you. I see why people take you for a joke. Goddammit *dude,* when are you gonna *man up!!!*"

If it was this easy, the wildebeest would tell the lion the jungle is now his, and it's he who's now the prey.

One's an animal, and one's a man, but they're both vertebrates that'll get their heads ripped clean off if they dare

challenge the established order. It'll take a princess of epic proportions to kiss this toad into a prince.
He begins letting doubt slip into his mind, and has become
certain she's playing him for a fool…………….

Until the phone chimes. A text lists an address, a time to be
there, and the number to a cab service?
His heart skips a beat and begins racing! Both energized and
filled with butterflies, he rolls up his trusty tarp and places it
inside his backpack and gets to his feet. In about twenty steps he
crosses the roof and climbs down the ladder.

Back on solid ground, he moves towards the tree line behind
the building, a short distance away is the club's back door. He's
in the back alleyway with five cars and a group of men standing
talking and laughing. A hint of something's in the air. It reminds
him of how he and his late brother used to sit in the back of his
restaurant and get stoned. It's been almost seven months since
he's been on the lamb, and seven months since he savored Mary
Jane's uplifting flavor. His cerebral palate badly desires a toke.
"Maybe I'll go find a bag once all this is over."
Alex has a habit of talking to himself.
Hunching in the brush, he dials the number to the cab, and after
eleven rings someone answers.
"Uhmn…Yes. I'd like to request a taxi at…twenty -two eighty
Covington highway, it's the Club Sandcastle."
The dispatcher asks him how many passengers, and what's his
destination?
"Just me, and the address is six seven zero Woodcrest Manor Dr.,
zip code three-zero-three-three-one."
She asks how he's paying?
"Cash."
She says the estimated time of arrival is in eighteen minutes, the
cost is forty five dollars, and asks if that's all?
"Yes."

And lastly she asks for his name.
But he hasn't even considered that part of the equation. Before she has the chance to repeat herself, in a very clear and confident voice he says: "Paine Bogart," having no idea where it came from.
She thanks him for choosing their service and ends the call.

An odd sense of certainty comes over him, and in a peculiar way feels driven by a sense of meaning, a sense of justice; *purpose*. But he knows he's a weakling, and his gusto meter is on zero. Where that name came from and what it means is pointless. All that matters is how powerful it makes him feel when he says it, and how much better it sounds than a diminutive name like Alexander Timothy Zarbin II. He says it again.
"Paine Bogart!......P-A-I-N! I think I'll drop the 'e'."

"Wow!!" He feels like somebody. What a difference a name makes!

For the next ten minutes he visualizes the most favorable outcome to tonight's mission, he envisions this fearless capped crusader who swoops from the shadows to free women and children from the grips of ruthless oppressors.
He imagines it morphing into a total disaster, falling from his fantasy into an acid rain of hot lead. After weighing the pros and cons of one versus the other, deciding there's no way this can have a good ending, and is about to chicken out, the phone chimes—except this time someone else is calling. He silences the ringer and stares at the number. It's a different one.
Taking a deep breath he answers.
It's the taxi driver calling to say he's out front.
His heart starts pounding again!
"Okay. I'll be right out."
The big mean gorilla is back, having characteristically commandeered his back, and is firmly weighing him down once again.

He was just beginning to feel like he's getting over the hump, but this species of primate seems to possess special powers, and no matter what it is he attempts, he never seems to be able to do it without feeling the burden of inadequacy. He was just at a high point, but now back in his typical lull of pessimism and self-doubt. The shot of bravado has worn off, replaced by the insecurity that controls his life. If Stockton were here he'd know just what to do.

Out of confusion he starts smacking himself in the face!

"Come on Alex. Stop being a bitch!......Pain Bogart!-PAIN BOGART!!......*PAIN BOGART!!!*"

He bangs his head against a tree several times until one of the men pointing his direction saying something.

Realizing he better go, he emerges from the brush and begins stumbling as if he's drunk.

One of them yells something but doesn't move. He continues with his manufactured gait until he rounds the building and is out of their line of sight.

Now clear he adjusts his style and dusts himself off, the noise and excitement of inebriated club goers calling it a night is suffocating. A warm gust of air brushes his cheek, and a fallen limb almost trips his feet; his well-worn *Braves* cap shrouds his face in mystery. Vehicles sit jammed into every available parking space, and even on the curbs. Though his back is turned and head down, he's still made uneasy by the squad car lurking a ways down. He scans the area but doesn't see the cab, looks over his shoulders, and it hits him like a jab! Right pass the officer, and straight through the teeth of the crowd. With no conviction his plan is sound, he makes for the sedan while scratching his balls wishing he was well endowed.

He catches the attention of a parking attendant.

"*Hey!*...Get the hell outta here!" the man yells coming towards him.

Moving for the sidewalk, Alex waves meekly and nods, but is

now exposed to the throngs of cars and people congesting the lot's exit. He's prime rib for any wasted douche bag looking for a laugh. Expectantly, he becomes the court jester, but doesn't first get a laugh, but rather a kick, a swift one right in his ass! *Now* comes the laugh—a howling one from two faux tough guys.

The blow is painful, the guy's booted foot meeting his glute causes him to grimace.

Fortunately they don't stop, just get their kicks and keep going. He does too, and with a little more fervor now, and can now see the cab. The driver is looking around, he still has a ways to go; and much to his horror, sees the sedan shift into gear and begin rolling.

Alex quickens into a jog/walk and is in the process of cupping his hands to shout when he hears the whistle of someone else trying to hail the cab. As it stops, a couple hurries to get there. Alex takes off running and reaches the car just as they're about to get inside.

"Excuse me sir," he begins, breathing hard. "I called for this taxi and ran from over there to try and catch it!"

The man looks at him strangely, up and down at his appearance. For several moments they stare at each other until the woman reaches for the man's arm.

"Go ahead sir, we'll get the next one...............Go ahead," she said politely, obviously sympathetic to his destitute look.

"Thank you miss."

He scoots around and gets in.

The driver who looks to be of foreign decent looks back at him as he sits behind the Plexiglas partition, in what's apparently an old police cruiser converted to a taxi. How fitting, considering he's in route to do God knows what. The cabin light goes out the second he shut the door, and the pale blue Dodge Charger pulls away. Alex looks over his shoulder. The guy is saying something to the woman, but she puts her arm around his waist and strolls him off.

Alex turns to see the eyes of the driver watching him in the rear view.

"You live around here or something?"

"No. I was just doing a job."

"Oh? What kind of work do you do?" asked the man with a Middle Eastern accent.

"….I'm a painter. I paint houses."

"Oh! You should make good money from that I would think."

"Not that much, work's kinda slow now."

"Aaaaaaaah."

He turns down a side street, cuts through an alley, and pops out four blocks down. Clear of the gridlock, he punches the destination into the G.P.S. bolted atop the dash. Once they're moving at a brisk 72 M.P.H., the driver situates the rear-view and returns his gaze to him.

"So where's all your paint and brushes?"

"…I leave my tools at the house I'm painting, the people I work for flip houses." Alex isn't a good liar.

The man's eyes brighten and reaches for the radio. An energetic pentatonic scale piece blasts from the speakers, while a woman sings quick rhythmic blips of sharp words and tones, while someone in the background vigorously plucks what sounds like a banjo. Another musician slaps frequencies of varying octaves from a hand drum, and some type of wind instrument croons back up.

"I saw something about that on television the other night," he shouted over the music. "I was telling my wife after we have our first son I want to start my own company. If Allah blesses me with this, I will be very grateful," he explained.

"I'm sure he will."

"Me too," and looks at the road singing with the song.

Maybe it's the fact he's from a third world country and doesn't understand American culture? Maybe it's the fact he's more concerned about being robbed than his passenger's fashion prowess.

Whatever it is, he doesn't seem to pay much attention to his dress.

In the dim light of the bulky sedan, Alex does his best to look at the small, no-frills analog phone she gave him. No new calls and no new texts. The ride is smooth, but his nerves are ragged as barbed wire.

In the distance there seems to be a vehicle trying to keep up with them?

You just sacred! Ain't nobody back there!

At this hour traffic is non-existent, and there isn't much to see other than the highway, the stars, and the green exit signs.

The driver has evidently acclimated himself with the operation of a motorcar, because he seems to be under the impression he's Aryton Senna. There's hardly anyone on the road, but for some reason he feels the need to routinely change lanes, and search for the apex of every curve. Currently, they're stuck in a curb-weight-increasing turn over Spaghetti Junction, the sedan shoots down the on-ramp, and jets onto Chamblee-Tucker Rd.

Alex decides it's time to put his seat belt on.

The click must've caught his attention because he reaches and turns the volume down, even though the steering wheel has its own controls.

"Ha-ha man! You scared or something?" he laughs.

"I'm good."

The driver snickers and turns the music back up, continuing his fun.

Alex should consider himself lucky to have run into a woman from his past. She seems to be an honest person who's only trying to do what she needs to survive. The fact she's so beautiful, and even seems to be somewhat educated causes him much confusion. Maybe it's because he's from rural Georgia and hasn't dealt with many women outside of his race. Since he can no longer use his adopted brother Stockton as a guiding light, he's falling back on the advice of his father. His pops was a good man who taught him the world is better with variety, and raised him to deal with people on a case-by-case basis.

He said to never allow racism to ruin him as it has so many others.

There's something magnetic about this woman of color. She's his exact opposite, and is convinced that helping her will put him back on his feet. He doesn't know where this will lead, but since he's a born follower, he'll follow his new leader. He should be euphoric, suspended in a state of bliss. He's been sleeping on the streets for the past eight months, and now about to have to chance to take a real shower and lay in a warm bed. Maybe it's his gut, or maybe it's his sixth sense, whichever it is, it's making him quite uneasy about the whole situation. The uneasiness increases when he looks at the G.P.S. and sees the destination is less than three miles away. The driver turns down a side street and drives for about two more minutes.

The device starts beeping!

After pressing a button it ceased.
"You must do pretty good painting. You live out here with the sheiks man." He doesn't have to be born in America to recognize the lifestyle of the rich and famous.
In terms of price and privilege, the area is quite high up the scale but not in the 'showy, new to money, look at me, I want to make people think I'm rich when I'm really not', kind. But the wealthy, 'I've been raking it in for a long time, don't want any of you broke-asses to know', kind. The comfort that generational success brings. "Old money".
The aggressive driver pulls the well-worn Charger into a Shell gas station and locks the doors.

"After you pay me I'll take you the rest of the way."

The jovial attitude is gone, and the cash tray attached to the Plexiglas partition pops open. *'$45.00' is* glowing red on the black box mounted on the dash, and his eyes are in the rearview peeled on him.

Alex doesn't hear any music, out of the corner of his eyes he sees a gray GMC Yukon pull into the lot, and roll to a halt beside them.

The attendant inside the gas station watches through the window.

Like an underhanded Washington lobbyist rearing its ugly head, from inside the dark expanse of the crime free neighborhood, emerges a van. Like a cunning wolf slinking out of a cave, it stops at the intersection and scans the street. Moments later, it runs the light, and sprints into the distance.

The cab driver looks over his shoulder.

"You don't live around here do you?" having determined his attire and said occupation doesn't match the neighborhood.

Alex extracts the money, unfolds the two twenty dollar bills, and pushes them in the tray.

The man retrieves it from the other side, and clicks the locks. As he prepares to put the car into gear and proceed to the address, something happens.

The passenger side window lowers and a face appears.

The cab driver looks strangely at them, and back at him.

"Are these your people?"

Alex is stuck. He's never seen this man a day in his life and sees no sign of Bailey Red.

Leaning over he lowers the window.

"Are you with Bailey?" sounding green as a pool table, and twice as square.

The man plays along.

"Yeah."

But he doesn't come across as an errand boy. *He's* an errand boy, so he knows the type. This guy is not in any way a peon, well at

least not in the physical sense. He's afraid and the guy can tell.
"Okay."
Chump!
The cab driver looks at him again, his unspoken words are in-
tense. Danger has a universal way of presenting itself.
Alex grabs his backpack and exits the vehicle.

No sooner than he's out, he's back in another. Except this one
is occupied by two occupants with mean faces and cold stares.
"You Tim?" his new driver questioned without looking at him.
The guy in the passenger seat is doing something in his lap, and
what he's hearing sounds like metal against metal. The type of
sharp sound made by a certain firing mechanism.
Alex is shaking like a crap game.
"Yes…………….Where's Bailey Red?"
The man hesitates and looks at his partner.
"Right around the corner," and pulls out the lot back onto the
main road.
The urge to vomit trickles around in his stomach like a fawn on
thin ice, his bowels begin stirring like blind mice in a snake's
belly.
In two quick turns they enter the same subdivision the van
emerged from. Some of the estates have spruce trees with
wrought iron fences, others charge gated entrances and *boule*
statues with the task of guarding master's property. They all sit
far back from the road, and could all be considered their own
little secret societies. There's no way on God's green earth an
exotic dancer can remotely afford to live in this neighborhood,
or anywhere in the vicinity.
The address they roll up on is different than the one on his
phone, and the house is so gigantic he can't see it all. It has a

gated entrance with the initial 'K.' emblazoned on it; but it's open. At this hour, the slightest tap can wake the entire neighborhood. He can see the property is well maintained and possesses a formidable brick wall, but sees no call box, and all of the garage doors are shut. Faint signs of light are inside the home, but no activity.

The phone vibrates in his pocket! It's Bailey.

He quickly hits the button and raises it to his ear.
"Hello," sounding like a timid telemarketer without a script.
The driver looks at him but the passenger is still doing whatever.
"It's me. Did you find the house okay," she asks.
Her tone sounds off?
"Yeah. I'm out front but it looks like the wrong address. It's not the one you texted me. What do you want me to do?"
On the other end he can hear people and music in the background. Something is definitely off.
She says she's having a hard time hearing him, and obviously didn't hear what he just said.
"Can you hear me?"
"The guy with you is cool. He's doing the favor for me. You can come on inside. The code is four-three-zero-one-five," she explained.
He didn't miss she said "guy" and "he", meaning singular, not plural. He doesn't believe her but what choice does he have.
"....Okay."
Before he can say another word the line goes dead.

The man in the passenger seat gets out and opens the door for him. He's holding a brown paper bag, and as he gets out pushes it into his chest.
"Be sure he gets this. The code is 13665," the man ordered.
HE?
His conscience screams abort!!!!!

Inside is something heavy and feels to be wrapped in clothes.

Heartbeat!

Heartbeat!!

Heartbeat!!!

After taking a step, he hesitates, just as the passenger door opens, and out gets the other man, gives him a long stare, puts something in his pocket, and nods at the driveway.
Alex knows he has no choice.
He closes the door, and heads for the front of the house.

The passenger is also in a suit, except his isn't tailored. It's a wool, two button offering. Moving purposefully he put an ear piece in his ear and his other hand drops to his side.
Alex nervously swallows as he heads up the inclined driveway looking at the lighting along the sides; they're off. As he reaches the garage door there's more landscape lights beneath the bushes spanning the front windows, and they too are out. Now the man is gone, the sound of the Yukon's engine decreases before ceasing completely. Now the only resonances are insect mating calls, and wind rustling through the trees. Four, white Genie® keypads are on each column, and one's flipped up with glowing digits waiting for input.
He punches in the numbers: *13665*

A core trait of the human experience is the desire to believe in something, an inherent hunger to represent a certain philosophy, a certain institution, a certain religion, or a certain party.

Beliefs are the adhesives which bind and break alliances. By playing on emotion rather than intellect, a compelling belief can delude the smartest man. One mustn't forget, there was a time when the world was thought to be flat. There was even a time preceding the Renaissance when no man could determine the worth of another man's art. It was widely believed there's no right, *or* wrong way when it comes to expressing one's talents. Feces, urine, and blood have even been used to create "art". This must be understood before "viewing" this piece.

Posted on the wall of the guest bed room is a 4 x 2 foot drawing. The word '*LIBERATOR* ' is titled across the top in red block letters with black trim. The canvas is laminated, and the background is gray; the light type, the color of a gloomy sky.
On it is a drawing of a metropolis being trampled by a grotesque "thing." A thing that looks like an immense robot of revulsion. In the background of this penciled image are depictions of the *Statue of Liberty*, the *Lincoln Memorial*, and various American cities. In the center of the poster, *and* trampling over these cites, this "thing" triggers fires; vast, destructive, orange blazes.
One of this thing's legs is a normal human leg; muscular, smooth, and white. Tied around its thigh is a ribbon which says:
'*World's Most Beautiful Leg*'.
The other leg is quite different however. It's raised and bent at the knees as if it's going to step on the *National Archives* building, the place where the U.S. constitution is kept.
In place of the missing foot is a missile which says:
'*Patriot*'. It's covered in blood.
The lower leg and upper thigh are made of rolls upon rolls of ammunition. In the center area where a normal torso would be, is a snare drum. Hanging from the drum, and directly *in* the pubic region, and directly over the burning flames of the cities, is the *Star of David*.
Connected directly to the top of the snare drum where a person's chest would normally be, there's a metal bird cage. In-

side this cage are African slaves dancing around with big pink lips and brown monkey faces. Posted on this cage is a small plaque which says:
'*Triumph of the Jitterbug*'.

Protruding out of the cage are arms, one on each side.
In the right hand is a Thompson sub-machine gun, better known as a "Tommy gun". The arm is covered with the sleeve of a black and white prison jumpsuit.

The other is an arm of a man wearing a pin-striped suit while holding a microphone. Both hands are white.
Directly above that set of arms are an additional set. One on each side. These arms are very muscular, very chiseled, and *very* black. The "artist" went to great lengths to get the black as he could.
From the left bicep hangs a rope and noose. In the hand is a vinyl record and a basketball.
In the right hand, is a fat sack of money, a white man in a business suit dangling from the bottom trying to hold on to it.

Sitting on the left shoulder sits an Indian woman wearing a feathered headdress. She's blowing a muted trumpet with a
'*Miss America*' banner wrapped around her waist.
On the right shoulder sits a white woman. She's holding an American flag wearing a banner around her which said
'*Miss Victory*'.
Around the neck of this filthy creature hangs a cloth necklace emblazoned with '*White Elks Front*.' Covering the face is the traditional cone shaped hat and mask.
Out of its back there's aircraft wings.
On one wing is word '*Uncle*'.
On the other is the word '*Sam*'.
A red pentagram is at the tip of each wing.
The entire propaganda artifice is quite creative, but

vomitous.

Done in the shade of #2 pencil by a meticulous illustrator with a demented hand, it's a horrible sight to see.

The mountain man visiting from the mountains can't find himself comfortable in the urban sprawl. Since he's going to be there for the week, mine as well go ahead and spruce up his temporary living quarters with some good ole' hate decor. Every time he views his drawing he gushes with pride. He's an *artist,* even if no one besides other bigots appreciates his hate fueled depictions. Somehow, his uncle made it all the way from the rural sticks of Ellijay, GA to the exclusive confines of Brookhaven. Owning a successful septic tank installation company will do that for a racist. He doesn't care that he had to crawl through shit and piss to get it. So much so, that he had to incorporate himself in the capital city so he could deal more efficiently with his growing list of metro Atlanta customers.

Now at three thirty-three in the morning he's awake again. But it's not the prospect of the bass fishing, or anxiety from the deer hunting, or the wild hogs getting away since he's gone; it's the sound of his most hated enemy.

Them!

He thinks he's dreaming, until he hears it again—it's them all right! He feels his temperature rise—partially from the lack of sleep, but mainly because he can't get away from them. They're everywhere he goes, they're in the schools, they're in the government, they're stealing all the jobs. He can't turn on the television without seeing their stupid faces. Between them, the Jews, the fags, and all the white women making babies with them; he's living in pure hell, a torment he's forced to endure in his own homeland.

He sighs angrily, agitated he has to deal with them even on the rich side of town! Getting out of bed he storms to the window! The barefoot bigot with a boar's pelt of hair growing from his back is wearing dingy beige underwear with a shit streak smeared

up his crack like a dragstrip of brown asphalt!
Outside he sees two black men.
"Fuckin' jigaboo coons!"
One's almost to the front door of the house next door, the other
is coming up the driveway from the direction of an SUV.
At the door to the garage he sees a white man punching
numbers into a keypad, seemly unaware of the approaching
darkies. The reckless redneck's initial thought is to yell out the
window, but his second one adds so much more appeal!

Wearing only a pair of boxers and a tank top, and his Springfield
30-06 hunting rifle, dash out of the room. Driven by the chance
to be a hero, he develops a scenario he *perceives* to be happening.
All the other white men are getting away with it, why can't he;
plus they have money. All he has to do is throw the new millennium catch phrase: He was "standing his ground".
Rumbling down the long stairway, he speeds down the short
hallway and into the kitchen to hurriedly unlock the double
door!
WOow-WOow-WOow-WOow-WOow!!!!!
The instant he opens it the penetrating ring of the
security system goes crazy!
Ducking down he ignores it, and heads for the tree line!
Upstairs lights coming on!
Psyching himself up with images of spicks invading his country,
and the slimy Jew at the bank telling him he's not qualified for
the loan; he uses the foliage to conceal his movements!
Heading into the neighbor's back yard, twigs and brush crush
under his bad feet. Being used to not wearing shoes, he expertly
navigates through the bushes until he comes upon the six foot
cedar wood fence. Peering between the planks he sees a black
man in a suit going through the house holding something. One
of the garage doors are up, but the white man is gone. Standing to his feet he tosses the rifle over, and runs behind a gazebo.
Images of Martin Luther King, Malcom X, and JFK cloud his

imbecile mind! He fancies himself as a Nazi S.S. officer beginning the extermination of an inferior race. Peeking over the top of the fence, his heart sinks when he sees the other black man is hunched at the corner of the garage preparing an ambush. The white enforcer remembers his uncle saying a prominent white family lives here, and knows these coons are up to no good. He didn't think he'd have the opportunity to hunt this week, but it seems his fortunes have changed!

The expert marksman chambers a round and moves. He knows backup can't be far behind. Once the rest of his relatives get up, there'll be seven trigger happy racists looking to protect their neighbor's from the attack of the savages. The rifle leads the way as he takes a deep breath and crosses the lawn, soft blades of chemically treated fescue spike between his toes.
A bright flood light comes on, lighting up the entire area!
The intruder inside sees it and begins looking out of a window! Realizing this could become a life or death situation, his hands begin trembling! Looking over his shoulder, he sees his dad standing on the back patio looking around. But he doesn't see him holding a gun.
The man inside the house takes off towards the other end!
Not wanting to give away his position, but wanting to get his father's attention, he thinks of a plan.
Deciding he has no choice, he puts two fingers together, starting to whistle. But as he inhales and is about to force a burst of wind over his vocal cords, he sees a pair legs lying on the floor behind a marble covered island in the large kitchen! As he looks closer he sees there's blood on the bottom of the foot, and a trail of debris scattered through the area. He now has clear indication he's stumbled upon something very bad.
That's when he becomes frozen with fear, hypnotized when he sees the other body on the floor! Even for a dumb bigot, killing a deer is not the same as seeing a dead human, especially one of his own race. Before he knows it, his eyes begin watering. Taking

a deep breath he gathers himself. With the rifle trembling in his hand, he realizes he's in way over his head, and needs to get back next door to call the police! He should've never let his hate for minorities cause him to compromise his own safety.
He races for the gazebo!

He's fresh out of prison after serving eight years for statutory rape, still hasn't registered as a sex offender, and gets no sympathy for the fact she was twelve years old and he was nineteen. Now ten years later, and three days from twenty nine, he's again involved in lewdness. The ex-con with the new gun hides beside the bush and watches for any sign of movement inside the four car garage. Two Benzes, a Beamer, and a SUV occupy the 1300 sq. ft. space. The garage has recently opened, but for some reason the automatic light is out.
The bona fide pedophile feels a great deal of anxiety for still being at the scene when they should be long gone, and fighting the urge to shit himself.
Why the hell do we need to frame a homeless man for the hit? We should be gone!
But as a lazy high school drop-out with felonies and no common sense, he has few choices. So if he wants to eat, he'd better get on with it. Behind his thoughts crickets chirp in the early morning hours of the Georgia night, in the distance a woodpecker bores a tree trunk for a meal. Over his left shoulder he sees lights begin coming on inside the house next door.
The tell-tell squeak of someone opening the screen door absorbs his attention!
With a ray of blinding light, the enclave becomes bright with color! The blast from the sawed-off shotgun disables him with momentary blindness and the inability to hear! Through the

subsiding ring he sees his partner burst through the door and blast another shot, blowing a hole in the water heater! The hiss of hot water and steam add to the chaos!

With his equilibrium knocked completely off kilter, he rises from his crouched position to offer assistance! But things are happening so fast he can't process them fast enough! He prides himself on womanizing school girls, not on shoot outs! With his weapon leading, the way he calls out to his partner!

"Which way?..........Which way did he go!!!!!"

But before his question can be answered, a panic-stricken man appears out of nowhere and downright bowls him over, sending him the gun, the keys, and the wallet hurtling to the pavement, almost tripping as he steps on his face!!!!

Before he can regain his footing, he reaches up and catches the cuff of the pant, and sends the fugitive hard to the pavement!

Alex skins his elbow and chin on the rough driveway as he skids on the concrete!

He crawls towards his gun just as his partner makes it out the garage, and is just about to put one in Alex's head!

BOOM!!!!

An earth shattering blast that literally explodes the back of his skull! The rear window of the luxury automobile becomes spattered with blood, shards of bone, and brain matter! The suit slumps against the vehicle, his leaning corpse grotesque as it sinks to the ground, his fate displayed to his partner on the ground in a debilitating state of shock! The puddle between his legs lets him know he's pissed himself.

"You make one fuckin' move and I'll blow your head clean off too," he said, pointing the elephant gun at him.

He closes his eyes and rolls onto his back. Out of the corner of his eye he sees the white man dash and pick up his wallet, gun, and keys.

"Don't shoot!!! This is my mother's house!!....*DON'T SHOOT!!!.....PLEASE!!*"

Alex takes off in a blaze down the driveway!!!

The racist seeing the man is white like him, returns his attention to the black man. Had he not let his skewed analytics sway his decision, he would've held him at gun point too. But since he didn't, the ten thousand dollar reward goes up in smoke.
He sees his nephew emerge from the backyard holding the rifle he was afraid to fire.
Meanwhile, Zarbin peels of down the street in a used Yukon!

Almost to the surface street, Alex stands on the brakes, the big SUV leans hard as it squeals to a halt! The vehicle is still rocking when the officer exits the gas station looking his direction holding something. While the yellow traffic device swing from the cable overhead, he watches him get inside the car and look at something in the vicinity of the center console. And moments later speak into the radio clipped to his shoulder.
The light bar starts flashing and the sirens go blaring!
He watches in horror as the car goes over the grass and comes off the curb heading straight for him. He's about to slam the gas and take him on a high speed chase, but before he can floor it the cruiser's careens across the intersection, and is on him!
Now he has to pee!
It's like the sun has instantly risen and is shining two feet from his face! He's being blinded by the brightest light he's ever seen! Squinting likes it's a bad horror flick, he puts his hand up and tries to see!
It's over!
He closes his eyes and readies for the inevitable!!!!!
But his vision returns, he sees the cars tail lights speeding into the nearby neighborhood!!!! Alex is so petrified he can taste the acid reflux and hot vomit sitting in the back of his mouth!
In a painful shallow he forces it down. The light is green, but he's

mummified by fear!
Get the hell outta here you idiot! His inner voice yells.
He snaps out his stupor and hits the gas! It dawns on him he's missing weight on his back, and plus he's bleeding! Wheeling the Yukon left, he disappears down the street!

Deux.

The well-to-do serenity which normally runs rampant in this sought-after zip code, is disturbed by a sea of flashing lights and armed men; many of the residents have never witnessed such a spectacle. It's going to be great for the gossip stirrers and blog columnists, but bad for property values and safety assessments. Despite the fact many of these high-worth individuals are offered a VIP brand of legal protection, their privilege can't buy their way out of their own neighborhood. The largest home in the community is a 9,550 sq. ft. wonder built by famed home designer Wilt Meland, and owned by the president of Southern Tell Communications. Threats of litigation aren't enough to persuade them to remove the blockade. The entire area is under temporary lockdown. When the wife and children of Atlanta's most powerful figure are brutally slain, it gets everyone's attention. The police major, the department's fourth in hierarchy, is on the scene, while the chief is on the phone being briefed on the situation, slew of his top detectives are dissecting the property with fine tooth combs. The head of the fugitive task force stands beside him as they watch more than seventy officers and vehicles completely take over the neighborhood. The fact a black man was killed by a white neighbor is more than enough to get the local news agencies on the scene, especially at four fifty-three on a Sunday morning, and especially in the South. The fact it's only a foretaste to the real story is icing on the cake. Male and female reporters stand about holding mics and pestering investigators for information.

The veteran lawman leans against the unmarked Mercury Marquis. Staring at the fog of deliberate movement and indistinguishable chatter, his thoughts become confined to a minefield of bureaucratic challenges, legal pitfalls, and political agendas. The fact the victims are amongst the city's elite makes the path towards accountability that much more precarious. From what has already been gathered, there was a murder of the family. Either during or after, it was stumbled upon by the next door neighbors, who just happened to be white supremacists.

The shit storm is brewing.

A voluntary search of their residence turns up a trove of hate material, ammunition, and firearms, and early reports are warning of heavy media embellishment. America's current climate of militarization of the police, and questionable shootings involving unarmed men have destabilized the state of law enforcement. The F.O.P (Fraternal Order of Police) is furious its officers are being made out to be criminals, instead of heroes. The public on the other hand are upset cops have seemingly become purveyors of unjustified deadly force, particularly when it involves a person of color. Major Russell "Tusk" Hall is of a contrasting position though, one which offset the hues of bright red both sides are seeing. Being a twenty three year vet, he understands the entire debate, and loathes men who use the shield as an instrument of domination, just as he dislikes citizens who think they can trample on the law by playing the race card. During his tenure as major, unscrupulous officers are swiftly dealt with, to such a point he's embattled in a departmental stalemate over his recent termination of four patrolmen. He's also disturbed by the fact that some members of minority communities are using this quandary to justify skirting the boundaries of law, while at the same time representing a large percentage of the city's criminal element. What happened here tonight will certainly add more fuel to a fire that's already a blaze.

The precinct commander is walking his direction holding a back pack. Beside him is a female forensic technician clad in a polyethylene jumpsuit. A barricade of yellow tape has the area in front of the house cautioned off, but reporters are still overstepping their bounds. Seeing the coroner emerge from the house causes several investigators to stroll over, followed by the news crews. Luckily, an officer prevents them from coming any closer. He can't however, stop them from turning on their cameras and bright lights. They sense something juicy developing.

"Sir, we found this bag under the Mercedes," he begins.
"What's in it," the major replied.
"Just some clothes, a blue tarp, and some miscellaneous hygiene products," replied the tech.
The name '*Hunt*' is written in black marker on his chest pocket.
"There's some type of proverb on it....No person was ever honored for what he received. Honor has been the reward for what he gave."
"That's a helluva message for a quadruple homicide," said Captain John Henry Peavey. "The neighbor says it belongs to the man they were trying to kill. But what I'm trying to under-

stand how he says he was ambushed in the garage by the men, saying they were trying to kill him too," Peavey continued. "It really bothers me claims he didn't shoot him because he believed he was a resident."

"Yeah. He blows the black man's head off, but let's the white guy run free," replied Maj., also a black man; boldly stating what everyone one else seems to want to avoid.

"It's become almost a guaranteed way lately to get away with homicide. I'm pretty certain the stand your ground cop-out was on his mind when he exited the house, especially when he claims the two black men were shooting at the white guy; not to mention the White Elks affiliation. Now he's lawyered-up and refuses to say anything else," concluded Peavey.

Major Hall doesn't have to be *William James Sidis* with his 275 IQ, *Philip Emeagwali* with his mind boggling mathematics equations, or the brainy *Marilyn Vos Savant* to figure out where this is headed. The media will fashion what looks to be a classic case of law abiding citizen exercising their civil liberties, into social lighting rod:

'Vigilante Supremacist Mows Down Black Man!!!'

Destructive riots are sure to ensue. The sub-plot will be the family murder of a powerful attorney/businessman; one which has all the makings of a professional hit. These weren't random pant-sagging, broke-joke thugs, they were hit men with clear and concise objectives. The mission was to eliminate the wife and children of Ed Denmark, who according to his law firm's website, just happens to be out of town.

From his vantage point, Maj. Tusk Hall has partly pieced to-gether the puzzle, but the real mystery lies with the man who got away. The items in the backpack only add more questions.

"I've spoken more in-depth with the officer who initially arrived at the scene," begins Peavey. "He didn't give me anything new, just reaffirmed what he said about being at the Shell station across the street when the call came in. I don't understand how he let the guy drive away. Back in my days on the beat, his ass would've been detained for questioning. I find it odd he let him go like that."

"Did he recall any other description of the driver?" asked Maj.

"Nah. Just white male with an Atlanta Braves cap."

"Put in a call to the GSP and get me an update on the APB. We may need to widen the search area. I need you to make that happen fast for me captain," he ordered.

"Yes sir!"

While Peavey places the call, Maj. returns his attention to the forensic scientist. As a man of authority, he wields his sword with honor and care, and isn't a big talker. He has a great sense of humor, but doesn't have time for games. His subordinates find him a hard man to gauge but a man who demands respect. Being a legendary college football lineman made him quite the popular figure, but his claim to fame is the work he's done since being an Atlanta Police Major. Imposing yet compassionate, undeterred but compromising; many of the women on the force find him quite appealing, a blue collar snack cake of mouth-watering muscle tone, and irresistible pheromones. Surprisingly though, he's yet to select a mate. He sired a daughter from an earlier marriage, but that's it. He's the epitome of a dedicated lawman, he's married to the game, and is used to winning. The most interesting part about him though, at least from a career stand point, is the fact he repeatedly turns down the chief position, even at the request of the mayor himself. After his predecessor, the late great, Gene "Mean" Primrose died, he recommended the current chief to take the position. Hall believes he's more effective as a major than chief. He isn't some power thirsty limp noodle who needs a gun and badge to make him feel like a man, but a gentleman who chooses not to use a gun until it's time to save a life—a legend in the world of law enforcement. But he does have enemies, both on the force, and amongst the civilian population.

Nobody likes a goody two shoes.

The coroner's staff are in the process of rolling the deceased to the van when he speaks. All heads raise attentively.

"Peavey. You and Detective Hickenlooper take it from here. This thing is about to blow, so prepare your sergeants for twelve-hour shifts, and Nguyen see if you can get those blood samples back ASAP. I want the identity of the one that got away. That's where the answers are."

"Yes sir," said Nguyen, the city's forensic scientist.

"Even if you have to drive them to Trion yourself, I really need those samples Joy."

"Yes sir. I'll see if I can have them back by Wednesday."

"Great."

Holding the brown bag, she turns and dives back into the ocean of activity.

Betrothed in lights, cameras, and action, the remainder of the group get the point the Maj. is finished talking. They gyrate forward, 1-½ somersault in the Pike position, *back* into the cobalt lagoon teaming with edgy hunters in blue suits. A watchful remora hangs beside the group like a fearsome piranha hovering over its brood.

The Maj. calls to that one.

"Peavey!"

Captain John Henry turns back.

"Sir?"

His uniform is in pristine condition, his boots shining like wet paint, polished badge gleaming proudly in the morning moonlight. Every medal he's been awarded is displayed on his shirt pocket, his smile is bright, and he's been blessed with a heart of gold. He wants all the world to see he's a *good* police officer, not one of these talentless jerks who got beat up as kids and need a gun and a box of doughnuts to feel tough. This is the major's favorite officer, the defining example of what a true police officer represents. Young, hungry, college educated, and with a voracious appetite for the pride, and virtue that comes with representing the Atlanta Police Force.

Not some shriveled dick scumbag discharged from the military with a chip on his shoulder.

He's a black man from one of the city's worst housing projects, the notorious East Lake Meadow's, also known as *"Little Vietnam."* His name *John Henry Peavey* made things even rougher on him, but it gave him an edge, one that comes in handy when fighting these new millennium criminals.

He does his job so well because he understands his duty is to protect, not harass, mistreat, subjugate, or intimidate.

Widely loved and revered, he maintains excellent relationships with comminutes on both the north, and south sides. Rumors swirl the new assistant chief from Detroit is upwardly mobile, and aiming for the state senate, but not Peavey, nor Hall are convinced he's the answer. He seems too concerned with popularity, and not with crime prevention. Plus the look in his eyes, and sly smile tells them not to trust Dagan Lacy.

"What's the feel you're getting on this?" asked Tusk.

"From what I'm thinking, these guys came to kill the family, but something goes wrong. The neighbor hears something and comes to see, and ends up shooting. For some reason, I'm feeling that bag didn't come from inside the house. You know how when you lose your hat or jacket, the first thing you do is smell it. That bag smells like something far from the rich smell of that house. Plus the items inside are off. Nothing matches this."

Meaning the shrewd luxury of the neighborhood.

The major nods and rubs his chin.

"Did you get anything from the suspect?" he asked.

"Nothing. He's in a state of shock from seeing his friend get his head blown off. They got him down at Grady undergoing a psyche eval. He's freaked out pretty good. The medics found skull fragments in his mouth."

"Hmmmn."

"Yep. So far they're saying it looks like the guy who got away may've been shot too, but they're not sure. The detectives found a blood trail leading out the garage down the driveway."

"Has anyone contacted Mr. Denmark?" questioned Maj.

"Yes sir. He's flying in immediately, and should be landing by noon."

"Do we know where he's coming in from?"

Peavey looks away. He knows he should've already had that information! Though he isn't a detective, Major Tusk Hall expects his officers to be versed in all facets of police work.

"No, but I can get it."

"Show me how fast."

John takes a few steps away and scrolls through his contact list, and in moments he's talking to someone on the other end.

Five corporals are tasked with the duty of keeping the press in control. Behind the throng of pushy people with mics, pens, recording devices, and agendas, are the residents; dozens of them, many very influential and very powerful. They too want answers. Though he's ducked between a group of low hanging Dogwoods tucked behind a barriers of cars, trucks, and emergency vehicles, the inquisitors are still able to sniff him out.

The department spokesperson, Tameka Parris is weaving her way through the mob, and coming under the caution tape heading his way.

"Beautiful morning huh major?"

"Quite."

"Shhhhhweeeeeeew...I just got here. It a mess out there. Have you seen Dresden?" (The surface street)

"No. But hopefully we can get this wrapped up soon. We're already pushing four hours."

"Have you decided on a statement because the press is getting pretty antsy? There's already false reports flooding the airwaves, and also the residents are starting to try to force their way pass the barricades. The media's right there waiting for an altercation so they can blame us. It's getting ugly major."

The patient and persevering leader strategizes his next play. "Before you come up with the answer let me brief you on some information I've found."
Switching on her Bluetooth® device she detracts the extension handle on her black, *Tumi® Alpha Compact* wheeled briefcase, heaves it up, and sits it on the hood. Producing a chunky manila file she opens it.
"I'm positive the press has done the same thing so we're kind of going be ahead of the curve........Now based on court documents, five months ago a lawyer representing his wife, Farah Denmark, filed a petition for legal separation. She also requested a temporary order of support and primary
custody of the kids. However, the petition was withdrawn a month later, but it looks like the order of support is still in place. I didn't find any TPO's (temporary order of protection). There's also these questionable dea-"
"What are the ages of the children," he interrupted. "What address did she list?" compiling a nightmarish scenario.
"The address she used is this one, but the kid's arrrrrrre...," pausing to search the documents.
Before she finds the answer, and he have any more vivid imaginings, a woman starts screaming! Cries so hysterical she's audible over *all* the noise and movement of a convoluted homicide scene. Overflowing with such a passionate charge of shock and awe, she fills the pale skies with the sad song of a mother's mourn. Unknowingly, she's bullied her way to the top of the major's To-Do list.
A call comes over the radio about a lady claiming to be the victim's mother being in a panic and causing an uproar—requests EMS, because it seems the woman's on the verge of a nervous breakdown.
The next thing said verifies the unsettling images he's seeing in

his mind.

The officer is telling his supervisor the lady keeps saying the news is reporting "*two*" children were slain. Where's the third one? She says there are three grandchildren who live in the residence. "He's right," Parris begins. "It lists three children as residents of the house, but only one is included in the support affidavit."

While she continues her detailed explanation of the documents, the major is digesting the chance he has a missing child on his hands!

Like the synergy between a quarterback, and his head coach, John Henry Peavey's back; one could even call him Johnny-on-the-spot.

"Sir I have that information for you."

The major has his phone to his lips about to update the chief on the developments.

"Shoot."

"Delta Airlines list's his departing city as Las Vegas, Nevada."

"Vegas huh,…Okay thanks. Good work. Forward it to the guys. I think we've got a missing kid."

The major's other phone starts chirping. It's Hickenlooper.

"What-cha' got Loop?" now with two phones to his ear.

He informs him they finally reviewed the tape of the store's surveillance cameras, and it shows a gray SUV and a taxi trading a passenger. It also shows a white van leaving from the direction of the neighborhood, followed by the same SUV several minutes later. The footage is too grainy to get an exact description, but they can tell it's a white cargo van with tented windows. Unfortunately, it didn't have any visible markings. He says the lab's gonna to try to clean it up but it may take a while.

Putting his hand over the phone he says to Peavey. "We got something," and removes it.

With the Dick on speaker phone, and the chief listening on speaker, Hall opens the car door and sits inside. In the center console is the same mobile information center a normal squad cars carries, but with more programs and more computing power. A press of the keyboard, and the screen comes to life. The major enters his access code, inputs a precise, two paragraph order for a high priority search bulletin for the two suspected vehicles—with the risk of a hostage situation. This is seen by the main dispatch center, as well as broadcast by way of 'robo-call' to the entire police force. The Georgia Highway Patrol and Georgia Bureau of Investigations are also made privy to the dragnet. An orange verification code starts flashing on the screen, meaning the order has been received, processed, and is now active. The fact it's been sent by the major of expedites the command. There's no need for further approval.

Hall says something to the chief, and ends the call.

Seconds later dozens of officers receiving the order on their radios crowd the area with even more chatter. Backs stiffen, scowls of determination intensify, grips on the investigation tighten as the brave servicemen acknowledge the order.

He doesn't need seventy two hours to hypothesize the third child is in the van, or that this was a clear and premeditated contract killing. Considering who these people are, and the magnitude of the stakes, any number of scenarios could be in play. If there's a silver lining to be unearthed within this madness, is the fact the perpetrators aren't that skillful. Either a rag-tag group of low level, easy to defeat opportunists, or ancillary cogs of a far bigger machine.

Some people find it difficult to walk and chew gum at the same time, but Major Hall displays excellent poise in this time of distress. After listening to Parris' information, he was able to coordinate the forces efforts, reply to his investigator, update the chief, and input data into the mainframe.

"Thanks for the info detective, and great work with the footage. Keep me in the know if you find out anything else."

Hickenlooper thanked him for the compliment and got back to work. Despite not being his direct supervisor, he greatly admires the major, and will follow his orders quicker than those coming from his own commander.

Many dimwitted managers use their position to demean and weaken subordinates, with hopes it increases their own miniscule amounts of both usefulness and might. But all it really does is exhibit their high level of low self-esteem, and dwindles the moral of the work force. These types of counterproductive tactics are often employed by spineless schmucks.

A true leader, a real lion amongst men doesn't deteriorate his kingdom by demonstrating the chickenhearted act of using the weak as fodder to validate his conquests. A virtuous man is submitted to by choice, thus attaining enduring clout. A tyrant has to manufacture the illusion of respect by way of fear and manipulation. Both means are effective, but only one deserves respect.

An unfortunate by-product of grief is the damage it does to ones sanity. The harpoon of heartache which pierces ones soul is the same one the drives ones will for answers. The mother finally breaks through the clog of officers guarding the perimeter, and runs across the front lawn screaming. News cameras pointed in any other direction immediately altered their bearing, and bare down on the developing ratings bonanza. With a signal strength of 10,000 watts, the gut-wrenching drama is thrust into million homes. Be it a Toni award winning Broadway musical, or a low-budget independent pilot, the face of death always looks the same, that same unapologetic stare of reality; one that always promises another sequel.

With compassion, a team of officers converge on the torn woman, and respectfully prohibit her from seeing what's already been decided. There's no need for her to validate what's been verified. She falls to the manicured grass. A grief counselor approaches and hugs her reassuringly—a wheelchair pulls up beside her.

And that's when Parris looks away, back at the major, who too is moved by the event. Concealed within this camouflage of men who aren't supposed to cry, and women who are to remain strong; are heads hung. Eyes water as the emotional toll of police work is explicitly showcased for all to see. A comforting arm of morning sun reaches from the heavens and graces the shattered home with kind rays of warming light. A hint of blissful juniper hangs to the breath of the easygoing Georgia breeze. It seems to be allowing the family's souls a peaceful passage into the afterlife. Soaring southern pines surround the congregation like a platoon of resplendent angels eulogizing the passing of a revered saint.

A shot goes off, splitting the ears of every officer issued a department radio!

The fist of justice squeezes! Fury seeps from their pores like fizzes of hot kerosene! The call ignites the officers with effervescent bits of red-hot moral, fortifying their mettle!
The suspect's vehicle has been spotted!
They want these assholes bad!

Fear and phobia affect individuals in a myriad of ways. Having been born and raised in the country, Alex should be used to spiders and small biting multi-legged insets. Arachnophobia is just one of the many knocks on the skittish fugitive hiding in a dark maintenance closet. The apartment community is East Hampton Hills. After narrowly escaping death, he headed for a hideout he thought of, but gets paranoid. He couldn't stop reliving the experience, he couldn't stop hearing voices, and kept thinking squad cars were scouring the area. Finally, he couldn't take any more and pulled into this complex. After having the bejesus scared out him, he developed a burning need to urinate.

While enjoying the sensation of the release, the night watchman who witnessed him enter the property saw him disappear behind the unit. He came and jotted down his tag number, and waited beside it. Alex never came back to it—the SUV is no longer an option.

The blood on his shirt from the spatter of the man's exploding head is making his skin crawl, plus he still hasn't dealt with his lacerated elbow. But being gullible, or lacking in problem solving ability isn't preventing him from thinking Bailey Red set him up. But he's a homeless drifter with nothing of value. What does he have that she wants?

The cheap Nokia analog relic he managed to hold on to starts buzzing in his pocket.

Pulling it out and looking at it, he sees he has absolutely no signal strength, but somehow Bailey is still calling?

Without thinking he answers.

"Where the hell are you!" he shout whispered, siting on what feels like a paint can in pitch black darkness.

He can smell the dankness of the space, and estimates it to be the size of a shed, and packed with stuff he can't make out. For all he knows, he can be in there with a butcher knife killer.

The first thing she says is, "Where are you?"

"Fuck no! You think I'm just gone tell you where I am after you just tried to get me killed!!" whispering with a little too much yell.

She accuses him of being crazy, and says he doesn't have anything she wants! Next he's called a lunatic and an ingrate for how he's treating her after she's risking her life to help him. She's still talking when he interrupts.

"So what was that back there; that guy was trying to kill me! Then some neighbor shoots him! I almost shitted on myself!" pausing to take a deep breath. "I mean *come on! Goddamnit* Bailey, what the hell," he spat.

"I didn't do anything, I don't know what's' going on!" she

screamed.

He can hear she's beginning to cry.

"Don't' you understand anything? I'm a mother and they're trying to kill me so they can send my daughter off to be groomed for sex work!"

"*Yeah!...*You told me that lie already! Who the hell are you lady?"

"A mother in need of help, you bastard!"

"Well call the police! Why are you trying to get me messed up, I'm already in deep shit! I'm just trying to get some cash so I can get the fuck outta dodge! You took my kindness for weakness, I knew I shouldn't have trusted you! You're just some slick ass stripper!"

She's crying now.

"*Shit!..* I'm sorry. I didn't mean that! But you don't understand, these two guys just tried to kill me."

"I get called names all day long, so it's nothing. You're just another asshole with a dick."

"People have punked me my entire life and I'm tired of it. But like I said, I apologize. We shouldn't be fighting each other, we're not the bad guys."

"I don't have long because a client is nearby. I'm only trying to help, and at the same time help myself! I can't gain anything from setting you up. Now make up your mind, where are you, or don't ever call her again because I'm in too great of danger to be playing games."

He only has seconds to decide, and only minutes before he has to get back on the move.

"*Bailey I swear If you---*"

But she cut him off and is about to hang up.

"I'm in some apartments off Pleasantdale....East Hampton I think."

"He's passed out drunk and I'm about to take his keys, but I'm feeling like saying forget you and do it alone today. I'm starting to regret ever asking you for help! And as far as going to the police, yeah right, so they can kill my daughter, no thanks! You think it's that easy to get away from these people? They have thousands of young women and girls they're doing this to, and even boys. You wouldn't believe it if I told you. You're just some country boy looking for a good time. You have no clue!"

"*Wait!* Bailey wait! I said I'm sorry, you don't know what just happened to me. Just come so we can figure this out, and I can get the hell out of this state."

She reaffirms that she's the one in danger and hopes she isn't making a mistake by trusting him.

"You're not. I'm not like that."

On that note she ends the call.

The architecture of the complex consists of twenty units, each with three floors. If his math is right, there's likely an occupied space on the other side of the far wall. There has to be because he just heard the sound of clanging pots and pans behind the voice of a female. Since their conversation is over, all he's left to do is stare into the darkness while listening to a mother prepare breakfast for her family. He on the other hand, is being overwhelmed by the fact he's just revealed his whereabouts to a person he barely knows, while simultaneously his gut provokingly chastises him with declarations that he's a fool.

As of now, he's been stowed away in this room for about three hours and somehow has even found a way to take a nap while sitting up. There's cob webs and whatever else is crawling around in his head, plus his knees are starting hurting being he suffers from rheumatoid arthritis.

He leans forward and stands up, his back cracking and face contorting as he enjoys the rush of relief. Looking at the floor he sees light coming under the door and can see his shoe in the trace of light creeping around the frame. His sight is compromised but his sense of touch can be used to feel his way around. He wraps his sweaty palm around the cold metal knob and prepares to take a peek. A quarter minute later, and a quarter spin of the knob, and the heavy door is swinging in his hand.

The first thing he sees through the two inch gap is the other side of the breezeway, and part of the cement floor; the rush of fresh air is stimulating. Not hearing any noise he pulls it open and sticks his head out. Looking as guilty as sin, he holds onto the door and steps completely out of the room.

Looking into the parking lot, he sees nothing but random cars and no people, but he does see the sun hanging over the tree tops. He turns back and using to light to view the room clearly.

It *is* a storage room. Rolls of carpet lean against the wall, gas cylinders, stacks of paint cans, garden tools, 2x4's, and a long list of other things he can't make out are stuffed inside.

His heart skips two beats when he sees the five gallon bucket he was just sitting on, and follows the wall upward! In the top corner is an intricate, and well-crafted web. In the center sits a massive black and yellow spider, which had been only inches from his head! Only a harmless garden spider, it just looks menacing; the same characteristic of most bullies supervisors and thugs.

A chill comes over him, realizing just how close he came to being bitten. Considering how dark it was, if he would've felt something crawling down the back of his neck with legs like that, he would've wrecked the entire room trying to get it off. The result would've been alerting the entire building that someone's under the steps. Clearly, he's not going back in there.

Alex walks to the end of the pavement and surveys the area. Five buildings over he sees the back of the SUV parked between two other cars, to his right he sees the expansive property and how still it is. His watch is gone, so a guess is used to predict the time. Estimating it to be around eleven, he turns and heads back the direction he came. At the opposite end of the breezeway, past the storage closet, and past the end of the concrete side walk, is the back of the unit. Through the woods he makes out a retention pond sparkling in the sunshine. The weather is spectacular, the start of a picturesque day.

But not for a man on the lam.

Turning his head both directions, he studies the area. The buildings are covered with wood siding and fitted with large sliding windows. The fluffy grass is lush. Green puppy-poop stations peg the length of the paved trail, wrought iron benches spaced along the tree line offer residents a chance to sit and enjoy nature's bounty.

Lost in his own world, he begins dazing. In the far recesses of his mind, his conscience is enamored with the consequences of his decisions. The word perpetrator, imitator, or clone may be harsh adjectives his inner-self is using to describe him, but they're applicable. He knows what he's done, but doesn't want to accept the position that he's a bad person. He feels like he was forced to do those things, and only agreed because he didn't have the strength to say no. It's always been easier for him to settle for being easily swayed, than hard to move. There are beatings immovable objects take. They are relentlessly peppered with the space-junk of a moralless world. They have to bare the solar winds of blistering character assignations, and unjustified public ridicule.

But still, they remain firm! They stand tall gallantly and represent what is good in the universe.

Alex wants no part of standing up against anything, not the police force, not the bullies who terrorized him when he was a kid, not his wife who told him she wears the pants, and the skirt; not anything. He can't even stand up to a woman.

She's calling again too!

"Hello," he answered sheepishly.

She says she's turning into the complex and wants to know where to go, and that she's scared and doesn't really know how to drive.

"Okay. I'll be out."

Scanning around as if the answer is written somewhere on the side of building, he gets up and jogs to the corner.

Stopping at the edge of the breezeway he 'one-eye looks' around. The coast is still clear.

He makes one last nervous scan of the area, and heads toward the front.

Ducked behind a shrub, he sees a slow moving luxury sedan rolling down the aisle, the windows are tented and the rims are factory. His palms are sweating profusely, so he rubs them against his thigh.

"Stop right here."

While the car is still moving he leaps from his blind and runs to the door, opens it and jumps inside!

Seeing the fear in her eyes, he knows she's in serious danger.

But *she* asked, "Are you okay?"

"I'm fine. Now what the hell happened? I thought that was your house I was at! Those freaking guys were trying to kill me!" and wipes a backhand across his forehead.

"Who got killed?...What are talking about," genuinely perplexed.

"The two guys in the truck tried to kill me when I got out. I knew something wasn't right with them. The neighbor popped out of nowhere and shot the guy. I wa-"

"What!...What guy?"

"Hell if I know, I don't know any of these people. These are your friends."

"That's a lie! No one's trying to kill you! You're just making this up! And they *are not* my friends!"

"*What!!!* Are you crazy or something lady! Some

guys were trying to kill me for real! Why would I make this up?" She stares at him.

"I've been out here a long time doing this and I'm tired! You could be some sicko just like the rest of these men. You ask yourself what you have to gain."

Alex is speechless!

She sees the blood stains and tears on his clothes! Her memory begins picturing all the acts of brutality she's suffered while being forced to work as a sex slave. The fact something bad may've actually happened brings more fear to her mind.

"Oh my god," she said, putting her hands over her mouth. "I thought you were at the hotel I was at! I had no clue he was doing something else! He's just some coke head I use to do favors for me. I know him from the club and have been trying to convince him for months to take me and my daughter to Missouri, but keeps saying he too busy and doesn't want his wife to find out about me. His parents are rich and live in a mansion off this street called Dresden! But it's really because he's terrified of Merciless. He watches me like a hawk and has his goons scare off anyone he thinks is getting close to me. Sometimes tricks fall in love with the girls and run off with them. He's not about to let me get away like that, that's why he keeps my daughter locked away somewhere to prevent me from escaping. I'm trying to help you so that you will help me. Kinda like eye for an eye."

Men who pay for sex are often called "tricks" because they are "tricked" into paying for what a real man gets for free.

"Merciless doesn't tell me what's up. I'm nothing to him. I'm just like all the others. We're just fun-girls he uses to make his money. Are you sure you saw somebody get shot?"

"*Very!* It's probably all over the news by now!"

She doesn't say anything at first.

"I've gotta get out of here before he harms my daughter!" panic heavy in her tone.

"So you work for him?"

"I already told you, didn't you hear anything I just said."

"Oh yeah. Sorry. My minds gone right now. I keep thinking about how those guys tried to kill me."

"I don't want to talk about it anyway. I just want to get away. I'm tired of this. If it wasn't for my child I'd commit suicide, I swear I would. Death is better than this."

"Well let's get the hell out of here!"

"Where do you want to go? But we gotta hurry, I'll be dead if he finds me here. You have family or something?"
"I already told you, there's nowhere for me to go. Just get me the hell out of here. If I could get out of town that'll be great."
Bailey's face goes from that of a staring woman trying to untangle the lies, to shocked Do-gooder.
"You're the guy the cops are looking for," she said astonished.
That's his cue.
Before she can make any more observations he's gone, I mean *gone!* Faster than Carl Lewis, Jerry Lewis, or even Usain Bolt; high-tailing it back the way he came, disappear down the breeze-way, and vanishes!

Bailey Red sits there staring at the passenger door swinging...... leans and shuts it—hits speed dial!

Alex is running full speed with no destination! His first thought is to head towards the pond, but gets another idea, and skids to a halt! The burn is his chest and the chafe in his throat remain as he beelines for a return to the maintenance closet! Overhead he sees a person looking at him from their third floor window, but he doesn't stick around to see what their next move is.
Luckily, the steel door didn't shut completely and lock him out. He doesn't have time to jimmy the latch again.

Back inside he quietly closes the door! It becomes just as dark as before. He's breathing so hard his hand is used to muffle his gasps! Remembering the spider chillin' in the corner, he stays far away from that area! Through the walls be can hear the morning is in full swing, and makes out at least three voices and a televi-sion.

Creeping around blind, he uses his hands to be his eyes. The thick dust on the floor has his steps slippery, and as much as he's terrified of capture, he's equally terrified of stumbling upon a biting insect, a wasp nest, or better yet a snake. Breathing way too hard, exhibiting way too little coordination, and not being able to see his hand in front of his face; he falls over something. Something big, something metal, and something loud!

Clang-Clang! BASH!...BAM!!!

Goes something falling from above, and hitting something else causing it to tumble over too.

"FUCK MEEEE!"

The television is instantly silenced!

The only thing he hears is the antagonizing sound of an empty can of WD-40® spinning on the floor like a twirling tin of torture!

Panicked by the shrill, he clumsily pushes himself upright and in the process makes more racket!

Clang- c-c-c-clang!

Getting on his knees, he starts sweeping his hands over the dusty floor like a demented maid! After nine more intense seconds he grabs the cold aluminum and clutches it angrily! Trying to squeeze the life out of it, he wants to slam it into the wall for pulling a stunt like that!!!

He gets to his feet.

Standing motionless he listens!

Through the walls he can hear hurried movement! He dusts himself off, and as he makes for the shimmer of light tracing the door frame, bends down and feels in front of him. Easing to the door he puts his right ear flat against the cold. All he can hear is blurred vibrations of human movement and the hushed echoes of nature. Turning the knob slowly, he cracks the door and peeks through. His eyes see nothing for concern.

He sits back down and tries to calm down. He fights to control his breathing that has him sounding like a panting hound.

As the seconds turn into minutes, and the match in his chest comes to an end, he gets sleepy again. His eyes grow heavy, he wiggles his frail tail in the seat to a more comfortable position. And wonders what happened to Maury?

A car door slams!

Radio chatter!!

Footsteps!!!

Someone's moving fast towards his position!

Paralyzed by fear, his muscles transform into stone trapping his fingers in a shaking claw of pulsing veins and chewed fingernails! The boots are close, and now speaking a request for backup!

A shadow appears under the door.

"Police! Anyone in there!"

Like a mini earthquake, the door begins shaking violently.

Alex knows it's over. The cheap lock won't hold up for long!! He watches in horror as the two blacks boot reposition themselves, and shoulder ram it.

BAM!!!!!

His mouth drops open!!!

BAM!!!!!

He steps away from the impending arrest!

BAM!!!!!

Hallucinogenic reminders of all the wrong he's done begin attacking him!

"Yeah! We've got the truck so we know he's around here somewhere," the officer says to someone nearby.

His vision shifts from clear sight of shock, to blurry phantom of impending doom! Waiting for the flashlights, the shouts, and the guns, he feels something crawling down his neck!!! It's right at the top on the inside his shirt!!! The way his heart starts racquetball-ing with his inner chest cavity, he suspects he's going to die from cardiac arrest!!!!!!!!!! With speed, he reaches back and smack-punches his upper back with fury, clutching a fistful of his shirt, and almost chocking himself unconscious in the process!!! The gritting teeth, and bucked eyes are clear indications of his mental state! With beads of hot sweat dripping down his forehead clouding his vision, more sweat is getting inside his mouth! Clutching his shirt as if he's arresting himself, he notices the shadow under the door is gone? Using his left hand he twists, and wrings his shirt until he hears a crunching sound!

And reluctantly let go! Gooey particles tumble down his back and into his pants like sandy jellybeans covered with tiny hairs! He's so terrified of making noise that he bares the anguish of dead creature parts touching his skin!

But before he can rejoice, it sounds like an officer is speaking to one of the tenants. He can't make out everything but he can hear a police offer questioning someone.

Petrified by confusion he moves for the door, and gets on his knees to look under.

He sees nothing.

Crawling on his belly he slides closer.

With his ear now closer to the outside, he makes out words, and multiple men with radios!!! Listening while panting, he hears what sounds like a lady telling an officer: *"I heard a lot of noise coming from in there. I think someone's inside."*

He hears a male respond: *"Which one? This one right here, or that one over there?"*

And she say: *"No, that one!"*

This tells Alex two things: There are multiple storages spaces, and she'd indeed heard him making noise.

As best as he can, he tries to think what to do! The longer he stands here shaking, the plainer it becomes! She had to have mistakenly directed the police to the wrong place! It has to be, because he can hear all the movement concentrated farther down.

Adrenaline pulses!

He sees a glimmer of hope!

This next decision could get him shot dead, but his choices are nil. With his back firmly against the wall, it's only one place to go from here! With the expectation of getting kicked in the face, or hit upside the head with a flashlight, he eases the door open! But he gets nether.

Nothing.
But he *can* hear men down ahead! His heart is beating like a high-octane piston, and he's about to blow a gasket! The signal that starts the dash is the sound of the authorities kicking in the door to the other space!
He swings the door and takes off for the trees!!!
Branches and vines smack his body as he tears through the dense brush like a buzz-saw through a corn field! Abandoning all sense of safety he runs,
and he runs,
and runs...and *runs!!!*
All the way until he can go no more and collapses to the ground! All he can see is the inside of his eye lids and the sensation of lying face down in wet leaves with twigs, grass, and wild mushrooms. He can taste the red clay in his mouth, and feel the granular debris sticking to his parched lips. The pain he feels over his aching body, coupled with the culmination of his impending demise, moves him to begin weeping. The man who'd done a lot of wrong is experiencing the ruthless karma of his actions.
"If only there was a way I could make up for it," he cried. *"If only I could make it right God I would. I'm sorry for the things I did! He made me do it,"* speaking with such conviction his body shudders.
"Please give me a chance to make it right, Please!"
Coming from the deep bowels of his torment, prone on the surface of a nondescript location, he implores the Creator for forgiveness. From his mouth saliva, mucus, and blood come forth in a shameful concoction of realization. The state of his condition pleads for mercy, pleads for understanding, pleads for redemption. But there's no alter to stage an offering, there's no sacred calf to be presented. What he's done is inexcusable, beyond forgivable. What's done is done, all he can do is await his fate.
As he tries to compose himself, he notices he still isn't in cuffs. Lifting his head he looks around cautiously.
He's sitting in the forest completely alone without a soul around

him.

Something is odd? There's no way he could've gotten away that fast?

"What's going on," he whispered.

A draft of chill bumps blow over him. The longer he remains still the more he wants to keep moving, but he's astonished.

Getting to his feet he hunches down and listens.

Still nothing?

Nothing in the distance either?

Maybe he really did lose them?

".....Hell no."

A rush of menacing wind storms through the trees and tackles him!

Birds rise to the heavens, locust, grasshoppers, butterflies take to the sky!

Shaken by the power of the Almighty, he takes off running away from the direction he came, trekking towards the pond like an all-terrain vehicle of spiritual proportions!

The thunderous crack of a tree branch falling from above further fuels his escape! He's certain he's running straight towards it, but somehow he's in a dense forest with no sight of water, or cops. Surveying his body he sees his shoes are caked with pounds of mud, his clothes are covered in grass stains, and dirt. Bits of organic debris cling to him like wet tissue. His face is filthy and sweaty with welted scratches. Moving forward, he pushes through the hilly terrain blanketed with soggy hay, dried leaves, angular boulders, and fallen limbs. He looks up at the sun sparking high above the canopy. To his right he sees a rusty generator reddened by the elements, remnants of the frame, and stiff corroded wires remain non-biodegraded. A brick structure overran with kudzu camouflages a badly deteriorated metallic tank. Cut sprigs of tarnished copper piping protruding from the base of the distiller gives a retrospective glimpse into its past.

Up ahead he sees the look of a sloping valley, and on the other side is a chain-link fence. There seems to be a clearing in the distance. Holding onto the trunk of an oak tree he looks and listens. Seeing nothing, he half slides, half walks down the decline. Using his hand like claws he makes it up the other side, and crouches at the fence. It's some kind of living community, and he's at the rear of the property scanning the expansive topography. The backyards are portioned by brick walls, and he knows there are probably cameras. Brushing his hands against his pants, he's pleased the phone is still there, and he also still has the wallet and ring of keys. But the gun is long gone. Reaching up he pulls himself over.

Running along the fence are a line of Callery pear trees. White, five-petaled blooms enclose him in a lively cocoon.

The residents love the charming feel they add to the vista. Bees are busy pollinating, short day breeders are mating, hummingbirds and brown thrashers jockey for air space; Alex is watchful and moving fast! Hugging the perimeter, he works his way past the tennis courts, swimming pools, and fitness center. Standing beside a unit, he realizes these are not apartments, but an independent living community for senior citizens. His suspicions are proved when he comes over the top of a crest and sees the main entrance in the distance. In various ways people can be seen moving slowly. Some under their own power, some on scooters, and some on golf carts. This is a silver paradise of the golden years.

Spying on the happy seniors enjoying the day, he sees lots of white, lots of plaid, and lots of boredom. If they see him it'll be a nitro shot to the varicose monotony of their routine lifestyle. This is the last place he needs to be. The elders may be slow, but their accuracy with punching emergency numbers is deadly. He hears the sounds of street traffic tarnishing the serene patina. Thinking of the best way to get his bearing, he ducks down and heads that direction. Still fairly hidden, and the right skin tone, so he may be okay. Luckily, he comes upon a trail and runs down the walkway until it goes left, and heads around the front of what looks like an activity building. It's covered with beige siding and single storied. The trio of running air conditioning units muffle his hurried movements.

Coming to the fence designed to protect the residents from people like him, and those traversing the side walk; the tall spruce trees add even more barriers. He crawls under and between a pair, and focuses on the surface street. About a quarter mile down there's an intersection, a restaurant, and a laundry mat. Across the street is a cafeteria and a grocery store. It wasn't until he sees the drug store, and the Mr. Cue's billiards parlor that the hair on the back of his neck stand on end! More beads of sweat sprout from his pores, he's hotter than he was a second ago! Here he is thinking he's out of danger, and he's only blocks away from where he started! With panic about to re-ignite, he queries the surrounding area for a solution. Driven by impatient befuddlement he stays on the good side of the fence and heads towards the intersection, knowing from past encounters the crossing streets are Chamblee-Tucker Rd. and Northcrest Dr. The plaza is the Embry Hills shopping center.

Void of a plan and overwhelmed with the fear of arrest, he emerges from cover, goes back down to the side walk, and starts running. But in meters, he's winded and back to a saunter.

Hearing voices, he leaps back to the protection of the spruces!

As the voices get louder he begins seeing people strolling down the walk-way, and in seconds they'll see a strange man standing at the fence attempting to hide amongst the trees! His only means of escape is over the fence, and onto the public road. A carefree laugh is heard, and he smells women's perfume! Iced by panic, he stands a moment too long! Sitting atop a burgundy Hoveround® scooter, she rolls to a halt and looks questioningly at the tattered man crouching at the fence. Like a photo captured in time, the two stare at each other. One with a look of fear laced exhaustion, and the other with a cup of rum spiked Maxwell House® with her head cocked to the side. She waves and smiles.

"Good morning," said the white haired woman wearing a star ruby on her pinky finger.

Alex shows his ass by leaping over the fence, falling over the other side, and taking off running holding his pants!

The heat of the sun immediately jumps him. Like a guppy in a den of ravenous feral cats, the man with the ten grand bounty on his head is showcased to willing bidders. Police are swarming the area and he's in the worst possible situation at this point. At any second there could be a person tackling him to the ground with hopes of securing the reward money. Between him and the intersection, a neighborhood sits across the street. The homes look safe and the entrance disappear down a hill. Glancing both ways he crosses and makes for it!

At the light, the sound of screeching tires catches his attention? A sedan is waiting to make a U-turn but there's a car in front. When he's sees it back up and drive across the concrete median, he breaks into a jog—a run is out of the question!

A person walking up their driveway flipping through a bundle of mail sees him enter the neighborhood, snatches off their sun-glasses, and focuses on the strange intruder.

"Hey!!!"

He hears him yelling but doesn't give him a chance to see his face.

The houses are decent, but nowhere near upscale, just a normal middle class subdivision. It's not until he hears the sound of more screeching tires, and the roar of a big V-8 that he half turns!

A car is coming towards him with a blinding sun glare reflecting of the windshield!!!!!!

He has nowhere to go! Playing dead only works in the wild. Somewhere on these grounds he knows he'll make his final hoo-rah! He can't go to jail, he won't make it in prison. He's fought a good fight, but he'll be sure his opponent kills him rather than surrender. Savoring every last morsel of life, he trespasses into a yard, runs to the back, and skids to a halt!

Next comes the slam of a car door, and heavy footsteps!
Under the back patio it is a two foot space, and like a roach
scurrying into a crack, he runs and slides just as legs fly around
the corner!

"You got ten seconds to come out with your hands up, or you're
dead Zarbin," instructed the voice of an angry man.

Alex begins crying. From under the wooden planks he can see
the expanse of the yard and the privacy fence. He thinks of the
time he saved the stray cat and wishes someone would save him.
"*Get...Your...Fucking...Ass...*Out-here-right-now!" kneeling on
one knee, pointing a gun at him, looking at the bottom half of
his body.

Prone on his hands and knees, the cold moist dirt crumbles
within the panic of his clutch! With his head nestled between
the wooden joists of the deck, he's immobilized, his brain is in
shock! The wasp nest tucked in the corner beside the stairs isn't
an issue at this point. He can't see the man's eyes, but knows
he's looking at him! All he can see are the lines of light squeezing between the floor planks above him, and the blue sky that
seems like another galaxy. As if the searing terror of impending
arrest isn't enough, fate heightens the instability of his sanity by
bringing a quaking shake to the structure! Dust and bits of saw
dust fall into his eyes! Instantly he feels the pain and tries to rub
it out! The burning tears are accompanied by the thunder of a
human being trouncing across the pressure treated lumber above
him!! A patio door smacks shut in the background! The familiar
action of a shotgun warns him of the presence of a 12-gauge
shotty.

An ear splitting boom gives his ears something to ring about,
and the trespassers a clue he means business!

"*Hey!* What the hell's going on! What are you doing back here!"
he shouts from the patio.

The man stands with his hands in the air.

"*Drop that pistol! Drop that pistol right now,*" squealed the homeowner, nervous and afraid, second blowing his chest out.

Alex watches a gloved hand lay a semi-automatic pistol on the grass beside his leather loafer.

"I'm a private investigator! Alex Zarbin, a wanted fugitive is under your patio! Please drop your weapon and allow me to apprehend him," responds the man, who has a foreign accent and doesn't sound like an investigator.

"Where's your badge," the homeowner demanded.

Before the wind blew another blade of fescue, Alex has crawled to the far end and is gone again, over the fence and into the next yard, climbing over into theirs!!! Before he disappears down the middle of the road, and heads for the tree line, the last thing he sees is a tall black man in a suit holding his hands in the air, while an older black man wearing a 'peace sign symbol' T- shirt and blue shorts points a shotgun at him.

The second his feet met the pavement, his quad cramps up, rendering him almost immobile! His arm drops to his thigh as he grimaces in pain! Through closed eyes he clutches his teeth and looks towards the heavens! But for a person like him there are no rays of protection, only blistering lasers of ultraviolet revenge, universal compensation for his transgressions.

About to collapse in pain, he sees the man he encounters upon first entering the neighborhood standing in his driveway with a phone to his ear. Parked on the curb at the mailbox is the running sedan of the man who claims to be a private investigator. Through sheer will he drags his battered body towards the vehicle!

The man yells for him to stop, and starts screaming for help.

He arrives at the vehicle, and gets in! Feeling the vibration of the engine, he slams the car in gear, and floors it!

The potent eight cylinder ignites the rear wheels. The smell of rubber, and the way the sedan leans as it jumps the curb careening onto the man's front lawn is more than a notion! Mud and pebbles spew like rooster tails from the spinning tires, as he slides out of a destructive U-turn back off the curb, leaving a trial of tire tracks, and a destroyed mailbox in his wake! As he flies up the hill and out of the neighborhood, he sees the man in the suit run from behind the house, and fire upon the vehicle! But the attempt is futile, Alex evades capture again.

Pressed for time and pressed for freedom, he hears sirens and runs the light at the intersection. Gassing down the street, in the distance he sees police cars swarming the area! Turning on Henderson Mill Rd., he speeds down the hill and sees he's driving a Chevrolet Impala, it's clean and smells like a rental. In the cup holder is a half empty bottle of water. The way his tongue is stuck to the roof of his mouth, and the congealing blood oozing from his cracked lips, there's no doubt about it. He lifts the bottle to his mouth and bites the plastic cap off—condensation dripping from the plastic heightening his angst.

But he drops it just as he was about to savor his first swig, his left foot and brake pedal are now thoroughly hydrated.

"You've got to be kidding me!" he shouted, reaching down to grab it.

Holding it before his face he sees there's only a third of what there was. He drinks it, and his throat is quite thankful for the few ounces.

With a placebo infused cocktail of sudden well-being, and the genuine health benefits of consuming two parts hydrogen and one part oxygen, he's beginning to feel confident about his chances. Looking at the fuel gauge, he again thanks his luck. There's almost a full tank at his disposal. Briskly but not speeding, he drives down the hill while thinking of a place from his childhood which may provide refuge. If only he can make it? The windows aren't tinted and he has no identification in case he gets pulled over.

His right hand drops from the wheel and digs inside the glove box. Pulling into a nondescript neighborhood, he empties the contents on the passenger seat.

Another wallet!

He counts the currency, and goes for the other stuff. A Florida driver's license is backed by a stack of business cards and a hotel key card. In another sleeve is a magnetic decal advertising cell phone repair, a tiny brass key, and a picture of a small child. No credit cards and no phone numbers.

After going to the stop sign and turning, he picks up the license again.

Jean Pierre Budry, born 4/30/72 lives at 908 Point Sumter Dr. in Hallandale Beach, FL He's 5' 10" and weighs 236 lbs.

Throwing it to the seat he picks up the keycard. It's plastic with a magnetic strip. The front has an advertisement for a local theme park and the words: *'Holiday Inn Select'* are in green letters. Returning to the road, he stops at a light and looks at the cars in a post office parking lot. Sailing the keycard, it hits the dash and falls to the floor. Leaning over he sweeps the glove box again. Nothing left but miscellaneous papers and a pen. Grabbing the first one he feels, he unfurls it and reads it. It's a receipt from the hotel, and states which room is provided, and for how long. Based on the receipt, the room is good for another week. He folds it back, stuffs it and the key card in his pocket.

Taking great care, he becomes one with the other motorists, and does nothing to draw attention. Looking straight ahead he avoids eye contact. The I-285 on-ramp is close, but what's on the hotel receipt keeps bothering him. It lists the address as Hampton. His heart skips a beat at his luck. If his memory's correct, that's the newly built one off Hudson Bridge, ten minutes from where he's already going.

He thinks about the authorities. Curiosity, and the prospect of benefiting from another's demise, tempts him with scenarios. Squad cars race down the expressway with sirens blaring, the beat of a chopper is in heights. Trapped by a red light, he taps his foot with nervous anxiety while searching the sky.

"Come on, come on, come on!"

The second it changes he's on the gas, down the ramp, and in the fast lane. Keeping in line with the posted 65 MPH speed limit, he tucks in between a motorcycle and a Ford dually towing a fishing boat. As he settles in for his attempt to Henry County, the sun comes over the horizon and blinds his view. Echoes of air turbulence, and the faint sound of music comes from the radio. He never claim to be an atheist like his adopted brother Stockton, so he has no problem with praying for help. The fact he possesses great compassion for animals, and likes to do charity work gives him confirmation he not a psychopath. When he was a boy, he would join his father in deeds of giving. Whether his dad was doing volunteer work at a nursing home, or taking a group of disadvantaged youth to a football game, he knew from a early age the act of giving is something he greatly enjoys. Considering they were what some would call "rich", he saw himself as a budding philanthropist.

But his kindhearted dad adopted Stockton.

What act of quantum physics caused his dimension to shift from that of honor, to that of horror? Despite not being the brightest apple, or the first to confront aggression, he's always felt a sense of connection, a link to something else, something spiritual, something extra. As far back as he can remember, he would see signs, strange patterns and trends that went unnoticed to others. Instances of unexplainable sensations, vivid experiences with unexplainable dreams, and heart-pounding daytime fantasies. Lost in his thoughts, he uses the time to search for answers. While the miles on the odometer flip, and the exits pass, he finds himself weeping more. The things he's done are eating him alive, they're consuming him from the inside. The fact he views himself as a patriot, and not a poison gives him the sickening feeling he's playing host to a repulsive parasite. The more it feeds on his soul, the worst he feels. Stockton once whipped him with a gun after he expressed regret something they did. There's no room for compassion in this world, is what he believed. The strong survive and the weak get steamrolled.

With the way things turned out for Stockton, maybe there's some truth to that.

As he merges onto I-675 S., he rounds the curve and has to foot the brake, traffic has come to a halt. Sitting on the overpass, he peers through the trees and sees flashing lights. Up ahead there something's going on? His first thought is accident. But it *could* be a road block!
Semi-trucks on both sides are boxing him in! The cars in front of him begins moving, and he has no choice but to follow! Out of habit he checks for his seat belt.
He isn't wearing one, and sticks his hand down to retrieve it.

But what he feels is no seat belt, but a handle to something?

Something that will change his life forever?

Abandoning the harness search, he lets the vehicle coast and reaches under as far as he can. He feels something behind his seat. Veering into her lane, the lady beside him swerves as he reaches over the seat, catches the hard handle, pulls it out, and sits it atop the seat.
This case isn't the brief type.
He returns his attention to the highway. As he rounds the curve, he's delighted to see a work crew performing a road repair. Calmly he passes and continues on his way.
Now focusing on the case, he wants to open it. It has a latch on all four sides, which strikes him as odd? It's rectangular, and three quarters the width of a traditional business carrier, but fifty percent longer, and black and constructed of hard plastic.
A Georgia State Patrol officer is up ahead!
Two of them!
He knows they've got a description of the vehicle and begins to

panic!

Something loud is coming up fast on his right!

He has nowhere to go! He's positive they're searching for his vehicle!

Vroommmmmmmmm!

Goes a motorcycle passing by at blistering speed!

He looks for a way to slow down but he's almost upon the squad cars!

One of them hit the lights and gives chase to the motor bike!

Heat comes up his neck as he's only feet from passing........without incident.

They're so focused on the bike that they paid no attention to him going by. He can't believe his "luck"! Now he really wants to get off the road!

Just as he sees an exit up ahead. On a billboard there's an announcement for a last chance liquidation sale at a furniture store. The action words:

"Don't Miss This Opportunity!!!" are spread over the top.

The next sign is both literal *and* metaphorical.

High above the trees a brown pole sprouts from the canopy. Like a top hat raised high above the crowd, the *Holiday Inn Select* insignia sign stands boldly.

Is the universe spurring him towards something? Could it be his ultimate destiny, or his foolish imagination intensified by the fact he's already having second thoughts about his other spot anyway? He hasn't been there in years. What if he gets there and it's gone, torn down to make way for a new development or something? Exacerbating his stress level is the fact there's a case with unknown contents in his possession. The table has been set in such an enticing way that he can't resist taking a bite.

The tempting delight on the seat is only the hors d'oeuvre?

His plan was to pull over, and peep inside, but since the exit is up ahead, he'll be a sitting duck on the side of the highway.
He elects to follow his gut.
Good decision.

Coming to a subtle stop at the light, he looks both ways and behind him.
And at the case.
Back at the road.
Gas stations, and hotels are divided evenly in both directions. But his destination is to the left, *right* behind a Huddle House diner. From his passing view, he sees patrons hunched over plates. The Holiday Inn sits behind it. With the lot sparsely speckled with vehicles, a fifty four foot tractor-trailer idles alone at the far end. He pulls around back near a group of other ve-hicles and puts it in park.
Just as he's put on his bib, grabs his utensils, and is about to dig in to the contents of the case, his peripherals detect a bored, and reluctant to sweep the parking lot worker, pop from around the building toting a backpack blower.

His gazed is affixed on the man sitting in the Impala® looking up to something.
Being a hotel service veteran, he's witnessed many shady
dealings take place right under the noses of hapless guests. To him, the man in the dark colored sedan is exhibiting the poten-tial for something interesting. He gets his camera phone ready to capture the action.

❑❑❑❑❑❑❑❑❑❑

The racket of the blower, and the stare of the man beckons him to pull the keycard from his pocket. Realizing the guy is purposely remaining close, he grabs the stuff and gets out.

Having developed a plan, he scans the area and heads for the door at the end of the twelve story, beige stucco building. At the end is an outdoor pool and lounge area. The glass door to the hotel glass door is controlled access to prevent outsiders from entering. Retrieving the card from his pocket, he slides it inside the digital box. The red light flips to green and beeps, followed by the click of a latch.

He grabs the handle and pulls the door.

The shrill scream of a young girl startles him!

Stopping halfway through the doorway, he turns around!

It isn't until he hears the laughter and splash that his heart calms.

Inside it's pleasantly fragrant. Wall sconces deliver soft light to the long, carpeted hallway. Ahead he hears activity. The smell of continental breakfast enamors him with desires to eat. But the elevator situated half way down speaks a different truth.

A woman's coming towards him pushing a cleaning cart.

He turns his back pretending to be lost, and digs the receipt out of his pocket.

Room 112

He feels a rush of apprehension when he notices he's standing in front of Room 136. He hangs his head and keeps towards the lady. Reading the receipt, he keeps one eye on the numbers, and one eye on her.

She watches as he passes.

Now closer, he notices another hallway intersecting at the common point, and the increased sound of yapping guests and clinging plates. Showing no part of his face he turns the corner, and before he can complete nine more steps, he's passing Room 122; and walks straight pass it. All the way to the end of the hallway.

With a drubbing heart, he looks out the door leading to the back side of the four-sided lot. With his chest deflated and sweat tricking down his neck, his conscience orates him that all viable options are bad, and all foreseeable outcomes are disparaging. He's well past the point of positive outcomes.

A door opening behind him produces a cast of light.

"..putting the things in the car. You want something from up front?"

A female respondent requests: "Something good, and a cup of coffee."

The man's voice is deep and he's probably big. His accent sounds northern, and most northerners don't like southerners.

Trembling, he inserts the card into the lock. The red light blinks green followed by a click.

As he stands holding the handle in panic, the presence of the man behind him worsens his fragile state.

What if someone's in there? What if it's the police?

"Excuse me sir, do you have the time?"

The Yankee is looking at him, breathing down his neck about the fucking time!!!!

In one swift motion he opens the door and slips inside.

All the polite gentleman saw was the side of his scruffy face, and the slab of lumber now blocking his view.

"Asshole."

Frozen to the other side like a stranded tax man hugging a sinking buoy in a sea of blood thirsty Great White tax protesters, he stands motionless. All he hears are vibrations of the man pacing away, and the heaving breaths of his own lungs. Staring at the drawn curtains, the sun light partially illuminates the dim room with traces of glowing streaks—a mahogany colored dresser is at the center of the wall. From his point, only the foot of the bed is visible. The design of the blanket is the same as all the other hotel rooms he's been in. The dark expanse of the bathroom present him with a partial view of the shower, and a partial view of a man!

His heart shutters.

But it's the image of himself reflecting off the vanity's wide mirror.

"Housekeeping….,"came his sad declaration. "Housekeeping! Housekeeping!"

After no response, he un-plasters himself from the door and ventures onward. Flipping the light switch inside the bathroom, he snatches the curtain back. The walls are wet, and a used rag is in the basin. On the sink is another used one.

Exiting he leaves the light on and rounds the corner to view the bed. It's queen sized with a nightstand on either side, and a lamp bolted over the head board. The wallpaper is artful and embossed, a short fridge, a microwave oven, and an office desk sit near the balcony. Steeping to it, he pushes back the curtains and observes. High above the horizon he can see for miles. Thirty miles to the north, the sprawling Atlanta skyline stands erect. The elegant manner in which the peaks penetrate the billowy clouds, an artiste would be hard pressed to find a more attractive setting.

Turning away, he opens the cabinet, and inside is a 32-inch LCDTV sided by a selection of alcoholic beverages. Behind him is an alcove for hanging clothes and a shelf.

Gathering he's safe for now, he sits atop the bed. Laying the case down beside him, he pulls at one of the metal latches but it won't open. Seeing the tiny key hole, he extracts the key from the wallet.

The slam of a door momentarily halts progress, causing him to get up and run to the peep hole!

Housekeeping.

He rushes back to the bed and proceeds to unlocking all four.

Having no clue what to expect, he clicks open the latches. There's no hinges at fixed points, so he has to completely separate the two halves. Placing one half on his lap he feels its full weight. As gravity exerts its force on the half he's holding, his eyes are captivated by the sight of so much steel! New, but dull, nice, but not in an endearing way. He's never experienced such weaponry before!

The carrier's insides are fitted with a rigid foam material.

As much as he wants to admire this half, it gets even better.

Secured behind elastic straps and sleeves, is another weapon. Shorter and more compact, but just as amazing.

Sitting it to the side, he returns to his initial selection.

Carefully, he unsecures, and lifts it out. The words: *LA2A1 Enfield (UK)* are stamped into the receiver, *7.62x39mm* is listed as the diameter of the bore. It's an exquisitely crafted firearm. He estimates it to be about nine pounds, and with a length of less than three feet. A long-ranged optic covered with rubber caps is secured atop. A box of ammunition and, a silencer each sit in their own individual compartments. He was raised around guns, just like almost everyone else in the South. Just about his entire family are avid hunters. He knows what a rifle looks like, but this is something made for sniping humans, not game.

Laying it back inside, he beholds the other. It's half as long, half as light, but just as deadly, and also has its own cadre of ammunition and equipment, including a 'noise suppressor' as they are properly called. It's listed as being a *Calico M960*. It seems to be a machine gun.

"Guess they can call me Kelly," he joked.

Under it, there's a compartment containing a semi-auto 9mm pistol equipped with an extended clip, a suppressor, and cache of titanium coated combat knives. The fact the man chasing him was carrying such lethal artillery makes him that more eager to vacate the premises. If he has access to this type of ordnance, there's no telling what other skills he possess. He's no match for a pool boy, better yet a trained assassin. The prospect moves him to get up and pace back and forth from door to window. From the look of things, he's better off till nightfall? Maybe that's when he can continue with his original idea.

While the sound of a vacuum cleaner breaches the walls of the 476 sq. ft. space, he looks at the weapon in his hand. At worst case scenario, he can shoot whoever returns. Walking to the desk he sits down. Parting the blinds he again searches the outside expanse, seeing no police and hearing no sirens. No caravan of black vehicles are moving toward his position, no ghetto bird is in the sky. (Street slang for police helicopter)
Allowing his brain to wander, he focuses his attention on the beam of sunlight stretched across the carpet. Floating bits of sparking nothings hover about like an enchanted breeze. The effects of extreme exhaustion are affecting his vision. The fact he's stationary, and for the time being not in a state of panic, his body involuntarily kicks into recovery mode.
The Sandman hits him with magic dust.
His head grows heavy, he has no control over his state. And in moments he's falling asleep.
His inner voice screams for him not to do it!
But the intoxicating relief of succumbing to a nap is too over-powering, the fat cushioned seat replicates the perfect bassinet. Behind his last specks of consciousness, he extends his legs. The pop of his bones, and the sensation of returning blood flow is euphoric.

Someone brought a piñata to the party and stashed it under the bed! And from the way it feels, it's stuffed with a trove of good-ies!

A thief assails his burgeoning dream, snatching the sleep from him. An incendiary image burns his mind with flames of being slaughtered while sleeping in the chair.

With his sight clearing, and a throbbing pain in his temple, his foot, and the section of a duffle bag underneath are the apples of his eye. With his biological engine initiating a sapped, and grudging start, it takes a few blinks of the second digit on the desk's digital clock before he regains his equilibrium. As his focus comes painfully clear, it only takes a millisecond for him to decide what to do.

He leans forward, grabs the bag, and pulls it fully into view. It's heavy and cumbersome.

What he's gazing upon is actually a military grade 'ditty bag'. A jumbo one, canvas and olive green, a Haitian flag is embroidered into the top center. There's various pockets attached to it, and two sturdy straps allow the wearer to transport it via back, or shoulder.

In the wild, competing males mark their territory by means of emitting scent. Low ranking members are frightened off by the mere essence of a dominant male. The redolence emanating from the bag permeates his psyche with indications of its owner's supremacy. Reluctant to even look inside, he stares at the buckled flap and at how round the bag is. Unlatching one of the pockets reveals a pre-pay cellphone still in the box, a stack of international calling cards, a charging hub, a digital compass, and a road atlas. Inside another produces what he'll later discover, are a pair of high powered, thermodynamic imaging, day/night vision binoculars, an eye glass case, and a high-tech flashlight. Clicking it on, and looking directly into the beam resulted in temporary blindness.

He put them back and opens the case.

Carefully unfolding the shades, he put them on. They look very dark from the outside, but from his view they're almost as clear as day, and his vision seems to be in hyper-HD! Things on the other side of the room are much sharper, the creases in the wall are more defined! To boot, in the corner of each lens a reflective sheen gives him the ability to see what's behind him while look-ing forward.

He been pretty down lately, but he really likes these!

Tucked away in the largest of the three pockets, is a shiny, silvery thing resembling a flashlight? Spinning it around he quickly gathers it's not that. It's quite heavy, with three raised metal-lic couplings joining what seems to be three separate parts. A rubber button is on one end, and a blue glass lens the size of a marble is on the other. Holding it perpendicular to the floor he presses the button.

Nothing happens, no light?

Spinning it around and looking at it, he questions its purpose? Shrugging his shoulders, he sits it on his lap and proceeds with the inspection.

When he unzips the flap and set sights on an image inside the cargo net, he knows this is something very different.

Very!

He doesn't know who the man is, but he finds it odd a per-son would place a picture right there. It gives the impression it's there for encouragement, or even worship?

What Alexander Zarbin, and soon to be *"Pain Bogart"* does not know, is the gentlemen in the photo is none other than Richard "The Iceman" Kuklinski, the American born assassin who in his lifetime killed over two hundred and fifty men, but refused to harm women and children.

Behind the framed photograph of the tall man standing between two young girls, is a book inside a protective sleeve. It's vintage but in almost mint condition. The cover is laminated paper, vio-let with a red outline of a slain individual. Titled:

Hit Man: A Technical Manual for Independent Contractors, it was published in 1983 by the Paladin Press, and subsequently banned in 1999 by the U.S. government after being the driv-ing force behind a brutal triple murder in Montgomery County,

Maryland.

Alex isn't presently wearing the special sunglasses; he doesn't have to. All he needs is a glance from his pupil.
A double take!!
Some unseen entity is inside the wall attempting to free itself by burning itself through! A smoldering ring the size of a wheat penny is growing into a fiery crater!
He jumps to his feet looking around, and back at the wall—a small blaze is ensuing!!!
Panicking like always, he prepares to run out when he notices the flames are reducing and beginning to smolder! He runs to the restroom holding the weapon, sits it on the counter, and grabs an unused wash cloth drenching it in water. Leaving the gun he runs back and smothers the flame with the rag! While pressing it to the wall he feels the heat of the burning material, and is dumbfounded? He's showing all the signs of hysteria, and can't determine the source of the fire! Suspended in sub-frenzy mode, he begin feeling a searing heat on the side of his foot, and immediately snatches it up! His sneaker has a tiny hole burned into his shoe, and a stinging sensation is working its way around his foot! About to take his shoe off, he sees the flashlight looking thing sitting on the floor with a thread of something emitting from it? Now that he's moved his foot, the rubber baseboard is the focus. When he sees the rubber turning to goo, he snatches it up and presses the button.
The click, and the warmth of the case tells him he's found the source.
He didn't think these existed! He was under the impression they're only fictional weapons! He's always felt his ex-wife's mother resembles Jabba the Hut, but didn't really think Luke Skywalker's light saber was real!
With his mouth again an "O" of fascination, he marvels at the laser producing device, and has completely forgotten about the burn on his foot.

He begins hurriedly gathering the things! With munitions like these he wants to get far, far away from this place! He wants no part of the owner! If Stockton would've been able to get his hands on items like these, there would've been *major* trouble in Dixie.

But there's no cash.

Taking a few careful minutes to properly secure his newly acquired arsenal, he's almost ready to leave. Taking a long drink from the bathroom faucet, he uses the back of his hand to wipe the dribble from his mouth. After performing one last check of the room, he reaches for the handle. With the keys in his hand, the shades on his face, and the tools of the murder trade, he turns the knob.

Lastly, a flip of the switch…but not before the ring of a phone! Stress and exhaustion causes his brain to jumble the data. He thinks he heard the faint sound of a helicopter!

Backing inside, the door closes on his own. Going to the room phone it rings again. He stares at it with discontent.

He can still hear the chopper!

His brain isn't processing the information correctly?

It isn't that one, but the one in his pocket.

It's Bailey Red, and she's looking for him.

Trois.

Tusk Hall respects the ability of his brave men and women, and knows his exemplary habits has rubbed off on them. He understands the pressures and fears that come with this line of work. He's not the commander of this precinct, there's already an established chain of command, but that didn't stop the chief from deeming him team leader: The senior officer who organizes the crisis response team, selects its members, plans and oversees training, and makes deployment decisions. His aim is not to show up and steal the glory—all he wants are the people freed. Experienced leaders understand important decisions are based on thought, rather than emotion. All of his abilities will be tested today. When the world is watching, and a deranged

man is threatening to kill hostages; each moment is critical.
Initially spotted heading south on GA-400, an attempt was
made to stop the vehicle but a chase ensued. Shortly thereafter,
the suspect's vehicle began experiencing mechanical failure, and
as a result abandoned it and ran into a restaurant. Not just any
eatery, but a historical staple.

Dante's Down the Hatch, Atlanta's quintessential fondue restaurant. After serving the community for nearly half a century, it
had recently closed its doors, but is now under new ownership
and back thriving. The live jazz band is back, the alligators are
back swimming, and the wooden ship is still providing patrons
with an unrivaled place to enjoy wildlife, exquisite dining,
soothing instrumentation, and unique ambiance. The building
itself was once a museum. One of the draws about the restaurant is that it comes furnished with its own folklore. Tales of
hidden passageways and secret vaults are just a few of the many
surprises. But customers are only allowed access to certain
areas; a substantial part of the building is off-limits.

What's different today is the cessation of business, and the
suffocating police presence. The entire perimeter is cordon off,
news choppers hover overhead, the SWAT team and their snipers are in position. Propaganda of black man being killed at the
hands of a racist is out, the media using it as the perfect topic
to piggy back on while the crisis unfolds. Minorities already
on edge from repeated occurrences are growing increasingly
agitated. Their numbers are continuing to swell, placing even
more strain on the situation. The mayor is livid, the governor
is getting impatient, and the chief is on the scene, but far from
the action. One of the two mobile command center buses is
his likely location. Parked with stabilizer arms extending from
both sides, a tall antenna protrudes from the top of each. A
negotiated release of three chefs, the line staff, and the waitress
was successful. The release of the child, twenty two patrons,
and the manger is still underway. The small alligators inside
are farm raised and de-toothed, but the captor is threatening

to toss the child in the tank. If it'd been a few hours later, the place would've been filled to capacity. The time is four twenty-nine in the evening, and he's been at it since one o'clock. Being fourth in command, he's the highest ranking official who actually performs field duty. He hates siting at that stupid desk, and all the things that doesn't involve police work that come with it. The closer you get to the top the more it becomes less about protecting the community, and more about politics.

Being he's not one to wear his feelings on his shoulder, it's difficult to get a read on him. Tucked away in an unmarked car, far from the action, he's in complete concert with the situation. While dozens of people hunker around, heavily armed and heavy anxious, he and his team stand resolved. Loop is across the street conversing with a group of other dicks, Parris is surrounded by boisterous media types with editorial deadlines, and Captain John Henry Peavey is leaning against the hood of a squad void of a light bar grilling his lap-top.

A man pushing an ice cream cart catches the major's attention?

With the amount of people watching from behind the barricade, it's a canny business move to hawk frozen treats. The Latino spectators seem to be very familiar with this particular vendor, but everyone else can be seen looking questioningly. Maj.'s attention returns to his duty. Maybe the airline information was bad? Maybe Delta is on the verge of an Eastern like meltdown? Whatever it is, it's wrong. Ed Denmark is far too wealthy, and far too egotistical to travel by such paltry means. He's a titan, a major figure in not only Atlanta, but globally. His Gulfstream 650 executive business jet landed at Peachtree-DeKalb airport an hour ago, and it's just come over the radio that he's on the scene.
Peavey looks up from his lap-top and at the major.
Hall hears the transmission but is fixated on the yellow straight

truck parked in the loading dock. The hydraulic lift-gate mounted to the rear is lowered and unfolded. An idea dawns on him, and he's about to call a play. Why hasn't anyone else not noticed what is now so obvious?

Before he can fully draw it up, he sees a throng of reporters disperse, and reconvene around two, black and heavily tented Mercedes-Benz Sprinters. From the outside they don't seem that spectacular. But once inside, the luxurious confines state the $169,000 price tag. The arrogant way that they've parked, flirting on the fringes of the police barricade trumpet his supercilious position. They even have the nerve to be equipped with strobe lights, even with the vehicles stopped, they continue flashing. Only a select few of the hundreds of people gathered actually knows who's inside. The rest just think some celebrity, or high ranking official has popped up on the scene.

Ed Denmark certainly has made quite an arrival.

Peavey sighs, and returns his focus to the screen. Being familiar with Denmark, it's something he doesn't like about him. However, he's in the minority. For anyone, even the P.O.T.U.S., you better have all your ducks in a row if thinking of stepping to a man this powerful. He has many friends, and they're all part of the one percent.

Maj. gets out of his car, and radios something. Peavey looks up, put his PC in sleep mode, and approaches from the rear.

Tusk initiates his march, Peavey follows.

As he rounds the side of a large armored vehicle, he cuts between a troop of beat cops. Now closer to the action, the commotion of restless bodies is more evident, and the civilian crowd is four times larger than before. Much of the yellow caution tape is replaced with metal barricades. There's more helicopters, and more ancillary personnel.

Stopping at the curb, camouflaged within the swarm of blue, he and Peavey watch as a gargantuan man of epic proportions emerges from the first vehicle, the conversion van literally rose

nine inches when he got out. Even from a distance of roughly
seventy five feet, Zeus, Denmark's personal bodyguard is an
unnerving site. Many of them have never laid eyes on that
much human before. His sheer mass has definitely increased
the temperature. Who needs protection like that? The well-
dressed giant walks to the side door, a set of folding stairs
automatically descend from the frame. With the experience of
a highly trained security agent, he stands beside the rear door
and waits.
A short breeze blows down the thoroughfare tumbling bits of
debris across the pavement. His stoic stance gives away nothing.
Out of the other van the side door opens on its own, two white
men in business suits emerge. Each van has drivers who stay
inside. They go and wait in the vicinity of Zeus, but not within
arm reach. He's the only one wearing shades. As if on que, he
reaches for the handle and pulls the door open.
The first person out is a woman, a smartly dressed one
wearing a stylish business suit with a briefcase in hand.
No sooner than both of her heels met the asphalt, another
individual emerges. His suit is tailored and his shoes are handmade English oxfords.
In a maneuver that completely disregards the obvious, Denmark steps out of the vehicle and whispers something to Zeus.
In one swift motion, the looming man pushes the sturdy
barricade aside as if it was a cotton ball, and Ed proceeds without the slightest regard for the offended officers opinions.
A rookie beat cop and his partner attempt to say something,
but are advised by a warning stare from Zeus.

Sensing the sudden movement, the stiffening backs, and angst
from the officer, Hall steps from his blind and intersects their
path. Peavey and six other uniforms follow.
The entourage of law, meets the entourage of power. Hall has
never met Denmark before but is well aware of the face. He

doesn't want to but extends his hand anyway.

"Russell Hall. Glad you could make it," his tone direct.

Zeus is watching him like a hawk, Peavey is watching Zeus, and the other six make a semi-circle around it all.

In the middle of Peachtree Rd. they size each other up.

Denmark only nods.

One of the men with him speak. Extending a hand to the major he begins.

"Brent Perminter, where are things currently? We hear a plan to go in has been devised."

No such decision has been made but the major plays along.

"We've been in continuous contact with the HT. Terms of a surrender are being developed and we should have an answer shortly."

Being experienced with high pressure situations the major takes control of the group.

"Let's get out of the street and let the negotiators do their job. Right this way please."

As he turns and leads them back to his vehicle, he thinks about the initial sight of Denmark. He doesn't have the panicked look of a man who just lost his wife and two stepsons. He catalogues this into his memory.

Before, his alcove on the backside of the building, adjacent to the back of a high rise condo, concealed by a row of Dogwood trees was a nice place for a major to coordinate the effort.

But since he's emerged and given away his position, it's now teaming with a lot more bodies. The shade alone is enough to attract a gang of personnel. The sun is still the sun and the unrelenting Georgia heat doesn't give them a reprieve because it's the third of September.

Hall and his men crowd to one side of the cul-de-sac created by the various vehicles, Ed and his people cling to the other. The female with them places her lap-top on the trunk of a squad car, and begins firing away key strokes. The other guy who's yet to speak is on a cell phone? Ed, Zeus, and Brent glare and wait. When working with the same crew for as long as he has, they can read each other and know the appropriate action. Loop having witnessed his arrival from afar decides the major can use his assistance, and he has questions of his own.

"Mr. Denmark, Detective Hickenlooper. He's our investigation lead," introduced Hall.

Again he only nods.

"Pleasure to meet you detective," Brent begins. "So where are things? Any leads on a suspect? Have you all figured out how Mr. Denmark's son can be returned to safety? We're approaching the fifth hour of this fiasco, and the sooner he can get him back, the sooner he can begin to grieve. This has been an extremely trying time and we want this thing ended as soon as possible detective."

"We're extremely sorry for his loss and are working diligently to get this solved. Any information you have will certainly help expedite things." Loop.

"I think the fact that my son is in the hands of a crazed lunatic should supersede the cause," answered Ed Denmark, in his deep sinister tone.

Tusk's antennas go up!

"It certainly does, but a cause will pave the way for us to gain leverage with the suspect *thus* promoting a resolution, or maybe even an immediate end to the stand-off. I understand this has been a great loss, one I can't imagine having to face. That being said, our main objective, to not only me, but every one of the officers you see, is to get these people safely returned to their loved ones. With all due respect sir, there's twenty-three other lives at stake besides your son. Be it information you have, or information we've gleaned from our intelligence, every little bit helps. If you find it more fitting, our headquarters may be a viable option. If we can, we'd like to get down there and see if we can get a bearing on all of this," clarifies Big

Man Hall.

Watching the eyes of Denmark, the feeling in his gut tells him which way he'll swing, but he still wanted to put it out there. If not for anything else but to get a feel for where he at emotionally. He gathers the two suits are most likely his lawyers.

The other guy has just ended his conversation on a Blackberry®. He can also hear the huge bodyguard breathing and makes a mental note to find out who he is.

The lady is still in deep focus on her MacBook Pro, seemingly unconcerned with what they're doing, but consistent in using her body and the vehicles rear window to shield their gaze from what she's doing. She's looking down but Hall knows she's well aware of what's going on.

"In light of all that's happened, and with the best interest of the family in mind, I think it'll be best if we avoid the attention of the headquarters at this time. In the coming days, the Denmark family will be releasing an official statement on the matter. We'd like to reserve the right of setting the appropriate time for a conference ajor," stated Brent.

Using Hall's momentary moment of silence as his opportunity, Hickenlopper jumps in.

"We understand this is an unfortunate time for your family, but there has been four homicides committed at Mr. Denmark's residence. T-"

"*Former* residence. He owns the property, but spends the majority of his time throughout the country and abroad," corrected Brent.

"..The hostage taker has now taken it upon himself to threaten to kill more people. I think the safety of all the hostages certainly supersedes the inconvenience of us asking a few questions."

Loop is an old school detective, and being in homicide has eroded his patience, especially when his instinct tells him he's looking at his primary suspect.

Hall gives him a warning glance, not because he interrupted, but because he's thinking the same thing and doesn't want to taint the investigation by giving Denmark a whiff they're on to him. They've both been with the force their entire careers, and are well aware of the many notorious rumors surrounding him. Hickenlooper sees it and proceeds accordingly.

But not before her.

"Armando Pena, born October, nineteen seventy-three in Tenancingo, Mexico. Member of the Kara Talvatruco "Killer Thugs" street gang, also known as *'KT thirty six.'* Deported in two thousand-nine, and two thousand thirteen by the federal government for convictions of international arms dealing, kidnapping, conspiracy to commit human trafficking, cocaine possession, and attempted murder. Parents deceased, no known children, and known to fancy men in drag....We're aware he's demanded a car be here by noon, or someone's going to die. Major, you being designated the lead, your role may overlap with that of the *on-scene commander,* who is the person in charge of the actual hostage crisis. Considering this individual is responsible for everything that goes on at the crisis scene, from establishing perimeters and traffic control, to directing the activity of negotiators, to deploying the tactical team, to liaising with emergency medical and community services; I think it'll be more appropriate that we speak to this person," she stated.

The woman who chose to make her presence known in this group of men, chose to let her request hang in the breeze without introducing herself, and doesn't even offer the well-respected major a customary hand shake.

Bitch! Loop said in his mind.

It's more than her short hair and masculine demeanor that display her military background. It's the accuracy of her information.

The major is so focused on the discussion, he doesn't notice

Tameka Parris has come up beside him.

Quickly she whispers something in his ear.

He shakes his head and thanks her.

The media seeing the shift of commanding bodies relocate to this new position, begin focusing their angst and movements, primed to pounce on any new developments.

The loud chop of a helicopter moving into position quickly drowns out the sounds of the group.

Snipers atop buildings, and police in tactical gear begin moving briskly.

A man emerges jogging from one of the two command buses, followed by two other gentlemen, and rushes over to the group holding his hand out with a smile.

The third guy with Denmark who was on the phone, and has yet to speak, is the first hand to reach out and accept the welcome. The smile and inconspicuous glances that follow tell the wise major these two men are associates.

It's Jack Stoker, the Georgia Bureau of Investigation's top negotiator, and on-scene commander of the hostage crisis. He shakes all of their hands, thanks Major Hall, and leads the entourage to the air-conditioned mobile operations center. Only the huge man remains outside, seemingly oblivious to the sun beaming on his charcoal colored face.

"We've got shots fired major!" Peavey, coming up to him holding his radio.

Relieved from dealing with Denmark, Hall makes a brisk return to his vehicle!

By the time he gets there, information is all over the place! A press of a button on the keyboard increases the volume of the force's communication transmissions.

Officer's cars and department radios are equipped with a new technology giving supervisors the ability to see exactly where personnel are positioned, which gives him the ability to make detailed moves on the fly.

A press of another key and a three dimensional map of the entire area materializes in crystal clear. With a direct link to main control, his orders are quickly relayed to the officers! Cops of varying rank track to and fro, each approaching the major with their own bits of valuable intelligence.

Communications come and go as the tense situation wears on. There seemed to be a break when the HT agreed to surrender under the promise that a member of the media will come and air his statement live, something rare in the history of hostage negotiation.

Department protocol sets guidelines for psychological principles and practices of hostage and crisis negotiation according to the needs of the situation. The standard operating procedure in hostage negotiations is to make the HT work for everything he gets by extracting a concession in return. This is to maintain a bargaining position without agitation. One of the defining characteristics of most hostage crises is the presence of some form of demand, which may range from the practical (food, transportation, cash) to the more grandiose (release of political prisoners, access to media) to the bizarre or psychotic (freedom from conspiratorial persecution, emancipation of downtrodden classes, dissolution of corporations).

At the recommendation of higher-ups, it was determined his demand to meet with the media is one they will not be willing to honor.

The HT must've found a megaphone, probably belonging to one of the kidnapped construction workers. In his anger, he's begin shouting threats to the police, and based on an analysis of his deranged speech, he seems to be under the influence of 'bath salts', a synthetic street drug known to cause severe panic attacks, agitation, paranoia, delusions, hallucinations, and violent behavior, including self-mutilation, suicide attempts, and homicidal activity.

"Nine one-one is receiving bomb threats from members of the HT's street gang, *KT-36* saying if anything happens to him

there'll be consequences," Hall informs Peavey. "Considering the intel on the HT doesn't list him as a high ranking member of the syndicate, this is most likely a macabre way for them to gain publicity for their criminal organization."
"That's no good major. I really hope it's just a threat." responds Peavey.

From that point communication has ceased, and the 'throw phone' was tossed out the front door of the restaurant by a blindfolded hostage with a rope tied to their neck.

It's been hours since the entourage entered the bus. The body-guard hasn't moved a muscle, not even when an unknowing investigator approached and questioned his purpose.
The crisis is now in its third, and most dangerous stage. All attempts have been made to avoid a tactical assault, which usually carries the highest casualty rate. The fact tactical intervention is necessary indicates all reasonable attempts to resolve the crisis by negotiation have failed. Either violence against the hostages has already taken place, or is imminent. However, if a fire fight ensues, the resulting panic and confusion may result in hostages being inadvertently killed or injured.

Reports keep coming in warning of a possible retaliation strike by the gang, but are largely being ignored. KT-36 are known traffickers of drugs and human cargo, with their fiercest rivals being the infamous 'Brownstone Locks'. While having a history of arson, extortion, car bombings, and execution style shootings; they aren't exactly purveyors of explosive devices. Centered on past experience, and reinforced by information gathered by a reliable informant, the authorities are thinking of something more on the lines of a low level attack.

Hall keeps pouring over the details of the petition filed by Denmark's spouse. There's no evidence of domestic abuse, though it's listed she'd once taken her and the children to a local shelter for battered women and children. The document filed with the request for separation, states she and the children remained there for three days until she and the husband reconciled, where she voluntarily agreed to return home. There's no other information on the incident.

Behind the chaos of chanting protestors, roving helicopters, and the relentless movement of dozens of armed personnel; the major begins noticing an influx of calls flooding the mainframe's data pool. This newly patented technology puts commanders even closer to the action, providing them access to real-time data regarding the volume of calls coming into the nine one-one center for a particular emergency, including the level of priority assigned by a computerized algorithm based on past crime stats, the geographical location of the calls, how many officers are assigned to each call, and what their badge numbers are. The dispatcher, by use of this information is able to either assign officers based on the computers recommendation, or override it and allow field sergeants to assign duties. This same technology also gives commanders and certain dispatch managers the ability to view live footage from the officer's body cam. This amazing technology epitomizes 21st century style police work. It's efficient, and it's fast.

The conversation of one of the choppers overhead is the one which poses the most informative to Hall. The pilot is telling the dispatcher an unidentified flying object, perhaps something on the line of a drone, has risen from below and is moving over the city. He says it's emitting a smoke trail from something dangling from underneath. The pilot advises the dispatcher to place an order of extreme caution as this object is gaining altitude, and moving with speed toward their position!

Hall immediately grabs a pair of binoculars from the glove box, jumps out of his cruiser and begins searching the sky!

Peavey standing just feet away runs up beside him!

"Something up?"

But the screams, and pointing by the crowds of bystanders answer his question!

Packs of news media jostle for new positions as tripods and cameras swing towards the lofty sight!

Moving briskly in the direction, Hall ducks under a low hanging tree limb, and splits between a groups of uniformed officers! A small entourage follows as he rushes to get in position to where the surrounding buildings aren't blocking his view!

That's when the call reaches everyone else, and a state of pandemonium issues! The mobs of barricaded bystanders, and shouting protestors grew stiff with awe as they see the ominous craft smoking in the sky. Though the streets are blocked, and the barricades keep the crowds a substantial distance away; shouting commands of *"Move back!"* and *"Clear the area!"* can be heard.

But the spectators are too preoccupied to pay them much attention! The simultaneous roar of starting diesel engines shake the ground, as big armored vehicles reposition in advance of whatever is coming their way! News choppers can be seen withdrawing to safe distances!

He sees it roving in the distance—smoke sending a plume of black trailing behind it like an elongated rat tail of combustion and sparks.

Focusing on the flying craft, it's quite a sight to see! Someone attached some sort of incendiary device to a line attached to the underside of a recreational drone, seemingly being controlled from a remote location. The smoke alone is enough to induce a terror! The fact it's a hundred feet over the city only exacerbates things.

The echo of the deranged HT using the megaphone shouts obscenities at the officers, remain steadfast; swearing allegiance to his street gang, vowing to remain undeterred, even while facing such a suffocating show of force!!!!

It's so much going on that Peavey has to grab the major's shoulder and direct his attention to the side of the restaurant!

Under the cover of excitement, combined with a new development, a twenty-four man tactical team is approaching the building from the east. There's no other option but to forcefully free the hostages.

Before Hall has time to fully comprehend the madness is ensuing around him, the identified flying object explodes!!!

BOOOOOOOO-oooooooo-ommmmm!!!!!!!!!!!!

A bone jarring, earth shattering strike shakes the afternoon heights! An orange mushroom cloud engulfs the upper expanse with 10,000 degree heat! Window panels of office towers, hotels, and high rise condos shatter. The shock wave sends burning shards of red hot shrapnel falling onto the spectators!!!!!! A swell of searing pain pours from the sky, knocking citizens off their feet; including the rescue team.

The tactical team halt their advance, and retreat back to the protection of their vehicles!!! Screams and blood curls take over the scene! The HT is shouting to the top of his lungs in Spanish while repeatedly firing a gun at an unknown target!

Peavey climbs to his feet and help his major up!

The once angry and agitated mob, has now turned into a stampede scattering for cover! Civilians, spectators, police officers, and birds alike run in every direction! People in buildings and towers are pouring out in endless rivers! For a moment Hall and Peavey are having a hard time finding their equilibrium, barely hearing in the midst of the chaos! With his men trying to shield him from danger, he fights them off, and runs back to his vehicle so he can find out what the hell is going on! When he arrives, information and commands are firing across the radio in hyper-drive! Now that a bomb strike has been carried out, agents from Federal Bureau of Investigation, Alcohol Tobacco and Firearms, local branch of the National Security Agency, and Department of Homeland Security are fast in route to the scene. The situation has just went from elevated to severe! The high drama is now being broadcast live across the entire country. Affiliates from BBC and Al-Jazeera are scrambling to get people on location!

The dust is starting to settle, and reports are saying the bomb originated from the drone, and is confirmed as being the work of KT-36.

Amazingly, Denmark's guard is standing in the exact same spot, and doesn't look to have flinched.

Peavey has a flip phone to his ear and a radio to his mouth.

His lap-top is brought back online and keys are punching. The computer screen in Hall's car is lighting up Mayday! One of his many work phones starts ringing!

It's assistant chief Dagan Lacy with a list of instructions from the chief.

Hall carefully listens to the directives and forwards them to central as he's relaying them. Next, he gives him the place and time of an emergency meeting.

In sixty three seconds the conversation is done, and with only three minutes before he's to be at the meeting, he takes a moment because he's gotten too worked up.

Calmed, he gets out of his car and is just about to update Peavey when he hears a call come over the radio that there's movement at the entrance!

He, Peavey, two sergeants, and Loop make a mad dash through the packs of officers and vehicles until they're across the street! Interwoven within the wall of armed vehicles and armed men, they focus on the front of the restaurant. As a result of the explosion, the deputy chief instructed Hall to increase the perimeter to a radius of ten blocks. Emergency vehicles tending to the wounded are to be allowed access, but no one else. In

the short time since the order was given, patrolmen have just
about cleared the area.

At the far end of the boulevard, Hall can see flashing lights and
squad cars blocking entrances, people are looking down from
buildings, distant echoes of thousands of panicked people per-
meate the spread. Radio chatter about difficulties being faced
while attempting to clear a popular Mexican café around the
corner is flowing—patrons are refusing to leave and are causing
a scene.

A man pushing an ice cream cart was seen in the area.

An old parking deck known to be a rest haven for the homeless is also presenting challenges. The day's barometric pressure,
compressed with the mounting pressure of all out chaos is
causing the air to moan with a low groan. Like hammocks of
elastic ribbons, endless yards of yellow tape twist in the breeze,
barricades lay turned on their side. Inside the "The Hatch",
the deranged man goes silent. The perpetual clip of chopper
blades provide a stirring accompaniment to the theater. Being
in the middle of a renovation, the new management decide
to offer customers multiple ways to enter the establishment.
Under the previous ownership, the only entrance was around
back. A simulated ocean dock, statues of wildlife, and antique
cars decorated the walkway leading inside. The tall, brow oak
doubles doors have been there since the initial build, but aren't
in use. The new lot gives customers a choice, as well as additional parking options. Being the sun is setting, and it's still
light out, the restaurant is lit up like a football stadium.
Slowly, the doors open!
But no person is seen.
Only the welcome booth, a wall covered with celebrity photos,
and an antique iron bench sit alone in the glare. Like the first
act of a terrible play, a huge card board box moves into view!
Slow and clumsily it moves! It doesn't take a genius to gather

someone's inside, possibly several people. It's a large shipping container, roughly 6x6 with a lid secured with packaging tape. From Hall's vantage, his binoculars gives him a clear view of the action. The box has something painted on it. *'KT-36'* in black letters are easy to make out. The others aren't so legible. "Fuck U Rick!" Hall reading the message aloud.

Blocking the entrance, this box of unidentified origin faces the nation. Three brick steps are at the entrance, and only feet from where the box sits. Like a big, uncoordinated string puppet, the box wobbles forward. It tips and rocks, three sets of legs are visible.

It stops!

There's no movement!

The regular authorities have no way of seeing inside. It has no eye holes cut out, and there's no way on knowing whether the HT has a gun or not. Really nothing they can do but watch. At this point, the best they can hope for is that the box topples over as they attempt to traverse down the stairs.

Inside the command buses, thermodynamic imaging cameras are already sending detailed pictures of the three occupants as human figures of reds, oranges, yellows, blues, purples, and greens. They're relayed to the scene and presently being viewed by the SWAT commander. He advises his men on how to maneuver.

Unfortunately, the box doesn't tip. Every few seconds it'll pop up, move a foot or two, and stop again—the three sets of legs moving in unison.

Denmark and his entourage are still inside the bus.

Hall's radio has a variety of channels he can access, many more than a normal patrolman's issue, and is already on the SWAT channel listening to their transmissions. From what he can gather, there's an individual, most likely the HT, underneath the box holding a gun to the head of the two people he's using as human shields. They hate the clever way he's using the box to keep them at bay. Even with snipers perched all around, they have no way of taking a safe shot. With the entire world watching, this has to be done with the upmost regard for civilian safety. If they screw this up, there's no way of gauging the fallout. The cauldron of public dissatisfaction has already reached its boiling point, they don't want it to superheat.

For a second time, SWAT members approach from opposite sides, but stay back, and only move when the box moves. Hall can see there's more messages.

Told u I was Comn!
KT-36

Is painted on another section, an undecipherable symbol used as the gangs emblem is beneath it.

He's also gathered they're using the outer edge of the lawn as their guide path, which seems to be leading down the walkway to the parking lot. With each agonizing moment, the force watches as the box continues moving unabated. If not for the hostages, this improvised contraption would've been filled with hot lead by now. The order from the top is not a single hostage is to be killed during the rescue attempt. It's impossible to predict if, or when the HT might decide to execute the hostages, there's too much at stake for there to be blunders.

Word he's reopened communication, and is on the line with the negotiator is good news. It temporarily alleviates some of their stress, and is also good for the media—new updates and breaking info spike television ratings. But whatever they're saying, isn't stopping his charge. Due to the excessive demand being placed on the cardboard, the once square cargo box has become wrinkled and rounded like a middle-aged water buffalo. Each time it moves, the people underneath bump into each other causing it to flex. A bend on one of the four corners is tearing from the top. Creases and seams begin revealing the colors and glimpses of the occupants.

A sniper reports to have a shot!!!!

But the box is still in one piece, and the only thing in its path is the loading dock, and the yellow Ryder truck. Due to its current location, it could easily be driven forward and out the parking lot. But not without having their head taken off. They'll have to show themselves at some point if they're to operate the vehicle. The best the HT can do is avoid considering that as an option. From the looks of things however, that's exactly where they're heading, but in every direction is a SWAT squad. There are multiple levels of security keeping whoever's under that box from going anywhere. If one was to make an intelligent guess, it'll be safe to assume a delivery of some sort was interrupted by something. Partly unloaded freight sits on the dock, the truck's lift gate is down, and the engine is still running. And, in something that baffles the minds of everyone looking, the box awkwardly situates itself atop the lift gate. And somehow the three sets of legs find a balance.

But one of them slips!

A child screams!!

The squad commander yells over the radio to stand down!!!

The surge of excitement almost causes one of the snipers to fire, while a jolt of panic rips through the major!

The child is grabbed by someone underneath and returned to footing!

This is the first time in his career he's witnessed a standoff evolve like this. They're completely powerless! How has one man managed to handcuff an entire police department? From three hundred feet, he listens as the motor whines, the lift-gate begins rising!

Confusion amongst the squad, and the command center is owning the airwaves! They report seeing no hand but the lift is still rising! Intelligence said nothing of anyone already being inside the truck, but technically it hasn't been verified. Due to the low hanging awning and sagging branches, no one can see if there's a person lying under the steering wheel or not.

Every possible option is being weighed in the seconds it takes for the ramp to stop! Once it does, the box immediately moves

inside. Without warning, someone breaks out of the box, grabs the strap, and yanks the door shut!!!
When it slams, the world exhales—the same words are on the tongues of millions!!!
What's happening inside the back of that truck?
What the news cameras can't capture, is the chief's phone is steaming with hot magma from fuming bureaucrats, the mayor has blown his top, the governor is an erupting volcano, and Senator *Sham*bliss is fending off lava from Washington! What results is infighting, and they still haven't determined if there are any more bombs. Reports of looting are trending. The embarrassment of letting the HT walk out of the restaurant is a knock-out punch to the state. The ripple effect from the drone strike hasn't even begin to take shape. The moment the door shut, the mission became a failure.

But things are about to get even worse. Anything that can go wrong, will.

An alarming call comes over the comm system! The command center is reporting movement! The "throw phone" given to the HT by the authorities is equipped with a GPS sensor. It's used to pinpoint an HT's exact position in the event he, or she has to be terminated.
There is verified movement, and it not anywhere near the delivery truck! But back inside the restaurant, which is still considered a "hot zone", deemed extremely dangerous because it hasn't been cleared.
All of their focus was foolishly fixated on the box, just like the HT planned.
They say the soul of a champion shines through when the game is at its most critical.
Abandoning his position amongst the rest of the officers, he turns and breaks through the crowd. In a situation of this magnitude, he's far from fourth in command, even the chief is

following someone else's orders. But that doesn't stop him from walking past the man-beast, and barge inside the gray command bus. The other Mobile Ops. unit is black, and teaming with its own group of shot callers. Dim, cool, and advanced, it's equipped with everything a stationary war room would have, and both sides are extended for increased work space. Banks of screens, radars, and monitors are operating at peak performance; thirteen people are crammed into this tight space. Denmark and his team are standing near the negotiator who's on the phone with several top officials. The chief is standing beside two gentleman in suits and the chief deputy Dagan. The two rescue squad commanders are too stressed to pay attention to him. Without hesitation, he politely grabs the chief by arm.

"Sir! Excuse me. Can I have a word with you please?"

Knowing his major doesn't make noise for nothing, he doesn't think twice about loaning his attention.

"I sure hope you've found some new intel Hall!......This fiasco might cost me my job," and wipes the back of his arm across his brow.

"We've gotta get in that restaurant! The HT's playing us! He's not in that truck and I know it! We're doing exactly what he wants! This is some plot to divert our attention, something somewhere else is about to happen. In all the years we've worked together I've had your back, now I need you to trust me on this and make the call! My guess is he's found another way out and is probably doing it as we speak. We can't afford to drop the ball again."

When a man is held in such high regard, his words hold weight.

"All right Hall. I'll see what I can do. Let me see how soon we can get 'em in. But I sure hope you're right, that building hasn't been sniffed. This can really get ugly if you're wrong."

Walks away.

Hall walks away too, back outside where he encounters Peavey waiting for him. The first thing that comes to Hall's mind is the image of a pitbull snarling at a rhino. The way he's mean-mugging Zeus is classic John Henry.

"John! Let do it."

Instead of returning to where they were before, the focused Tusk quickens his pace and heads for his car, the fearless John Henry Peavey jogging beside ready to protect and serve.

Thirty seconds is all it takes for the duo to fight through the fudge of investigators, officers, and support staff.

"I need you to listen carefully! Get me a detailed map of this area, specifically the surrounding mile! And I need it fast!"

By the time he grabs his lap-top out of his car and closes the door, Tusk's hand is inserting the key and turning the ignition. John Henry's leg is barely inside before the engine revs. Considering they're blocked in from every angle by vehicles of all sorts, the manicured lawn of the office complex running parallel with the side road is his only option.

The beefy Ford lunges forward and jumps the curb, chunks of grass and dirt flying from the spinning wheels! Driven by sheer determination, Maj. Tusk yanks the wheel right, sending the vehicle sideways of the curb in a tire screeching skid onto a paved walkway! Careening down the walkway bouncing and bumping, Peavey is on his computer while the right mirror mows down rows of decorative bushes as they woosh by!

Peavey sees the end of the walkway up ahead and holds his breath!

The major doesn't blink as the car goes airborne off the concrete stairs, over a grass median, and bounces back onto the lawn of another commercial property!

Peavey looks over his shoulder and sees an entire section of aluminum railing bent and destroyed! When he feels the centrifugal force pushing him into the major's shoulder, he turns to see they're back on a public road, the lack of traffic and people make for a swift transition from one scene to the next! As the image materializes in his mind, Hall uses his free hand to slam data info into his command console. The information coming back assures him he's on the right track! Word that simultaneous assaults on the restaurant, and the delivery van were initiated causes his chest swell with pride. The chief is with him! His first instinct tells him to get to the Mexican grill. When he does, it's indeed quite popular. It's been there since his high school days, but today it's the scene of a burgeoning riot. Another corner, and Hall can see the heavy police presence, and the '*Taco Del Rico*' sign up ahead.

As he skids up beside a brawny crowd control vehicle and row of squad cars, he grabs one of the three radios clipped to the dash and selects the channel. Radioing the sergeant at the scene, he tells him to be on the lookout for a man pushing an ice cream cart; his gut telling him to hold off on a full APB. Resources are already stretched to the limit, and all that will do is add more confusion. He didn't understand it at first, but there's a reason he kept catching his eye. Stepping out, he scans the area, and despite earlier reports of a man seen heading this way selling ice cream, he sees no sight of anyone fitting that description.

He gets back to the car and reaches for another radio.

"Got it sir!" alerted Peavey.

With the chatter of three radios monitoring developments at multiple locations, he studies the map Peavey provided. It's a crisp 3-D layout of the surrounding area out to a mile. A press of a key and it zooms down to a "street view", providing the perspective of a person standing at the point of the actual coordinates.

Searching the map with a fine toothed stare, the only thing jumping out is the old abandoned parking deck. It had been scheduled for demolition, but public outcry over it being a refuge for the homeless caused the plans to be scratched.

Just as he suspects, over the radio word comes that the HT

is not in the back of the truck!!! It's only a male and female hostage, and a young child. They're still trying to verify if it's Denmark's son, when second word comes they're bound together by some sort of crude bomb equipped with transmitter for a remote detonation! Eyes at the scene are saying it looks to be sticks of dynamite wired together, and fortunately not that difficult to disarm.

Hall wasn't afraid before, but now his heart is pounding! The weight of the potential loss of life is crushing. Beads of sweat squeeze from every pore in on his body, anxiety rockets through him like bombardments of cruise missiles. The harder his chest heaves the clearer the picture becomes.

Over the radio comes word that the siege on the building yielded no suspect, but there are casualties.

Even at five blocks away, the restaurant and the parking deck are perfectly in line with each other; he notices a run of railroad tracks disappearing underground about a half mile to the west. Taco Del Rico is three blocks away from the parking deck! When the pound in his chest reaches the point of almost knocking him off his feet, the equation has been solved! He doesn't have the clearance to command the rescue mission, but he does have the respect of his men. The situation at the taco joint is now secondary, there's no way he's going to be out smarted by KT-36.

Without a second to spare, he reaches for the proper radio and presses the button.

"All officers! Call sign Red! Number three-six-nine. Be on the lookout for a person pushing an ice cream cart! Approach with extreme caution!"

He repeats himself twice, and loads the order into the mainframe.

In seconds he hears dispatch on Peavey's radio broadcasting the order area wide.

And that's all the time he can spare. He starts the engine, puts the car in reverse, and floors it!! The car takes off backwards, and spins around in a cloud of burning rubber and screeching asphalt! Throwing it into drive, he stands on the gas! The 4.6L pulls with the muscle! Knowing Atlanta like the back of his hand, and after studying the map, it doesn't take him long to find the parking deck.

In eighty-one seconds he's there.

Looking at the gloomy deteriorating structure, the fence around the perimeter is cut in many places, and completely torn down in others. The gate preventing cars from entering the property is destroyed, and junk is strewn form here to there.

Hall turns left onto a gravel path and coasts down.

The deck is seven levels high, and at one time could hold as many as fifteen hundred cars. The sublevel garage can be accessed by driving down a pair of concrete ramps. As they circle the area, they search the tent city for any sign of the suspect.

Elevated over the area is Monroe Blvd., and a wide run of train tracks. When a train comes overhead it makes for a deafening experience. Even with the noise of non-stop traffic drowning the area, it's still enough to give one an ear ache.

But today it's calm, only the echoes of curious people watching the slow moving car.

Back at the main road, patrol cars are flying by with sirens wailing.

He slams on brakes and backs up! From the distance in which he's heading, another cruiser pulls up and the two officers talk through the windows. After sitting for a second, one of the cruisers pull onto the property and begin canvassing the area near the far end. The foliage is wild and uninviting, construction debris from failed restoration attempts litters the expanse with jagged boulders, warped lumber, and spikes of twisted re-bar.

Pulling inside the ground level, the shade darkens, the sun is completely blocked, and the electricity has been off since

2005. The walls of the decommissioned beast are littered with graffiti. A man sits against a pillar wearing a tattered military jacket, the pillow he's sitting on, and the mattress beside him holds his scant possessions. The wheeled suitcase sitting upright with the handle extended is only an attaché. A group of men stand around a steel drum chatting, an elderly man pushing a shopping cart overflowing with belongings pass behind them. Speckled far and wide are makeshift shacks, each trying to be as far from the other as possible. Even in real estate as unfortunate as this, location is still key.

As the car rolls forward under its own power into the bowels of the deck, his headlights met the faces of more individuals. A woman sits on a crate. In her lap is a small child, the teddy bear clutched in her arm is matted and dingy. Between them, a rusted car rim lined with plastic trash bags still shows signs of water. The soap and rag in a baggie, and the towel draped over a crate tells a grim story. Feet away, a man and boy sit in before a tent hosting a game of checkers atop a crate provides laughter. A wheeled suitcase with the handle extended waits beside them. When they look up and see the car passing, Tusk looks away. There's no need to get out and question these people, they aren't who he's looking for. Though they're tres-passing on private property, he feels that he's the one doing the intruding. Only a cold-hearted sonofabitch can view this sight and not feel something.

Peavey attentively scans the area with his own pair of binocu-lars. Not wanting to hit anyone, Hall is careful not to move too hastily. His heart skips a beat when he sees a woman pass him eating something! Over the radio information is coming in that the rescue team located a secret cellar leading to the city's sewer system with signs it's recently been accessed. In light of the new discovery units are being dispatched to all area manholes, street grates, and, spillways. Sixty percent of the entire police force is now being expended on one situation. Even personnel from other departments are being pulled and sent here.

Now fully certain he's on the right track, his adrenaline kicks into hyper-drive! Mashing the gas, he reverses outside in search of the woman! He sees her heading toward the street and rumbles up beside so fast that the startle from his presence causes her to drop what she's eating. When he sees the orange sherbet spilling out of the Push-Up®, he becomes possessed! He throws the car in park, thumbs the trunk release, and runs around back!

The woman freezes!

Peavey doesn't have to be told to meet him there! With speed he opens the truck and grabs a steel reinforced flak jacket, and tosses another to Peavey! While one hand fastens the Velcro® straps, the other prepares his weaponry. Making sure it's loaded, he hands John Henry the 12 gauge pistol gripped pump loaded with six buck shots. He selects "Aunt Betty", a military issue M-16 equipped with long range optics, a laser beam, an ultra-high intensity flashlight, and a specially fabricated sixty round drum.

The woman unthaws herself and takes off in a mad dash!

Tusk takes of his major hat, tosses it inside the truck, and slams it! Running back to the driver's side, he grabs two of his three radios, and clip them on!

Peavey is on the other side readying his equipment!

Stuffing the keys in his pocket, Hall shuts the door and dashes back inside the deck!

Using his finger/thumb he lowers the volume on his radios to a whisper. People watching from a distance gasp, those in his path move, others run, and pigeons scatter at the burst of unexpected activity! Moving with vigor, he powers on the light! The brave duo enters the belly!

The humidity is noticeably higher down here, but the temperature is much lower. The smell of urine is intense, and the scurry of squeaking rats resonate of the walls. Worn parking lines chip on the floor, while faded letters guide the direction. Hopeless faces can be seeing peeking from their structures, light fixtures bolted to the ceiling are gutted leaving frayed wires exposed, fire extinguisher cases are being used as storage lockers.

A child cries in the vastness!

The fact these people aren't frightened by two men with guns is unfortunate. They'd been so battered and beaten by the drudgeries of life, that two men wielding guns doesn't faze them.

This side of the aisle is coming to an end, and the corner of the other aisle rounds up ahead. Tusk can't see around the corner yet, but something up ahead causes the hair on his neck to stand on end!!!!

He kills the light, and signals Peavey!

Now in low light, his keen vision zooms in on a man with tattoos on his arm. From the rear he doesn't move like a homeless person, his demeanor seems abnormal for these conditions.

Hunched like a lion, he repositions himself in a sideways profile making himself less of a target, and steers as far from center as possible!

The man is doing something they can't see!

Sticking to the far left, he signal Peavey to go man the position behind a slab a fallen concrete!

With the weight of a feather, Hall tip-toes forward! When he sees the cart with the umbrella sticking out of it, and the clothes on the ground beside it, he steels his nerves.

....And slows his breathing.

The man is healthy as an ox with a gun in his waistband.

He gives another hand signal to Peavey!

3!

2!

1!

"DROP THE WEAPON!!!!!!"

But the HT does the opposite by swinging around with the weapon raised! But he didn't get a chance to fire!

When Hall pulled the trigger, the 5.56×45mm NATO round slams him to the wall! The sound of gun fire sends what seemed to be a place void of much activity, in a temple buzzing with energy!

A man appears in his line of fire darting up the aisle!

The split second delay was all the HT needed to make a move!!!

He lunges forward and grabs a helpless woman as she attempts to flee!

"AAAAAAAAAAAAAAAAH!!!!!!" she screamed, as he uses her body to shield his, chocking the woman from behind, fire at Hall!!!

Having no shot, he ducks for cover!!!

"Let the woman go!!!....Drop the gun!!....DROP IT NOW!!!!!"

The woman is struggling and the HT bleeding from the shoulder! He can hear Peavey on the radio calling for backup!!

The HT shouts: "Let'cha balls hang you fuckin' pussy!!!!........ This shit ain't gone be easy motherfucker!.......I ain't going alive homie!...Now get back pig before I waste this *bitch*!!!!"

Coupled with the blood of another person staining her garment, and the terror of being killed, causes the small woman to struggle mightily! Major watches as she begins stomping his foot, and scratching at his face!

Hall raises the scope to his eyes! With his finger on the trigger he looks for his shot!

Foolishly, the drug fueled gangbanger raises the pistol and attempts to strike the woman in the head! The moment his hand reaches its apex....Tusk fires!

The gun goes flying to the ground, the woman breaks free and runs into the darkness!!!

The sound of dozens of police arriving at the scene is deafening!

He exhales.

The crisis is over.

Quatre.

*H*is eyes shoot open!
Heart is racing and body is drenched in cold sweat, he kicks off the thick blanket and sits on the edge of the bed! Looking at his wet feet, he cups his face in his hands. They're shaking, and he's feeling an extreme sense of terror; panic and horror like he's never experienced before! Shortness of breath, and the throb of the migraine gripping his cranium hits him with blow after blow!
He stands to his feet and stumbles to the bathroom! Nausea, paranoia, and depictions of death and murder assault his mind with violent intentions!
He's fighting the urge to run and leap out of his bedroom win-

dow! His brain is instructing him to get his gun and commit suicide!

Images of white bodies with police dogs gunning down black men are everywhere he looks! And his head is on all the officers' shoulders! Giant police badges fly around like saucers spewing blood money! Visions of Native Americans lay dead in endless seas of slaughter, while chants of Thanksgiving are blown from bugles held by America's four fathers! Riding atop an enormous tornado, St. Nick sends lightning bolts of mutilated corpses clothed in wrapping paper down on millions of blindfolded citizens, a murderous reindeer tramples them as they run for the safety of a slave ship!

He grits his teeth as what he's seeing cuts him to his core, drool seeps down his chin as he reaches the bathroom and flips the light switch. The sudden glare of light causes him to squint, and only partly see the plagued reflection in the mirror. His face is puffed and hideously discolored, eyes burning and reddened with dilated pupils. Veins pulsate on his forehead like bulging pipelines. Dark rings circle his eyes.

He drops to his knees and tries to vomit!

Voices from overhead tell him he's the lowest of the low! He gags and feigns, but nothing comes forth!

"God help me," he pleads. *"God!..Help!...Me!"*

Guidance from deep within keeps shouting he's nothing, and there's one only option!!!

Do it!...Do it!.............YOU PIECE OF SHIT!!!!

He tries to ignore it, and spurs himself to get back up!!!!

"Hold it together Russell!!..You're losing it!..........Don't do it!"

He tries to breathe.

Turning on the tap, he splashes water on his face!

Definitions of his unworthiness capture his mind. Examples he's nowhere near the man people think he is overwhelms his mind! He flips off the light and rushes out the bathroom banging and bumping! Using both banisters to steady his decent, he leans against the corner of the foyer, and falls to his knees.

Tears of pain and worthlessness drip down his cheeks. Presenters from inside his head do a visual presentation on his inability to make the kill. A macabre projection of him electing to shoot the HT twice instead of putting one in his head demonstrate his cowardice! Internal strife between his beliefs and his badge are overburdening his moral compass.

He runs through the kitchen, bowls through the laundry room, and out onto the patio into pouring rain!

In seconds, the fast-acting ointment of Mother Nature begin healing his soul! He's soaking wet wearing nothing but his boxer briefs.

After regaining his composure, he goes back inside and peels of his undergarment. Leaning against the wall, he's glad the pain has subsided.

How on God's green earth did the Atlanta Police Force allow a high value suspect to die while the international media is watching?

Conflicting reports are still surfacing, and many of the details are sketchy. But the most credible version has the HT being taken to Grady Hospital under armed guard. Once in the ER, his anesthesia was switched, causing him a fatal allergic reaction. Apparently, all attempts to resuscitate him were taken, but failed.

The media is reporting a different version.

Based on their sources, the man was dead when he arrived at the ER. The medics claim to have been ordered by members of SWAT riding with them, that the HT was not to be unrestrained from the stretcher, even though the medical attention he required dictated such.

Another vague, and widely considered totally unreliable report a medic alleged that a group of strange men were seen surrounding the HT before he was placed in the ambulance, and he was alive because he was throwing gang signs, and shouting obscenities at the officers. But she later recanted the statement, claiming to have mistaken the federal investigators for outsiders.

The fire storm is ragging and the media is stoking—marches and spot protests are popping up all over the city. KT-36 is threatening more bombings, civil rights leaders are condemning the act, proclaiming a deliberate cover-up. Being the HT was of Hispanic decent, the local chapter of the National Society for Latino Americans are rallying. The black community, angry over repeated incidents of police brutality have joined forces with the NSLA, and other human rights groups. Now they're all storming the capital demanding justice. The mayor considered enacting a city wide curfew, but in a city of six million, that will be close to impossible. The fear is that such an extreme measure will only increase the ire of citizens, further deteriorating the situation.

But things aren't right. Not with this case, not with the take over, not with him, not with anything! In the pit of his stomach he has this sour feeling that the HT was killed on purpose. The magnitude of what he may've said could've been the reason why. He could be wrong, but the medic's claims about strange men hovering around him has merit. The fact she later recanted shows classic signs of correction through intimidation.

"You're okay now…Pull yourself together man."
But whispers still pester him with tauntings of being a nice guy, too caught up in his make-believe world where honor and justice actually mean something.

In the real world people do whatever it takes to survive. Everyman for himself is the usual moniker. Nice guys finish last is what they say. If they don't, why is he slouched on the floor at 2:56 a.m. feeling like a spineless worm. He can't understand his instinctual desire to avoid taking a life. His main focus was to free the hostage, and apprehend the HT, not kill him.

But what if the HT would've somehow had a second firearm or, somehow had not have been affected by the shot, and went on to kill the hostage? His reluctance to terminate could have caused the woman her life. Plus, if he'd went on and killed him, the department wouldn't be dealing with the issue of a suspect mysteriously dying in custody.

You took the weak way out! You're no Tusk!

He gets off the floor, grabs a jug of water from the fridge, and takes a long drink.

Heading to the living room, he grabs the card off the counter and continues into the den. Gather himself, he flops down on the sofa and inhales deeply.

With regained mental stability, his chest stops heaving and his heart slows down.

Anytime there's an officer involved shooting, especially in this age of 24/7 news cycles, department policy requires that the officer(s) be placed on administrative leave, pending the outcome of the investigation. But in certain circumstances, protracted examinations are unwarranted. The major was clearly justified and immediately cleared. The investigation was done in three hours. The force can't afford to lose his leadership, not even for the three days it takes for a preliminary investigation to be completed. Considering the countless witnesses, nearby officers, the radio communications, and evidence gathered at the scene; it was quickly determined Maj. Hall responded appropriately by shooting the HT.

Holding the card to his assigned support member, he flips it over and sees the name and number, and can't believe he's actually considering calling; but wants to be reassured he'd actually done the right thing.

Atop the fireplace's mantle sits a picture of a woman—she isn't his little princess any more. Even canvas and oil paint is not enough to dim the sparkle in her eyes. Other framed memories of him and her captured in time adorn the mantle. At the time, the decision seemed the right one to make. But in retrospect, he wonders if it was the best one. He can see she's happy and loves him dearly. But the question *is,* whether it's enough for *him?* Can he live with the outcome of things? Can his natural penchant for over analysis allow him to accept the outcome? Did his inherent desire to critique everything, and perceive every trend lead him to develop unrealistic expectations for himself, and for others? Or did his habitual use of advanced science, and mystical reasoning cause him to become out of touch with reality? There's something to be said about his marriage only lasting three years; the ex claiming she could no longer endure his constant elucidations regarding her inability to *"find her purpose",* and his constant quest for perfection. To her, life isn't a stone that should be meticulously chiseled until it becomes a flawless gem.

The fact that even during their final goodbyes, she still claimed to love and admire him, gave him a subtle warmth in his heart. He'd wanted to string the marriage along until their daughter was out of high school, but that proved futile—their time was up. It was time for them to move forward on separate journeys, and it was best for her that they did. Not only for the wife, but their daughter as well. In the early stages of his new life as an ex-spouse, he feared she'd suffer from the loss of his daily in-sight and unrelenting guidance. He feared her readiness for the world would be adversely affected by the void created by him not being there. Evidently, his tactic proved beneficial. She's grown to become a valedictorian, and summa cum lade college grad. So far so good and from the looks of things, he'd raised a child properly prepared to compete in today's world of mass of deception and singular progression.

But the idea of his daughter in the arms of another man still causes his heart to miss a beat.

He exhales, realizing she's already set sail, and he'll have to accept the fact he can't control the weather.

Feeling powerful and mighty again, he raises his athletic build off the sofa and stretches his naked body.

"UuuuuuuuAaaaaaaaaaaaahhhuh…….."

He shakes the reminder of earlier from his mind.

When he hears the fax machine beep and come alive, he takes that as a cue from the universe it's time to get back to business.

In the guest room which doubles as an office is a basket of clean clothes he was supposed to put up. After putting on a fresh T-shirt and a pair of boxers, he turns his attention to the printer, set to automatically receive and print incoming transmissions.

The ink-jets hum to life!

"Wow. That was strange."

The paper feeder initializes and begins printing.

Good thing his daughter is with her mother leaving the house to himself. He flips the switch, pulls up a chair, sits down, and begins reviewing the documents.

The first one he selects is still warm from printing. Nguyen has the test results back from the lab, and isn't surprised Loop is up at this hour. Part of what makes him such a good detective is the fact he gets so immersed in his work. Loop often tells a story of how he stayed up nine straight days working the trail of a suspect. He's probably pouring through case files over coffee with his hand stroking his chin. For some, insomnia is just part of being a police officer.

In the few minutes it took him to read the document, six more are waiting. Two of the blood samples returned profile hits matching the two suspects they already have, but the last is unknown. The items in the backpack were also tested, which too matched the profile of the unknown sample—meaning they likely came from the same person. The picture is taking shape, and what it's beginning to resemble isn't good. On one hand, you have a powerful businessman with a legal practice involved

in a marital separation has a hit carried out on his family, while
a third mystery person is at the residence during the commission of the murders. The question that'll tie the web together is
whether this unknown was part of the hit team, or part of the
target. To a civilian mind, it may seem implausible that a man
such as Ed Denmark would aid and abet a violent fugitive.
But to him, it's more than plausible. Who is the unknown to
Denmark, and why did he want him dead? Could he have been
involved in an affair with the wife?
If this is true, it'll answer a lot of questions as to why he was at
the residence, and why he was targeted. The hit team must've
had intel he would be there? The family getting killed could've
been collateral damage? But why take the kid, and why KT-36?
Though Denmark has not a blemish on his record, and has
never been convicted of any crimes, he's still a shadowy
figure. Rumors swirl about his double life, one in which he
rules an underworld crime syndicate involved in everything
from corporate espionage, to arms dealing, to human trafficking, to extortion, to murder. To many, including Denmark,
it's all just talk, baseless lies fabricated by his foes. When
questioned about it, he rarely gives more than a smirk. But on
one occasion, he challenged anyone with a shred of evidence
connecting him to anything to come forth. And to this day, no
one has been able to meet it.
These latest events may've altered the spectrum.
At the mild end Denmark, and his family were random targets
of a gangbanging fugitive.
What did the HT mean by *"Rick?"*
What did the forewarned indication *"he was coming"* mean?
At the extreme end, he's the mastermind and funded the entire
operation on the fact that his wife was involved in an affair,
and he was about to lose custody of his son—two children from
a previous relationship killed, and his biological son kid-
napped, was no accident; the evidence tells that much.
Looking at a color copy of the unknown suspect getting out

of the taxi pulled from the gas stations surveillance system, he doesn't come across to Hall as a gangbanger. It's grainy with bad angles, and gives no view of the face. By studying what he has, he sees no mention of gang activity, or ties to any criminal organizations. He actually looks rather dorky, and perhaps even timid. Just from his meek walk, he bares all the signs of a person who knows nothing about gang life. He seems the polar opposite of Denmark, and maybe just the kind of man that could wittingly sweep an unhappy housewife off her feet. But he isn't married to this theory.

He couldn't help but notice, when they were at the hostage scene, Denmark seemed very familiar with many of the officials, which meant politics could be at play? Which meant facts could be compromised? The haughty way he pulled into a restricted area spoke volumes about the sureness he has in his position. He himself was surprised no one stopped him.

The more documents he studies, the more he's able to hypothesize the information he doesn't have. Mixed within the pages of material is a thirty day calendar of community events, and departmental meetings he's scheduled to attend. Two conferences with the police union are listed but dates have yet to be determined, plus he still has the quarterly budget proposal for the south precinct to finish. Pulling these to the side, he continues studying under the white light of the ceiling fan. Behind him, the silence of the late night stillness serenade him with peace and quiet. He knows there's nine investigators working the case, and isn't the person specifically tasked with solving them. He's a major whose main job is to, ensure compliance with department policies and procedures, precinct management, infrastructure development, and community relations. But there's no rule stating a senior official is prohibited from assisting subordinates in active investigations. The phone records from the entire family are being analyzed. Loop just faxed the lists of all the names and numbers that have connected with any of the phones belonging to the victims. The powerful computer program, TraceCross®, designed to find patterns and trends in phone data, was employed. It red flagged eighteen numbers based on analytics such as frequency of use, call duration, time it was placed, geographical location of incoming calls, and date of initial contact.

The next document that slides into the tray, is the signed statement of the cab driver. A man named Pidwas Badu, employed by the Halal Cab Company, claims to have picked up a man who went by the name 'Payne Bogart' at a nightclub. He wrote that he took this gentlemen to the Shell gas station around the same time of the murders, going on to say he got in a silver SUV with some other guys and left heading in the direction of Denmark's neighborhood. He also supplied a number from which the call originated. Looking at the other document, it isn't on the list of eighteen flagged by TraceCross. He takes a short time to read the document.

By the time the clock chimes five am, he's been up for almost three hours. He now has concrete evidence the unknown was purposely at the Denmark residence, and from the look of the evidence, could've even been part of the hit team. But the fact he rendezvoused with a third party before continuing to the home confuses things. Right when he looks to be getting somewhere, he ends up right back at square one. Denmark being out of town and his wife home at the time of the unknown's arrival doesn't offer much towards determining the scope of the relationship, nor if she knew him at all.

He feels it's too premature to say with certainty that the person was there for the misses. There's currently no evidence indicating Denmark even suspected infidelity. However, the fact that only his biological son was spared seems like it was meant to be that way. But it doesn't solve the puzzle. If this was supposed to be a hit, why did the HT take the kid in the first place? Surely the hitman wouldn't have wanted to complicate the mission, so something had to happen to where he felt forced to take that action? What happened to make them turn on the unknown, and try to kill him too? All of his equations keep having the same common denominator.

He goes to the kitchen and fills the coffee maker. Once ready, he pours a cup and returns to his seat. It's still dark out, but traces of light are creeping across the sky. He doesn't care much for television, so he logs
onto Google® and enters the name 'Rick.'
In .48 seconds, the search engine returns 6,480,000 results.
But the link at the top of the page in bold blue says it all.

'World renowned economist, Richford Chuld found dead in New York mansion.'

He clicks the link. The *'Fuck U Rick'* annotation now has a basis.
Published at 2:13 a.m. on today's date, the news site explains he was found at approximately 11:09 p.m. by his housekeeper inside his wine cellar with a "self-inflicted" gunshot wound to the head. No one else was harmed. The author of the piece goes on to highlight the life and career of Richford "Rick" Chuld.
Embattled with legal problems stemming from allegations he was a key cog in a global currency valuation scheme involving trillions of dollars. He started Chuld Index Inc., which grew to become the world's leading name in currency valuation, and also sat on the board of some of the world's leading investment banks. His wife of twenty seven years had recently divorced him.

The eight paragraph article is detailed and expertly written. But it's the comprehensive level of investigative journalism which deserved the most praise.

In 1993 Chuld was charged with the death of a beautiful young screenwriter. After enjoying an evening of fine dining, the twenty four year old SCAD (Savannah College of Art and Design) graduate was found dead in a Lake Tahoe suite registered to Chuld. He was later arrested and charged with her murder. Represented by lawyer, Eldrin Denmark, the expensive and highly publicized trial resulted in him being found not guilty. But in the civil suit that followed, he was found guilty of her murder and required to pay the family damages in the amount of eight hundred-thousand. Chuld would go on to become a respected authority in determining the value of money. The authorities aren't releasing information on whether they suspect foul play.

Gold, the world's leading hard currency, is used to value the worth of a countries paper currency, by the actual amount of gold bullion the said country holds in their treasury. People like Chuld, who gain this almost impossible status, wield immense leverage on world markets, and control vast sums of money. He was the definition of elite, the epitome of the one percentile. But as of late, his organization, and others alike have become the faces of income inequality, being blamed as one of the key contributors to the problem. He'd spent millions lobbying for a one world currency with the hopes of widening the gap even further. The catastrophic result he and his cohorts at the Federal Reserve are hoping for, is they will ultimately gain an iron clad monopoly on the entire trade of currency, thus making them the sole power in the known world.

He remembers seeing him on television facing a congressional inquiry, and can still see the smug and remorseless way Chuld sat there and claimed the playing field is level, and people are paid a fair wage, even had the audacity to say the corporations are the ones losing.

It's one calamity after the next. He now has definitive proof there's something sinister at work, and wonder's if Loop has seen this? He reaches for one of his many phones, sends him the link, and forwards it to Peavey.

Why was the HT having dealings with a figure like Chuld? This make absolutely no sense! What could billionaire Richford Chuld possibly gain from a KT-36 gangbanger?

A few more minutes were spent reading email, and sifting documents for anything else that may catch his eye—the sweaty smell on his body moves him to take a shower.

By a quarter to six, he's in full uniform and ready to go; unheard of for a man of his rank. He shows no signs of insomnia, no indication of a panic attack, no signs his confidence is wavering, and shows no hints of a man with a shaken resolve. He doesn't have the luxury of being burnt out. People look to him as a pillar of endurance; someone they can lean on. At a time like this, he has to put his problems aside, and the problems of others at the forefront. The department is under attack, the city is gripped by fear anger and anarchy, and at the center of it all, is Ed Denmark.

Around all of life, there exists an electromagnetic field, one which encompasses all of space, and all of time. All forms of creation share like characteristics with this filed. Some life forms have more positive (+) energy, others have more neutral (N), while others have more negative (-) charges. The combination of these magnetisms determine the overall charge of the being, or a mass.

Teeming with positive energy, Hall is able to plug into this environment, and become part of its pulse. By performing this fissioning, he amplifies his frequency towards impacting its development in a *"positive way"*. Chemical contents of self-regeneration, and key signatures of nutritious sub-atomic isotopes buzz through his conscious with impulses of reassuring encouragement. Reminders of past experiences tell him the universe has specifically chosen him for this mission; assuring him that the thunder in his chest is part of the increase in divine enlightenment. A feeling of optimism and protection warms over him as he prepares to report for duty. Performing a mental check of his gear, the bulk of his primary effects remain inside his vehicle, but both arms and hands are lugging something.

A chime notifies him a text message has been received. Sitting the leather briefcase on the ground, he unlocks the phone and clicks the envelope icon.

It's an urgent message from Loop.

But before he could read the first word, two more notifications come in. One from the arrival of a new email, and the other from a text on his personal phone. They're messages telling him a cell phone believed to belong to the unknown has been tracked to a proximate location. Though he's up there with the deputy chief, the assistant chief, and the chief of Police, he can always be found somewhere close to the action, down in the trenches getting his hands dirty; hard-nosed police work with a focus on integrity and respect. He loves doing what he calls "getting it out the mud". It makes him feel like a man when he looks himself in the eye.

The house phone starts ringing, and the fax machine starts beeping.

He isn't even out of port yet but already he's commanding his fleet. Sitting his major hat atop his head, he resumes course towards greatness.

The information Bailey gave him stopped him in his tracks!

Alex is so paranoid and out of his mind that reality and fantasy have merged into one. He's so stricken with hunger pains, that the acids in his empty stomach are burning into its lining; the cramps and twists are intense. It's telling him not to trust anything she says. He knows he should've never answered the phone, he could've been five hundred miles away by now, and feels like fool for staying. Emotion and irrational thinking had him thinking flee, but the magnetic Bailey Red and her spellbinding words now have him thinking stay. She keeps playing the same broken record.

She and her daughter are being threatened with their lives, and can really use his help.

Just like him, she too has a desire to live, and has convinced him bunkering down in a safe place is his best option, claiming she overheard the guy chasing him isn't getting out of jail anytime soon because he's some kind of foreign mercenary on the FBI's watch list, plus Merciless has more men hunting for him, and has beaten her with a gun believing she had something to do with it. For all he knows, that's a lie. What could be waiting out there for him is horrifying. His mind keeps playing tricks on his vision with shocking scenes of his capture, while her words are echo through his mind like laughs of a sadistic clown. She has everything to gain, and he has nothing to lose.

Being on the run is expensive, and he's broke. All options to generate cash are on the table because he's running out of time, with no way of knowing which day will be his last—being where he is now could lead to his demise; anywhere inside six hundred miles of Atlanta is bad. The sooner he gets some dough, the sooner he can leave. There's no way of knowing if she's playing him for a dumb white boy, but she's not the only one who's learning the ways of the streets. Should he double cross her the first chance he gets? Maybe, because at this point he's not concerned about anything other than his own survival, and will use whatever means available to evade capture.

It's all beginning to click. The fact his life has turned into a minute by minute crisis has forced him to tap into reserves he never knew he had. In his mind he has to expect she's trying to fuck him over. He's not going to *get caught slipping* any more. His eyes are open now. That's why he got rid of the phone, he was too easy to contact and doesn't want anyone to be able to communicate with him. Like he learned from Stockton, things run smoother when one dog leads the pack. Indications the police were trying to track the phone already had him spooked, but when she kept demanding he tell her his whereabouts, he hung up and took the battery out. Earlier today he tossed it in the bed of a landscaping truck, and has since been staked out across the street. Eight hours in a stolen car with no A/C in the sweltering Georgia humidity is punishment in itself. His skin is sweaty, and balls of lint and dust have him itchy. The seat is leaned all the way back, so from afar it looks like an empty car sitting in front of Bishop Bankers Auto Auction, which is across the street from Dream Kings. Being that it's closed, it offers the perfect blind for him to surveil the entrance he once sleep in front of in secret. Pulled between other cars sitting before the auction's main building, he draws no attention, the cars in the surrounding lot make him invisible. At two fifty-seven in the morning, he still hasn't eaten, his mouth is dry, and his lips are like gator back. So when he finally sees the car pull up, he's relieved.

Fear sets in!

When he sees Troy Merciless get out of the sedan and go into the club, he knows it's time!

Now all of a sudden he has to use the restroom.

Letting the seat up, he starts the car, and for encouragement, glances over his shoulder and looks at the weapons case and ditty bag. The club he's spent many nights sleeping before advertises adult entertainment, but is really a front for human trafficking. Merciless has underage girls working for him that are usually more desirable than the others because of their "exotic" nature. The variety of girls he has gives the tricks and johns a plethora of ways to spend their bucks. Asians and Eastern European girls are hot right now, but his constant stock of Latino, White, and Black girls are always in plentiful supply.

Before he can think about whether he really wants to do this, Merciless emerges from the club with two barely-dressed women. One gets in the front, one gets in the back, the scum gets in the driver's seat.
Alex backs out and prepares to follow, as the supercharged Chrysler 300 shifts into gear, and pulls onto the street.
With his heart racing and forehead sweating, he pulls out behind it, but is so nervous he almost forgets to turn the headlights on; not to mention the police cruiser sitting in front of the club.

The sedan is moving fast, but he stays back enough to keep him in sight. Merciless goes nine lights, makes three turns, and gets on the interstate. That's when he really puts the pedal to the medal. Heading east on 20, he pushes the 300 to almost 100 MPH. Alex knows he's going to get spotted, but he has no choice if he wants a meal. Almost a half mile back, he sees the speck that is Merciless light up red, and get off on Boulevard Ave. Afraid he may lose him, he presses the accelerator until the Impala closes the gap.
He begins to panic! He can't see them!
Relief sets in when he rounds the bend and sees the car sitting at the end of the exit ramp. Thinking he could've been spotted, he pretends to turn right, though the sedan is turning left.
As he coasts to an easy halt, the light turns green and Merciless turns left and speeds over the hill.
Alex pulls out right, turns left, and follows—a risky move for a fugitive.
The area turns dark and unsettling. While he continues with

caution down Boulevard, he studies his surroundings. The houses become increasingly ragged, the potholes get worse, and the cars get older. As the 300 turns left three blocks ahead, he notices beings shrouded in darkness hunched in movement. Shadows can be seen moving about—inside squalid dwellings lights flicker. He drives past the turn and looks down. The tail-lights of the racy 300 are turning into a driveway. Seeing the neighborhood is laid in blocks, he goes to the next street and turns left.

The street is named '*Hilliard*'.

At the first stop sign he turns left again. The dim road is lined with cars and the sound of distance voices is apparent.

A siren wails!

He turns left again. Two hundred feet on the right is a small shopping center. The barber shop, grocery store, laundry mat, and the Chinese restaurant are closed and heavily fortified with alarms, bars, floodlights, and gates. From the end of the lot, a car comes heading from around back. While looking in the direction of the house Merciless pulled into, he glances back to his left and sees there's cars parked behind the shopping center. This hits him as being very strange, considering the stores are closed, and the area is mostly inactive.

He sees the 300!

It's parked at the end of a long driveway between some other cars, and there looks to be movement under, what from a distance, looks like a side door. Alex keeps going and doesn't slow down until he's back where Merciless initially turned. While waiting for the car coming down the hill to pass, his heart drops when he sees it's a police cruiser!

He closes his eyes!

"*Stay calm! Stay calm! Stay calm!*"

The dark blue Crown Victoria with red letters continues pass and disappears over the hill.

Whatever he's going to do, he better get on with it. Riding around at night in this area isn't a good idea. He signals with

the blinker and turns left, and comes to another light. Waiting
for this one to turn, a person to his right is waving from the
sidewalk. Through the window he hears them saying: *"What's
up? What's up?"*
Living on the street has taught him some of the "G-codes".
What's going on, is that a man dressed as a woman is mistaking
him for a customer looking for sex.
He ignores him and pulls forward, turns, and by the time he
comes to the next turn, has an idea. Upon making *another*
turn he pulls into the shopping center from the preceding end,
drives around back and kills the lights. Coasting forward, he
sees the houses are separated from the lot by a barbed wired
fencing. With his head on a swivel, he sees cars parked under a
light. And that's when he sees the reflection of Merciless' car on
the other side. Realizing this is it, he takes a deep breath and
pulls beside a green trash dumpster, turns off the car, and sits
in silence.
Now he doesn't know what to do, and on top of that, he's
scared starving and being searched for. Being crunch time, his
brain is feeding his gut bad information. The new figures coming in, has him being conned from the start, she's
going to have him killed, and go collect the reward money. To
her, he's just a cracker with a bounty on his head. This business
about her trying to get her and this made up child to some safe
house in Missouri is bullshit! When the head lights of a car pull
out of nowhere, he jumps into the backseat and grabs the case!
The van swerves in so fast that it runs into a stack of flattened
cardboard boxes! When Alex sees how the stack of aluminum
ladders are shift, he knows they're going to tumble on the car.
The driver stumbles out and looks right at him.
"Heeeeeey essay. Time to get some poo-see huh?....*Ha-Haaaa!"*
And staggers away.
The words are still registering, he's so jacked he was about to
shoot that drunk!
"Shit!" Wipes the back of his hand across his face, and sits the

case back behind the seat.

Cupping his shaking hands in his face he sees a box on the ground. Focusing more, he sees it's actually an empty box of condoms. While the man goes to the end of the alleyway and squeezes through a hole in the fence, Alex figures out what's going on. There seems to be some kind of sexual service being offered in the house.

Maybe she isn't lying?

The plan is to rob Merciless, and escape out of town with the proceeds. He's supposed to meet up with Bailey afterwards, but has decided to renege on the rescue part.

He's blinded by a flashlight. All the blood leaves his face and drops his mouth open!

"Hey man, you straight?" asked a guy standing near the trunk.

His voice is gone!

"You can't be sitting out here like this pimp. This shit hot. You gone have to gone inside or get from round here buddy."

"Okay," Alex whispered. "I'm a little drunk. Sorry about that," pretending to be inebriated.

"Yeah," waiting for him to get out.

The situation is now out of his hands.

Putting the keys in his pocket he sits up. Keeping his face shielded under the 'A' baseball cap, he gets out stumbling like the other guy; heart whamming like a bass drum!

It isn't until he makes it to the hole in the fence that the man turns away.

But another man is waiting on the other side. Merciless' car is right there! It's empty with no sign of him, or the passengers. The door to the house opens where a second man guards the inside. A potent odor of cheap perfume brushes under his nose. Merciless bursts through the door and looks right at him!

In the darkness of the Georgia night, everything becomes still. It's unadulterated fear its purest form! The wetness between his legs removes all feelings he has of being a man.

It isn't until Merciless looks away and says something to the doorman that he exhales. Somehow he didn't recognize him? He hears the roar of the engine echoing off the side of the house, and almost falls to his knees. He's seeing stars.
After auto-starting the car, and unlocking the doors with a click of the key fob, Merciless gets inside, and slams the door with authority!
The feel of cold urine running down his leg is the only thing keeping him upright! The Xenon® headlights of the 300 illuminate the side of his body as he backs out. The rumble of the tires over gravel is the only sound he's comprehending.
 "What-chu need man?" asked a deep voice.
"..............Uhmn............I'm just...... trying to get a girl. M-My friend, frie---"
You're about to die!
"Spit it out man!" the man shouts. "Da fuck you want?"
"...j-just came in before me. I couldn't keep up," he slurred.
"What-chu drunk or sum?"
"Yeah I guess. A little bit."
"Man don't puke in this house!"
"Nah, I won't. It looks bad but I'm cool. I been like this all day?"
"You got some money?"
"Yeah. You don't remember me from last time. I spend big money here."
Ding! Ding! Ding!
Without further questions, the man pulls the door open, and it's the opening of Satan's lair.
Stumbling forward, he sees the man inside looking him square in the face. The second both of his feet are inside, the brute rudely bumps him aside.
Slam!
Goes the door, locked with a deadbolt.
He stares into him with deep black eyes, before nodding to keep moving.

The scent is sickening, sticky, and uncomfortable. The walls are cracking with faux wood paneling, low hanging ceilings showcase tiles of yellow tint with mildew coating, moans and gasps of unseen customers are heard in the background. The odd color of the paint establishes the bad tone humming from its core. A set of stairs at the rear of a large room leading down to another level, a cluttered kitchen is off of it. His heart pounds as he looks at the filthy carpet matted with ages of filth, the smell of vomit and bleach is bullying him to gag. Traversing downward, light is even dimmer. Bare red bulbs hanging from a string guide the way.

He gasps so deeply that he almost cries out!!!!!!

An older woman with a cigarette stuck to her lip, and large sagging breasts that resemble cantaloupes in trash bags; herds girls out of a room for the man who came in before him to choose. Two of them look to be with the pair with

Merciless. They're all lined up for the man to see, and all scantily clad in reveling treads. The soul-jolting looks in their eyes is nothing but pain.

He can't be a bad person, he feels extreme sympathy for these women. Several look like they should be in high school, but are all staring at the ground with fake smiles. Some have polish chipping from their toes—they're all different ethnicities, and different sizes.

They all carry scars, both inside and out.

The hallway behind them is lined with doors on either side.

He thinks of their parents, and wonders how they got here?

When the trick chooses the one he wants, he hands the old hag the money, and him and the girl disappears in a room.

She turns her attention to him.

But he looks away because another door has opened. And out emerges a man sweating noticeably with a young lady behind him. Red marks are around her throat and chest, and the immaturity of her breasts tells him she can't be a day over 14.

An anger greater than any he's ever experienced constricts his

throat like the hand of God!!!! At this precise moment, a vigilante seed is planted *deep* within his consciousness!!The horror
of what he's witnessing brands him ferocious with rage!
His spirit wants to *KILL!*
NOW!

The man glances at him and goes up the stairs.
From the bowels of the hallway comes a scream!
Gritting his teeth and balling his fist, he can only image the
atrocities behind it! He thinks of all the women and young
girls in his family and imagines if this was them!!!!!
The woman who doesn't look American stares strangely at him.
The girls lining the wall stand meekly awaiting his selection.
He stands there looking completely out of place snarling!
"Hurry up!...Which one?" she asked impatiently.
But he's too shocked to speak, and so dazed that he doesn't
even hear what she's saying, though he's staring right at her.
Out of a door along the hallway, a huge guy emerges. Enforcer
is written all over him.
"Where's your money?" she asked in a foreign accent.
"............................"
The guy comes and gets in his face.
"Check-em,'" she said.
The man pushes him into the wall, pats him down, and
squeeze his pockets. When he touches the wet spot between his
legs he jumps back.
"What the fuck!.........."
And pushes him in the chest.
"This drunk muthafucka ain't got no money!"
Is the last thing he said before he grabs him by the throat, and
rams his head into the wall!
The madam yells something and the girls scurry back down the
hall and vanish inside different rooms.
When the last door slams, he's snatched from the wall and
kicked up the stairs! He stumbles going up causing the man

behind him strike him in the head, the ringing sensation in
his ear knocks off his balance to the point he grabs the wall to
steady himself!
"What I tell y'all about coming here broke! This ain't no fuckin'
charity!"
When he gets to the top step, the guy at the door comes and
slings him down!
"Where you from? I ain't never seen you?"
Sprawled on the floor in pain, he tries to find his breath.
"The guy I was with brought me here. He said it's on him. I'm
just looking for a good time. I'm not trying to play any games."
"Well I guess you fucked then, cuz ain't shit good going on
here."
Before he could recover from the first, a foot kicks him in the
ribs! Seconds later what feels like a heavy rubber hose, smacks
against the side of his face and nose, almost
knocking him unconscious! He knows he's about to die when
he feels the same thing being wrapped around his neck! Blood
begins coming from his nostrils, the goon twisting it around
his throat trying to put him to sleep! Teetering on the brink of
collapse, he feels himself lifted to his feet and thrown outdoors,
sending his face, cheek, and forehead raking across the ground!
Clutching his neck, he fights to untie whatever it is before he
blacks out!!! Coughing, gasping, wheezing, with saliva dripping
from his mouth, he waits for the bullet to the head!!!!!!!
"There's your good time asshole!.......Bring some fuckin' money
next time!"
The second he gets the thing off his throat, he rolls onto his
back and sees the sky!
WHAM!!
The last thing he remembers is something hard strike him in
the head!..

....

....

.................*He wants to lay there and die, his will to live is gone.*

The ugly karma he's set up for himself is enacting its retribution. The reprehensible things he's done are inexcusable, and the law of free will is proving costly. And for him, it's a fitting punishment.
The man seeing he hasn't gotten off the ground yet, comes and peps him up with another kick!!! He crawls to his feet, and this time his stumble is real. Looking over his shoulder to make sure the man isn't about to hit him again, he sees a black, thirty six inch dildo laying on the ground, and his head is throbbing with pain! This is obviously protocol for customers who come empty handed.
The doorman grabs the dildo, and goes back inside; slamming the door!

Back in the car with his stability completely off kilter, he begins crying. Feeling the tears running down his face, he falls to the passenger seat. Loud, deep, painful tears pour forth, his body shudders and jerks! Mucus runs out of his nose and into his mouth. He screams in anguish for doing this to himself, he hates being in this body, he reviles this skin that did those things! He's in no way prepared to deal with the repercussions of his actions. He'd been deceived by a man who said he loved him.
"We were supposed to be brothers!" he cries. *"We were supposed to be friends!"*
Sobbing under the sparkling canopy, he accepts the fact the stars have aligned against him. The disgust he feels for himself is nauseating, scenes from the crimes are haunting him like poltergeists with bullhorns. He thought he'd reached rock bottom before, but had no idea there are subterranean levels of lowliness. Locked inside this underworld of anger and regret, he unearths a gem, a topaz of innovation; a new element for him to exploit. A more efficient fossil fuel for his soul. As far back as he can remember, he's been fed upon by wolves, dominant males have used him as a pissing bush to mark their terri-

tory. Now there's nothing left for them to devour, they'd eaten him to the bone, his carcass left to rot in a barren wasteland of pain and suffering. Within this pit of despair, he's stripped of all his emotional possessions, bags he's carried his entire life are engulfed by the wildfire of awakening, inferior complexities he's possessed since childhood are banished. His cognitive physique is torn down and rebuilt. An exoskeleton of impenetrable conviction is fitted for his new disposition, cutting-edge programs are installed on his hard drive. Through the blur of eyes puffy with stress and the haze of dilated pupils, he watches his life pass. He was once a boy with hopes and dreams. Now he's a man stuck in a perpetual nightmare.

When Alex sits up and wipes the internal rubble from his face, he feels reborn. The evocative experience he just lived through was like the commencement of a boy transitioned to adulthood. Looking in the rearview, he doesn't recognize the man he encounters, he hasn't seen these eyes before. The jaw line seems hardened, veins pulsate on his neck and forehead that weren't there before. There's confidence is his chest. The calmness of mind and acceptance of self is something new. He seems recreated, a reengineered man hell-bent on righting all his wrongs. The growl in his stomach no longer craves food, it craves confirmation. Verification that he's a top predator who knows how to rip the throat out of his prey!

The first step a hunter takes when tracking is attainment of the high ground. From there the terrain can be studied to determine where game are likely to gather. Over his shoulder he reaches and grabs the case. Out to a hundred and fifty yards, his accuracy is deadly. Being condemned to the hotel room, he's familiarized himself with the weapons and its accessories.

He also read the book. The treasures discovered within are now sparkling with thoughts of brilliance. He grabs the multi-vision (Meaning capable of seeing in day, night, and heat signatures) binoculars and hangs them around his neck. They're noticeably heavier than normal types. As if something taps him on the shoulder and tells him to look, much to his delight there's a trusty roof access ladder tucked in the corner, perfectly camouflaged by a grease trap and trash compactor.

Opening the door, he gets out and stuffs the keys in his pocket. Immediately he looks towards the fence. The light is on but sees no movement. He turns and makes for the ladder. To keep people like him out, it's elevated seven feet of the deck. Having prior experience with sleeping atop buildings, he's up the chute in minutes. The surrounding area is a neighborhood of urban blight. He can see Georgia Baptist Hospital and the peak of the gold-domed State Capital building.
Placing the optics on his face he tightens the strap, it's like having scuba goggles on but the difference is clear. With a press of the power button everything becomes green, and darkness lights up like high noon. Alex is astounded by the amount of detail he can see! He was mistaken when he thought the area was dead! Pockets of people can now be seen everywhere, even those standing in dark alcoves are exposed!
A twist of the knob, and the intensity increases or decreases, depending on which way he turns. Too much and the view becomes too bright, too low and it goes black. Leaving it at the mid-point, he pushes the other button. The view transforms from glowing green, to dark with rainbow color—he sees what the night vision can't. The thermal imager opens the window to a whole new world! In the trees he can see colorful figures of squirrels and birds, a dog with vibrant hues of red, lime, orange, yellow, purple, and blue can be seen ambling down the street.
Even more people are out there! He can now see them sitting

in cars, and even some inside of houses! The doorman unseen before, is now lit up in a colorful kaleidoscope, a woman sitting on her porch is smoking something!

Pressing the zoom button and the perspective increased 10x. The level of detail is astonishing! The heat signature from the cigarette smoke is like a red wave of floating haze. He clicks the button again, and the vision returns back to normal. Amazingly, even without it he can see, can even read the street sign down at the corner!

Irwin St. is the name but someone has spray painted a line through it, and vandalized it with the slogan: *The Blade.* Defacing the side of a boarded up home are black graffiti letters spelling out the words: *Pink City.*

Alex pulls the binoculars off and walks to the far end of the roof. Kneeling to one knee he quietly sits the case down and unlatches the four sides. Separating them in two he extracts the L42A1 sniper rifle. It's in three sections so he screws them together. Once assembled, he sights and loads. Even in the warm humid air, the 7.62 x 39mm round is cold to the touch.

He has no reason to wear gloves.

Laying the rifle on the roof's ledge he focuses on his target. Since the roof top is four feet lower than the sidewall spanning the perimeter, he has a blind to hide his body, and a stable place to set the rifle. It's like the perfect deer stand. He pulls the binoculars back over his face, and presses the button to night vision.

There in his cross hairs is the target talking on a cell phone, and smoking something brown fat and long. Based on his upbringing with guns, and his experience with it in the hotel room, he's certain that based on the dope, in ideal conditions the weapon will fire accurately to five hundred yards. But at this short distance things like wind speed, air pressure, and gravitational pull wouldn't have any effect on the bullets trajectory. This is just like shooting a wild hog. All he has to do is slow his breathing and wait for his shot.

Because of the focus, the links of the fence are appearing as translucent fog when looking through the scope. But the man's face however is clear as crystal. He's busy on the phone pacing near the doorway.

The nervous pace that normally attacks his heart during times like this, is gone. When the leech turns to take a step, he wraps his index finger around the trigger. As if he couldn't have picked a better position, the man puts the cigarette in his mouth, the phone on the ground, unzips his pants, and starts urinating.

"We are who we are before we are born...So let God judge me." And pulls the trigger.

The soft whisper from the end of the barrel is like a sneeze. There's no muzzle flash. The instant burst of red spatter on the side of the house sends the slime slumping on the dirt still holding his cock! The place he fell is perfect. If someone comes out the door, they won't immediately see him. They'll have to come completely out and walk to the rear corner. Even a john can miss him if they aren't looking.

He releases his breath and clears the chamber. The smoking cartridge ejects and lands beside his foot.

The feeling is invigorating!

Quickly he rises and slides the binoculars off his face. Combining the two halves, he locks the case and dashes for the ladder.

Once on the ground, he takes a cautious look around before continuing. Going to the hood of the car, he sits the case atop and reopens it. Extracting the silenced pistol and submachine gun, he attaches the strap, fully loads it, and hangs it over his shoulder—the silenced 9mm goes in his waistband.

Opening the car door, he tosses the two halves in the backseat and shuts it. Walking in a dark alleyway behind a shopping center in crime riddled 4th. Ward, he heads for the fence with four deadly weapons on his person.

A treat!

He smells marijuana in the air and get excited!

The door opens, and out heads the drunk trick. The girls look to have sobered him up a bit. Thinking of how young that one girl look, a mean sneer comes over his face! If he's going to kill him, he better get ready because he's coming through the hole in the fence, and hasn't seen the body. He's looking around expecting to see the doorman, but keeps heading to his car.

He dashes and hides behind the dumpster! When he hears the keys jingle, he reaches to his leg and unsheathes the Becker® BK9, a combat knife with the 17-3/8 inch blade. The swift whisper of the steel startles the man causing him to spin around.

He lunges, grabs him, and sinks the blade in his chest all in the same motion.

"Aaaaaagggggg-hhhhhhuuuh!"

And snatches it out in a nice, spinning half-turn!

The blood loss is spectacular! The killer hasn't bathed in days and smells like an animal!

"Who...........are......... you," the dying man gasped, blood gurgling from his mouth, falling back against the van clutching his chest as he collapses to the pavement!

"Pain Bogart!"

Slices his throat, and returns the knife to its sheath strapped to his leg. A puddle of blood creeps from under the trick's body as he expires looking towards the heavens.

He pulls the key from his clutch. The police certainly have a description of the Impala, the work van will be perfect for the type of work he plans on doing.

In forty five seconds he's taken the few items remaining in the Impala, and put them in the Ford® Econoline. After the swap is finished, he readies his weapon and set his sights on the house. Dressed in donated clothes with another man's blood peppered across his face, shirt, shoes, and pants, he looks like death.

With the binoculars swaying around his neck, he steps through the hole in the fence; the weapon on his back taps the link as he passes.

Eon's earlier, this night was written, predestined from birth. With the rifle to his eye and finger on the trigger, he moves like a military man.
The door opens from the inside, and there a huge figure stands! The instant their eyes met, he knows he's looking at his executioner! The point blank impact blows the man back inside the doorway with the top half of his face missing in action! The entire alcove is chuck full of brain matter, bone shrapnel, and shredded muscle fibers.
He's been craving a toke for months, and retrieves the marijuana blunt burning on the ground.
"SwuuUUUUUUUUUUUUUU-ew!"
After pulling it a few more times, he put it and out stuffs it in his pocket. The taste is similar to bubble gum flavored gasoline, the smell like ammonia. Next, he robs the deceased of anything valuable; a cell phone, a ring of keys, and a money clip. He pushes the booty in pocket and stands up. The effects of the herb are immediate. He's already on cloud nine. Finally, he kicks the lifeless legs to the side and quietly shuts the door.

Now inside, he throws the deadbolt. This business is closed! Hearing the woman talking to someone, he trades weapons. The submachine gun is now in his grips and the rifle is over his shoulder. Stepping forward he peers around the corner and sees the stairs leading downward, and through the door he sees the kitchen, and to his right is a hallway. With the gun leading the way he tip-toes forward and looks around. There's two large door-less rooms with junk strewn everywhere. A bathroom that looks like it belongs in a junk yard is filthy with rust-colored water dripping from the faucet. He heads back and creeps into the kitchen, and to his surprise there's a door he hadn't seen from his previous position. Plastered to the wall, he sticks his head inside and sees it's a room. Easing back out, he looks down the stairs; seeing the carpet, he can't see the lady, or the person she's talking to. Coming up with a quick strategy, he pulls the money clip, and peels off a hundred dollar bill. From his thigh he unsheathes the knife, still stained with the trick's blood. Thinking of how much he used to enjoy origami, he folds it into a paper plane and flies it down. It flutters and lands out of sight.

The lady stops talking!

He hears the deep tone of the man who beat him up.

Stepping into the kitchen, he waits for the ambush.

The vibration of someone coming up the stairs quickens his breathing!

The goon does the right thing by looking around the corner first.

But the wrong thing by not already having his pistol ready.

He shoves the blade into his neck with such force that it comes out the other side! Blood spews like a ruptured pipeline of red wine! The goon shrieks like a bitch and grabs his throat!

He slams the blade into his stomach, and again into his crotch; feeling the thud of it pierce his pelvic bone!

His body locks up like a concrete pillar! He hit him again, this time in the center of his back, severing his spinal cord by way of bilateral thoracotomy!

The mortally wounded filth falls to the floor with blood hosing everywhere!!!

Like a psycho superhero, he leaps down the stairs and strikes the old biddy in the head with the gun!

She falls to the floor and starts screaming!

"Where's the money!"

"Please! Please! Don't kill me!! You can have it all!"

Women emerge from rooms! Rushed movement ignites to air! Seeing a blood covered man holding a gun causes the same reaction in most people.

"AAAAAAAAAAAAAAAAAA!!!!!!!!!!!!!!!!!!!!!"

"WHERE IS IT BITCH!!!!"

"…AAAAAAAAAAAAAAAAAAAAAAAAAAAAA!!!!!!!!!!!!!!!!!!"
"Okay! Okay!"
More women emerge screaming!!!!!!!!
He waves to gun at them!
They all run back!
The madam crawls down the hall! Seeing him coming their way, women scream, slam doors, and scramble for cover! Yells, and cries are coming from everywhere!!!!!!!!!!! He hears children crying!!!!!!
The barefooted madam in the night gown, pushes open the first door on the left, and crawls inside.
He flips the light!
The room stinks something serious, and has nothing but a grimy mattress, an old T.V, and a dresser. A bottle huge of Astroglide® brand personal lubricant, and a big box of condoms on top of it. A roll of paper towels and a can of feminine deodorant spray is on the floor. A blood stained pair of panties are tossed in the corner, and a family of roaches dot the collapsing ceiling.
She opens the bottom drawer and pulls out a brown grocery bag!
Snatching it from her, he looks inside the large bag and sees nothing but cold hard cash.
He spits on her, shoots her in the head, and walks out!
He runs around opening doors!
"GO! GO! YOU'RE FREE NOW! GO!!! YOU'RE FREE!"
the bloodied raider shouted.
But since many of the woman are heavily drugged and heavy dependent on their kidnappers, they scream and run from him!
He thinks his eyes are deceiving him when he sees a school-aged girl emerge from a room!!! The sight of her with make-up on wearing a school teacher costume is paralyzing! Out comes a little boy made-up like a ballerina with lips stick on crying!
He can't be seeing this. This can't be real.

He can't take any more, and runs out of the room, up the stairs, and makes for the exit!! Running full speed toward the van, people had heard the late night screams and are emerging from the darkness to investigate!
Pew!-Pew!
Dropping the person who got in his way!
Now the man who'd questioned him earlier is coming towards him yelling something!
He doesn't yell for long. The sub-machine gun fills him with hot lead!

Back at the truck he jumps inside, cranks up, and speeds off! Pink City is left with five dead sex traffickers. Once on the interstate he lights up the confiscated grass, and gets ghost!

If there was a way to zero gravity a phrase, a way to free the words from the page; they would sail through the sky, sharp and escalating, thrusting like the flap of a raven's wing, the songs of insects mating chants fly like the wind. Behind them, the chorus of frogs gripped by the torrent of recent rain call to nearby amphibians with croaks of *rrrrrrib-it!.......rrrrrrib-it!* Neighbors three houses down are enjoying the autumn night with fiends and laughter, the aromatic smell of grilled meat infuses the air, good music serenades the listeners with spine-tingling vocals arranged into superb melodies. Meanwhile, a man sits on his patio sipping a beverage. Allowing the warm night and good tunes to relax his body, he closes his eyes and creates his own get-together. Embarking on a cerebral journey he goes back, back to the place where he used to dream of doing this very thing. He used to illustrate scenes like this in his writing. Now that he's been given this new opportunity, he

won't disappoint. Being older, the errors of youthful stubborn-
ness painfully become clear. Many decisions were made out of
desperation, others due to a lack of information, many because
they seemed good at the time. But for him, the elusive hand of
fate has reached out and sucked him through a Pandora's Box,
transforming him into a time-shifting supernova. He's now all
the things he desires to be. The new opportunities are endless.
In this new dimension, he has the chance to make good on all
his promises. Things once considered unattainable are only a
fingertip away. He's always dreamed of being a philanthropist,
well now is his chance. His new found celebrity has given him
the platform he always wished for.
A voice!
Which to him, is worth more than the fame and money. All
the money's done is make him more of who he is. Through
experience he's learned, that to become who we are, we must
stop being who we were. If this is true, he's a caterpillar fresh
out of the cocoon as a butterfly of second chances. That chunk
of space and time he lost can never be retrieved. But many lessons were gained on the extraordinary journey. Now that he's
been resurrected, he can focus on building the table; the one
he's built hundreds of times in his mind. The table he periodi-
cally sits at and attempts to create positive elements of world
change. Thirty six years ago he was born a genesis. Now he has
the brawn to go with it.
For the build, he selects from an arrangement of special materials, rare metals amalgamated with divine understanding.
It has only two seats, four legs, and a flat translucent surface
that emits glowing light. He and she are a pair of *9's* working
under the same life number. Here, he and this special woman
will attempt to create custom mechanics, and innovative appa-
ratuses engineered to benefit all of humanity. For the duration
of their lives, this "light-working" bench will be their place of
sacrifice, progress, and aid—designed to uplift their fellow human. In his estimation, there are others around the world who

too have crafted benches of their own, and together they form a network of individuals who use the power of light to combat the forces of darkness. In their short time developing products, they've already created four offerings for the betterment of God's people.

A good designed to protect children from abduction. A low cost, high quality, organic, food protein designed to end world hunger. A brilliant new product which gives customers a profitable DIY option for left over hygiene products. An innovative toy designed for all ages to be used playfully at home, but transformed into a battle weapon on the half-pipe.

Proceeds from these products will go towards furthering the humanitarian effort. A program aimed at rehabilitating the homeless shall be realized. Health-giving refuges for battered woman will become globally available. A hand of love for all the forgotten children will be extended world-wide. Pushing the foundation to the forefront of international philanthropy is the aim.

Let the light shine forever.

The fact he still hasn't called is worse than actually hearing his voice when he does. It's been almost two days since it happened. It's not enough that the hit on the family went bad, and the cops are sniffing up there ass like thirsty bloodhounds; he had to screw this up too. He'd just left and was only two streets over checking some money, and the spot gets laid down. (Street slang for robbed) Twenty two-thousand taken, and five people killed. Everyone over there knows whose "pussy house" that was, thought Merciless.

They've never seen him, but they sure know the legend.

"White Man Ed" is a revering figure who's been elevated to

mythical status by the hoods of the inner city. Since kids, they'd heard the epic stories of stash houses with money hidden in the walls, the annihilation of the *"Miami Boys"* street gang when they tried to move in on his Atlanta operation. Notorious kingpins like Terry Height and Charles Smack are rumored to be supplied by him. Three of the city's most feared enforcers, Bruce Samson, Boceif "Jet" James, and Rolle "Iron Head" Swickter, all work for him. It's also said that he's the controlling hand behind almost all of the city's strip clubs. He's the man over Wooren "Wo" Baywood and Sharice "Speckle Neck" Marriot, the leaders of "The Bluff"s multi-million dollar heroin trade; a treacherous section of town minutes from the state capital, synonymous for having the Southeast's largest concentration of heroin users. This area has historically been a stain on Atlanta.

These are just a few things that come to mind when one concerns themselves with White Man Ed.

Now the chump who calls himself *Troy Merciless,* has to deal with his wrath. Though it's 1:39 p.m., this is a business and it should be booming. This is *Rio,* an adult entertainment establishment catering to the city's Latin community. A fresh batch of girls straight from Queens has come in, so the money should been moving, especially since this is one of the organization's most profitable locations.

The thing when dealing with foreigners, is they are generally less likely to talk to police, and are often untrusting of law enforcement. Unfortunately, this works against them. But it does work in favor of the criminals who control them. They can feast on a demographic with little to no regard for prosecution. But when dealing with American born girls, it's a little harder. Whether they're runaways who've been forced into the sex trade, or girls from good homes who've been misled by vile men, it's always more risk involved when dealing with natives. That's why the global tide has shifted towards hosting foreign women in a foreign land. If a trafficker has possession of an

American girl outside of the country, she'll certainly command top dollar. The most attractive and heathy girls are often taken by the traffickers for themselves. Disbelievingly, many go on to become wives and mothers, who continue the vicious cycle. Down in Tenancingo, another group of kidnapped girls are being "prepped" for life in the sex trade. Vegas, Chicago, Queens, Houston, and Atlanta are the primary points of distribution. Every few months girls are rotated and restocked with girls from other cities and new arrivals from around the globe. This gives victims less time to learn their surroundings, while also making it hard for authorities to track them.

Sitting at the stained wood bar is a black man in a suit. He's trash, and he's a "real nigga". Not by my words, but his. Latin dance hits jam from the system around him. Being up since yesterday, "snowed in" on a cocaine binge, he's in first-class asshole mode. He's not seeing the errors in his way of handling things because his drug fueled ego has him thinking he's a bloody genius and it's everyone else who's messing up. His foot keeps tapping the stoop and his fingers keep tapping the bar. He can feel "the drain" of the recent line. The *Newport® 100* keeps making its way to his mouth. A bottle of *Tito's® Handmade Vodka* is half empty, an empty glass with watered down ice sits beside it, his cellphone sits to his left in plain view. It's like a belt waiting atop the counter that his father will use it to beat him with when he gets home from work. It's just a smartphone but to him it's an assault weapon. There's approximately twenty patrons and fifteen girls, but he doesn't see anyone heading to the VIP rooms.

The phone rings; the humming vibration emitting from the phone percolating atop the polished oak is like an alarm clock waking him on the dawn of his death. He's not looking forward to the conversation. But in his current predicament, if he lets the boss call and he not answer, something as simple as this could mean the end of his existence. The yola (cocaine) already

has his heart racing, but his fear of Ed Denmark is something to the tenth power.
He snatches up the phone.
"My lord."

It's been almost thirty seconds and the voice on the other end hasn't made a sound. He doesn't hear him breathing, he doesn't hear him moving, and he doesn't hear any noise in the background either. He doesn't hear Zeus but knows he's somewhere close by. While sweat beads squeeze out of his pores and drip down his nose, he contemplates the dangers of repeating himself.
"Do I ask too much of you archon," Denmark begins.
"No my lord."
"...Do you feel that I've wronged you in any way?"
"Certainly not my lord."

He goes silent again, this time for a while.

"So in your estimation, how shall I take it that you have wronged me?"
The perspiring Terry Bostic sits there out of breath, floored by the unexpected left hook to his solar plexus. When he tries to produce the beginning of his explanation as to what happened at the brothel, it falls on deaf ears.
"I'm going to tell you how. So listen closely you *feebleminded fuck!* This is exactly how you're going to proceed."
In his right ear he gives him his instructions. After that, he explicitly conveys his disdain for the sound of his voice, and advises him it will be best that he not speak.
With words which hold a dense monotone of both fear and admiration, Bostic listens quietly. The one hundred-seventy words of adjectives, verbs, nouns, and vowels is the verbiage of a mad man. When he's finished with Bostic, he doesn't ask whether he got it all, or if he understands his orders. The line

simply goes dead.

Terry lays the phone down, picks up the bottle, and pours another shot—the Tito® burns on the way down. From the inside pocket of his blazer, he extracts a 14k gold vile, unscrews the gold cap, and pours two lines on the counter. Screw closing the cap he put it back in his pocket. Using his index finger, he closes his right nostril and leans forward. With his face smashed against the bar, he vacuums up the powder.
The bartender looks in disgust but doesn't say anything. A few nearby patrons gasp and snicker. Others look on, wishing they had some too.
Rising to his feet, he gathers his phone and keys, and grabs the bottle. Stepping down the bar he makes for the exit. A half-naked stripper comes and blocks his path with her bare breast and long nipples, sticking them in his face while her hand grabs his pencil dick.
He pushes her aside and continues on.
The bartender is also the "house man". The one who oversees the prostitution, collects the money, and makes sure it's right when it's picked up. He's behind the bar drying glasses, and has been giving him dirty glances the entire time he's been sitting at the bar. Even though he knows Merciless' position, he doesn't *know* Merciless. He's from an affiliate in Chicago, and is new to the way he runs things. Plus he's 6'4" with tattoos.
Merciless steps through the waist-high swinging door, and smacks the Vodka bottle across his head, sending him stumbling to the floor holding his face. Before he hits the ground, he bashes him a second time, shattering the bottle, sending liquor and glass everywhere!
Standing over the bleeding man he says: "The three months you been skimming equal seventy five-thousand. You got seventy two hours to live faggot. He wants his money returned or your family dies too."
Steps over the man, and walks out of the establishment.

□□□□□□□□□□□

Outside the day is dreary. Just moments ago it was so nice and sunny, but now it's wet and gloomy. The sky has wept on everything. It seems to be the prelude of a coming event. Bostic gets inside his 300 and speeds off. With the throaty drone of the 425 HP engine, and the growl of the dual exhaust; the heavy tint shields him from view. From his perspective, he should be the big man. After all, he's the one from the hood, he's the one raised on the mean streets of West Atlanta, he's the one people see every day, he's the one out here "putting in work". He's just some Russian immigrant! Why is he letting this pussy cracka rule his city, the city he was born, the city he claims! Denmark disliked Bailey Red from the start, saying she's trouble and causes him to lose focus. But since he hadn't, this is his punishment. The more he thought of it, the angrier he becomes. He doesn't want to do it. He's infatuated with her and wants to keep her for himself. He wants her to love him. He almost lost his mind when Denmark took her to his vacation estate and kept her for six days. From that day on he wanted to kill him.

Strangely though, in the other lobe of his sick mind, he hates her. He hates her because she's so magnetic, so strong, so persevering. He wants the tricks and johns to cause her pain when they ravage her. With as much as he's done to break her will, she's still unbroken, and still has the heart to fight. To kill her spirt, he's beat her until she's begged for mercy. Afterwards he'd hate himself. He'd think of his mother and beat her again. He'd remember being molested and molest her too. But if he doesn't do it, Denmark will make him disappear; and her too, so it's a lose lose either way.

That's all he has; fury, rage, but no power. He knows this is where his prowess stops. Denmark is the commander-in-chief, the one who too rose from poverty to influential capitalist. All

Bostic chooses to be is a thug. So it's fitting he holds the position he does. His envy and jealously of Denmark has caused him to become foolish. At every turn he's living the life and making the moves of a real boss, while he plays flunky.

Bostic has a problem with seeing himself as something he's not; believing the lies he tells himself. The placebo effect resulting from the mirage of perceived power has sent the wrong signals to his pee-brain. He wants the top spot, he wants to be the king, but all he is, is a servant.

He slams the gas and takes out his frustration on the SRT®!

In the fourteen minutes it took for him to conjure up more delusions of grandeur, he's entered the parking lot of the other club. The very upscale and very exclusive, Kobalt Gentleman's Club, owned by a shell corporation of Denmark Enterprises. He pulls the 300 into his personal parking space and gets out. This is the only 'private' gentleman's club in the state with a license to serve alcohol.

The huge doorman holds the door for him.

He walks up the aisle and goes in without out looking at him. With accents of crown molding and plated gold, wood paneling of cherry and mahogany; the décor is plush and well-appointed. The women here are the best of the best— goddesses to the rich men who come to venerate their exceptional wares. The lights are low and seductive, the air cool and mild; the fragrance hi-life. Twenty five-hundred dollar bottles of Louis XIII® pour like water in these confines.

To working stiffs, these are working hours. But to millionaire businessmen, and wealthy boss ballers, this is just another day at the office. The fact it's a weekday at 2:41 p.m. is irrelevant— these people live different lives from the average Joes and Janes caught in the rat race.

Merciless tightens up his act in here. He doesn't want news of him making a scene in one of Denmark's key establishments to get back. Coolly, he signals the bartender to get him a drink. The man in the stylish tux and perfect groom, takes his request and provides a drink and smile.

Siting at the expansive glass block bar, he looks at the architectural master work. It's a pristine palace of high-class lust which attracts international interest. The profits it generates are astronomical, the members list said to be of Atlanta's most powerful, and rumored to be kept inside a vault. There are no qualifications for membership. It is strictly determined on a case-by-case basis. If accepted, the name of an animal is assigned to the member. Along with it, a history of the animal, and all of its characteristics, including life span, region of habitat, tendencies, and enemies. The member decides how they wish to display the animal. Some chose to make it into jewelry, others have it fashioned into their clothing, many use it on their cars. All the rule states is that it must be visible to the doorman, and easy to detect. Non-member guests are limited to two per visit. After the conclusion of the experience, they must either apply for membership, or never return again. But the thing that draws the world's elite to this place, beside the women, is no money changes hands. There is absolutely no money anywhere in the building. Dues are paid on a yearly basis, with packages ranging from $25,000 to $175,000, with each providing there own level of benefits. The type of package dictates the type of experience, and also what areas may be accessed. This is done to prevent a billionaire from being bothered with the company of a mere millionaire while he enjoys his consumption of vintage champagne, Cuban cigars, escargot, and exotic anatomy.

There she is, sitting in the lap of a Middle Eastern gentleman wearing a business suit and keffiyeh. Merciless sees her notice him, but she doesn't let her client see. Bailey is his most valuable commodity, one he constantly exploits; fueled by his hate for women, stemming from abuse and abandonment by his mother.

Bailey Red has a complexion that makes men weak. Brown, but not like coconut, but brown like cinnamon hinted with undertones of burgundy and amber. Her locks are kissed with the color of peach nectar. A reddish-caramel sex symbol that brings titans to their knees.

She's also a mother and a human being.

But the people who used her aren't. Many of the members of this establishment are nothing more than perverts, sociopaths, and pedophiles in nice cars and fancy suits.
But seven in her present state, she's a survivor; one who hasn't given up on her promise to make it out. She would rather jump of a cliff holding her daughter, than have her endure the pain she has.

While sipping aged spirits in this cesspool of fire and brimstone, Merciless thinks back to the first time he met her.

Bailey Red, born Cailida Bailey Floriano, on November 25th, 1994 in Tenancingo, Mexico. Her father was a Cuban truck driver who frequented the brothel where her mother lived. She was his favorite girl, and he dealt exclusively with her for years. In her village brothels were the "only" economy. Everyone was too poor for indulgences like cocaine, and marijuana, so prostitution became the drug of choice. There were dozens in every neighborhood, and all ran by local gangs with protection from the authorities. Ninety nine percent of the young boys aspired to be pimps, and ninety nine percent of the girls wished they were boys so they wouldn't have to face the prospect of life as a "fun girl."
The remaining one percent had unrealistic aspirations of being a farmer, a builder, or nurse. However, one boy got the opportunity to play baseball in America. But that was only because he was the son of a powerful sex trafficker. To the

rest, they were lucky if they lived to see thirty. Crossing the
border illegally to sleep on the streets of America was a more
realistic dream. Unfortunately, sex work was the best paying
job, and the preeminent way of feeding a family. To keep her
daughter from growing up to the same fate, she convinced the
Cuban trick that little Cailida was his daughter, and offered
him money to take her across the border to a distant relative in
Texas. The fact he was a dark-skinned Cuban, people mistook
him for being black until they heard him speak. This is what
gives Cailida her gorgeous African/Mexican/Panamanian look,
making her ripe for the sex trade. He agreed to do it for a
thousand dollars. In the year 2000, that was roughly fifteen
thousand pesos. The top girls could skim a hundred-sixty pesos
a week from their captors, which roughly translates to ten
American dollars. The younger, the more desirable, so one can
only fathom the things a thirty eight year old mother had to
do to reach that figure. Her mother made it her life's mission
to raise the money, and after grinding eight grueling months,
she had it. Somehow she came up with a thousand dollars in
a city where the per-capita income was less than $859.00, *if*
they were lucky. Luckily, Catholic missionaries cared enough to
routinely visit the town. Being that Tenancingo is surrounded
by mountains and forests, and relatively isolated; the fact the
travelers trekked through dense jungle and dirt roads to spread
the Catholic faith is commendable.
Her mother developed a relationship with one of these women,
and was informed about their willingness to rescue her, and
any others who wanted to escape; claiming to have sanctuaries
in the U.S. where they provide help for women and children.

Afraid to tell the others fearing they may tell the local gang
leader, she didn't tell a soul. Spending the next few months she
prepared six year old Cailida's escape. Like a gift and a curse,
word came there will be a group of girls sent north soon.
Due to her mother's age, she'd fallen out of favor with the

tricks and was being "retired" to madam duty. Initially, her mother was going to come, but backed out at the last minute from fear of gang retaliation against the family she leaves behind. If she stays they only can punish her. So, under the cover darkness on the day of young Cailida's seventh birthday, she smuggled her to the edge of the town where her father agreed to meet. After being nearly five hours late when he arrived, he reluctantly took the money and his daughter, promising to deliver her to the address. She kissed her young crying daughter, and hugged her tightly. In her sack of belongings she included a ceramic statue of a girl kneeled in prayer, and wrote the address of the place in America she was going, along with her full name. She didn't have any paper so she wrote it in black ink on a square of fabric torn from her dress. After thanking the trick for his kindness she ran back to her village, never to be seen again. When they found out what she did, they killed her.

The man did as agreed by getting his daughter across the border, but in the small town of San Manuel-Linn, they got out at a truck stop near the Lower Rio Grande Valley National Wildlife Refuge, for a rest. He instructed her to go use the restroom, and when she came back out he was gone. Abandoned at a remote truck stop within spitting distance of the Mexican border, she sat alone in a foreign land. After siting for a few hours, a group of believers heading home from a humanitarian mission entered from the bus station across the street to wait out their layover. One of the women sat beside Cailida and asked where her parents where. Speaking no English, she just mumbled and shook her head. Doing what's humane, she notified the police officer sitting in the parking lot that a young girl is alone in the truck stop. He in turn informed her there's always abandoned children in that truck stop, and his best advice would be to leave her and let the border patrol deal with it; warning her that she's probably an illegal and they're known to carry infectious diseases.

Refusing to accept that mindset, she fed little Cailida and told her a story from the Bible. When her bus arrived four hours later, it was the middle of the night and the truck stop was deserted. Believing a good saint wouldn't just leave a child alone at a truck stop, she grabbed her and her belongings and carried them with her; all fourteen hundred miles back to Utah.

In the state of the Great Salt Lake, people of color are far and few between. Even on a religious compound where people pretended to be holier than thou, racism and still bigotry existed. Being she couldn't have children, and wasn't likely to find a husband, she took Cailida as a gift from God. In a miraculous twist of fate, she was able to get a birth certificate and citizenship for her in the name on the piece of cloth found with her, *Cailida Bailey Floriano*.

As a way to make Cailida, her own, she gave her the nickname "Bailey Red", after a very rare, and very striking type of rose. The thorns are larger than those of a normal rose, and known to cause painful injuries if handled improperly.

In the face of criticism and ostracism, she did what felt right in her heart, and raised her as her own, even under extreme and rigid religious doctrines. All the way until she died of complications from Lupus. After her death, and subsequent death of the sect's leader, a new "Prophet" was ordained, one with a focus on material wealth and worldly pleasure. Being the only life she knew, Cailida was subject to the same desires for love and compassion as anyone else, and fell for the new leader, and embarked on a three year love affair, one that produced a child out of wedlock. A major violation, and greatly frowned upon by their brand of faith. In order to avoid the embarrassment, he demanded she marry him immediately. She accepted and became queen of the compound. But the new "chosen one" became lustful and tyrannical, wanting multiple wives and lewd orgies. He also became abusive and alcoholic. When he required she undergo female circumcision, she began planning her escape.

During a night celebration commemorating the death of a
revered prophet, she and her daughter left. Still in possession
of her mother's note, she prepared to get to the address; now
eighteen and a mother herself. Surprisingly, the address was
still good, and the person on the phone informed her there's
many wonderful things awaiting her when she came.
Cailida had only limited knowledge of the area surrounding
the compound, but did remember there was a market, some
restaurants, a post office, a church, and a truck stop in town.
Considering this was how her mother got her to safety those
many years ago, she did the same thing. Abandoning the religious garb for the secular look, she ran.
While trying to hitchhike a ride with a trucker, she was conned
into preforming oral sex on him at the promise he would at
least get her to Las Vegas. While her daughter slept in the
sleeper of the rig, she performed sessions on him as he drove
five hundred miles to Sin City. It was during this passage that
the naive girl from a religious compound learned a valuable
lesson about men and sex. In times of desperation it can be
traded for favors and used as a means of control.
This new place she found herself in was full of bright lights,
noisy gambling machines, and bustling with tourists heading
to and fro. By this time, she still wasn't sure she was safe
because the *Squad of Saints*, the religious faction's security
wing, was hot on her trail. In grave danger and pressed for
time, she began asking for directions. Based on what her
mother told her about them, she avoided the authorities at all
costs. Reading from a free pamphlet detailing local attractions,
she was drawn to a ranch a few miles away which had lots of
smiling women on the cover. Seeing that one of them
resembled her ethnicity, her flustered mind told her there is
where she could find help. Directed by a local, she and her
daughter walked the few miles to the remote outpost, which

turned out to be a ranch house with a gate and lots of cars.
When she informed the well-dressed man she and her daughter were in need of help, he smiled and welcomed them. One
inside, an older woman gave them food and drink. Cailida seeing that many beautiful woman lived there, became comforted
and trusting enough to tell them her story. It wasn't long before
he started telling her how pretty she was, and about ways she
could make lots of money for her and her daughter; saying in
a few months she could make enough for her to get to her address. After days of hot baths and good food, she grew open to
hearing more about the man's proposal.

A man showed up promising to get her to her destination.

That was five years ago, and she still hasn't made it.

Part of Bostic's issue is, he's unaware his abuse has turned her
into a woman out for revenge on those who holding her
daughter hostage as a way to make her sell her body. She refuses to accept the life of a sex slave, and knows there's more to
life than "working the line".
Her mother strongly believed life is about nothing but pain
and sadness, and nothing else. She told Cailida to never dream
about being rich, or being a famous, or having a car to drive.
Only about making it to the next day.
But she doesn't want to accept that, she doesn't want to become
a madam. They get old and die, rotting until they wither away
while their seeds are damned to a life of sex work. In this realm
of dungeons and demons, it's common for mothers to see the
daughters they'd birthed, many from rape or the johns impreg-
nating them; being sold to anyone willing to pay.
Merciless recently informed her that her little girl is almost
ready to "join the line". He keeps saying "she's getting close".
An unfortunate fact about brothels is, if in one long enough
children begin emerging from the shadows. They know the

men are mommy's customers who buy sex from her. While daddy drinks all day, mommy puts food on the table by going into her room and closing the door with those men.

Merciless watches as Bailey thanks the gentlemen, and avoids heading his way by stopping to chat with other guests.

At first, his plan was to reel her in slow. He'd dealt with runaways and drug addicted, spoiled rich girls before, but never a fugitive from a religious cult. He was shocked by her unfamiliarity with simple things, like social media and reality television. She could read and had decent education, but he could tell she'd been in a vacuum her whole life. She was so unbelievably gullible that it was easy to gain her trust by appearing at the house with gifts and food. He would bring shoes for her daughter, and have the house madam bake her cookies. Being the ranch sat on property owned by Denmark Enterprises, he had the upper hand. Over the next few months he changed her hair from plain and straight, to seductive and enticing. Her nails showed new color, and her dress went from a drab on-piece, to heels and miniskirts. One evening, though she'd never driven before, he let her drive his fancy car through the desert. And at the end of the night forced himself on her. To smooth it over he claimed to do it out of love, saying he only did it because he wanted her to be his wife.

Things went bad; he took her identification and her daughter disappeared, followed by demands that she sleep with strange men—he'd take the money. Drugs were being shot into her arm, violent and perverse sex acts became rampant. He deprived her of sleep; locking her in closets for days became a pastime. Beatings with newspaper rolls, and wearing dog collars became her lot. He'd make her urine while on all fours. Promises to rape her little girl, and chop her to pieces are his favorite threats.

Through the haze of drug concoctions, physical abuse, and isolation, she agreed to work the clubs and turn tricks in exchange for access and protection for her child. From Vegas to Chicago, from Houston to Queens, from Miami to Oakland; in every city they visited, she slept with men.
This went on for years, many times of which she had no clue of her daughter's whereabouts.
When she did see her, she always seemed unhappy, but looked healthy.

Bailey ran out of customers between him and her, so she comes to the bar and sits beside him. She's there but her mind isn't. So many times she wants to give up and just accept this life. But can't let go of what life could be like if she can make it to the address.

If she can find a way to keep fighting, maybe things will get better.

She feels him bump her with his elbow.
"Did you hear what I said hoe?"
She mumbles something and shakes her head no.
"Go get dressed!" He sips his drink. " We got somewhere to be."
She gets up and walks away like he's not even there.

Ten minutes later she returns wearing designer jeans, a designer purse, designer shoes, and a designer shirt.
Her demeanor is designed by despair.

Outside, he extracts the vial and takes a snort before pulling away. While the vehicle wheels onto the street, she looks out the window. The normal world seems so close through the dark tint, it seems just an open door away. But she knows it's a mirage. Stopping at the light, the family in the minivan beside them admire the sleek 300. But little do they know, there's a prisoner locked inside desperate for their help.

"You hear anything from him yet?"

"No."

"Fuck you mean no bitch?"

"...It goes straight to voicemail or something."

"I know you set that shit up too. I know you did! I don't believe shit that comes out yo lying ass mouth. Soon as I find out ahma fuck you up."

"I didn't."

"You know I don't fuckin' play bitch!"

"No."

"You better get rid of that funky ass attitude too! You think cuz I let you have a little freedom you top bitch all of a sudden? Bitch the only reason I give you freedom hoe is so you can get my money! Know dat tramp!"

"Okay."

"Hey look at me when I'm talking to you bitch!"

She hears him yelling at the back of her head but she's in a day dream. She doesn't care anymore about being hit. They all just melt into her perpetual haze. She can't see the crystals of cocaine in his nostrils but can tell he's geeked out of his mind. She feels him pull her hair to get her attention!

The person she sees is nothing but a physical entity, he's not even a person. When he speaks, she doesn't see his face or hear his voice. She feels and hears him, but in her world he's nonexistent. To cope, long ago she learned the art of daydreaming. The honed craft of removing herself from her earthly body and getting lost. Behind the abstract hues of her flight, she can feel the car make a U-turn and hears the voice's profane language and heightened volume.

She's in a thicket of strawberries spinning around in a summer dress.

He yanks her head into his lap, and forces his penis into her mouth!

She's dancing with a handsome knight.....

He becomes disgusted with her disobedience and pushes her off of him!

To her she's floating on a majestic lake.

Vitriol flies from his mouth! He strikes her with the back of his hand!

She watches the migration of a flock of mallards on a cool fall morning. Thunderous herds of buffalo stampede across the plain. Soaring like an eagle gliding over the Sierra-Nevada Mountains, she studies the plateaus and peaks that move under her.........The aroma of her mother making fresh bread, and her father tilling the field welcomes her with smiles and a laughter as she stands on the front porch waving.
The car stops! He comes around the front!
She's a Hollywood star, a valet is coming to hold the door so she can strut down the red carpet.

He reaches and pulls her out!...His hand again meets her face!

Her toes sink in the sand as she plays along an ocean coast.

Until the clock strikes midnight, she's lost in her world of make believe and fantasy. Hour upon hour elapsed as he viciously raped and beat her. Guns were put down her throat, belts were used to bind her body. On her he blamed all of his failures. She's the cause of his inability to rise to the upper echelons of the syndicate.
As the clocked ticked, he snorted line after line. Sweating, spiting, cursing, and crying, she stayed far, far away. Banging his

head into the walls, he accused her of being a liar and a slut.
She stood accused of being the source of his failures as a man.
He swore on his dead mother's grave that he loved her.
Finally, after six arduous hours, gripped by paranoia he crawled
into a closet with his gun crying that he wouldn't come out
until she promised she won't kill him if he falls asleep.

At seven minutes past midnight, she listens to him snore while
she lay naked on the bed tied to the head board.
A tear drops her eye.
*Even from 92.96 million miles away, she's able to feel its warmth.
Its reddish-orange glow tans her face with luminous rays...The
sunset is beautiful.*

Cinq.

*H*am Brennery, the beloved helicopter pilot who'd been giving Atlantans their morning traffic report since elementary school, died this morning. The sound of his voice on morning radio is a welcome memory. They were fresh from Hong Kong looking to make Avondale Estates the new home of the Yuen family. Somehow, his father all the way from China had found the perfect suburban enclave to raise his family.
While cruising in the fast lane heading to visit him, he thinks off how far he and his siblings have come. If it weren't for his father's courage they never would've realized the American Dream. Being his father originated from the region's Hans majority, he was able to maneuver unabated to the top of the

power structure. His father was elected the regions first chief executive, and his uncle was a senior government official within the state's justice department.

But this was all before war tore their country apart.

His father became a successful entrepreneur with a chain of urban clothing stores, his mother went on to become a pediatrician, and his sister a computer programmer. So him becoming the county's assistant district attorney is right in line with the legacy his father has established. Becoming head of the city's special investigations division is right in line with what he envisioned for himself. After trying twenty four homicide cases, and performing valiantly over a sixteen year career, he was deemed head prosecutor on the case. The case is already a media sensation, and just like a supporting actor, whoever tries it will be at the center of the frenzy as well.

Kam Yuen will soon become a household name. He hasn't even gotten out of the first scene before there was a reworking of the script. Despite the iron clad efforts of the DA's office to keep it from getting out, it was leaked that after almost four weeks of investigation, there's word of an impending warrant out for Ed Denmark's arrest. Being he's an industry titan, and uber powerful businessman, he won't be facing the same arresting procedures as normal folk. The general public won't get the privilege of seeing an elitist paraded in front of cameras in cuffs with his head hung.

Nineteen days ago Denmark turned himself in under the cover of darkness, where he was charged with three counts of conspiracy to commit murder. It was discussed whether it's best to charge him with as many adjoining crimes as possible in an effort to get him on something, or charge him with the most serious offenses, and focus their efforts on getting him on those. The prosecution requested that bond be withheld, but in a rarely seen action, the ranking superior court judge overruled,

and granted him a bond in the astronomical amount of fifteen
million dollars; the highest in state history. This was before
Denmark had even been arrested; unheard of, and considered
by some to be illegal, and gross example of judiciary malfeasance. It was agreed that in the event of arrest, Denmark would
post the bail with fifty percent cash, and fifty percent assets.
All other terms of the surrender were sealed. At the request of
higher up's, it was determined that it would "harm the ongoing
investigation" if details were released.

The real reason however, is to keep the public from knowing
Denmark is being granted special conditions, unparalleled with
any case before it. When the hand of corruption extends from
the very peaks of state government, a man who commands
untold amounts of wealth can easily buy the services he needs.
No cuffs were placed on his hands, he saw the inside of no cell,
and not one officer dared pat him down. He came inside the
jail with his lawyers, signed a few documents, and went back
out. Mr. Denmark will also be granted a preliminary hearing to
determine if there's enough facts to dictate a trial.
 Today's the eve of the hearing, and at nine o'clock tomorrow
morning, it's game on.

After being with the city for coming up on sixteen years, Yuen
has never been this embarrassed to represent the badge. He's
the man listed as the head prosecutor, but is being told exactly
how he's going to proceed with trying Denmark. Never in
his career has he experienced this level of convolution with a
case. He knew the second it was given to him that it's a double
edged sword. The entire night he stared at the ceiling thinking about why they gave it to him when there's attorneys more
qualified to take it on. He can think of five right off the top of
his head. Why give it to the Asian guy, and the African-American woman? This is the type of case that only comes around
once every few hundred years, why give it to two minorities?

In a state where the confederate flag still flies high and proud,
why put them out there to represent the state?
After hours of negation between a team comprised of him
and other state officials, against Denmark's team of four, he's
frustrated with how things have gone; all the key decisions are
being made without his input.
His grandfather used to tell him stories of how things were in
communist China. Emperors are considered living gods, mystical deities who rule the heavens and earth. Subjects are never to
consider themselves on par with the emperor.

Turning onto Mt. Vernon Rd., Kam takes the back way in.
This is one of the city's more snobbish malls. The city of
Dunwoody is the jealous little brother of Buckhead. With both
having their fair share of glitz and glamour, this is the junior
varsity zip code. There's money here, but not like Buckhead.
Surrounded by restaurants, boutiques, and bars favored by de-
mographics with high incomes, this is a prime location for his
dad's venture. It's not his latest one, but his first; the one that
started it all. He has four spread across the city, but none are as
special as this.
The entire mall is under renovation. On all sides are construction vehicles and caution signs. Over the top of the building
cranes can be seen lifting commercial air conditioning units to
the roof. Concrete trucks are behind cordon off sections of the
lot. Landscapers are planting shrubs around the entrance to
Dillard's department store.
Kam parks and hops out.
The weather has just finished pouring rain so steam is rising
from the asphalt, customers dodge puddles as they head inside.
With everything going on, he thought it would be good to pay
his father a visit. Upon calling, he said he's at the store getting
the remainder of stuff hauled out. A chain store originating in
England purchased not only his space, but the other six stores
in the wing adjoining his to make way for their eight thousand

square foot bazaar. His somber mood brightens when his feet meets the familiar black marbled tile. A maintenance worker is repairing a cracked section, the female working at the welcome desk works to get his attention. As she watches him work the power tool from his knees, with her right hand, she works the middle spot under her dress.

Windows that used to be laced with the hottest in urban fashion, are now bare. Sales floor that used to be packed with boisterous hipsters, is barren and lifeless. Walls that once show-cased sneakers and head wear, are nothing but pale drywall and jagged edges. Behind the check-out is a long mirror mounted on the wall. Kam looks at the suited man before it with the emptiness of a vacant retail space in the foreground. Vibrant carpet is gone, only the dull stare of naked concrete remains. A pile of dust sided by a push broom sits in the corner where the dressing rooms once were.
Heading through the walk way into the once stockroom, there are no more boxes stacked to the ceiling with employees and merchandise. It's only a hollow space filled with the desolation of a ghost town. Coming through the back door/emergency exit, his dad comes through the heavy steel door leading to the service hallway, which leads to the loading docks, which lead to the trash dumpsters. He's shorter than him but with more gray. And even at seventy one, his father still moves with energy.
The rapid-fire way in which he's working the straw broom, the determined look, and the veins pulsing in his skinny forearms; Kam sees strength in the aged body.
When he looks up and sees his son, he kind-of smiles, kind-of waves, and put him right to work.
"How'd you get here so fast? You say you were thirty minutes away. You should stop driving so fast.....Come, get that box and follow me to the dumpster. You're right on time," said the man.
Though his father speaks great Hànyǔ, specifically Mandarin,

even some Wu; he prefers to speak English when dealing with
people who can speak it.
"That was forty minutes ago Ba. I'm late."

In Chinese culture children often refer to their father as
"Ba-Ba " or "Ba. "

"Oh…Well how are you son?" he asked, closing the door and
turning down the hallway.
"I could be better. I had a pretty bad day today."
At the end of the cinder block hall is a freight elevator.
Manually pulling open the doors, they step inside. His lean
father looks at him without pressing the 'UP' button on the
operating panel.
"Better how? Have you eaten today?"
"Yes. Why?"
"Well your day is good then."
And turns his back and presses the button.
"You should be thankful."

The elevator hums and kicks into motion. The dim light in the
ceiling dims noticeably while the car drones to the next level.
A clank and a beep, and the vertical metal doors separate in the
center. Using his foot, he press down the bottom gate because
it jammed about a foot above the floor. Still holding the box,
they exit through another door and end up outside surrounded
by delivery trucks and service vehicles. In the distance, the
resounding echo of an I-Beam being pounded into the ground
at a nearby construction site hammers the air with the noise
of productivity. They walk to the closest one and toss the box
inside. A sensor on the door triggers the compressor to compact. The mechanical sound of the plate pressing trash to the
back of the dumpster cracks and crushes behind them as they
return inside. The second the tension controlled door slams
shut, they're back in the seclusion of the long corridor. On the

other side of the back door/emergency exits of the other spaces, they hear sales people conversing.

"Yes indeed. I am. It's just hard trying to deal with some people. It's like I just want to give it to someone else and let them deal with it."

"Having to flee Guangzhou after the war with thousands of other migrant workers and their families was hard. You have it easy."

A medallion with the *Emblem of Hong Kong* stamped in a metal loop dangles from the key ring in his grasp.

Getting back on the elevator, he whistles the anthem '*March of the Volunteers*'.

Kam looks at the ground and smiles.

His father sees him.

"See. All better."

By the time the door reopens, his father has straightened his back, raises his chin, and begins high stepping like a brave general while he sings the lyrics.

"You're something else," said Kam amused.

Back inside, he returns to gathering the last remnants of the store that started it all.

"Look around Kam, this was my first store. It was swept out right from under me. I can do nothing about it now, I cannot be like you with your thoughts of defeat. Even in times of discomfort, one must learn to appreciate what one has accomplished. It is not the samurai who lays wounded on the battle field and dies from the first blow who gets the glory. It's the one who has the courage to get up and fight on—he's the one who'll be remembered."

Leaning on a support pillar striped of drywall, he looks at the man move about, and wonders what he's experienced in life that gave him so much fortitude? Where is this well that can be tapped in times of thirst? Because his father has this relentless make up of unwavering tenacity, he thinks all people can just hit a switch, and get a full tank of resolve. Kam is his son, but isn't blessed with his exact build. He wasn't raised in China, he didn't witness the atrocities of the Japanese occupation, he didn't see the bodies of his fellow countrymen floating among the rice paddies.

"I thought you came here to talk," said his father coming across the room.

"I actually came to talk over lunch. I was thinking you could use some food."

"Ahhh..Well I don't see any bowls sticks or spoons?"

Kam chuckles. His father is a sort of comedian. This is one of the reasons he needed to see him. He always brightens his mood, and loves Phở, a Vietnamese noodle soup consisting of broth, rice noodles called *bánh phở*, herbs, and meat; primarily beef or pork.

"You don't usually eat phở during the summer months Ba. I was thinking of taking you up to Cumulus."

When he said that his father looks at him.

"Ooooooooah! Well maybe I should change?"

"You look fine. Now if it was after dark, *then* you would need a different attire."

His father looks at his clothes, dusts himself off, and leans the broom against the wall.

"Well I guess you would know. Give me a second to wash," and trots to the restroom.

Initializing a slow stroll, Kam traces the inner perimeter of the space. Looking at the vinyl baseboard and the wooden strips that used to hold the carpet to the floor, he reminisces on how many days he's toiled here. He recalls the long rides on public transportation to get here after school. He remembers the pride he felt after buying his first car with his own money. He remembers all his friends coming to the store and shopping. He remembers the jeers and dirty looks because the Asian family decided to sell clothing that didn't exactly fit their opinion of what's others felt what's appropriate for this zip-code. He recalls members of the demographic they catered to, coming and trashing the store, angry that foreigners were looking to profit off their culture. He remembers the mall manager telling them the food they were cooking in the back of the store was repugnant to the customers. Before this same window one evening he was cleaning, and a girl who'd later become his wife, caused him to fall off the ladder as a result of her splendor. The noise of a group of professionals charging through the lower level entrance heading for the food court catches his attention. A 24x12ft. advertisement banner hangs in center court. The product today is a newly release novel titled: *'Coming of the Hour'* written by the great, *Harrison Charles.* The logo is burgundy. *Buttress Publishing Company* is the outfit sponsoring the advertisement. It's hanging between the two escalators that carry shoppers either up or down. A tall teen is jumping in the air trying to touch the bottom of the banner. Kam looks to see if his father is done yet. He can hear the faucet running and movement coming from the restroom, but doesn't see him yet.

A loud celebration erupts in the center court!!!

He walks out and into the common area to get a better perspective. For some reason he notices the lady at the welcome booth is smelling her fingers, and tries to get the maintenance guy that's repairing the floor to smell them too....

A loud whistling and yelling erupts!!

A large group of teens are throwing a "flash mob" in front of a restaurant. They're so loud he can hear them all the way at the front entrance. They're shouting something about ending capital punishment and freeing America's wrongly accused prisoners. One of the teens is wearing an orange inmate uniform holding a picket sign while wearing a horse mask. People are taking pictures shouting and laughing. The group is making quite a scene, and one hell of a statement. But many of the patrons have angry looks, pissed they're ruining their shopping experience—two mall security guys come running towards them from the opposite end.

Kam laughs, thinking this is something he would've done back in his day.

"What's all the fuss about?" asked his father, kneeling to one knee locking the space's glass doors.

Kam paced the few feet back to him.

"Just some kids clowning around."

"Oh?....They sound like you then. You liked to play lots of pranks on me and your mother when you were a boy," rising to his feet, about to head towards the escalators, but he redirects him.

"It's this way Ba."

"Aaaah," turning around.

Kam holds the door, and goes to hold the second set.

A water fountain sits beside the stairs leading to the upper level. In the center are jets of water tumbling over a round structure of boulders and marble. Thousands of coins are in the bottom.

"I remember the time you pranked your mother with the wasabi sauce in her toothpaste. She was very angry at you for that. I know seeing those kids reminds you of when you were young."

"I can't believe I did that. What in the world was I thinking? I felt so bad when she couldn't get it to stop burning. I remember you hit me in the head and sent me to bed without dinner. Ma came and said she forgave me."

"I bet you don't remember how she repaid you?"

"Oh yes I do! She put fish sauce in my book bag. I didn't realize it until I got on the school bus and started smelling it. All the kids were holding their noses and laughing at me. I'll never forget, this girl told me that I smelled like rotten sushi. I was so embarrassed."

His father laughed noticeably, his shoulders shaking with

amusement.

Before they knew it, they're upon the restaurant.

But Cumulus isn't really a restaurant. Attached to the front of the mall, it's the first thing customers see when entering from Ashford-Dunwoody Rd. It's behind the valet area between the Cheesecake Factory and Maggiano's. It can't be described as bar, it's not billed as a night club, and doesn't want to be considered a pub. What it is, is an establishment that serves great American food and exotic spirits, while jazz hits purr from the rafters. It's quite impressive, and a favorite lair of the well-to-do. Regular people have a place where they can hang with the money, and maybe even catch a celebrity sighting or two. In the center of one of its two entrances, is a revolving door encased in spotless glass and shiny brass. Beside it is a set of swinging doors. Overhead is a fabric canopy artfully over-ran with vines of kudzu. Concrete benches made to look like Roman sculptures sit on either side of the walkway. Bushes of rosemary blossoms aerate the alcove with botanical scents. His father spins in one section, and he spins in the section behind him.

When they spin out the other side, they're catapulted into a world of air conditioned to the perfect temperature. Tall, angular, textured walls have sparkling water cascading down them like endless flows of Perrier®. The lights are low and recessed, the often buffed floor is like a fjord of platinum brilliance. The seating is contemporary and private. A wondrous glass wine cellar runs from floor to ceiling. A smartly dressed server stands atop its spiraled staircase selecting a bottle from their world class collection. To their right is a welcome podium. Since this isn't the evening hour, *and* the fact they don't represent the wrong demographic, the lady doesn't say anything about the father's attire. Plus the son has on a suit, so it didn't throw off the ambiance. A concentrated effort is made to keep the riffraff out. She walks them to a section on the back left side, and seats them at a booth overlooking the water fountain and main parking lot. Through the blinds, slivers of sunlight draw lines across the table. The valet is full of luxury cars, the walkway teams with people anxious to spend.

She presses a button and two digital menus appear on screens built seamlessly into the glass table, and she details today's specials. After she walked away, a perfectly groomed gentleman wearing spotless clothing delivers two glasses, and pours water from a stainless-steel pitcher. When he walks away, the black box clipped to his waist with an ear piece can be seen.

"How did they get these T.V's in here like this?" said Ba, looking under the table."

"Dad!"

"Oh yeah I forgot. I'm supposed to be acting like a snob."

Kam almost spits his water out!

"I swear you could make millions as a comedian! You're out of this world!" laughing while wiping the dribble from his mouth.

"Ha! Money never made me happy. It's not even worth the paper it's printed on. I have more interesting things I want to spend my life chasing. Let the fools chase the green back."

"Well there's a lot of fools out here then Ba."

"Yes. There's also lots of coal. But there are only a few diamonds."

"You're a wise man."

"No. I just have common sense."

"Well let's see what they have. I haven't been here since they remolded everything. It looks pretty good," said Kam looking around.

On the upper level he can see they've built a second bar and more seating.

"This booth is so soft I could sleep on it," replied Ba.

"I used to come here pretty often, but it's been a while since I last did. I like what they've done," stated Kam.

"Mmmmm…."

His father looks at the glowing menu.

"How do you use this thing?"

Kam reaches over and swipes the screen with his hand.
"Aaaaaaaah."
Kam badly wants a drink, but won't dare disrespect his father
by consuming spirits in his presence.
"No baijiu I see," noticed his father.
"You know they don't serve that here Ba."
"I know. I was just checking."
"When did you start drinking anyway?"
"I didn't."
"Hmmmmmm!" Kam replied, smirking at his father.
His father chuckles.
"So, what are you thinking?
"I usually get the Hawaiian steak, with whipped potatoes and
asparagus. It's really good."
"Well I'll have the same thing," said the elder Yuen.
Kam presses a button, the server returns, and he gives her
their orders. After she's gone, his phone buzzes in his pocket.
Looking at it, he sees it's someone from the office, and quickly
hits 'Ignore.' He's still upset with everything that went on
today, and isn't ready to speak to the person on the other end.
Kam has a bad habit of wearing his emotions on his shoulder.
Throughout his life, his father constantly reminds him that
this is something he should change. But pushing forty, he still
hasn't conquered it.
"Your wife needing you? Or maybe your mistress," he chided.
"No. That was the office. More hassle probably."
"Well you should answer, it could be something important."
"It's nothing. I'll call them back later."
"Hmm, I understand...So I thought you wanted to talk?
"It's just this job Ba. Sometimes I think I'm just wasting my
time. There's no impact for me to make there. It's just case after
case, nothing changes. I'm just working for a check. When I
first took this job, I had plans of making a difference. I wanted
to do something to better things...Now I realize I've been tricking myself. It's all just a big game. There's no honor to be had

doing this type of work."

"There is *always* honor in doing what is just my son. Each person has a desire that is woven into their spirit. It is in this that we find our ultimate happiness. It is there that we discover the secret of the golden flower. When we ignore our inner light, it is then that we become confused by darkness. When on one's quest for understanding, one's desire must remain vigilant!..Like a serpents back, the road to enlightenment is long and winding. It may seem like it leads nowhere. But one must stay patient and determined to see what rewards lie ahead."

".....Yeah. But sometimes that's easier said than done Ba."

"Well who told you life would be easy, who said you were guaranteed a smooth ride? I'd like to find the master who taught you that thinking."

Ba reaches in his pocket, and grabs his wallet. Inside is a photo. "Look how young I was. Look at your beautiful mother. Notice the age of your sister. Look at how immature your brother looks. Now imagine having to be in my shoes, and feeling the same as you do now. I did not have the luxury of failing. It was succeed or my family die. I had no option but to make it. I did not want to raise my family in China. I didn't not want the government telling me that I can only sire one child. You have to take whatever is bothering you Kam, and make it your mission. You must commit to it! You must use every part of yourself to see it through....If I may ask son, what is it that's causing you so much discomfort? What is it that has brought my wonderful son down here to see me today?"

He loves the ground this man walks on. He loves him so much he wants to return to a boy so he can sit in his lap and hug him like he used to. But he can't. That's only wishful thinking. He's a man now, he's the state's representative in the case against dynast, Ed Denmark. There's no time for embrace.

It's against the code of ethics to discuss matters of an investigation with outside parties, especially in a case like this.

But this is different, this is his father. How can he not cite his opinion?

"Ba. I know you got all this going on with the store. I didn't mean to come down here and get you involved with my mess. I just w-"

"My son. You don't have to explain. Just tell me what bothers you. I can see in your eyes something is there?"

"......It's this guy named Ed Denmark, you've probably heard of him."

His father shakes his head no, and say no.

"He's this hi-powered guy who's suspected of hiring hitmen to kill his family. All the fingers say he did it, but there's little evidence to support it. He has so many powerful friends he's almost untouchable. Even within our department he has loyalists. My investigation is being hampered by unseen forces, and I'm ashamed to be a part of it. They assigned me and an associate of mine the case. It's like we're the laughing stock of the department right now, the two fools who think they can challenge Ed Denmark. They're sabotaging the case from the inside, and I just know we're going to be the idiots the world blames. Our careers will be destroyed, labeled as incompetents by the legal community. There's no way we can win this case with the connections he has. We're just fall guys. That's why they gave a case of this magnitude to two minorities. Blame it on the chink, and the black girl," and goes silent.

His father doesn't immediately speak. He take a few moments to absorb what he said.

A rare, 60's rendition of *'Sunny'*, by Japanese soul singer "Miko", whispers to patrons. The tone of their body language display their appreciation for the selection. Recorded on a vintage Sony® Superscope reel-to-reel tape recorder, the warm, deep, analog sound, gives listeners a musical delicacy to accompany their delicious food and drink.

"Sài wēng shī ma, yān zhī fēi fú," his Ba-Ba begins, and pauses for a moment.

In English he continues with: "A bad thing may become a good thing under certain conditions...There's a story about an old man living in a border region of Yushu, Qinghai, who lost his horse. People from his village came to comfort him, but he said 'This may be a blessing in disguise, who knows?' Indeed, the horse later returns to the man and brought with him a better horse. So now he had two...Every step leaves its own print my son. Work steadily and make solid progress. I too have faced playing with a deck that was stacked against me. But if I win, it gives me greater prominence.....You've come so far Kam. Look at you," he gushed with pride. "You've come so far son. I still remember the day I first held you in my arms. My firstborn son. It's a day I'll never forget."

He reaches across the table and grabs his hand.

"I'm so proud of you Kam. You're all a father could hope for. You make everything I've done in my life worthwhile. But you can't give up now. If this is your passion, if you feel this is your duty, you *must* proceed—you must fear the wolf in front, *and* the tiger behind. I don't know your work son so I can't tell you exactly how to deal with everything you're facing. But I can tell you a little bit about life. If you back out now, if you do anything that lessens the intensity of your punch, you make it easier for these forces of evil to defeat you. I understand it may be difficult. Even a dragon, looking from the outside in, finds it hard to control a snake in its own haunt. But this is all part of it Kam, this is all part of the journey! This is the path you must travel if you aspire to become a grand master. On treks across great distances, we are only concerned with reaching the destination. We are in such a rush to get where we are going, that we miss all the gifts to be had along the way. I know you son, I have never known you to be fearful. I have always known you to be a fierce Bengal. I have faith that you will surmount this adversity, and prove victorious."

"Thanks Ba-Ba…..How's Ma?"

"As beautiful as always. She asked about you earlier. I told her I would tell her when I see you. You should call. She would be glad to hear from you."

"I know. I just get so busy sometime. I talked to Jian yesterday though. He says he's doing well."

"Yes he is doing well. Bao is graduating this year and will be looking to become a surgeon. She also is a dou di zhu addict," and laughs aloud.

"I can never beat her. She's always winning my money," and laughs. "You've done a great job with us Ba. I mean, how did you do it? How did you take your family so far? You've done something amazing with so little. Bringing us from the other side of the world and providing us with an opportunity to do things we never could've dreamed back home."

"…….A bad workman always blames his tools my son. Patience and persistence can break through anything, no matter how great the obstacle."

Nineteen more minutes of conversation and laughter, their food arrived.

Twenty nine more minutes of relaxed eating, while being serenaded with delightful music dipped in a superb setting; they concluded their meal and returned to the space.

Five minutes of goodbyes, he's back in his car with a full tank of determination. For the rest of the day he envisions himself as the great general, Attila the Hun about to face the Battle of Chalons.

After leaving the office Kam arrived home and was delighted to see his wife turned a cow into beef lo mein, and his son and daughter have turned their grades into a delicacy called 'honor roll'. After a couple hours of family time, he's back out.

Pacing in circles he's sweaty and breathing hard. At the completion of each revolution, he'll glance at himself in the mirror that runs the length of the wall. His shirt is off and his feet are bare. His black hair is no longer slick and stylish, but wet and weighty. His fist are balled, and the wooden dummy is begging for more punishment. Two nearby students watch in awe as he works. Montages of all things martial arts adorn the walls of the school. Photos of the grandmaster squaring off with some of the world's best fighters are displayed for their viewing pleasure. At ten till ten, it's dark out and many of the students are gone for the day. Being the rules for acceptance are very strict, there isn't a large number of bodies to clutter the training area.

This is *Jason Lau's* vision, his official school for Wing Chun. Kam has been under his tutelage for seven years now. He's no 'Ip Man', but he's no slouch either. His shirt is tossed on the floor but his black pants are on, the red belt with a yellow strip on each end is tied around his waist. The inscription stitched below the front pocket states his degree: *Si Fan Duan*, a 2nd Duan Wing Chun master. Meaning Kam is capable of bringing death to a man in a matter of seconds.

The school will be closing soon, but that's the last thing on his mind. The fact he has to face Denmark in the morning is. Just like every other legal professional in Atlanta, he knows of his legacy, and has already been steamrolled by his firm twice before. On both occasions they proved their prowess in the field of law to be vastly superior to his; it wasn't even a close contest. In his first experience, he thought he had a case that was strong enough to take their client to trial. Not only did it not go to

trial, but got completely tossed on a technicality. The second time facing them dealt another painful defeat.
He walks back to the wooden dummy.

Called a *'Mook Yan Jong'* – literally translates "wood man post", or "jong" for short. The dummy consists of a body with two upper arms at shoulder level, a lower arm at stomach height, and one leg suspended on a framework by two crosspieces.

Kam believes there's two contrasting forces in the world. He prides himself on representing what is good. Men like Denmark represent the other side. He knows the stories about him, but it wasn't until today that he knows he's part of something much larger. This case has the stench of injustice all over it. He could feel the sinister aura emanating from him. He knows he isn't an ineffectual lawyer, he knows his capability isn't the issue. It's the fact that Denmark is cheating!
"YAAAAAAAAAAAAAAAAAAAA!!!!!"
Kam sends a flurry of strikes to the dummy!
The two students snap to attention with their mouths agape!
"HU-HAA!................DEEEEEEEE-Huuuuuah!!!
Assaulting the dummy with blows capable of killing a person.
"HOOSE!!! HOOSE!!! HOOSE!!!............WIN-TILE!!!" each strike a fatal blow!
Gritting his teeth there's blood on his knuckles and traces on the dummy.
And everything turns to a blur!
Sequences of precise moves fly in rapid fire! It's a chain of dissimilar paper dolls; each move delivering tons of force to the dummy! His arms wave, his elbows jab, his shoulder rolls, his stance shifts! Altering from fist to palm, knee to elbow; his waist bends and twists, flipping like a vicious Rubik's Cube!
The precision of the lethal dance is a sight to behold!

Exhausted and spent, he stares the dummy down looking for

any sign it wants more! He imagines Denmark's face laughing at him.

You know you will never beat me!

YOU DON'T KNOW THE RULES!!!

You're a fool Kam!......Just like your father!!!!!

Kam commenced to beating the dummy some more! Feeling that wasn't enough, he goes for the weapons.

In the center of the wall is a locked cabinet with the code given only to masters, and grandmasters.

He opens it, selects the items he wants, and heads to the center of the room with his toes gripping the hardwood. Through the window behind him, the reflection of the outside area can be seen in the mirror. In each hand is a 'Ba Zhan Dao' or butterfly sword. Designed with a guard which protects the hand during combat, in close range the hand guard can also be used like a pair of brass knuckles to smash the opponent. A hook starts from the top of the handle, and follows behind the back, but shorter than the blade itself.

Like a jet throttling at the end of a runway, the whirl from him swinging the blades in an interlocking circle produce a sustained whistle, and noticeable wind. The razor sharp rapiers cut through the air only inches from his body. With his back slightly humped, he moves forward, back, and around—cycloning the blades at an invisible adversary; into a thousand pieces he slices the image he sees in his mind. Exhibiting his prowess for controlled destruction, he knows annihilating tomorrow's opponent will take more than fists knives and kicks.

Six.

The night for Kam was sleepless. The night for her was sleepless. They're the state's chosen gladiators, pitted against the region's reigning despot and his band of Ivy League sentinels. Sitting at the prosecution's bench sided by the badger that is Myra Keith, they wait for the defendant to enter the colosseum. There's standing room only and the walls blocked by the media. One cannot appreciate the new floor covering because human beings have turned the room into a can of sardines. Cameras and bodies are packed together like toes in a pointed shoe. The thirteen rows of seating make courtroom 4-E capable of occupying a crowd of one hundred and twenty-five, but today it's almost twice that many. Any fire marshal in his right mind will quickly recognize the hazard. The short wall erected to keep observers separated from litigants, is today acting as a retaining wall.

Behind him he can feel the heat coming from all the people and lights cramming the space, the hotness around his neck is causing his tie to irritate his skin, and there's no way he's taking his suit coat off so that everyone can see the wetness saturating his underarms.

Due to the high profile nature of the hearing, eight bailiffs are on hand, the witness box is empty but the jury one has a butt in each of the fourteen chairs. There's no verdict yet, but the deliberating room around the hall is packed with people too. The defendant table is topped by a pitcher of water and stack of plastic cups, two corded microphones and three empty chairs are there too. The judge is not on the bench and the door leading to his camber is closed.

Looking at the name presiding over today's hearing, he finds solace. The man who wears the black robe in this room is known for being no-nonsense and tough, with a long history of being fair and impartial. Kam counts this as a small victory. Wearing his best suit, he consults his Breitling® Navitimer; the only nice watch he owns. The time 9:03. He'll kiss the ground if Denmark pulls a no-show. But he knows he's coming, there's no way he'll bow out gracefully; especially when international news agencies are stationed in the courtroom, the hallway, downstairs in the lobby, in the main corridor, out on the street, and in the air.

Tapping his foot on the floor, beside him assistant prosecutor Keith reads over today's material. Seeing his nervousness, she pats his leg with a smile of confidence.

"Don't worry. We'll get him," and returns to the file.

It's their job to let the evidence determine the outcome, and it's sound legal practice to avoid forming options. Counselors are taught to avoid developing a personal connection with the cases because it's said to produce poor conviction rates, or cases which are later overturned on appeal. But both parts of this pair believe he's guilty, even if the evidence is circumstantial. In the days leading up to the hearing they've collectively spent two hundred and fifty plus hours preparing the case. Atop the desk are stacks of binders, folders, and bundles. The flimsy filing box beside his foot is stuffed so tightly that the lid won't lay flat. Cob webs can be seen blowing from the vents of the vaulted ceiling. A retractable projector screen attached to the far wall's ceiling is fronted by the unmanned podium with a skinny microphone protruding from the top.

The table is set, the only thing left is the main course. The reporters are hungry for a storyline, and the state starving for a conviction.

There's a commotion in the hallway! People turn towards the exits!

Keith looks at him?

Three bailiffs walk out to investigate?

A notification comes over Kam's cell. Opening the message with a swipe of his thumb reveals the text. Denmark is on the way up!

Like an underdog fighting an overwhelming favorite, his heart begins throwing uppercuts at his chest!

In the corner of the room is a door accessing the hallway used by court personnel. Out of it comes two gentlemen in suits. They don't sit down, or say a word. The bailiffs say nothing to them, and they have no visible badges or labeling. Just two older white men with straight faces and wingtip shoes.

The bailiff standing near the door begins clearing the aisle of people.

Keith puts the file down and places her briefcase on the floor.

Like trained infantrymen, the ranks of cameras swing towards the impending arrival! Anchors ready themselves!

When the doors swing, it feels as if he's been waiting since midnight, ample time for him to convince himself he's prepared.

The use of flashes are prohibited inside the building, but the shutter clicks coming from the droves of photographers mimic the sound of ten manual typewriters in a speed typing contest.

Kam isn't going to turn around and welcome him like he's some god! He doesn't move a muscle. Just sits there with his hands clasped on his lap, and legs crossed looking at the judge's bench. Over his left shoulder he hears the short divider door swing. Out of the corner of his eye he sees one man followed by another, and a hazy figure sit down between them—he can smell their cologne.

Kam leans over and whispers in Myra's ear.

She shakes her head accordingly, and goes to whisper something to the bailiff.

He in turn goes to one of the women sitting near the clerk's box and says something to her.

She nods, goes through the door behind the judge's bench, enters an access code, disappears inside, and shuts the door.

Cameras are still flashing and there's a lot of movement behind him.

Turning to peek at the crowd, he catches a glimpse of one of his lawyers.

The suit flicks a toothless smile and nods. Not like two friends greeting each other, but like two war dogs about to battle.

Kam nods back but holds the gaze a moment too long.

Denmark leans back and sends a laser to his pupils! The heat is searing and the burn penetrating!

Without knowing it he turns it into a stare down, they're locked in a duel of dominance. The first male to look away signals the loser.

"All riiiise!" the bailiff begins. "In the presence of the flag in our country, emblem of our constitution; remember the prin-

ciples for which they stand. The Fulton County Superior court is now in session. The honorable judge Julius Baxter is presiding. Please be seated. Come to order!"

They call it a draw.

The towering black man with the flowing black robe sits down and adjusts the microphone. The room is silent and he doesn't look at anyone. Reading something that can't be seen, he leans forward and he writes something down. After a few strokes he's finished.
"Denmark vs Georgia, case number three-nine-nine-three-six six. Counselors please state your designation," his voice disconcertingly robust.
"Kam Yuen, prosecution."
"Myra Keith, assistant counsel."
"Brent Perminter, for Eldrin Denmark."
"John Brogan, Mr. Denmark. Thank you your honor."
The man who seems muscular and lean under the robe shows the stern look of a seasoned magistrate. His face is square with a defined jaw, with skin that is dark brown and leathery; his eyes are deep and give away nothing. Being a proud graduate of the Thurgood Marshall School of Law, he wears it with unapologetic pride. Pouring himself a glass of water, his crisp and exact moves aren't rehearsed or showy. Leaning in his intimating chair, he looks down on them and exhales.
"We are here today to determine if there is probable cause to bound this case over to a higher court, where it will be held for trial. As you can see, we have an extremely large crowd here this morning. I ask that members of the media and citizens alike, remain quiet and that all cell phones be turned off. If there is space, may you please pack in tightly, for we have many people standing that would like a seat. Mr. Brogan you may commence your opening statements."
"Thank you judge...I'd like to call my first witness, Dean

Cromwell."

From behind the wall separating the preceding area from the seating area, a man rises and approaches.
The bailiff swings the waist high door, while he passes and takes the witness box. Sitting down he unbuttons his suit and sits up straight.
"Mr. Cromwell, can you state your name and occupation for the court please?"
"Certainly. My name is Dean Cromwell. I work as a senior investment advisor at Gleeman Brothers Securities."
"How long have you been employed with them?"
"For approximately twelve years."
"And during this time, who was the co-chairman of this corporation."
"That would be Rick Chuld."
"While working there, what was your relationship with Mr. Chuld?"
Kam is up!
"I object your honor! The line of questioning leaves the door open for speculation, which like opinion, can't be proven."
"....Sustained. Counselor streamline your questioning."
"Mr. Cromwell, on an average day, did your *job description* require you to come in direct contact with Mr. Chuld?"
"Yes it did."
"In what capacity?"
"As a member of his executive staff, I worked in close concert with him on all sorts of company business."
"Now…If I may ask…Being he was your supervisor, did you consider him a friend?"
"I object your honor! That is clear speculation. The person in question is deceased. That question has nothing to do with the evidence, and he's also unable to offer his own testimony. I ask that it be removed from the record your honor?"
"Judge I am trying to show the court the witness' opinion of

how he viewed his supervisor, *not* how he thought his superior viewed him. I find it very reasonable, and relevant for the
witness to state *his* opinion of Mr. Chuld, not the other way
around your honor."
"Overruled."
Kam sits back down.
"You may answer the question Mr. Cromwell?"
"Yes. I would consider him a friend."
"Can you expound on that please."
"I've worked at Gleeman almost my entire career. It was the
second job I've held since graduating college. Throughout my
tenure, I developed a close relationship with Mr. Chuld from
his extensive work as a world renowned economist. I've been
to his home on many occasions. My kids have played with his
kids. I even visited him when he was in the hospital recently. In
my opinion, our relationship extended outside the professional
level."
"Have you ever been out of the state with Mr. Chuld?"
"Yes. Not only Georgia, but the entire country. We have
gone on dozens of business related events, both domestic and
abroad."
"While on these trips, was it unheard of for there to be adjoining parties?"
"It was not."
The defense lawyer pauses a moment to let that soak while he
grabs something from a file atop the desk. Holding it to his
chest, he strolls back to the witness.
"Now....you have already admitted that there were *other parties*
who often joined you on these expeditions. Did this contingent
consist of members of only the company body?"
"No," the witness replied emphatically.
"In your recollection, had you encountered anyone from the
Chuld family on these outings before?"
"I object your honor! The witness is not qualified to recognize
every member of the family. He is not related to Mr. Chuld in

any way, so there is no reasonable way for the court to assume
he knows all the deceased's relatives."

"....Sustained. Let's stick to what's valid Mr. Brogan."

"Mr. Cromwell, being we have already established you're an
executive level officer, in your estimation, had your supervisor
and company co-chair ever brought along with him anyone
you recognized as *not*…being a member of Gleeman Brothers
executive body?"

Kam wants to object again but has no grounds. He's
beginning to perspire more.

"Yes."

"Your honor, I would like to include this as exhibit A."

And hands it to the bailiff, who and hands it to the judge, who
looks at it, and passes it back so he can give it to the prosecution.

After showing it to all the parties, he hands it back to Brogan,
who displays the photo to the witness.

"Have you ever known this woman to be part of Gleeman
Brothers executive body?"

"No, not in my estimation."

"Have you ever seen her before?"

"Yes."

"Can you tell the court where you recall seeing her?"

"I first met her at a fundraiser in New York, where she was
accompanied by Mr. Chuld. Since that date, I'd become
familiar with her as being a regular acquaintance of Mr.
Chuld's."

"At that time, did you know who she was?"

"All I remember was her saying that her name was Farah?"

"At that time, did you know Mr. Chuld to be still married?"

"To my understanding he was."

"At this juncture in your career, had you ever heard of Ed
Demark?"

"Yes."

"How so?"

"I knew that he was a prominent figure in the legal
community, but I knew him more as a business person."
"At this time, did you know that your supervisor, Mr. Chuld,
was once accused of murderer, and was acquitted while being
represented by Mr. Denmark?"
"Yes"
"Did you know this was the spouse of Mr. Denmark?"
"No."
Oooohs! Break out in the courtroom. In unison, the media be-
gin scribbling on note pads, and photogs start snapping shots.
The judge picks up his gavel and taps it twice.
"Order in the court!" and nods for Brogan to continue.

For twenty minutes, he grills his witness; introducing more
exhibits, and poking more holes in the state's case. Kam objects
more, and so does Keith.

On cross, Kam tries to cast doubt on the witness's testimony,
by pointing out he'd once been admitted into a rehabilitation
facility for cocaine addiction.

The defense built him back up, by pointing out that this was
under his own free will, despite him never being arrested for
any type of drug offense, and having no convictions of any
sort.
The next witness the defense calls is the sister of Farah Denmark. Under oath, she states her sister confided in her on many
occasions that Rick Chuld constantly begged her to leave Mr.
Denmark so that they could get married. Adding, her sister
enjoyed the lifestyle of being a wealthy housewife, and would
only dissolve the marriage if she had assurances her standard of
living would be maintained, if not elevated.

Under cross, Myra Keith was able to prove the sister is a former
identity thief with a questionable past, including the mysteri-

ous disappearance of two of her former husbands, one of which was a police officer with the state of Georgia.

The third witness called, is a man from Wyoming claiming to be a childhood friend of Chuld, who states under oath that Chuld propositioned him about a contract to kill someone. The defense uses phones records to show the parties had communicated many times in the months leading up to the killings.
The prosecution scores a point, by pointing this same man is an ex-con with a rap sheet a mile long who can't be trusted. Kam thinks he reaches a turning point when it's revealed that Mr. Chuld, by way of his lawyer, filed a restraining order against this same man for stalking and terroristic threats. The witness admits that Mr. Chuld never once said he wanted him to kill Denmark's wife, or anyone in his family.

The fourth and fifth witnesses his team call, are Joy Nguyen, the city's chief forensic scientist, followed by the county medical examiner. They both testify that DNA belonging to an unknown suspect had been found at the scene.

Nor Kam or Keith elect to cross examine these witnesses.

Until now, the most damning testimony comes when the investigation head, Detective Mitch Hickenlooper takes the stand, and admits they have nothing but circumstantial evidence connecting Denmark to the crimes.
That's when a woman in a business suit rises from the crowd and passes him something.
"I assume this person is co-counsel Mr. Brogan?"
"Correct your honor. I *do* apologize for this occurrence. But I have been informed of a new piece of evidence that has recently come available. I would like to request it be admitted," he explained.

Kam is almost dead in the water, and needs time to regroup because he's running out of steam. He has an idea what this new evidence is and he wants the judge hearing no part of it. He heard there's possibly a video, but it was said to be a rumor since no one could verify its existence. He knew it could become an issue, but since he's already outmatched and not being given a fair investigation, he took the gamble.

"Your honor, in light of this new discovery, I request a recess to view this new material? Considering its source, I don't find it unreasonable for the court to determine where it originated, especially since it was not included in the discovery?"

"...Denied."

Kam is losing his cool while his inner self works desperately to calm him! There goes his emotions showing on his sleeves again.

"Counselors approach the bench."

From the persecution's table only Kam goes up.

From the other side, Brogan is stationed near the jury box and goes over.

Clicks of camera shutters fill the room!

In hushed conversation, the group convene. The judge is the first to speak.

"Mr. Brogan, how has this new article just so happen to come available on the morning of the hearing? Was this some sort of concentrated effort aimed at stymieing the state's case?"

"No your h-"

Baxter puts his hand up.

"In a case of this magnitude, I think it will be wise for all parties to avoid the conventional subterfuges."

"Your honor, again I apologize about this. We had every intention of sharing this with the state once we actually had it. Due to the sensitive nature of our source, especially considering we are in the middle of civil litigation; by releasing the details of how we came across it, may at this point decrease our

options for exonerating my client. During our negotiations
with Mr. Yuen and his staff, we advised them to be more judi-
cious with their investigative approach, and also advised them
not to let their over zealousness and desire to charge my client
lead them to overlook certain details. We repeatedly asked the
state to hold off on moving forward with the warrant until
this new evidence was thoroughly examined. We thoroughly
explained it had the potential to fully exonerate my client, and
that patience should be exercised. He had access the same info
that we had, but apparently did not give it the due diligence of
a comprehensive analysis."
"The state has not had the opportunity to verify this new
evidence, and therefore I would ask you to disqualify this
article until further review," Kam rebutted. "Considering, we
are dealing with an experienced lawyer with endless resources, I
think it would be fair to the case, and to the victims if we fully
understand the nature of this information."
That's the best he could come up with.
Judge Baxter looks at him.
And back at Brogan.
"Let me see this new evidence you have."

In his ultra-tense state, all of Kam's senses are heightened.
His 20/20 vision is sharp, his keen observation scanning for
anomalies. As Brogan hands the judge the material, he notices
a strange looking ring on his finger. It's the size of a class ring
but that's the only similarity. It's subtle, yet quite intricate. But
it's not until his eyes follow it from the judge's hand to the desk
that the real mystery begins. Being the sleeves of Baxter's black
robe don't extend the same length as the shirt he's wearing beneath, he's able to see the white cuffs and the Rolex watch he's
wearing. But that's not what commands his attention. It's the
cuff links. They look to be the same type of symbolism as what
Brogan has on his finger.
And just as fast as they appear, they're gone. Baxter's has moved

his arm, and so has Brogan.

His brain is attempting to understand what just happened.

While Baxter studies the information, the antsy crowd uses this time to resituate themselves on the pews, the media takes this opportunity to get on their phones and text the developments to interns and producers.

Kam is feeling heat seep from his collar spill over his body. His black slacks are sticking to his leg and he badly wants to use the restroom.

Brogan sees the defeat in his body language.

He smirks. *This is too easy.*

Kam looks away and consults his watch.

In his mind, he envisions himself sending a violent kick to his face, delivering a death strike to Denmark's esophagus. He's regretting the way he's handled this case, and painfully realizing his lust for a conviction, coupled with his righteous, save-the-world mindset, has caused him to overplay his hand; even employing trumps he doesn't have. Now he fully understands the reason he was chose to try this case. The rage burning inside him is akin to molten lava!!! All he can do is clench his teeth and try to steady his composure. A ball of sweat rolls down his temple, the court clerk is looking him right in the face.

"If what you say is true Mr. Brogan, you Mr. Yuen have opened the door for a potential lawsuit. I'm certain you were aware that the details of this interview would be used as evidence. Did you include the notification of the impending release of this interview when you filed your warrant application?"

"....No your honor I did not."

"Didn't you consider it important to the investigation?"

"Yes your honor I did. But in my experience, I did not think that it would undermine the guilt of Mr. Denmark. Considering the HT was a key figure in the original murder, and an

admitted gang member guilty of many violent crimes, I did
not think his testimony would be considered anything close to
reliable. The fact he changed his story five times from his initial
statement only strengthened my position that it wouldn't be
considered factual. Citing, Hood vs the State: Evidence supplied by the prosecution in an attempt to prove that vehicular
homicide suspect, Eric Hood was guilty, was not admitted due
to the unwillingness by the state to provide proof of its authenticity."
His justification is understandable, but still negligent. The statues in that case aren't the same as the ones of a potential felony
murder trial.
"Legitimacy should be determined by the court, not by the
opinion Mr. Yuen," Baxter stated flatly.
Writes something down, hands it to the bailiff, who takes it
and disappears out the door in the corner.

After instructing them to return to their positions, he informs
another bailiff to put the disc into the player. A white
projection screen extends from the ceiling. While they
prepare for the show, Kam and Myra flip through files, whispering in the other's ear and nodding in agreement.
And just like in the theater, the lights dim.

When the video starts, it has everyone's undivided attention.
It's the HT handcuffed to a stretcher, swollen with stitches and
bandages on his face. His left arm is in a sling, and his lips are
fat as Ball Park Franks®. There are IV's going into his arms, and
sticky things on his chest. On either side are two men who's
faces can't be seen. He starts by vividly explaining how Rick
Chuld was directly involved in money laundering and arms
distribution, saying five years ago he was in a meeting with
other high ranking gang members when they met a person in
the banking industry with overseas interests who were looking
to get into the black market game of washing cartel profits by

exchanging it for gold bullion. He highlights how two months later they did a test run of five million dollars, and how an associate of this same person introduced him and his gang to a person who had access to unlimited stores of Russian weapons and ammunition. He follows with a gripping story about how he and his KT-36 gang are more than a common street click, but a global influence with twenty thousand adherents, and political backing; saying they pride themselves on being corporate gangsters with diverse portfolios. He explains he had no idea who Chuld was until word started buzzing about a contract out on American born arms dealer for four million dollars. Just so happens, it turns out to be the seller they'd developed a trusted business relationship with.

Looking for protection, he approached the ranking leaders of the gangs U.S. branch and pleads for security. In return, he promised to supply them with unlimited qualities of untraceable weapons at thirty percent of their market value, deliverable to anywhere in the world. In addition, he offered to introduce them to a supplier with the ability to supply them with as much as ten tons a month of the cleanest, purest, crystal methamphetamine in the Western Hemisphere. By taking the offer he understood it would risk the relationship with their banking affiliate, and to offset this loss, he provided three Middle Eastern firms, and one in Switzerland with the ability to offer them the same service, but at even better rates. He claimed to have connections with Jewish rabbis who use their synagogues as fronts to wash millions of dollars. With the global potential the deal offered, they took it. Now part of their organization, the defector spilled the beans on the entire operation, explaining how the world's billionaire elite make untold amounts of untraceable, tax free earnings by dealing in strictly gold bullion. The HT details in stunning clarity how this same person even claimed to have access the tons of totem gold or "death gold", that was pried from the teeth and fingers of French Jews during the Holocaust, melted down, and secretly stashed in

Swiss bank vaults. He said behind it all was the man at the very top of the currency valuation industry, Richford Chuld. The HT goes on saying: That as the months passed there started being assassination attempts on the gang's top members, and that after his entire family was killed in a car bombing, he made killing Chuld his mission. Based on what he now knows was purposely reported misinformation, a source believed to be reliable sent word an address of Chuld had been gleaned. Once it was verified as accurate, his gang employed a group of black low level street thugs to make the hit because he didn't want his KT-36 gang connected, and recommended the killers find a person to frame, saying a "street bum" would be the easiest option. Driven by personal vendetta, he foolishly went along so he could be the one to put the fatal bullet in Chuld's head. He didn't realize the information was bad until it was too late.

With all the trappings of a Hollywood blockbuster, the camera captures the footage of the HT coughing. A wheeze is followed by the alarm of a machine, which causes a medic to check its reading. A hand does something to a device beside the stretcher, but it doesn't help. The restrained killer winces and starts mumbling blood, the chains and shackles clank when he tries to touch his chest, the camera begins shuddering, but the unseen men continue their interrogation.

Another medic comes into view, and that's when the video ends.

When the audiovisual stops, there's silence in the courtroom. The judge is writing something.

As the morning wears into afternoon, a one hour recess is given. The media vans camped for blocks around the courthouse is the epicenter of the action, the courthouse stairs are blanketed with people. The developments are being broadcast live to the world. The fact that famed economist Rick Chuld was allegedly involved in global crime ring is a rating extravaganza. The slant being pushed, is that his dealings with "drug lords" contributed to his death. No mention of the gold bouillon scheme is being mentioned; not a word!
This has just turned into the case of the century. Some of the country's most recognizable anchors are now on the scene. The police presence is overwhelming, and so is public interest. Nothing garners public attention like a good scandal, especially when it involves the high and mighty.

By the time the session reconvenes, the preceding is the top story in America *and* Europe. Some estimates are predicting the fallout could plunge the stock market, with ripple effects spreading to all the world's economies. The sheer scale and magnitude of what's been alleged today, is more than Kam, Ms. Keith, or anyone in the judicial system could've ever imagined. By the time the latest witness takes the stand, Kam is uncertain if he'll have a job tomorrow.

The defense calls four more witnesses, with each providing their own cutlass of facts.
Kam calls two witnesses, and Myra calls two of her own. Those were the only credible people they could find willing to take the stand against Denmark, and two are law enforcement.

In the face of insurmountable odds, the team performs valiantly. With every bone in his body, Kam squeezes out objection after objection. With every drop of will Myra can muster, she tries to beat home her point that Eldrin Denmark is not the person he appears to be. Citing example after example they attempt to show it's reasonable to believe Denmark has lots to gain from the death of his wife.

When the smoke clears, Kam's suit coat is tossed over the back of the chair, and Myra is spent. Each time he looks at Denmark, he's stone faced. He knows the power he commands, and it shows.

Pushing six o'clock, they're all ready to hear the judge's decision. When he walks in, and the bailiff says all rise, Kam is visibly shaken and emotionally wasted. Even facing so much adversity, he still believes there's a chance it will be bound over. With all that's been alleged today, there's no way a judge like Julius Baxter is going to let Denmark just walk out of the courtroom. There's just no way!

"...........As written under Georgia section code four-three six-one, dash two-three-seven-G, and based on the evidence and the testimony by the witnesses. The court finds there is *not* enough probable cause to bound this case over for trial. Therefore the case is dismissed."

The courtroom goes into an uproar!!!!!!!!!! Cameras click with reckless abandon! Many in the crowd boisterously voicing their disapproval of the ruling! Bailiffs determined to keep the situation under control, move into action!
"ORDER!" he yells, banging the wooden gavel on the desk. "ORDER! ORDER IN THE COURT!"
Denmark's lawyers simultaneously stand, and in the blink of an eye, grab their belt buckles and quickly flip them inside out and back again while standing towards the bench. To the naked eye it just looks like they were situating there trousers. But Kam is educated and observant enough to recognize the unique angle at which the lawyers are holding their feet to form perpendicular angles. It goes completely unseen to the

spectators. But to the judge, and six other men in this room, it's *all* that matters.

By the time the commotion subsides, and the people begin spilling out, he sees Denmark and his lawyers grin as they exit the courtroom under heavy guard.

Leaning in the chair staring at the ceiling, he's floored by the ruling. He forgot about the cameras and people, and disappears into a deep daydream; one that takes him back to his days as a young boy in China, and the day his tooth got knocked out for playing hero to a boy being bullied on the playground.

By the time Keith taps him on the shoulder they are the only two in the room. It takes several minutes for her to help him gather his things, and usher him out.

Heading to the elevator his legs are so weak that he has to retreat to the restroom. What begins as a few splashes against his face turns into forty minutes of tears?

While standing outside with tears of her own, she waits patiently while he mourns his loss.

Abernathy Blvd. is streaming with bright lights and fast cars. The rich, and upper-middle class are out in droves tonight. The streetscape is a landscape of sophisticated bars, trendy hotel, VIP parties, and inebriated sexism. The 64° temperature washed with the just right amount of pressure and humidity, has the city just right for fun. No one's marching, rioting, or protesting out here. The fact unarmed suspects are getting killed by cops is the farthest thing from their mind. They're more concerned about getting their Yorkies groomed, and brunch at Chateau Elan, than what's going on down in the dreaded inner-city. The news about the hostage crisis, and drone bombing is losing steam; Ed Denmark is the only topic. Though the residents of N. Atlanta live comfortably, and have substantial income, they're not of the same ilk as him; so his quandary is just that more interesting. Whispers, laughs, stares, and comments, are coming from the mouths of random people as they discuss their view of the titan, and how he beat the case. Conspiracy theories, and Ed Denmark fan clubs are popping up all over the internet. Memes and Emoji's are pasted on just about every social media site. The hottest selling memorabilia at the moment happens to be an article on Atlanta Magazine's website. It offers its own take on how Denmark beat the charge. It's rife with tales of collusion and preferential treatment of the wealthy in not only the legal system, but in all walks of life. But it's the photo included with the article that's causing all the fuss.

Pictured is a man behind bars. On one half the inmate is wearing an orange jumpsuit with the face of Ed Denmark. On the other half he's wearing a business suit with the face of Satan. Inside the cell with him is a man sitting on a bunk with the black robe of a judge and the head of a donkey. Around its neck hangs a plaque saying: *Dishonorable Baxtard.*

Due to the convention in town, the city's packed with visitors. Now that the work is done, it's playtime; making Cumulus a hot spot tonight. In the day it's a low-key den for snobby professionals and bored socialites. But at night it becomes the addiction of a select few. A door man is now posted at both entrances, and patrons can no longer waltz right in. Attire is meticulously checked, and reservations are strongly encouraged. No longer is the main entrance of the mall flourishing with families and singles from all walks of life. At this hour, the mall is closed, and the premier scene in the area is at Cumulus. The valet is a show of Italian luxury and German engineering, the outdoor patio is transformed into an oasis for high earners and heavyweights; shuttle buses wait to whisk guests to and fro. The stars in the sky, and the diamonds on their person engage in games of competitive flair, each trying to out shine the other.

Postured in the far corner of the upper level bar, a well put together man enjoys his drink; doing so in the most discerning type of way. His ensemble for the evening is stunning, and his subtle selection for eye wear is appropriate. With his new found prosperity, he can now mingle amongst a new demographic. With his new found identity he can now be a new person. Shrouded by the cloak of money and privilege, he's even harder for the authorities to find. They definitely aren't searching around here. But this is only temporary. By tomorrow he'll be out of the country, and hopefully with enough cash to keep him out of view until he decides his next move. The person he's meeting will have a lot to do with where things go in the next forty eight hours. If what she's offering turns out to be true, he may never be apprehended.

With music so full of class, and decor so exquisite, the aroma of the food and the sight of so many beautiful people; he's already gotten used to this life. If all he has to do to maintain it is kill more evil men, so be it.

The limbic system is a complex set of brain structures located on both sides of the thalamus, right under the cerebrum. It supports a variety of functions, including epinephrine flow, emotion, behavior, motivation, long-term memory, and olfaction. Emotional life is principally housed in the limbic system, and also has a great deal to do with the formation of memories. Due to *trauma*, birth defects, or long term drug usage, this can become *impaired*.

For him, it was the sequence of violent assaults at the brothel which caused him to become this altered person.

Having previously promised to arrive at the agreed time, she's prompt and equally spectacular. Pain doesn't see Merciless but is certain he's there. Watching the men admire the sample strutting up the stairs, he can't keep fooling himself. She does something to him that he hasn't felt before, not in a sexual way, but in a way he can't define; the flutter in his chest reminds him of a distant memory. The vixen in the black evening gown reminds him of man's inherent duty to protect the woman.
He stands and welcomes her with a kiss on the back of her hand.
A nearby gentleman admires her while he holds the barstool. Her fragrance is sweet and sensual; the ladylike crossing of her legs takes the on-looker's breath away.
With her here, he's certainly separated himself from the pack.
"You must be Bailey," he greets, like an experienced lady's man. "*I hardly recognized you with those stupid shades*," she whispered. "…Yes! You must be Mr. Bogart?"
"That's correct. But my friends call me Pain."

The first part of the plan is for him to pretend to be a john meeting for a date. But she's having a hard time understanding what she's seeing. It's been three weeks since she last saw him, and the last she checked, he was a fugitive on the run. Now he's sitting there dressed like a fashion model?
"What are you thinking about?"
She plays it off with a seductive head throw and hand wave.
"Nothing."
The bartender comes to assist.
"Good evening sir. May I get the lady started with a beverage?"
"I'll have a Shirley Temple with a splash of lime," she answered for him.
A nod of the head signifies his understanding.

While he prepares her drink, she looks at her date and smiles. But inside she's having all sorts of paranoid thoughts. Ones ranging from him being a con artist, to him setting her up to kill her, then eat her.

"You seem nervous," he commented.

"I am."

The bartender places a velvety napkin down topped with her drink.

"Thanks," and elegantly takes a sip.

She has to make it look real. She can't let Merciless get the idea he really isn't a trick about to pay her three grand for her services.

Having gone step by step with him over the phone regarding strategy, he produces an envelope from his inside pocket and causally slides it across the table.

Picking it up she slides it into her sequins clutch. From where ever he's watching, Merciless won't suspect much now that payment has been received.

"So how long are you in town on business?"

"I'll be leaving tomorrow. I'm only here to attend a convention at the World Congress Center. How about you?"

"I'll be leaving as well. Off to the Midwest to attend a spiritual retreat," Bailey hinted.

"Oh? So does that mean you're into solving mysteries of the unseen?"

She laughs, pats her hair, and sips another taste of her drink.

"No. It means I understand the fact that I'll never truly understand life's mysteries. Somehow everything happens for a reason."

"True indeed," he agreed.

And downs the remainder of his Johnnie Walker® Blue Label.

"So what do you have in mind for the evening? You look as if this night will be a special one," he hinted too.

She smirks at his wit.

"Well I hope you're ready for a night you won't forget."

"I can't wait to get started. I just hope you can practice what you preach? I'd hate to be disappointed," he states.

"Let me tell you something sweetheart. When you deal with me, satisfaction is *always* guaranteed."

"Well must I wait any longer? The night is young."

"Good things come to those who wait."

He isn't a customer, but he's still a man. She has to employ all of her powers of persuasion to be sure he doesn't back out. After planning this for months, this is her only shot at escape. After tonight, no man will ever harm her again. This will be the last time she has to subject herself to be used. After already being forced to sleep with hundreds of men, this is nothing. All she has to do is remember her daughter. She's cried more than she can remember, and been through more pain than imaginable. She knows Merciless will kill her if he finds her. But this is the first time in years she sees a glimmer of hope.

Just this one last time Cailida…Come on girl! You can do it!

She leans forward, and seductively touches his penis.

He shoots her a cold stare and pushes her hand away!

For a moment she thinks she's tearing up, but quickly gathers herself.

"So where are you staying?"

"Don't do that again. It makes me feel cheap…But to answer your question, I have a suite at Crown Plaza."

"Is everything okay sir," the bartender interrupted. "Would you like anything else for the lady?"

"We won't be having anything else. We'd like the check please," she informs.

"Certainly," and turns away.

"It amazing that such a beautiful woman has been through the things you have. No one would never know what you've lived through."

"I learned long ago you can't wear your life story on your
sleeve. It can be dangerous."
"Yes it can."
From the exterior he looks like a rich man, but when he speaks,
his teeth bare the signs of malnutrition and the effects of life
on the street. If one was to look closer, they would see the frail
physique bleeding through the designer suit. An even closer
inspection would reveal he's not sporting a hundred dollar
haircut, but a self-employed clip-clip in a mirror; accentuated
by a comb and styling gel.
The bartender sits the bill on the counter.
Bogart opens it and places two bills inside.
"So shall we get our evening started?"
She takes another sip off her drink and leaves the rest.
"I was just thinking the same thing."
Carrying himself like a perfect gentleman, the pair heads
downstairs and makes for the exit.

Merciless is downstairs sitting in a booth near the wine cellar.
Watching her and the john leave out, he picks up his phone
and sends her a text.
He puts the phone down and picks up the menu. While she's
making his money, he has a taste for blood. At first he didn't
trust Bailey enough to let her have a phone. But over this past
year she convinced him that she could make him more money
if she was able to meet tricks at their location. Now business is
booming, his pockets are fatter than ever. But unfortunately,
Denmark has given him a month to get rid of her, and this is
day twenty nine. If he screws this up too, he knows he'll be
dead. He can't understand why he turned sour on Bailey, to
such a point that he wants her gone immediately. She's the best
worker he has, and he wants to squeeze ever last drop out of
here before selling her to their Queens affiliate. They agreed
on a price of seventy five thousand, but he has to throw in the
daughter too. He wants to keep her for himself, because as long

as she stays disease free, she has the potential to be worth more than the mother.

Initially, he didn't want the girls asking the tricks to use condoms. Tricks are willing to pay a premium to have unprotected sex with the girls. But after so many of them kept contracting venereal infections, he as well as many of the other associates realized it's bad for business if they don't start protecting their investments.

His phone rings.

It's the host enquiring about his arrival.

While he talks, Bailey and her "trick" head across the parking lot. The night is starting off well. He takes his mind off her and focuses on other matters.

Standing at the curb, she and her date look marvelous as they wait for the crosswalk to give them the signal. The night is abnormally warm, and the sky is free of clouds; the stars wink spontaneously. It's as if they're hinting at the good fortunes to come. Part act and part natural, she grips her dates arm. This is the first time in her life she's actually looking forward to something, the first time she feels like a normal person.

As they walk in silence toward the hotel, she thinks about the devastating toll being born in the sex trade has taken on her. She's void of family, and void of help in a foreign land. She's terrified of Merciless and wouldn't dare attempt escaping unless she's certain she can make it. But when she found out he's about to send her daughter to Chicago, she knew she had to go. If he sends her off, she knows she'll never see her again.

She'll take both of their lives before she allows that to happen.

Due the perpetual horror she's experienced, she's never believed in God. But as of late, she's been having these spiritual feelings of protection. Something, or someone sent this man her way. She sees the death in his eyes. But there's something principled about him, he seems to be searching for something; or even destined. She doesn't want to get into praying or anything, but the warm feeling coming over her makes her want to thank somebody.

Coming onto the property they're meet by floral bushes and low hanging trees, a brick walkway lined with bright bulbs guides the way. Cars, shuttles, taxis, and vans team in the half circled driveway before the bank of glass doors. Men in suits, women in push-up bras, and congeries with carts, move about as they help guests unload their luggage.
They slip through the crowd, and through the automatic doors, and not one security personnel bats an eye.
Standing in the expanse of the lobby, beige marble and golden brass entertain the eye with striking displays of ultra-contemporary design.
Sliding onto the elevator, she takes a subtle glance of her surroundings. She doesn't see Merciless but she keeps feeling he's near. After being captive so long, she's become emotionally dependent on him. Her mind keeps telling her she doesn't need him, but her body is telling her the world will eat her alive without his guidance and protection.
Getting on the elevator she trips over the threshold and almost fall, but Mr. Bogart keeps her from hitting the inside wall.
"You okay?"
"Yeah. Wasn't watching where I was going I guess."
Pain looks at her in the doors reflection, he looks at himself. Somehow he's inside an elevator as a wanted man about to commit more crimes with a stripper he slept with years ago. As a child he dreamed of being a superhero and helping others, but he wouldn't have believed life would play out like this, even if it was shown it to him. They're as opposite as opposite can be. You can't find two people more different.

Opposites attract.

Getting off on the 12th floor, they step into the carpeted corridor. The same piano tune that was playing in the elevator is playing from the ceiling.

"I probably don't want to know, but how did you manage to get this room?"

"I didn't."

At the end of the hall is door '2016'.

Looking over his shoulder he moves to the door with something from his pocket in his hand, and in seconds the door is open.

"Come on."

She slips inside as he shuts the door behind her.

Inside this huge suite there's plastic sheeting over everything, the walls are stripped bare and the electrical receptacles have wires hanging out, paint cans and building materials are scattered about, the bed is up against the wall, the mattresses are covered with drop cloths, and the furniture is pushed to the far corner near the balcony.

"How did you find this?"

"Being homeless forces you to find places to sleep."

"You sure no one's coming in here? There sure is a lot of stuff in here? I'm sure somebody's watching it."

"And that's why we need to figure out what we're gonna do so we can get out of here?"

"I thought we already agreed on what we're gonna do?"

To her it sounds like he's having second thoughts. Her heart starts racing! She can't let him back out now!

"Right."

He moves to the closet, and reaches into the ceiling.

The workers removed the drywall which made it easy for him to hide his equipment without much difficulty. He grabs the gun case and ditty bag.

She looks for any signs of reluctance—he doesn't seem confident anymore, and doesn't look like a killer. His posture has slumped and his movements go uneasy.

She steps to him and takes his hands.

"Hey. Are you all right? You're not about to leave me hanging are you?" She leans forward and kisses his lips. They're cold and hard, and his upper lip is stinky. The look on his body says startled and uncomfortable, his eyes say please stop—he can't even look at her.

Sex is a weapon that works on men. It's all she knows. Disobeying his earlier warning, she reaches for his penis again. The second she does, it grows stiff.

And that's when he grabs her hand and steps back.

"That's not what I'm here for Bailey. You're about to ruin everything."

She's genuinely surprised and taken aback! A piece of her is even offended...Now comes the hurt.

"So what? I'm not good enough for you? You don't like what you see or something," she snaps.

"No. I just don't want to be like all the other men. I don't want to be just another guy who takes advantage of you."

"Well you did it before!"

"I did a lot of things before. But this is now, and I don't have to do them again."

"That's not what it is! You think I'm disgusting don't you? Go ahead, tell me! Tell the fucking truth, I can take it! I'm a big girl! Tell me I'm a whore and you think I'm nasty! You know you want to!..All men want is pussy! Pussy-pussy-pussy! You're all sick!"

"I don't Bailey."

"Why not? Why not huh!" beginning to cry, her emotions all over the place.

 She can see all the horrible men who used to touch her when she was a child. She remembers how the tricks would come for her mom, but later come to her room and try to get in bed with her. She remembers how the compound's high priest took her virginity against her will.

"Well you'll be the first," and wipes her face. "I'm tired of crying."

"Me too."

"You know I can't go back don't you? You know if you back out now, they'll kill me? If you're having second thoughts, at least let me know now so I can still have chance to save my daughter?"

"I'm not going to back out Bailey. At least this way I can put my wrongs to good use before I die."

"...Do you believe in God?" she asked.

"I think so. Yes. Do you?"

"I don't know why but I do. I have every reason not to, but in my heart I feel in some strange way he's with me."

"Well you shouldn't be afraid...They say that he works in mysterious ways."

"Do you think you're going to hell if you end up killing these people?"

"I don't know. That's not for me to decide."

"Do you think I'll go to hell?"

"No."

"Why?"

"Because God requires man to kill. Death is a key element of life."

"I'm ready to do whatever I have to do get away from these people. No, I mean animals. They're not even people. People don't do things like this to other people. I don't care anymore. If they die, they shouldn't be doing these things in the first place. I know God sees what they're doing, he knows what they're doing to all these girls. There destroying thousands of lives with all the women, girls and boys they're kidnapping. It's so awful. Many of them need surgery from all the rough sex and tears to their insides....," and pauses. "Well you know. But, and other things like the girls not being able to hold their urine."

"So you're saying there's girls walking around with *inconti-*

nence!" a look of disbelief on his face.

Bailey looks confused, she doesn't know what that means.

"But yeah, I wish the world can see what's going on. I wish God would do something to help all these girls. I wish some one would expose these people."

"He will..............Somehow this mess all makes sense. We just aren't smart enough to understand God's plan."

"I'm scared, but I'm ready to do it? How long do you want to wait?"

"You said that the game starts around ten, so we should probably be leaving soon.................If we make it out, where will you go? Are you going to the police?"

"No. I'm just getting as far away from Atlanta as I can. The cops can't do anything, some of them are in on it too. These gangs pay handsomely for protection. You'll never believe how many players there are. The right amount of money will turn the most honest man corrupt......But yeah, I don't care what happens to them. I just want to get me and my daughter some-where safe."

"What if she's not there?"

"She's there, I know she is. I can feel it."

"What about all the other girls? You said there are thousands. They need someone to save them too? Maybe God has chosen you to be their hero," he asked.

"Maybe you're right.........But you're the hero, not me."

"If the cops find me the last thing I'll be is a hero."

"Well screw them! They should do something to stop this— the government too! They spend all this money on wars, and bombs when the war is right here! They should deal with this human trafficking first before dealing with that other stuff. Fire a missile on at all these brothels and disgusting strip clubs and massage parlors that have women locked up inside them!"

She takes her dress and wipes the tears from her eyes.

"You know what?"

"What?"

"Believe it or not…I write."

"Oh yeah."

"Yep.....It helps me get my mind away from all this. I write these poems when I get down. I have this one I wrote........You wanna hear it?"

"Sure."

"Okay now don't laugh......It's called Pierced by a Rose..........
My mother called me a rose, now the seedling of me has taken root. Sometimes I walk in my own garden and get lost in the beauty that surrounds me. I'm a rare flower that grows on mountains high in the sky. Beyond my field of red petals and green stems, the world is dark. The cold wind blows like an angry storm over my savanna; I am strengthened by the push. I grow in this storm to become lovely. Captivated by my blossom, a gardener steals me and wants to implant his seed. Blinded by beauty, he doesn't notice my thorns are unable to be contained. He cuts me down anyway and takes me to a faraway land. Unable to grow, my petals wither and darken. My red turns deep with the color of pain. Parts of me are washed away by the erosion of life. Falling to the ground, an angel rescues me. Planted in a new plot I bring hopes of a new harvest. People from all around come to anticipate my bloom. They call me their sacred floret, a gift from grace with the power to bring light to gloom. This flower of the heavens must not be misused. For like the birth of an angel, her display only has one bloom."

"Stupid huh?"

"I thought it was wonderful. That sent chills up my spine Bailey. *Pierced by a Rose* huh, that was all right."

They hear movement in the hallway going past the room. It reminds them of the reason they're there.

"You sure no one's coming in here?" she asked again.

"Probably not tonight, but I'm sure they'll be back at some point. Probably in the morning."

"Oh………Well do you want to go over anything?"

"I have it all."

He sits the items down and heads to the restroom.

In the three minute he's in there, he does something he rarely does. He gets on his knees and prays. Why, what, and to who, doesn't matter. He did it for him. And it felt good.
When he emerges, he's surprised to see her doing the same thing. While she whispers words to her higher power, he readies the items.

In minutes they're gone.

The Swimming Pig, is one of the top three restaurants in the city, if not the Southeast. Depending on who you ask, an argument can be made that it's actually the best restaurant in Atlanta. It's fairly small, secluded, and doesn't have a marketing budget. There's only one sign, and it's barely legible. It caters to people who value separation and distinction, not wannabes masquerading as big shots. The dress code is cocktail, and all the tables have white cloths. The main area is rectangular with wood floors, but the isles are carpeted. Under the carpet is white ceramic tile. There's no echo, only cozy and inviting. The art consists of oil paintings of some of history's most abhorrent men.
King Leopold II, the Belgian tyrant who monopolized the world's rubber trade by committing genocide in the African Congo, is posted near the hostess podium.
Vlad the Impaler, the original Dracula, and member of the House of Drăculeşti. Vested by the 'Order of the Dragon'; he was also known as "the king of terror" and used Orthodox Christianity as a vehicle to spread barbarism, excessive cruelty, and relentless slaughter across Eastern Europe, leaving

tens of thousands dead; is idolized near the humidor.

She recognizes Bailey, but not the gentlemen she's with. Earlier that day, she lied about returning this evening with a guest of Merciless'. Believing this, the woman doesn't ask any questions. Private sections of four person booths lines the walls. In the rear of the room sits a raised floor. There, a trio consisting of a flutist, a pianist, and a tenor saxophonist make blissful music without the use of vocals. To the opposite end, sits a hallway with elevator doors of polished walnut. Situated in the center of the expanse, is a full service kitchen capable of feeding a limited number of guest incredible cuisine without the use of heat. Patrons can watch in astonishment while their food is prepared by expert chefs versed in this fine and sought-after art of cooking. If more privacy is desired, the second floor offers better accommodations.

Unlike the rectangular shaped ground level, it's built in circular design. Around this atrium sits eight alcoves with curtains. Within each, a table capable of seating six keep guests separated from others. A window overlooking the Chattahoochee River adds breathtaking views of downtown and Buckhead.

A bar with four stools has one bartender making drinks in the rear. The elevator hides at the end of the hall pass the restrooms. In the center of the atrium sits a round, three-dimensional, 25x25 ft. topographical map of the entire world. Every city has tiny life-like skyscrapers, the coasts of the continents have water and waves, the landscape has trees, and the valleys have peaks, the Swiss Alp's seems like you're in the heavens standing over them the great Caspian Sea is scaled to perfection, the Ho Chi Minh trial can be traced with a pencil point, the island of Madagascar is the size of a cigarette litter as it rises from the Indian Ocean. Yellowstone National Park is green with detail and colorful with Rocky Mountains, the glaciers of Greenland are jagged and immense, the Sahara desert is the size of a bumper pool table, Dubai looks just as spectacular as it does in real life. Surrounded by an elegant bannister, this stunning piece is both impressive and imposing; giving viewers the sensation they're gods looking down on planet earth.

But at this hour the restaurant is closed for the night. The few staff members who remain have finished the clean-up and are preparing to leave. The chef is gone, and the hostesses is chatting her goodbyes to the manager. The musicians were paid for the night and sent home with their usual gourmet meal and tips. The $1,250 a week each member earns is paid on a weekly basis and never taxed. Most of the lights are off, making their walk more climactic.

Bailey's hands begin shaking and her mouth turns bitter; a nauseating feeling in her stomach commences churning. They are almost at the elevator and she still doesn't know what he's carrying in the case. But she knows it's not money like the hostess probably assumes. Now she's the one having second thoughts!

Only "circle lords" and working girls are allowed downstairs. No bodyguards, no drivers, and no personal assistants. They all have to remain upstairs until the individual reemerges. Once the restaurant upstairs closes, drivers and security wait in the back alley in their limos and Sprinter® vans until the game is over. The VIP's share nothing with their staff about the dealings of the sub-level. Only the manager and the hostess know about the gambling. The elevator only allows them access to the upper level.

The ladies room is to her right, causing her to excuse herself and leave him waiting in the hall.

The lavatory/lounge is posh and perfumed with a fat sofa and vintage make-up counter in her midst. Her mind keeps telling her to stop! But her heart keeps telling her to save herself and her child by any means necessary! She's just a girl from Tenancingo, she doesn't know anything about killing!!! But she didn't know anything about performing oral sex until Merciless

beat her into mastering. Just like she had to be shown how to be "in the life", and how to scheme and plot. She can now be shown the art of murder. Merciless mercilessly prepared her body for the rigors of the sex trade by repeatedly raping her until she became desensitized. Now she will have to lose her feelings of compassion for these dogs portraying men.
Nobody cares about you!..Whores like you come a dime a dozen!
Merciless never shows any sympathy to her or the other girls, so why should she show sympathy now. Her mother believed in eye for an eye, so why does she have tears in her's?
Looking at herself in the mirror, she sees a product of a sick being's creation.
"A mother's duty is to protect her child Bailey. Fuck them!"
She can't swallow, so she takes a deep breath and opens the door.

Pain is still standing where she left him, and doesn't say a word when she comes out. Only looks her in the eye and presses the elevator button—his rock hard demeanor giving her mind calm She prepares to face the rest of her life shrunk into minutes. When the doors open, the hostess looks over her shoulder. The last thing they see before the doors shut, is her picking up a phone.

On the brass panel is six buttons. The numbers *1* and *2, Up, Down, Open Doors, Close Doors,* and *Emergency Stop.*
Bailey reaches on her tippy toes, presses a tiny button hidden in the corner, and presses the emergency button twice while holding the '1 and 2' buttons simultaneously.
She feels the jerk of car beginning its descent!

The sub-level houses storage spaces, another restroom, the electrical closet, etc. A smaller loading dock different from the one on the ground level leads to a curved alley concealed by tall pines and thick bushes. Controlled access, it requires a pass-

code to open the gate. Leading to Hammond Dr. it gives VIP's
easy access to the interstate.
The car is slow and steady, she prays she's done everything
right! She will need more than luck tonight, especially with
the doorman being there like always. The night with him was
one of the worst in her life. He was extremely rough, abusive
and demeaning. He got off on fisting and liked to spit in her
mouth. He told her she smelled like a wet back, but fucked like
a half-breed nigger. Bailey is not a forgiving person, so she's
apprehensively anxious to see bodily harm enacted on him. She
told her "war dad" to make sure he gets him good.
The elevator stops with a slight jolt.
In three seconds it opens!
The man sitting at the table stands the second he sees them.
Bailey kicks into survival mode.
Go get 'em girl!

"This is my date for the evening. He's looking to come out the
box."

"*Come out the box*", is the code phrase known only by those
with knowledge of the game.

"Right this way," said the suited man.
The lights are dim. There's a green, stained glass lamp
hanging over the players table. There's thirteen button leather
seats around this large table with a burgundy suede top. The
hallway to the far right leads to where Bailey suspects the real
horrors lie. She knows from her years in this trade there are
locations around the city where traffickers stage girls that are
being received, or transported from other cities. Her motherly
instinct tells her that her daughter is somewhere down that
hall. She badly wants to run down there and get her, but knows
that will be foolish. She steels her nerves and pretends to be
patiently waiting.

The way the operation remains under the radar of the authorities, is to move small numbers of people, usually less than six, many times per a month. It's easier to control small groups and they're easier to conceal.

Other things goes on here as well.

Deep within the clandestine world of the elite, is a game of cards said to have destroyed empires. A version of the game is said to have been played as early as 600 A.D., and has since become the game of emperors, barons, oil magnates, sheiks, and Wall street bankers.

Circle 13.

Little of this game is known to the masses, but exists in abundance in the hearts of the rich and powerful.

Each player picks a card from a deck of 52, which are called "souls". No two players can "wager" the same "soul". A player can wager as many souls as he likes, as long no other "circle lord" has already "taken possession" of that soul. There is no limit on the betting amount, and there is no set ending to the game. They routinely last for days, and at any given round of betting, as much as ten million dollars can be at stake.

When in the act of playing the game, players are considered "circle lords." There are two players that have a permanent advantage over the other players.

One, is the man sitting at the table called "The Gatekeeper." He sits at the head of the table and pulls one card at a time from a sacred box called the "coffin". His advantage is, he can win the money of other players without having to wager his own soul, which can only be done at the start of every hand.

The man at the other end is called, "The Scepter", and he has
the other advantage; which is after he cuts the cards, he takes
the one on the very bottom as his "soul." If in cahoots with
each other, these two "circle lords" can work in concert to cheat
the other players out of their souls, thus winning the majority
of the bets. Their positions are for the duration of the game,
unless they decide to sell it to one of the players.

The remaining players at the table are called "The Eleven
Burdened Goats". Each player picks a card (soul) from the deck
of 52. Before the "Gatekeeper" pulls a card out of the "coffin".
Each player must wager his soul against all the other souls at
the table, that his soul will "sacrifice" theirs for his benefit.
Once all bets are placed, the Gatekeeper begins pulling souls
out the coffin one by one, until they have all been sacrificed.
The soul standing at the end of the hand wins.

In this elite underworld, clients are not subject to rude and
obtrusive pat downs. If you're here, you're trusted. That's the
main reason Bailey is so terrified. She's on deaths doorstep, one
wrong bat of the eye can be fatal.
A man in a tuxedo approaches holding a tray with a white
cloth draped over his forearm.
The second he approaches, the other gentlemen turns and
heads back to his seat.
Bailey has them believing this man is Merciless' client and
should be treated as such. Them knowing her as his
"bottom bitch/girlfriend" they trust her word without a second
thought.
"Will you be enjoying a beverage with your game sir?" asked
the man with the British accent.
"I won't."
"Certainly."
Before he can get to his next question, Bailey interrupts politely.

"I'll leave you to your game. Good luck," and sashays away to take a seat on a long leather sofa.
From this point on, he's in the driver's seat.

"In that case sir, what number may I get you started with?"
Meaning, what quantity of chips is he going to purchase.
This is the second layer of security. If he answers this question wrong, he'll immediately be asked again. If he answers wrong a second time again, he'll be detained, strip searched, and interrogated about how he became privy to the whereabouts of this ultra-secret game. If he's really Merciless' client, he should know the correct answer. The seven men at the table are one percenters, so he has to act like he's used to being around influence. Through the cigar smoke he can see random glances his direction. He stays calm and composed.
"There wouldn't by chance be a counting room available would there?"
The expressionless host looking him directly in the eye says:
"...Right this way sir."
Turns and leads him to a nook the size of a bathroom.

Inside is a chair and a mahogany counter. On the other side of the alcove, is a room. A foot high partition separates the two sides, and an opening cut in the section is the runway for the transaction.
Pain doesn't sit.
 The host appears on the other side and waits for him to initiate the next step.
He sits his case on the table and opens it.
He reaches into the compartment where the cadre of combat knives are kept, and grabs the stack of cash. It's only ten thousand, a pale comparison to the hundreds of thousands that pass through this room in a month, but enough for what he's about to do.
He pushes it through the runway.

On the other side, he hears the man pop the band and put it in a money counter.

Pain places his hand on the silenced 9mm.

The cash is exchanged for chips made from narwhal tusk, and just as the man turns to secure the cash in a drawer. He raises the gun!

The bullet penetrates his skull, and sends him falling to the floor in a quiet heap, so quiet it even surprised him!

Pain coughs twice, and clears his throat!

Trusting Bailey heard the signal he quickly places the pistol in his waistband, and pulls out the compact *L42A1* sniper rifle. With speed he assembles it!

Exiting the nook, he goes back into the hallway!

Standing at the corner awaiting the diversion, he hears the players talking. They don't suspect a thing.

He hears Bailey say it!!!

He chambers the 7.62mm round, takes three steps and swings around the wall!!!

Dead center in his sights is the man who Bailey said sodomized her! The round hit him in the left eye and comes out the back of his head! The 6'3" doorman tips over backwards, and falls into the table sending chips, and Bicycle® playing cards every-where!!!

In a split second, he clears cartridge and chambers another round!!!

These are multi-million dollar men who rarely, if ever, have seen anything like this!!!!

Three duck and scream, four are in shock, and two still think he's playing! He pulls the hair trigger and blows the man's lower clavicle off, killing him instantly!!!

And chambers another round!

"NO!!!!!!!!!PLEASE!!!!!! GOD NOOOO!!!" the other lord yells and leaps under the table.

In .68 of a second, he spins his aim towards another man and shoots him in the head, sending him slumping out the chair to the floor!!! His legs hideously twisted, eyes and mouth open and moving!!!

The second he chambers another round, a lord leaps in reaction of sheer panic, his body's catatonic response to imminent death. But trips on the person beside him and falls to the floor!!!

He didn't get a chance to get up before the round enters his back and explodes his heart like a nuked pomegranate!!!! Seeds of his blood soak his back and front, his reflexes lock him in a horrid statue of his final moment!!!!

Like a Wild West gunslinger, he pulls the pistol and sends five hot projectiles into two other men's skulls, rendering them obsolete, claiming their souls for himself!!!!!

Bailey tries not to scream when blood spatter from the dead fat-cat mists her face and arms!!!

"*AAAAAAAAAAAAAAAAAAANOOOOOooooooooooo!!!*" a burdened goat cried.

Slumping in his chair, gasping loudly at the ceiling; gigantic veins pulse up his neck, bulge out his forehead like vines up a tree! Smoke is still rising from the chamber when he begins foaming at the mouth! By the time his eyes whiten, and his heart attack becomes fatal, Pain has already chambered another round!

BAM!

Goes his body falling out of the chair, his eternal sleep initiated!

The acrid smell of noxious gun powder is like fog, the smell of death potent and suffocating. The waning moans of lives being lost whispers like soft jazz. On the side of the room stands a deranged man with a smoking gun, desperate to add meaning to his suffering, desperately searching for redemption!

The two circle lords left are burdened by the realization that the wages of evil is death, and there's is imminent!!!

"Where are the girls?" Pain asked sternly.

Atlanta is a music mecca, and this is the head of a world famous record label. This year alone, his company has generated one hundred and twenty-five million dollars in record sales. At his overseas villa is where he hides his sex slaves. So far, he's invested sixteen million into his harem.

"I think down there!!!!" mumbling and trembling with piss dripping down his leg.

"How many?"

"...I don't know!!" he can barely speak.

Pain Bogart looks into his eyes and sees the sinister slant to his pupil. He sees the funny looking black ring on his finger, he sees the amulet.

He doesn't need to see more.

"…Open your mouth."

But he doesn't give his lips red from the wine and grapes a chance to open. He slams the pistol in his mouth while the man's eyes bulge and twitch!!!!!

He pulls trigger!

The weight of the man falling forward is immediately on him! Like a hog on a pitch fork, he turns and slings the roach dropping to the floor with the rest of the dead insects!!!!

"Noooooooooooooo!. Please, no more!!!" Bailey cried, curled on the couch in the fetal position.

Bogart acts as if she said nothing, and looks at the "last soul standing", who's shivering under the table! He's not acting like he just won the game, he's sliding on his side while his tailored suit drags like a dust mop through blood and guts.

His hands go in the air as Pain approaches!!! He tries to speak but is muted by fright!!!

"...Af....Ge.....PL.....wl!!!" his words fractured and incommunicable.

"Come get the gun Bailey," cool, clam, and collected.

The man is gagging on disbelief! It's taking all he has to gasp out a sentence! And he inhales a huge breath of air, as if he's just surfaced after almost drowning!

"*They keep the money in the other room!!!..Please, my family needs me! I have a daughter in college...I can have twenty million dollars here in an hour! Please spare me! Please! Don't kill me! Please just don't kill me,*" the powerful circle lord sobbed.

Crawls from under the table, and starts kissing the Payless® shoes of the executioner!

But she's sin shock, her brain isn't processing the mayhem she's witnessing.

"Come get the gun!...*Bailey!!!*" he shot.

Slowly she stands and comes to him, but has to cover her mouth to keep from vomiting. She steps over the dead man's legs and reaches for the gun. The Ruger® is trembling, her first time in life holding a gun.

Pain has no time for pep talks.

"Take me to where the women are kept," he demanded.

The terrified man has no clue what he's referring to! He knows nothing about the girls! Though, he's a real estate tycoon with holdings in thirty one countries, he honestly isn't there for that purpose, he's there only for the game.

Bogart is angered by his silence and is about to shoot.

He hears Bailey scream!!!!

The man flinches and closes his eyes, thinking he was dead! Pain looks around but doesn't see her! He sees the dim light coming from down the hall, and hears her crying and the sound of someone banging a door!

"Get up and move fast!"

The man crawls to his feet, but falls back down!

Bogart raises his foot and kicks his ass into gear! In seconds he's back up with the blood of his fellow circle lord soiling his attire.

Heading down the hallway, they pass another short hall splitting off of it, which is likely where the room leading to the other side of the counting room is. This corridor is just as lavish and comfortable as the rest. There's a sofa on the side and

more art. But Bailey hasn't stopped screaming!
"Look around and tell me what you see..*Hurry up!*" pressing
the rifle against the back of his neck.
*"I see the woman standing at a door crying!!! Uh, and some more
doors!!!"*
He pushes him forward, rounds the corner, heads to Bailey,
and pushes the man to the floor, putting his foot on his head.
In the top center on the tall mahogany door is a window
into another world, another realm; one filled with two dozen
children, teens, and young adults from all nationalities and all
places! And behind this door is a metal gate leading to the stag-
ing area. There's a table in the center of the room topped with
bottles of water, and bags of belongings. No one's talking, and
there's a hole cut in the floor with a grate over it. His eyes
instantly begin tearing up, rage courses through him!
When he sees the human excrement, he reaches back and
stomps on his head!!!
"YOU PIECE OF SHIT!!!!
He shoulder rams the heavy door but it doesn't open!
Bailey is going hysterical now that she's seeing her
precious daughter in the cargo hold!! And starts banging the
butt of the gun into the window she's looking through!
Get up and get that fucking door open or you die!...*GET THE
FUCKING DOOR OPEN..NOW!"*
The terrified man is in panic! He raises his Valentino loafer and
kicks the door!.......He kicks it again, and rams it! Seeing the
man gritting his teeth pointing a gun to his face, he begins crying, realizing the door isn't coming down! He punches it like a
weak lamb, and hit again!
Bailey is in such disbelief that she's in a state of incoherence!
She's about to fire the gun at the door.
He takes it from her, and she falls to her knees in agony, her
hands clawed, and raking at her face!!
"GET IT OPEN MOTHERFUCKER!!!!!" And sticks the gun
to his ear.

"OPEN IT!!!

The tycoon feels his saliva on the side of his face, he smells his foul breath! If he's about to die, he would rather be killed by a door than a bullet to the head! He steps back as much as the hall would allow, and sends his body into the solid wood door as hard as he can!!

It burst open as the bolt tears from the frame splintering the wood like toothpicks!!!! His momentum careening him into the metal gate like a fierce linebacker, knocking him unconscious, and bleeding from the head!

"Moooooo-mmmmmmmy!" the little girl screams in panic. Bailey runs and embraces her daughter through the barred gate! Feeling her child is a dose of adrenaline!!!

Though many of the people can't speak English, they know something isn't right, and back away from the gate. A girl in the corner is saying something and moving her arms!

"Get back! Everybody move back!" he shouted.

But it wasn't until he raises the rifle that they scatter. Some begin screaming and crying! Guns are the last thing they want to see!

"MOVE! MOVE!"

Takes aim, and shoots the lock! The wisp of the bullet followed by the mechanical recoil action, and the lock is obliterated! Bailey wastes no time in going in!! She picks her daughter up!!!!! Tears of joy come forth uncontrollably. She can feel the energy transferring from her body to hers. Cailida Floriano becomes lethal like only a cornered mother protecting her cub can. He mind instantly becomes clear and she no longer feels bad about what she's done!

It's at this very moment, he has validation there's redemption in what he's doing. There's life to be found in death. He can't erase the past, but there's a gratifying feeling of atonement in his heart today!

But he refocuses.

"Let's go, we gotta go move!"

She removes her embrace and turns, but doesn't let go of her hand.

"Stay with me! We still gotta get outta here!"

"What are we going to do about them? We can't just leave them!"

"We aren't! I have it all figured out! But we gotta move!"

She takes one last look at the confused people, pushes the gate completely open, and turns away!

"Ready your weapon!"

The rescues stayed behind him as he heads back the way they came, but makes a detour to the cash room!

He raises his weapon and shoots the door, the bolt lever staying open meaning he's out of ammo. He kicks it open and goes inside. The door bumps the dead concierge sprawled on the floor as he pushes his way past. Pain reaches over the small divider grabs the gun case, releases the clip, and reloads!

The room is simple, only a counter topped with a counting machine, and a vintage dresser chest. Pulling the top drawer by the handle he sees nothing but poker chips in thirteen rows of colors! He opens the next drawer and sees nothing but plastic currency bags and books of deposit slips! In the third and final drawer, there's racks upon racks of cold hard cash. For a moment he's mesmerized, this is the most money he's ever seen in one place in his entire life. He's stunned by the sight of so much green, but remembers the people in the cages, and gets angry all over again! He grabs a plastic bag and starts stuffing! In seconds it's full, he grabs another and stuffs it! And he grabs another! He stuffs $10,000 band after band into whatever space he can find! By the time the drawer is empty, he's carrying thirty extra pounds of weight, not including the money stashed on his person.

Emerging from the room he hands a bag to Bailey, and one to her little girl!

"You hold that tight okay."

She nods her head.

And says to Bailey: "Stay here. When I get back just follow the
plan!"
"Okay."
He runs back to the hold!

When he reemerges a minute later, he's holding a cell phone!
"Let's get out of here!"
Due to the fact this is a select club, there's no need for security.
The restaurant is open to the public but random people don't
come here. The mood has always been laid back and
reserved; so loose that after regular business hours the only
person upstairs is usually the hostess. She stays until midnight,
locks up and leaves. The car they arrived in is a black sedan
which could pass for an executive service vehicle, or a premium
class business rental, but it's parked down the street. They have
to get to the car, and come back so Bailey can escape in the
doorman's vehicle, which unfortunately is parked inside the
secured lot out back teaming with the waiting limousines and
vans of the dead circle lords.
"Cover her eyes!"
Bailey grabs her around the shoulder, and uses her hand to
smother her face to her side to prevent her from seeing the
massacre. She can feel the point of the money stacks, as the
bags in her daughter's hands bump into her knee..
Bogart sits the case down and searches the dead doorman's
pockets until he finds his keys and his cell phone, and holds
them up to Bailey!
She shakes her head yes!
He snatches the case, moves for the elevator, and presses the
button. Checking his weapon, he's sweating profusely with a
dry mouth! Looking at the scared mother and daughter behind
him, he thinks of the people in the back! The odor of death
is overpowering the haze of cigar smoke. Bailey pats her back
until the elevator arrives. When it does, he points the rifle at its
emptiness, and ushers them in!

Once they've doors close, Bailey's anxiety really kicks in! After being held captive for much of her adult life, she's jumpy with apprehension!

"Please get us out of here! They're going to kill me Alex," she pleads.

"Shhh, stay calm, be ready to fire! You have to stay calm and aim!"

While he's kneeling at the open case, stacks of money are everywhere, and he's having a hard time bending at the hip because there's money all around his waist. He quickly disassembles the sniper rifle, sits it inside and extracts the sub-machine gun! After checking the cartridge he shuts the case, grabs the money and case in the same hand; in his right is the Calico®.

He hit the '1' button but it doesn't move!

For a second she panics, but remembers she has to perform the proper sequence. She does, the elevator begins rising.

They all lean against the far wall breathing heavily, the child is still crying and visibly shaken! It's no telling what she's been through. Bailey offers a quick prayer and now has to go out on faith!

The elevator stops.

Bogart steps into the dark silence swinging the weapon in all directions!

"All right! Let's go!"

Their footsteps now seem 10x louder than were before! The sound of the air conditioner adds an eerie undertone to the climate. They rush through the kitchen and dash for the exit. The moonlight creeping through the windows, and the dim light of the dining room sconces is all they have! At the rear of the building they push through a pair of swinging doors and come into a stock room! Through the room, Bogart spins around looking, seeing the other short hall, and the management office and dishwashing area! His heart paces faster when he spots the exit sign at the end!

"This way!"

Moments later, they're standing beside a roll-up garage door, and the steel swinging door leading to freedom! But it's locked! He aims at the area where the bolt slides into the frame, fires three shots, and bumps it with his shoulder! But it won't open!
"Oh nooooooo!" Bailey cries.
He shoots it again!
And realizes he has to push the panic bar to free the latch. He bumps it with his side and their out!

The rush of air is manna from heaven!

Holding the door he hurries them out!
They're now under the awning of the loading dock. Quickly, they run down the stairs and head for the front!
The quiet Georgia night is muggy with moisture, the leaves on the trees have already changed color.
Without a moment to spare they cut onto the grass and enter the woods beyond the tree line! Pushing through the thick brush makes carrying the load even harder! Her daughter is wearing a pair of cheap rubber sandals and keeps saying she's scared and the vines are scratching her arms!
Mommy assures her everything will be all right, and that they're almost home.
After coming out behind an office building and dashing across a well-lit parking lot, they're behind the gas station where the car is parked! But there's people at the pumps filling their tanks, a man is sitting in his car talking on the phone beside a drive-thru car wash.
They have no choice but to expose themselves. He kneels in the pathway and secures the weapon back in the case!
"Come on!"
Holding three bags of money and a thing that looks like a instrument case, the trio emerge from the blind and make for the car!
Seeing them coming his way, the man seems startled by their

sudden appearance, and by the time they get to the car, he's already pulling away.
Bogart unlocks the door and put them in! Once inside, he goes around to the other side and hops in! Slamming the keys in the ignition, he takes off!

The plan may seem odd to a normal person, but to them it's their best option. Neither of them are in a position to search Craigslist® for a car. The easiest, and quickest way is to take one of theirs. Once she and her daughter are safe, she can ditch it and continue to her destination.

Turning down the narrow street, he goes around a curve and comes to a small driveway which can be missed if not careful. Turning left, he cuts down it!
Bailey and her daughter are in the backseat ducked down!
In another five hundred feet he sees the back of the restaurant and the access gate! Through the wrought iron fence he sees several waiting limousines, all black and all running.
He eases to the gate!
"What's the code!"
"Five-three-one-two-seven, equal sign, then nine," Bailey said from behind the seat.
He lowers the window and fingers it into the glowing screen. Seconds after entering the final digit, it opens.
An alarm remote is built into the key fob, and when he sees the 'peace sign' medallion, he instantly knows what to look for!
Before the gate is fully open, he pulls forward! Soon as he's inside it closes!
Through the windshield he sees what couldn't be seen from the other side. Backed into a parking space is a black Mercedes Benz®. He pulls in beside it!
From here he's visible to all the waiting vehicles, and can feel them looking!
He reaches and switches the dome light to 'Off' to prevent

them from seeing inside when the door opens!

Having come too far to turn back know, he puts on the hat on the seat, and gets out!

The drone of the running engines is more pronounced now. He can feel the pressure of the moment twisting his innards!

Employing his best chauffeur impersonation, he first opens the back door of the Benz, followed the back driver's door of the car!

Looking at the terrified people hunched down, he knows there's a good chance they can race all this way, only to die at the finish line.

Bailey is frozen with fear!!!!

"Hurry! You have to," he whispered.

She's already put on the wig, and the shades he was wearing when they met are on her face. She sits up and grabs her daughter!

"Hurry!!!!"

She's too afraid!

"God help me!!!"

"BAILEY HURRYYYYYYY!!!!!"

Taking a deep breath, she squeezes her child's hand, clutches the bags of money, and gets out!!!!!

The second she rose, car lights appear at the gate!

 He pushes her and the girl into the backseat, tosses her the keys, and shuts the door!

Moving back to his car he gets inside and throws it in gear!

The car at the gate is waiting for it to open!

It turns out to be another van, not a luxurious Sprinter® like the others; but the white delivery type. It doesn't take a genius to figure out who the van is for. It pulls in and backs to the loading dock.

Bogart presses the gas! As he pulls to the gate he sees a man standing near one of the limos looking at him!

Acting like any other rich snob, he sticks his nose in the air and pays him no attention.

Upon entering the code the gate opens! But by the time it fully does, the Benz still hasn't moved, and the lights are still off! Looking in the rearview, he impatiently taps the steering wheel.

"Come on Bailey! ..... What are you doing!!!!!!!!"

One second!

Two seconds!!

Three seconds!!!

Four seconds!!!!

Five seconds!!!!!

......Something's wrong!

He has two choices: Either leave in one piece with the money and his freedom?

Or turn back and risk certain death for a woman and child he barely knows?

Pain put the car in reverse and was just about to go back when the lights come on! The engine revs loudly, the E500 lunges forward!

Bogart throws the shifter back in drive and floors it!!!!!!! Out the gate they go like two bats out of hell!!!!!! With Bailey hot on his tail, he drives with purpose back the way they came!!!! Looking over his shoulder he doesn't see any lights following them!

"AAAAAAAAAAAAAAAAAAAAAAAAAAAAAAH!!" he shouted as they turn onto Hammond Dr.

He feels unstoppable!!!!!

He's a deranged super hero!!!!!

He feels wonderful about what he just did!!!!

"AAAAAAAAAAAAAAAAAAAAAAAAAAAAAAAAAAAAA!!!!!!!!!!!! FUCK YOU MOTHERFUCKERS!!!!!! TAKE THAT ASS-HOLES!!!!!" spit flying out of his mouth, and punches the seat with excitement!!!!!

He feels like he can walk on water!!!!!!!!!!

But there's one last thing to do.

He pulls the cellphone out of his pocket and dials nine-one-one.

The operator answers on the first ring.

"There's been a massacre in the basement of the Swimming Pig!
Be sure to bring back up…*You'll need it!*"
He throws the phone out the window!

Sept.

$\mathcal{O}$n the way home from visiting his beloved grandmother, a young man rides in his '92 Toyota Camry down I-72. He grins as he relives the day's events. The seventy three year old woman was once again making improvements to her home, her latest being installing new siding on the back of the house. To assist in the job she enlists the help of her favorite grandson. Ray leaped at the chance to help the person who's been like a mother to him. He laughed aloud as he passes Sparkman Dr. heading towards the I-431 junction. He can't believe she was dancing to that rap song. Her and her fanny pack and that measuring tape.

Ray exhales aloud, the mere thought of her takes his breath

away. "Granny" is by far his favorite person in the world. Through all his trials and tribulations, and bone head decisions, she stuck by him and always believed he would eventually turn it around and prove "all the turkeys wrong".

She ended up being right, he's finally gotten his life together and is on the track to greatness. He's graduated from college where he met the love of his life. They've since gotten married and have a new baby. His career in the engineering filed is blossoming well, and next month they'll be closing on their first home. After starting off bad, his life has made a drastic turnaround. He's thankful he had her to lean on when everyone else left him for dead. She always said it's how you finish that matters.
On the passenger seat, his cellphone signals an incoming call. Picking it up he smiles. It's his other favorite woman.
"What's up baby? I'm just about to be there."
On the other end she sounds afraid. With all the stuff going on right now, the bombing, the riots and protests, the hostage thing, the murders and stuff, and now just last week some guy goes in a restaurant and kills a bunch of "innocent" people "playing bingo", which also a doubled as a privately run "shelter for the homeless"; even being two hundred and fifty miles away from Atlanta in Huntsville, Ala., she's still on edge. Considering those things are happening in another state, he thinks she's being a little dramatic. Now she's asking if he can hurry home because there's a strange car circling the parking lot, adding when she and the baby came home there were two guys in a car watching her, and on top of that, her girlfriend a few buildings down said she saw the same car near her building too, and that the car has Georgia tags. She also said the girl and the child who recently moved in with the old lady upstairs has just gotten home too.
"Well make sure the door's locked. I'll be there in a minute, I'm like five minutes away. Just *hold* on. Papa's coming home baby,"

he jokingly replied.
She says okay and thanks him with a kiss.
He hangs up and tosses the phone on the seat.
Having a long and embattled history with the DMV because
of his need for speed, he knows he shouldn't do it. But already
in a great mood from the wonderful day with his grandmother,
and with the warm mountain air gushing in through the
windows; his wife just gave him an excuse to test the old 2.2L.
With only the weight of his 165lb. frame, the 2,600lb sedan
can move pretty good. Ray reaches and gives the volume some
love. Now the music in his ears has him feeling the groove.
65.....75.....85.....95.....105 MPH!

But before he knows, the fun is over and he has to get on the
brake. After getting off, he drives the few remaining miles
and turns into the complex. Even at ten thirteen on a Sunday
night, the first thing he sees is a group of men leaning on a car
drinking beer and smoking something. The sooner the closing
date comes the better.
Driving around back to their building, he pulls in beside the
fancy Mercedes their new neighbor drives. When he parks and
gets out looking around, he doesn't see any circling car. But he
does see the new girl and someone else sitting in the car talking. And it looks like one of them is on a cellphone.
He minds his business, and firms his grip on the lemon Jell-O®
cake his grandmother baked for him helping her today.
Coming through the door to the sounds of his barking dog and
his smiling wife, he puts the cake down and hugs her tightly,
his dog tugs at his pants with his tail wagging.
"I'm so glad you're home baby, I missed you. I was getting
scared."
"Well I'm here to protect you now so you don't have to worry."
And kisses her on the cheek.
He loves his wife immensely, but the cake is still warm, and his
mouth is watering.

He pulls away, and heads for the fridge.

"Where's my little buddy?"

"Oh he's sleep. I fed him and put him down for the night. I want to try to get some school work in before going to bed."

"When you become a pharmacist, I'm gonna kick back at the house and fish all day. Like this week, you know those crappies are on the bed right now. All they waiting for is a cricket and a hook. A good, five pound largemouth will be even better though really."

"You can go right ahead too baby. I can't wait to do some nice things for you. You work so hard for us, that's why I love you so much," she gushed. And sits on the couch.

"I wonder why that girl is always sitting in the car late at night talking on the phone?" he asked from the kitchen.

"I don't know...Why, you like her or something? I know you think she's pretty, you'll be lying if you say you don't," she joked.

"Yeah she's pretty, but I'm happy with you. Looking at that car she drives, she's not dealing with no regular guy like me anyway."

 "Oh okay, I was just checking. But to answer your question, maybe she doesn't want the lady she lives with in her business. She's probably her mother or something. Why, is she out there now?"

"Yep. Her and some other girl."

"Oh yeah?" and gets up to peek out the window.

Through the tint she sees two figures inside, turns away, and sits back down.

"You remember the time we went downtown and did the food drive for the homeless?" she asked.

"Yes," sitting a heaping slice of the cake on a plate.

"Well I don't know if I told you or not, but the lady told me the next day that she saw us taking the boxes of food to the car and asked if we work at a shelter or something. I told her we were going to a food drive, and she tells me she works with

battered women and abandoned youth. She said she's in
Atlanta a lot doing community work, and she goes into these
massage parlors and strip clubs and tries to find girls in need of
help. She also does a lot of humanitarian work here in
Huntsville too and asked if wanted to help."
"Well that sounds great. So what did you tell her?" and raises
the glass of milk to his lips.
"I told her I would love to he-"
POP-POP-POP-POP-POP-POP!!!!!!!!!!

He drops the glass!

BOOM-BOOM-BOOM!!!

She dives to the floor! The deafening sound of gun shots are
right outside their window!
The dog goes hysterical and runs to the window barking like
crazy!

POP-POP-POP-POP-POP-POP-POP!!!!!!!!!!!

Two figures run past their patio window, their front door, and
take off down the breezeway!
He runs for his gun!
The baby begins crying!!
She runs to the bedroom for her child!!!
The dog is still in the living room barking at the window when
he grabs his rifle and dashes to the other room!!!!!!!
"You okay! You okay! How's the baby! Is he hit?" looking at him
with his heart racing!!!
"No, no! He looks fine!" picking him up and feeling him all over,
wrapping him in a blanket!
He steers them into the bedroom!
"What the hell was that!" he exclaimed.
"I think they were shooting at the car with those girls in it! *Oh*

God I hope they didn't shoot those girls," she sobbed, tears up.
He runs to the window, looks out, and can see bullet holes in
the driver's side window and doors!
"You're right! They shot up the whole car!" his jaw hanging in
disbelief.
Tears well up in his eyes. The way they were firing he knows
those ladies are hurt.
"Oh, God no! Don't tell me they shot those girls, " cries his wife.
*"I knew something was up with that car!......I told you! I told
youuuuu-uh, "* she cried, and tries to look, but he blocks the
window.
"Come on baby," and sits her back down.
The dog is still barking!!!!!
Ray runs back up front and drags him from the window by his
collar, and pushes him in the bedroom!
He immediately goes to the other window and starts barking!
"Shhhhhhh Ram! Quiet boy! Hey! Quiet!...Ram!"
The dog finally stops, and sits down with his ears erect
growling at the window.
"Stay here till I get back! Ahma go see if they're okay! Call
nine-one-one!"
"Okay, but what if they're still out there?"
"I'll be okay! I just want to get to them and see if they're okay!"
"Okay baby. Please, be safe."
"I will!" and closes the door.
Ray goes down the hallway flipping off lights, cocks his rifle
and goes out the door!
The first thing he sees is the empty playground!
Looking around he doesn't see anyone else! He steps out and
makes for the car cautiously going to the driver's side! Through
the shattered window, he sees the driver leaned over in the
passenger seat with holes in her back, behind the seat the other
person on the floor not moving.
Residents are in windows looking out, people are beginning to
emerge.

Ray sees a man and woman coming his way.
"Call nine-one-one! Someone's been shot!" he yells.
They stop in their tracks and say something to each other.
Running back inside, he sits the rifle behind the door, and goes
back out. He can hear police sirens and more residents heading
out, and lights from the apartment upstairs come on.
With every person who views the damage, the more he knows
what he initially saw is all that he needs to see. It's clear there
are casualties.
He goes back inside and tells his wife everything is all bad, she
say she's not leaving the room until the police arrive. By the
time he kisses her and his son on the cheek, there's blue lights
and sirens in front of the unit. By the time he makes it to the
walkway, the lady upstairs is coming out. In the time it takes
the woman to make it down the stairs, an ambulance and
four squad cars are on the scene. One of the neighbors already
tipped the police that she may be the victim's mother.
It dawns on the older woman what happened, and she eagerly
tries to approach car, but is prevented by an officer from seeing
it.
When he sees the woman hang her head and begin weeping,
his fears are confirmed.

Several hours later he's exhausted from peeking through the
blinds with his gun, and pacing the floor. Ray goes to the
fridge and grabs a bottled water . At three hours from the time
he has to face Monday morning, he grabs his rifle and steps
outside.
Standing beside a tall bush he looks at the spot where the car
sat. The tow truck and police are gone, and strips of yellow
tape is still tied to his patio. People have already placed a me-

morial of flowers and candles on the ground. The story gathered so far, has one girl visiting Huntsville from Atlanta with her daughter when some guys shows up at the door asking the older woman if she's housing a woman and child. A few days later this other woman shows up saying she's going to help her get somewhere in Missouri she was apparently trying to get to. One of the victims was pronounced dead at the scene, and the other one was rushed to the hospital. The child has yet to be seen.

Ray raises the bottle to his mouth. Looking at the liquid drain into his throat he sees a light ray twinkle in the water. He lowers the bottle and turns his head just as a slow moving car is coming his way. He grips his rifle and ducks behind the bush! The slow moving car creeps up and stops in front of his building. The man inside rolls down the window, looks at the ground, and looks at the building. After sitting for several moments he pulls off.

An eerie feeling washes over him. The first signal his brain tells him is, that was the killer. From watching Lifetime® with his wife, he learned killers have a propensity for coming back to the scene and reliving the murder. Luckily, he was able to get the tag number as the sedan coasted by. The only other information he'll be able to tell police is that the car was a white Chrysler® 300.

Back in Atlanta, the attack on the two women doesn't even break into radio news cycle, better yet be mentioned on television; they have their own bundles of bad news to deliver. As bad as he didn't want to, Russell accepted the advice and took a three day vacation from law enforcement.
But now he's really pissed, to such a degree that he's made the

decision to do something drastic. He performed the same exercise he does before for making all major decisions; he slept on it. But the more he thinks about everything he's witnessing, the more encouraged he becomes. Being a spiritual man hasn't changed his belief in the validity of science, if anything it's increased it. The more he's learns about creation, the more he understands the Creator. He's also a student of advanced mathematics and numerology. In his theoretical statement, the theorems he uses to determine the sum of a man's morality deduces that: Integrity is an invariant coefficient that should not be lessened when faced with a complex problem.

In the face of the intense pressure the department is facing, the leadership is caving to outside demands. He knew something was up when he was "advised" not to testify at the preliminary hearing because it was considered a "conflict of interest". It made no sense. He's far too intelligent to believe that was the reason why. The other thing he finds odd is, in the midst of increasing protests, in wake of the bombing and hostage crisis, the shooting, and all the other troubles the force is facing; it was "strongly encouraged" he take a few days off to settle his mind.

But this stuff with the massacre at the restaurant is where he has to take a step back and ask himself, what is it that he's actually a part of? The fact the department engineered a blatant cover-up to mislead public about what really happened at The Swimming Pig, is wrong. Why not tell the truth? The citizens have a right to know a restaurant owned by an affiliate of Ed Denmark was a front for gambling and human trafficking. It infuriates him to know officers who took an oath to the protect the people of Atlanta, are now switching allegiances to side with a crook like Denmark. He's experiencing first hand why the name "White Man Ed" rings bells in Atlanta; the extent of his power on full display.

Earlier this week he requested a meeting with the chief, but with so much going on, he flaked him off. First instance he's ever done that. However, he did schedule a meeting with the assistant chief, the force's second in command; the young slickster who'd made a name for himself by cleaning up Detroit after the mess mayor Kilpatrick left. Nevertheless, he has his doubts. For starters, he never shows much affinity for police work, all he does is flaunt his degrees and special clearances. The way he chums up with the mayor and other ranking members of the legislative body, his public service is building relationships for his political aspirations, not being a police officer. He reminds him of a cheap car with fancy rims and shiny paint, there's more flash than actual substance.

Normally after working a long day's work, he comes home and tries to relax a bit, and does more work. Very seldom is he not doing something related to his duty; not his job, but his *duty*. But today he's not at home, he's still at the office, the same one he's been all day.

Warning! Warning! Warning! Warning! Warning!

Goes the shrill speaker malfunctioning in the elevator. Being his office is thirty from it, he can hear it each time it emits another false alarm that the doors are jammed. The maintenance team has been working all day to fix the problem, but at this juncture are still unsuccessful.

Today's paper is still on his desk. On the other side of his ajar door he can hear the voices and movements of other officers as they pass. The blather about Denmark is still a trending topic. On the front page is a satirical portrayal of a man in an orange suit locked behind bars; their response to the spoof published in Atlanta Magazine. Just like in theirs, this too features a cell with a bunk and cinder blocks. But sitting on the bottom of this bunk is another man in an orange suit. His is the face of Governor Yates, the man standing in front holding the bars is Ed Denmark. The piece goes on to highlight in stunning detail how Denmark's power and privilege propelled from the grips of a murder charge. The fact the editor named the APD's senior cabinet as being a significant cog in the broad reaching aim to protect Denmark bothered him greatly. People are now coming to him with questions, and looking at him suspiciously. But the facts included in the article are undeniable. The way in which the reporter slanted the scope conceptualizes the public's growing sentiment with the government and their lack of transparency. Included is a map of Atlanta showing all the properties owned, or affiliated with Denmark Enterprises L.L.C. Him being managing partner at Denmark & Perminter is nothing new, everyone knows about that. But they didn't know about Denmark Enterprises Inc., or all of his other DBA's, affiliations, shell companies, and partnerships. They didn't know he's the man behind L. Burgan Tussley Construction Inc., one of the largest land development firms in the South. They didn't know he's on the board of the banks they entrust with their money. They don't understand how he gets to meet the president, and are confused by all the bad things he's alleged to be involved in. It's no way Ed Denmark can possibly be guilty of the things this lady is insinuating. From drug smuggling, to arms dealing, to human trafficking, to extortion, to bribery, to tax evasion, to murder. They were shocked to know he represented Richford Chuld in his '90's acquittal involving the murder of a young screenwriter. They were just as shocked to hear allegations that Chuld later returned the favor by having an affair with Denmark's wife. The piece closes with statistics from the last hundred cases similar to Denmark's where all but one case was bound over for trial, which did nothing but add more kerosene to the anti-government blaze sweeping the land.

His office phone rings.
Hall takes the call from the deputy chief. He says he just got back in the office but isn't going to be in long, pierced if he wants to come meet with him, he has a minute to spare.
He accepts the invitation and hangs up.
After spending a minute or so gathering items, he locks the

door and exits. At the other end of the floor in the last office on the left is his. The door is open when he approaches.

'Office of the Deputy Chief, Dagan Lacy' is emblazoned on a brass plaque to the right of it. The APD's coat of arms is embossed across the top.

Lacy is sitting at his workstation with his back turned when he taps the side of the frame with his heavy hand.

He spins around in the chair.

And there go those unnaturally white teeth and that disingenuous smile.

"*Major Haaall,*" he sings.

And gets up extending his hand.

"All I hear is good things about you. It's a pleasure again major."

"The pleasure's all mines," but no smile.

Dagan isn't wearing a highly decorated uniform like he his, but a designer wool suit from overseas, and shoes far too expensive for a man on an officer's salary; even in a senior role. Not many officials are wearing Brunello Cucinelli® oxfords, especially to work.

"Thanks for having me. I see you're a busy man these days."

"Yes, yes. But come on in! Take a seat major."

Closing the door, he holds his arm to either of the chairs before his desk. And goes around to his side and pulls up his fat buttoned-leather one. His desk isn't sacked with files and swamped with spreadsheets like his. But clean and organized with a fancy gold pen.

"I'm just getting back from a meeting with the regional director of the DHS. I apologize for not being able to get to you sooner. The chief sends his apologies for not being able to see you as well; he asked me to pass that to you."

"No apologies needed."

"Well thank you...So, how've things been? Looks like the

time off gave you time to sharpen the ole' blade. You look refreshed."

Lacy's the one who suggested he take a few days off, using a non-compulsory departmental policy as his scapegoat.

"It did indeed…Not to spend too much of your time, I'd like to get your take on a few things."

"Okay," Lacy said, putting on his game face.

"One of the things I'd like to discuss, is a recent submission concerning a review of my budget proposal for the fourth quarter. I received an email stating it's under third party review for revisions. In my tenure as major chief of staff, my determinations were until this point final. I'd like to request a formal explanation for this action. These cuts will have undesirable impact on officer safety. Another-…"

"Excuse me major if I may interrupt. Allow me to answer your first question……As you know, the department's under heavy duress right now. We're being attacked from all angles, by the media, by the public, and even our own damn officials. I am aware you requested to speak with the chief, but it was me who asked him if I may take his place and meet with you instead. Being I work closely with our chief, I saw an opportunity to lessen the load while at the same time getting to know more about my fellow men. What has it been major, a year almost? I think we've maybe only spoken three times. I see how much the men love and revere you and wanted to reach out, and see if there's a chance for me to get to know more about your strategies and experiences as an APD officer. I also want to say I was impressed to hear how integral you were in cleaning up the Red Dog task force. But to answer your original question, the chief ordered me to find a way to trim one point seven million off the budget. I'm the one who suggested the changes to your proposal, not the chief………"

While Dagan goes on about his opinion of his numbers and his desire to protect the department, Hall is taking it all in. Never before has the chief sent messages to him through another person, and can't recall a time when the chief didn't trust his numbers; to such a point he gave them to another person to review. He knows the chief is under pressure, but never before has he seemed so unavailable; especially in a time of crisis. This is usually a time when they close ranks, and congeal as a team; not splinter and fight on separate fronts. Being a very wise man, much wiser than most, he knows the chief is a good man and it's obvious his subordinate is having an influence on his judgement. Lacy, with his fast talk and fake smile can fool a lot of people. But if he thinks it'll work on him, he's wrong. He didn't miss how he buttered him up with complements before getting to the real reason for wanting to meet him either.

"….You know major, I must admit, you're not like other men I've met."
"Thank you for the complement. But I'd like to know what you think of Ed Denmark?"
"*Aaaaaaaaaaaaah*…Ed Denmark, White Man Ed, The Grey Russian, The Denmark Jew. I've heard them all," he sighed.
Hall watches him closely.
Lacy leans in his chair and crosses his arms.
"I think this city has a fascination with this guy. I think it's some make-believe obsession people have here. It must be something in the Georgia air that lulls people into this fairy-tale world. Maybe that's why you have your, Margret Mitchells, your Paul Hemphills, your Harrison Charles', and your Gone with the Winds; some of the world's greatest literature comes from here. People down here love enchantment. And I think he's just the latest victim of their love of mystery. I think until he's convicted of a crime, people should hold their judgment……………People become imperiled by their conviction in what it is that they believe," and pauses a second to reach inside his desk.
While waiting for him to reveal what it is, Hall replied:

"They certainty do."

Lacy sits an old rusty hex-bolt atop his desk. It's the size of a man's index finger. The threads are corroded and damaged, and chucks are missing, and it's leaning like the Tower of Pisa as it sits on its chipped head.

"Do you mind if I share something with you major?"

"Do."

"I not sure if I told you, or you know or not, but I was born in Detroit, Michigan. My father was a factory worker at a battery plant and my mother worked as a receptionist at Dana Communications. I had an uncle who was heavily into drugs, would come to our home and steal things to support his habit. One day he stole my mother's finest china and silverware. She got so furious she threatened to shoot him if he ever came back into our home. But my father being a church deacon, said *no*,.........he's a good man, he knoweth not what he do.....He repeatedly came back and stole from us, and ultimately ended up killing my father when he shot him dead for his wallet as he stood in the driveway of his own home holding the Holy Bible. This sole event pushed me to want to be in law enforcement, I wanted to make a difference......When I got older I joined the Detroit PD, going into it with this save the world mentality with the idea that I could right all the world's wrongs; believing that I alone could prevent any other boy from losing their father the way I had........After about four years on the force, I'll never forget. It was this cold winter night, *blisteringly* cold. We'd just had this big snowfall the day before, and about three in the morning I get a call about a man reporting to have found a young girl in a storm drain—bleeding and unconscious, but possibly alive. So I race to the scene speeding across snow and ice so I could get there and save this girl's life. When I do, the man who called has somehow taken up this steel grate up that weighed hundreds of pounds, and pulled her out. We later find out she'd been raped and stabbed multiple times in an abandoned house across the street, and dumped with the hopes of being washed away. The girl ends up surviving luckily. I was so captivated by this gentlemen's heroic effort, that I kept one of the bolts he removed from the grate. A decade later, I hear this same man is poisoned to death by his wife who said he was a shithead felon who dealt drugs, shot people, and was the worst person she's ever met……..As you may suspect, this incident greatly affected my outlook on life major…..How we chose to look at a person has nothing to do with who they actually are. Belief can be a dangerous thing my friend."

And picks up the bolt, tapping it on the desk.

"I'm reminded of it every time I look at this."

"That it a gripping story. I'm pleased to know the victim pulled through. But if I may speak candidly."

"I would expect nothing less," Lacy replied.

"You've made a true reference, but I think the result should be the focus, rather than the person. In my experience, the conclusion is more important the beginning………..I was once at a home where there was a dispute between a gay couple, the next door neighbor, and a social worker. The neighbor violated a court order to stay away from the couple by attacking the social worker who came to check on the teenaged foster child living with them. Her argument was that she didn't think the state should allow gay couples to adopt kids, and would become enraged every time she saw something her religious values disagreed with. I explained to the woman that though she may not agree with their sexual preference, the home with the gay couple is better than a state facility, explaining that many of these youth are living on the streets, and just like straight and singles; gay couples too have giving hearts and seek to better the lives of others. I knew I could get into hot water for discussing this subject with a civilian, but I felt this fell directly under an officer serving his community. Like I tell my men and women, often times too much emphasis is placed on the source of the help, and not on the appreciation that help has been offered, and that a persons, color, creed, nationality, religious

affiliation, or sexual preference shouldn't outweigh a person's contributions; as long as there are just. As long as there are honorable. Because the gentlemen became a felon doesn't erase the fact that he saved the girl. Just like I teach all my detectives, when investigating a crimes, good results are what we're after."
"So who determines what's honorable and just...Your beliefs?"
"The result determine what is just. The honor comes from the outcome.... A belief is an asshole. They stink and they're everywhere!"
"Well major, I'm glad you brought that up. Since I see you're a man of insight, I'd like to know your opinion on something... Let's just say for the sake of conversation you're hanging off a cliff. Below you is imminent death...."

Warning! Warning! Warning! Warning! Warning!

Goes the alarm in this distance, the timing uncannily coincidental!

Lacy hears it too, pauses for a moment, and continues over the noise.
"You're hanging off a cliff and beneath you is imminent death. You look up to see a hand appear, but it's the hand of Satan. Do you reach out and let him pull you to safety, or do you stay there and fall to your death?"
Hall imagines the scene. He in a fit of desperation about to fall into a bottomless valley.......But he notices something watching from afar.....A winged being radiating light floating in the clouds!
"I face my fate."
"...That's a little contradictory major?"
"Well that's your belief."
Lacy is quiet. The warning alarm stops.
"I believe Mr. Denmark is innocent until proven guilty in a court of law. I think he's do his constitutional right just like

any another American citizen. Do you have some new information you would like to share major?"
He did, but not anymore.
"I have other issues to discuss, he's not the reason for my request. I just wanted to know your professional opinion."
"Well I just thought I should ask…..Let's just cut to the chase major. You didn't come in here to discuss a budget. You probably don't like the cuts I made, but that's not all. But since you inquired, we're running low on money and the mayor's on everybody's back. But you're really here because you want to know why we're not telling the real story to the public about the restaurant massacre. That's the real reason you hung around all afternoon until I got back…I'm a thinking man as well major…The chief was right when he said you're going to want an explanation, and after the service you've given the force, I don't blame you. You're not the only person around here wondering…..Now follow me closely here Hall. I know you and I may not have always had the same vision for this department, and at times have conflicting agendas. But for a second put aside whatever dislike you may have of me, and what you *think* I represent. This matter with Denmark is *no touch*, I mean hands *off.* Not one word of this leaves this room. I'm serious as can be Hall. This entire investigation has been taken out of our hands by the attorney general. We're getting orders to shelve it completely and let the Feds take over."
"Orders from who," Hall spoke.
"Orders from Washington!"
The room is relatively silent while he lets that soak.
He continues.
"The day after the hearing, they came and seized every shred of evidence we had. His lawyers were at the courthouse trying to get the transcripts from the hearing destroyed after successfully getting the entries on his record expunged. That's all I know. From this point forward you are not to not comment on any questions regarding Ed Denmark. This is from the chief….I

want to pin his ass just as much as you Hall. I'm not blind major, I know that where there's smoke there's fire. But at this point, until we get something rock solid, we're just sticking our thumbs up our ass."

From a vantage position approximately fifty meters from the target, he watches him through high powered binoculars. The target has just gotten out of his car and is heading inside. The warrantless search of the property revealed nothing abnormal. It showed the reclusive existence of a lonely single man living the honest life of a dedicated police officer, not a shred of contraband was found. They found no evidence of illegal activities, but a listening device was installed inside the Wi-Fi modem anyway; his computers raided and scrubbed. To prevent him from detecting foul play, a virus made to look like its operating system has crashed, was loaded into the hard drive. While his service vehicle was in the shop for routine maintenance, a GPS tacking sensor was placed inside the muffler, and the number to his department issued cellular phone was placed under 24-hour surveillance.

The expert in advanced surveillance techniques watches Hall go through the door and enter his home, and is watching to see if he notices any signs of a break-in. Once he goes into the restroom and prepares to take a shower, the reconnaissance mission is ended.
The day has been a success, they achieved all they set out to. Now he would return the material to his superior and await further instructions.
He climbs down from his blind and returns to his vehicle.

Once inside, he extracts the phone and makes the call.
"It's done. I have all the materials you require. Where shall I meet you my lord?"
The person gives him an address and thanks him for his service to his country.
"It is an honor my lord. I'll arrive at the location as instructed."
And waits for "his lord" to hang up.

Though he's a foreign agent, he traverses the city like a life-long resident. He's not a diplomat but does have immunity.

The target lives in a gated community in expensive East Cobb. The meeting with his associate is to be off Collier Rd, In twenty eight minutes he's there. Within walking distance of Brookwood Square, with its breathtaking views of Ardmore Park, is an old English style mansion. The manicured kudzu growing over the estate makes it lush with sophistication. The guard at the entrance is expecting his arrival, and upon recognizing the symbol, is permitted entry. From the street, all passerbys can see is a gate with two concrete pillars, a stone mailbox, and a call box. Behind the gate a driveway leads between a section of trees. Coming upon the main house is quite an intimidating experience for first time visitors. With a cobblestone drive way and separate guest parking area, the owner of the home showcases his sense of taste, while at the same time exhibiting his wealth. Beside the water fountain in the center of the circle, a valet opens the door.

Familiar with the procedure the driver puts the car in park and gets out. Waiting in the cut is a black Maybach 62 with the rear curtain drawn. The valet gets inside his vehicle and pulls it forward to the guest area.
As he heads towards the hulking sedan, the driver gets out and opens the rear door.

He nods and slips inside.
Wasting no time, he hands him the material.
The man opens it, and takes a visual inspection of the items.
On the back of the front passenger seat is a data center. He
spends a few seconds inputting information and waits.
He still hasn't spoken to his guest.
The laptop on his retractable desk flashes and beeps
something.
He responds by punching something back.
On the burl wood console between the two front seats, a
printer/fax/scanner/copier is built into the lap of luxury. Out
of it comes a document.
He hands it to him.
He doesn't read it in his lord's presence, so he just holds it.
The man punches a code into a nondescript keypad to the right
of his knee, and a small safe opens.
"Your payment has been delivered."
"It's been a pleasure to serve you my lord."
"Your sacrifices will not be forgotten."
He doesn't twitch a muscle while looking at the low ranker,
which means it's time for him to leave.
He hops out and heads back to his vehicle.

When the driver gets back inside, the lord reaches into his
fridge and extracts a can of Russian sturgeon caviar; the most
elite natural delicacy available on the modern culinary market
today. As he prepares his tiny plastic spoon to scoop out the
salty gelatinous black pearls, he notifies his attendant.
"Tell him we're ready."
"Yes sir."
He takes the spoon, digs out approximately twenty eggs,
puts them inside, and rolls his tongue towards the roof of his
mouth, bursting them like oceanic grapes. While enjoying the
satin finish of the savory roe, three men show up outside the
car. One man opens the door, other watches, and the last one

gets in. The man who was watching, comes around the hood and gets in the driver's seat.

The man sitting behind the passenger seat raises the partition. The big sedan rolls into gear and in seconds they were off. The ride is akin to a luxury hotel being inside a spaceship.

"So how was your visit? Did you enjoy yourself?" asked the power broker.

"It was excellent, I really enjoyed the evening. The estate was unbelievable, I've never seen anything like it."

"Well great. I assume you were treated well?"

"I've never been treated better sir, thank you."

He too has material to share, having already spent the day sharing it with the influential men inside the mansion. Now he's going to personally visit "The Ruppell's Nest" and speak to the doyen master himself. Hopefully the material will reaffirm what he's already shared with the parliament.

"Would you care for some?"

"No sir. Thank you," replied the inside man.

"You seem tense."

"No. I'm just trying to make sure everything is in order. I don't have anything to be afraid of."

"*Oh*. But you should. We should all be afraid of something."

"The only thing I'm afraid of is poverty. The quickest way to a billion is the route for me."

"I *see!* Is that why you got into the judicial sector? Is that where you think your *billions* lie?"

"I guess you can say that. I realized when I was in college that those who control the laws, control the money."

"...We all like our control don't we," he smiles.

And takes another spoon of the thousand dollar an oz. beluga sturgeon eggs.

Returning to the workstation back to its idle position, he reclines the seat eight inches. For the rest of the ride the man with the crossed legs and manicured nails enjoys his caviar and vintage melodies. On the 17in. LCD screen below the privacy partition is a concert being performed by the late composer Marvin Hamlisch; the suspenseful piano and outstanding orchestra crisp and harmonious. The treble's perfect setting is showcased in the flute, a cymbal chimes repetitiously like an African casaba, violins whine and purr to elegant highs. Blissful lows bring the bottom out of the trombones, while tubas thunder like lightning strikes.

The white, hand-stitched nappa leather smells distinctive. Completely overwhelmed is the guest with palatial elegance.

The house and the property were more than ever imagined. He's always pictured himself becoming a giant in the world. And now here he is rubbing shoulders with colossal figures— sitting in the cabin of a half million dollar

flagship on his way to meet the ruling tyrant himself. He's being treated like a specially invited guest, and even allowed to eat at the table with them. All they want is certainty that the information he provides is always comprehensive and precise. In turn they'll open doors he'll never be able to get through on his own. He has big dreams and high hopes on sitting on Capitol Hill, and knows this small cost will return big dividends, which will hopefully increase throughout the life of the partnership. His father was nice guy, but his brother was a wise guy. He always told him, whatever he chooses to be—be the best at it. In this world you're either a shark or a guppy, but you can't be both. He remembers how as a boy he would make him watch him slaughter a lamb, saying that if he wants to eat meat, he must pay the price for enjoying it. He must be able to stomach the blood and guts of the kill if he wants to enjoy the flavor of the loin. A lion must sometimes take a wounded calf if that's all he can get. He taught him to not look at life in terms of right and wrong, but in terms of instinct and survival; saying when he becomes a man, if he wants to have the quality of life that conveys might, prestige, and achievement, he must learn to consume men in his quest. If a man isn't willing to see the carcasses of those he's devoured, he shouldn't make wealth his pursuit.

So here today as an early forties man, he has no conscience for what he's doing. He doesn't care that it may destroy careers, he doesn't care if lives are lost. All he knows is that he's worked long and hard to get where he is, and is now in a position where he has a shot at the big time.

When the car comes to a halt, he notices they've pulled into the main entrance of the Westin Peachtree Plaza, but the black Maybach doesn't stop, it eases past the crowds of taxis, shuttles and tourists of average people, and slips around to a dimly lit driveway into the secluded VIP entrance. The security guard at the booth seeing the sticker on the windshield opens the gate. The lord picks up a phone in the console.
"Inform him that his guest has arrived and is on his way up."
And places it back.
"It's been a pleasure speaking with you again. I hope you've enjoyed your evening. A gentleman will be arriving to escort you to your appointment. Thank you again for gifting us with your company. It was most enjoyable."
And holds out his hand.
He takes it and is shocked by how cold and hard it is. It feels like holding a dead snake.
"I'm the one who's been treated. Thank *you* sir for the welcome you've shown me today," replying with that big counterfeit smile.
A suited gentlemen appears and opens the door.
He nods, grabs his briefcase and gets out.
"Remember. We shall all be afraid of something my dear boy."
And signals his assistant to close the door.

Called him a boy.

He's quickly enveloped by the cool night air, much different
than the controlled confines of the heavily tinted 62.
As he's escorted through the pair of sliding glass doors, the big
Benz pulls away. His oxfords click across the marble floor. The
cognac colored walls are accented with gold tones and dark
woods. Passing through another set of doors, he's in a large
mezzanine. An opulent bar spanning three floors hangs to the
side of the atrium like a Spider Man of sparkling granite. Up
ahead he sees a walkway with a pole and a rope across it. It's
near the entrance to the expansive bar, but secluded; there but
hidden.
Two gentlemen in suits stand guard. One steps forward and
drops the rope as they approach.
Once the guest has been escorted to this point, the other
gentleman turns back.

The *Westin Peachtree Plaza* is a lavish, seventy three story
auberge known for its mirrored glass finish, luxurious
amenities, upscale clientele, and fine dining. For connoisseurs
of stunning French cuisine, it hosts a three-star Michelin
restaurant ready to cater to their palate. An attraction of
residents and tourists alike, is the elevator that runs in a glass
shaft up the outside of the skyscraper. From the ground level to
the top, the ride takes about eighty five seconds, and has been
known the induce labor and trigger seizures. So warnings are
now posted to inform riders of the risks.
But that was in the late 90's. It's since been upgraded 21st century style. The single, box shaped car is gone. Now three sleek,
bullet shaped cars hurl passengers from base to peak in half
that time. An operator is on each car, and there are no more
free rides. If they don't have a room at the hotel, or a reserva-
tion at the restaurant, there's a fee of twenty five dollars per
person.

One of the gentleman enters the elevator with him while the other one stays. The operator inside says nothing.

The doors close.

The guest isn't new to the state, he knows about the hotel because it's the tallest building in the city. It's on every post card of Atlanta; you can't help but see it. But he's never visited or heard of the popular elevator and restaurant at the top. If he had, he would've certainly objected to this means of travel. For those desiring a less thrilling experience, there's several traditional elevators available throughout the hotel.

The carpeted floor is thick and soft, the glass is clean and void of fingerprints, the brass rails are sturdy and polished. In the dim light he sees the reflection of the man standing beside him. The car begins rising—a torpedo out of a cannon; the balconies and windows woosh past his face in blurs of color! He sees the roof of the lower structure!

Like a rocket into the stars, the lights of the city rise like a wave around him; his heart almost stops! He grabs the rail, terrified of heights!!

The escort grabs and steadies him.

It's akin to having to endure the load of a person crushing you into the ground while more and more people join! The higher it goes, the harder he breathes! He sees the tops of buildings that keep getting smaller!

The elevator operator turns and looks at him.

He thinks he's hallucinating when he sees an enormous stone mountain in the distance! The car is moving so fast that he knows he's about to embarrass himself out of an opportunity! He fights to keep it together so he won't look so weak! But the more he wished for it to stop, the more it keeps climbing, reaching higher and higher! It's the most nauseating pressure he's felt in his life!

His uncles' words ring in his head!

He takes a hard dry swallow and pushes his mind to will his body to keep its food down!

Like a slowing turbine, the car eases to and silky smooth stop.
The doors open like nothing ever happened.

When the hand in the small of his back ushers him forward,
he's sweating and nervous!
That will probably go down as one of the worst experiences
ever!
Looking around, he's standing on an overhang looking down at
the people eating, he looks at the seats above, and around. He's
in *The Sundial*, a restaurant sitting seven hundred and twenty-
three feet above the city, which gifts guests with extraordinary
views of the skyline while they dine from a four-star menu.
At first he thinks he's about to lose consciousness when he
notices the room is moving!
But it's actually the floor of the lower seating area. While customers eat it rotates the entire time, giving them 360° sights of
downtown Atlanta.
He's escorted around on a path hanging too close to the tall
panel windows, through which he sees the blinking lights of
a helicopter. Up a set of velvety stairs a man is standing at the
corner of a hallway. There's no ropes or crowd control stands,
only a man in a suit.
He nods to the gentleman with him.
"Right this way sir," said his new escort.
He clutches his material and follows the man down the low
hanging passageway. At the end of a corner, the escort stops
and holds out his arm halting him. He can't see around the yet,
but when he does, he's in a small vestibule. His heart flutters
when he sees another set of elevator doors! But the man standing in front of them is more frightening than any man he's ever
laid eyes on!
He looks seven feet tall, and every bit of four hundred
pounds!!! He's shocked by his mass!!!! The menacing look of
those shades and that suit is utterly terrifying!!!!
For the first time today, he's beginning to question his

decision to do this. At this very moment he grasps the magnitude of the game he chose to play, and begins feeling woefully inadequate. The material in his hand isn't giving him the comfort it once did. The Hulk-like man approaches and stares him down. In less than a second he's forced to look away, cowered be the close proximity of this elephantine being.

He takes his briefcase and runs a wand over it. It beeps green twice, gives it back to him, and taps his watch.

"Abu, your guest is here," notified the beastly tone.

He looks around and is glad to see no more clouds. He wipes the sweat from his brow.

"He's ready to see you," and moves towards the elevator.

With a press of the button the door opens, the mammalian gives him the eye.

He immediately steps forward, wondering what other surprises are in store. He expects the man to get inside and smash him into the wall, but he doesn't get on. He presses a button on the outside and the door shuts.

Feeling the rise of motion and slight jolt in his stomach, he prepares his mind for another hellacious ride.

But just as quick as it begins, it's over.

The door opens.

His heart drops again when the first thing he sees is the sky!

Stepping onto fawn colored carpet that swallows his shoes, to his left is an exquisitely paneled wall; the design is flawlessly executed.

To his right are windows overlooking the city. He can hear the sound of the sky and smell the aroma of outside air. The hiss of brisk wind and the accelerated breeze tells him this room is open to the elements!

What the fuck am I doing!

The sound of a fork hitting ceramic reverberates of the glass.

He's rocked with fear when he realizes he's standing on the very top of a metropolitan city!!

He gets light-headed and thinks he's about to faint!!!

But wills himself to pull it together out of fear of dying if he passes out. Surely, no one's going to resuscitate him. It's not that type of party. After a few deep breaths, he continues on. There's three tables covered with white table cloths, but only a single person dines.

In the far table he sits. With one leg crossed over the other, his hands are clasped on his lap. There's a dark uncorked bottle, and a gold rimmed wine glass waiting at the side of his elbow. His shoes were handmade in Italy, and took four months to craft. The fabric of his three-piece suit is of the finest money can buy. Ultra-rare Super 200 Australian merino wool, isn't for lasting durability. It's for the ultimate in comfort and distinction, and not ideal for frequent use.

The timepiece on his wrist retails for $1.9 million, but isn't dripping in diamonds and gold—hewn from silicon, a material half the weight of titanium, yet four times harder.

He doesn't get up to welcome his guest, only smiles and extends his palm towards a seat at his table.

"I'm glad you could make it. Your trip went well I assume."

"Yes," clear his throat. "Yes," flattened by the being before him. He still hasn't gotten back right, and is still taking in the extreme height and close proximity to death.

Knowing he's trying to pretend he doesn't see what's on the table, the figure looks into him. He's used to having this effect on men; cowering mere mortals by his presence. He breaks men's spirit without saying a single word.

"Would you like to taste?"

"No sir. Thank you. Your people have feed me well."

"Well good."

He keeps trying not to stare, but he knows it's bothering him. This is all part of his mind game. He takes his time studying the man, and sees he has decent style, and has made an honest effort at impressing him. He sees the entry level Rado® peering from under his sleeve. With the rush of the wind whistling and gusting around them, he sees how he's making every attempt at avoiding his gaze.

He dislikes this.

"Would you like to know what it is?"

For a moment he plays like he didn't know what he's referring to.

"*Oh*. You mean the food? I was kind-of wondering what it is. My first thought was snake, but I don't think that's correct."

Denmark smirks sarcastically, and picks up the utensils.

"...Do you take me as one who enjoys the taste of serpent?"

His heart flutters, he didn't mean to offend him! Heat creeps up his collar like a rouge space heater! Now he meets his piercing stare.

"Well no,...I was just assuming it's a possibility but was uncertain. That's why I didn't mention it."

He keeps watching him, and looks down to the forks the meat curled in the bowl.

"While visiting the Far East I became accustomed to its health benefits. The consumption of tiger penis soup has been proven to aid the increase of cerebral function."

In Asia, as well as across the world, tigers are considered endangered species, but are still illegal poached and sold on the black market as a sought-after delicacy and medicinal item.

"Oh!....I've never heard that. I would assume it's an acquired taste?"

He cuts a piece of the phallus accentuated with ginseng and ginger root.

The visitor is able to discern the other dish is an egg, but the shell is leathery, and is not of the 'Grade A' variety.

A Filipino delicacy called *'Balut'*, which is a fertilized egg— "usually" from a duck or chicken—that has an almost-developed embryo. It's boiled and eaten right out of the shell.

"Or an innate thirst," Denmark alluded.

He pauses to look to his left at the stainless-steel framing, and the thick Plexiglas® slabs of the penthouse hideout that is "The Ruppell's Nest". The vaulted ceiling, the colored carpet, the hardwoods, are all expertly crafted to convey the pinnacle of luxury.
"This is a very impressive sitting area you have here. It's quite captivating. It gives the sensation of a man on top of the world—a man at the peak of his game. I can see why a man of your caliber would enjoy a place like this."

Ed Denmark is a rude individual, but also very perceptive. He places the fork and knife down, and using his bare hands slides the dish with the egg in front of him, and pushes the soup aside. Taking it in his fingertips he speaks.
"So what caliber of man do you fancy me?"

He prides himself on being a fast talker and a fast thinker, but he's outmatched. He keeps trying to hold his stare but every time he looks into his eyes, it's like a bayonet goring his pupils. He can stare at the sun longer than he can look at the being siting across the table.
Atop the surround buildings are blinking lights and antennas. He looks at him again; it's similar to riding a wild bull. If he can last eight seconds, he's achieved something.
"Honestly sir, all I know is what I've heard. I haven't been privileged with the chance to meet you, so I can only go by what I see. And to me you seem like a man who appreciates quality."
Denmark responds by cracking the egg. Inside is the grotesque, dark colored fetus, of a giant ibis boiled in coca plant and duck stock.

The '*Giant ibis*' has been declared the most endangered and evolutionarily distinctive bird on the face of the earth. Native to the marshes, rivers, and seasonal water meadows of Northern Cambodia, this is known as the world's rarest bird.

The guest watches in repulsion as Denmark takes his three fingers, pulls the lump of flesh from the shell, and put it into his mouth. When he sees a drip of the juice seep out of the corner of his mouth, he almost pukes, but holds the hot acid reflux in his mouth, knowing it will be bad on so many levels to let it out.

Denmark takes a cloth napkin and dabs his mouth. Once he'd finished savoring the pungent flavor of the bits of embryo rolling around in his mouth, he speaks: "I'm a man who also appreciates trustworthiness."
"You can trust me Mr. Denmark. I'm honestly a decent person you can depend on."
He doesn't immediately speak.

"You excogitate yourself an honest man do you?"

"I would say so."

"...Well why are you here with sensitive information you've filched from your employer?"

The question catches him off guard! A blind kick to the face! Denmark sees the pulse thumping on his neck.

The guest thought he had his fear of height under control until he imagines the big gorilla bursting through the door and throwing him off the roof! Unconsciously, he takes his hand and loosens his collar.

"Loyalty will take you farther than honesty ever will. I could give two fucks about honesty....Men die over loyalty."

"Yes sir," was all he said.

Denmark pours himself a glass of
Domaine de la Romanee-Conti Montrachet Grand Cru, Cote de Beaune, France.
Swirling the white wine around in the glass, he teases his nose with the multi-dimensional aromas of honey, graphite, pear, pineapple, orange peel, and vanilla. Out of a compartment hidden in the wall, he retrieves his burning instrument, and sits it on the table. He takes a sip.

The water pipe atop the table cloth is made from a gourd found in the mountains of Kathmandu. The neck is made from the antler of a Yak, and the mouthpiece from the hollowed tooth of an Amazonian payara.

Ed takes the book of matches and strikes one.

As the smell of sulfur and prosperous prickle his nose, he watches Denmark grab the bizarre water pipe, lights it, takes a pull, and inhales deeply.
Sitting it back on the table he releases the smoke.
The guest is a connoisseur of cannabis himself, but the stuff he has is like tear gas. It gets hard to breathe, the potent odor is unlike any marijuana he's ever smelled. He's thankful the wind blew, and took the fog out.

But what he's smelling is not pot, but it what 18[th.] century Ottomans referred to as: The drug which enhances the art of alchemists: Opium, fresh from Burma.

Denmark returns his hand to clasped on his lap and his leg

back crossed.

"You would have been correct had you quantified me as one who enjoys serpent...My favorite is the Blue Krait...You remind me of one in many ways.

He pauses to hit the Burmese opium again.

"...They are the most deadly species in Asia and Indonesia, known hunters and killers of other snakes; even cannibalizing their own....They are a nocturnal breed, and are only aggressive under the cover of darkness. *However*, they are quite *timid*, and will often attempt to hide rather than fight...You will be contacted if your services are deemed useful. Be sure not to forget your briefcase."

Speechless!

His brain hasn't triggered his body to get up—armpits awash in perspiration, he's not comprehending what he just said meant leave.
No sooner than Ed grabs the pipe, and is about to light it again, the elevator door opens, and out comes the behemoth. He jumps to his feet so fast that he accidentally bumps the table!
"Thank you very much for the evening sir. I hope you find my offer useful and know that it will not only be me who will be at your beg and call, but my vast network of contributors who are in key positions as well...And again, thank you Mr. Denmark for the wonderful evening sir."
And turns and walks away before the behemoth has a chance to put his behemoth hand on his shoulder.
Now comes the mounting anxiety and terror from remembering he has to ride that elevator back down!!

Huit.

Things are going just as Kam had foreseen. Instead of being lauded as the man who brought down Ed Denmark, he's being lampooned as the man who floundered; viewed with sympathy, pity, and repugnance. People keep patting him on the back with words of encouragement, others whisper when they see him; everywhere he looks there's eyes staring at him. Unable to take any more, he left the office and went to the law library to research case files. Even there he was getting stares, and had to find a seat in the corner of the third floor just to find peace. By the time he got home, his kids were glad to see him, and later made passionate love to his wife.

The following morning starts with the sight of her in his arms

and the bright rays of the sun steaming through the curtains.
After preparing a delicious breakfast, he and the family sat
on the patio and ate together. Currently pushing 8:57, he has
court at nine, but has just gotten to the office. Lucky for him
traffic was abnormally light, or he wouldn't be here yet. Along
the way he kept receiving calls and texts, but due to his phones
lack of a charge, he was unable to talk text and drive. The
vibration from the last message killed it, and it hasn't recharged
enough to where he can use it while being plugged in.

So making it to his office, the first thing he does is sit his things
down, plug it up, and try not to draw attention to himself.
He's the Asian running back who fumbled the case against Ed
Denmark.
He goes into the file cabinet behind his desk and unlocks it, he
needs to hurry because he has morning arraignment. Stepping
forward he turns his computer on, selects the file, and shuts
the cabinet. He hears the tune of the smartphone powering up,
and looks at his watch, and takes a minute to check his email.
The sound of another message.
Irritated he sighs, spins in the chair, and snatches it up. There's
seventeen messages in total, five voicemails and the rest texts.
He opens his incoming text folder and sees mostly messages
from his co-workers. He clicks the one from Myra Keith, who
is asking about the link she set him? The next one asks whether
he's seen the new story about Denmark in the Creative Loafing
that everyone's talking about?
He closes that one and scrolls through the others. They're all
referencing this same article.
Just two days ago the Atlanta Journal and Constitution article
was tearing up the airwaves, now this. His day is starting off
bad again. The sick feeling in the pit of his stomach returns.

The Creative Loafing, the city's second team news source, it too
has millions of readers and a loyal following. But they represent

the urban Atlantans, the art and technology community, the
cool kids who invent things, and smoke doobies before and after college exams, the people likely to date outside of their race
who don't care much for religion. They cater to the opposite
of what the AJC does, and are known to be edgy controver-
sial and pioneering. Not wanting to be bested by their rival,
Creative Loafing runs their own feature on Ed Denmark. Staying true to their nature, they do it a little differently though.
Instead of putting the face of Denmark on the face of a man
inside a cell wearing an orange jumpsuit, they put *him* on the
front of their weekly paper. Copying from the theme of a notorious, real-life gangster from the 70's, whom they purposely
didn't mention; is Ed Denmark *himself* on the cover. In his best
suit and coldest stare, depicted as being Godzilla standing over
the city. The word '*Untouchable*' is in bold black letters across
the top. The paper offered him a hundred thousand dollars to
do the photo, but he agreed to do it for free once he saw the
finished product.
In the article, the writer used the fable of: Powerful attorney
and businessman Denmark being an undercover crime boss, as
the carrot for reader's appetites. They highlighted all the
unsavory stories the AJC chose to omit. They pushed hard on
the elitist conspiracy theories. They dug up profits sources the
other papers and magazines couldn't find. They located former
associates who said things other's hadn't.

By the time Kam reads the article it's nine twenty-one, and the
clerk is calling him from courtroom 5C telling him the judge is
about to take the bench.
But he's at a loss for words, but snaps out of it, grabs his things,
and dashes for the door.

He makes it to the courthouse next door by the time the judge
takes the bench. He's there, but just to get it over with; literally
just going through the motions. The moment they recessed, he

was mobbed by the lawyers of clients who'd been waiting all morning to speak with him.

By the time he makes it back home, he's certain that if he could go back, he would've never accepted the responsibility of trying the case. On the days he's home by seven he usually catches the ABC World News. He's already missed the top story but has a chance to catch the start of the next one. His daughter is looking in his ear with her plastic otoscope wearing a Doctor McStuffins outfit. His son, dressed as a WWE wrestler is trying to put his leg in an arm lock. That's when he sees the image of the magazine cover to the right of the anchorman's head. While his kids use him for a lab specimen and a training dummy, he watches as the story from the Creative Loafing is broadcast worldwide. Included is a clip of him in the court-room after the case got dismissed, followed by a clip of the statement he gave to the media afterwards. Also highlighted is the vast wealth and influence Denmark commands. The story ends with an excerpt and the image of the Denmark towering over Atlanta.

"If the wrong man uses the right means, the right means work in the wrong way."

To the contrary of how the corporate owned media may be swaying things with the aim of producing maximum ratings, everyone's not fascinated by Ed Denmark. Just like any other powerful man, he has his share of enemies. But his biggest foe has always been a man with the kind of power that money can't buy.

In his chambers at the Federal Justice Center, sits the chief justice. Being the court's swing voter with a history of voting across party lines, he's a true centrist; one whose moves can't be predicted—the court's nine month term has just started. Members of this court don't answer to constituents, raise money for campaigns, or respond to pressing threats to the nation's security. The existence of a Supreme Court justice is one of an isolated existence, one withdrawn from the rest of the world. There's isn't a lot of collaboration or collective thinking, justices don't partake in cultural gatherings, or social events. Clerks do much of the administrative work, things like sorting through the thousands of petitions the court receives, summarizing memos, etc. Holed up inside his chamber, characterized as an independent law firm, he silently reads and drafts documents, and is currently in the middle stages of crafting a one hundred and thirty-five page opinion on a selected case. Atop of his vast slab of wood are the two recent articles. During his twenty eight years on the Supreme Court, he's kept close tabs on the man who everyone seems to fear and revere. He knew since first meeting him, that he would one day become a problem. On the winds in the lofty world of the high and mighty rides lyrics and melodies of his reprehensible dealings. Hymns of his ruthlessness and brutality are sung from state to state. To him, Denmark is nothing more than an international despot in exquisite wool. Bitter the constitutional doctrines he's dedicated his life toward have been made irrelevant by the moderates' compromises, he's finally reached the point where he wants to do something that actually changes something.

Denmark knows the arrogant way he uses his influence to throw salt in face of the justice system is bad for business, but his inflated ego won't let him stop. What he doesn't know, is by agreeing the do the incendiary photo in the Creative Loafing, that one single act will ultimately lead to his demise.

Having already placed a call to his direct number, Chief Justice Masterson hears the phone ring.
After two rings he answers.
"Hello Mr. President."

With $154,765, even a person clinically diagnosed as being mentally handicapped can find a way out of a city with that kind of bread. Bailey took the other $170,000 with her and her daughter so that they can start a new life in Missouri. He hasn't seen or heard from her in almost a week and is worried. The plan was she would link up with a close friend, who was also trying to escape to freedom, where they would head to Alabama, and on to Missouri. He was supposed to head to Mexico, and hopefully overseas.
Being fresh from the clutches of captivity, she was afraid disoriented and confused, having so much money and a child made it even harder. Feeling a connection to her and an uncanny sense of obligation to protect her, he followed them across state lines to Huntsville. There she met up with a girl, and on to an apartment to rest and prepare the second leg of her journey. Over a long and tearful goodbye, she thanked him for all he's done for her and wished him well. They promised to stay in contact once a day until she made it to Missouri, which was supposedly planned within seventy two hours.

For the past seventy three hours her phone has been going straight to voicemail, and he's about to blow his top. Being he was out of the state, and was heading west anyway, he saw no reason to go back to Georgia. So by way of the internet and a cellphone, he found a trailer for rent in a rural municipality just outside of Madison. The guy was eager to get someone

in there, and didn't ask any questions when he presented him
with the money. On this hundred and fifty acre property, he
sits in his rented single-wide trailer on a Thursday afternoon
fully dressed and prepares to leave for Mexico. While sitting on
an old couch in the back room of the badly deteriorated mobile home with no running water, no cable, and a gas generator
for electricity; he keeps having this horrible feeling something
has gone terribly wrong. He keeps reliving the scene in the restaurant and he keeps seeing those face in the cage. The taste in
his mouth becomes sour when he thinks how he tried so hard
to do something good, only for it to end up going bad. He
blames himself for allowing her to leave and for not escorting
her all the way to Missouri. The more he looks out the window
into the forest, the more he feels like he's been in here sleeping while her and her child are out there calling for him. Now
angry, and going on the fifth day, he's wavering over whether
he should go back to the apartment and check things out. But
there are so many things that can go wrong if he does.
On the property where he leases the trailer is a Spanish guy
who maintains the land, tends to the horses and chicken
houses, speaks decent English, and knows the area well. For
five hundred bucks he was downright giddy at the chance to
make half his month's salary for driving him just seventy miles
to Huntsville. He's arrived with the car and blows the horn.

Gathering the things he's taking he exits the trailer and
locks the door. The best part about the Spanish guy, is that
at night, he runs his car as a cab service. It's properly licensed
and fitted with everything a normal taxi would have, it's just
in a green, 1998 Ford Tarsus that was once a police car with
203,401 miles on it.
 Along the way he sees police car after police car, and by the
time they make it to Huntsville, he's decided he's going to offer
him ten thousand to drive him to Mexico.

Now they're pulling into the complex.

Rolling over three speed breakers, he continues around towards Building F. He sees the unit where he dropped her off and tells Jesús to pull over. There's some sort of memorial at the curb? He quickly jumps out! Candles flowers and stuffed animals are sitting on the ground? He's looking at it, but he's not putting it together? In the parking space there's bits of broken glass! To his left he sees a man walking a pit-bull coming his way.

He comes and speaks.

"It a shame huh pastor how they did them girls. How can people do things like that? You come to pray with the family or something?" thinking him to be a pastor since he's wearing a clergyman's cassock. A gold cross with a beaded rope hangs around his neck. The white stole, the skufia, and the fake beard have him looking holy. The bible in his right hand seals the deal.

Pain feels something strike him down!

Asking him to repeat himself after agreeing that he *is* a pastor who's has come to see the family; the man tells him what happened!

"From what I heard, she and this other girl who just moved in got shot up by her ex-boyfriend. It's been a week and people haven't forgotten about it. It's all everyone's talking about. We praying for her too reverend. I think there was something on the news the other day about they found out who the guy is, and they say the police are looking for him."

He becomes washed with disbelief! Guilt is sucking him down like quicksand! But he's clinging to the hope the guy's mistaken, or either he's mistaken, and is somehow at the wrong apartment!

But he sees the playground and knows this is the right building!

Now there's fear is in his voice!!!!!

"So!... So did they do something to somebody or something! Did something happen! Are you sure it was the new girl or just a girl that looks like her! I gave her a ride her from church last week and

she said she was heading out of town!!!! You think it could've been another person maybe!!!"

"Yes revered. I put my right hand 'fore God, it was the girls that stay in this building. Cuz I used to see her and her little girl out here playing on the swing. My neighbor across the hall said he spoke to her a few times, and I remember him saying that he thought she was black, but she was really maybe Puerto Rican or mixed with something because she had a Spanish accent."

Pain's heart skips a beat! He takes a deep breath and turns towards the parking space!!! He pictures her sitting in this very spot getting shot!!!!

WHY DID HE LET HER OUT OF HIS SIGHT! YOU STUPID FOOL!!!!

He's out of breath, feeling himself gritting his teeth!!! He wants to cause himself pain to make him pay for his stupidity!!!! He wants to cry—the emotion seething deep in his soul!!!! He wants to kill this man because he should've done something to save her!!!!!!! Perspiring at an alarming rate, his entire body begins itching!!!!

Vision of horror begin playing tricks on his mind!!!!

"…I have to find her," he murmured.

NO-NO-NO-NO- NO!!!!! I have to find out what happened! There has to be more to the story!!!! Bailey can't really be dead! She can't be!!!

The man watches him morph into an unidentified object, and realizes it's time to go.

"I gotta get to the store pastor. You take care."

And continues down the side walk, disappearing around the corner looking over his shoulder.

He wants to follow and ask him more but he's stuck!! His legs won't move!!! He stands there staring at the memorial in disbelief, as if it's going to give him the explanation he so desperately desires! He hears the door of the upstairs apartment open.

When he looks up the woman slams the door!
He looks around and runs towards the stairwell, the
handrail is chipping with white paint. Rushing to the top he
heads to the door and knocks!
Someone's standing on the other side of the door rustling their
feet while looking through the peep hole.
He knocks again.
"...May I help you?" asked an older woman.
"Yes!" out of breath. "I dropped a young lady and a child off
here last week, and is here to take them to Bible study with me!
Are they here?" close to panic, trying to keep his emotions at
bay enough to find out what happened!!!!
After a few seconds the door cracks, and a round face and short
body of a woman in her mid-to-late 60's peeks through.
She looks him in the eyes, and up and down at his attire.
"You sure you're from the church revered?" she asked
suspiciously.
"Yes ma'am I am! Sanctuary of Grace Methodist in Valhermoso
Springs, about ten minutes from Redstone Arsenal! I was
supposed to be picking Bailey up so she can get to Bible study!
I didn't mean to startle you!"
She's still suspicious and the chain is still on the door. Plus he's
a little too keyed up.
"I really need to find Bailey ma'am! Can you please tell me if
she's here? I assure you I mean no harm!"
The woman sees the fear in his eyes and hears the worry in his
voice.
"There's some bad stuff goin' on in this world revered. The
devil is hard at work looking for souls to eat. But I'm just an
old lady trying help these girls get off these corners and these
truck stops, and get back to their families. I ain't meanin' no
harm."
"He sure does ma'am, and that's why I'm here! I'm just a
person who's trying to help as well! I'm out her slaying these
demons every day!"

She keeps watching him?
"…Lawd have mercy……Come on in child."
Shuts the door and removes the chain.
She opens the door and he steps inside.
"Sorry about that pastor. There's been some bad people coming
around here lately," and closes it, locking it behind him.

He emerges moving fast fifty four minutes later fast!!! Down
the stairs he goes with the cross bouncing against his chest, and
his clergy shirt wet with sweat!!! His silk stole scarf
inscribed with gold crosses is flying in the wind like the cape
of Zorro!!!! His skufia (a soft-sided cap worn by monastics) is
sliding off his head!! By the time he gets inside the car and tells
Jesús to pull off, he's no longer thinking about Mexico. He's
thinking about slaughter!

On the way back to get his gear, his car and get on the road, he
has Jesús pull into a gas satiation, who runs inside and comes
out with the day's paper and hands it to him.
Bogart yanks out the section he wants and tosses the rest aside!
Pursing his lips so hard they're losing color, he scowls at the
newspaper like it's his worst enemy! Being that most of the
story is based on witness statements, yellow journalism, and information leaked at the hospital; it's not all that accurate. Some
of the things written in the small, down home editorial are just
plain lies. He sees that the authorities have named a suspect
as being a man in a white Chrysler 300 with Georgia tags,
with it coming back as being registered to a "Terry Bostic" of
Mechanicsville, GA. After the unidentified girl who'd been shot
multiples times, condition stabilized, she was moved to a recovery unit. But later vanished. Authorities believe she is with the

man in question, and is in extreme danger. The story ends with Bostic being considered armed and dangerous and not to be approached. If seen, the public is advised to avoid contact and call police immediately.

He tosses the periodical aside and goes inside his bag.
Before dropping her off that evening, she gave him a small token of her appreciation. She took the poem she shared with him at the hotel, wrote it on a square of cloth, placed it inside an embroidered picture frame and gave it to him as gift.
He reads her words:
My mother called me a rose, now the seedling of me has taken root. Sometimes I walk in my own garden. I get lost in the beauty that surrounds me. I'm a rare flower that grows on mountains high in the sky. Beyond my field of red petals and green stems, the world is dark. The cold wind blows like an angry storm over my savanna; I am strengthened by the push. I grow in this storm to become lovely. Captivated by my blossom, a gardener steals me and wants to implant his seed. Blinded by beauty, he doesn't notice my thorns are unable to be contained. He cuts me down anyway, and takes me to a faraway land. Unable to grow, my petals wither and darken. My red turns deep with the color of pain. Parts of me are washed away by the erosion of life. Falling to the ground, an angel rescues me. Planted in a new plot I bring hopes of a new harvest. People from all around come to anticipate my bloom. They call me their sacred floret, a gift from grace with the power to bring light to gloom. This flower of the heavens must not be misused, for like the birth of an angel, her display only has one bloom.

A tear drops his eye.

"…I'm going to find you Bailey. Just hold on," he whispered.

The authorities don't know where Bostic is heading, but he does. He's going to turn Queens upside down looking for him!

☐☐☐☐☐☐☐☐☐☐☐

For a Friday morning, the office is busy and people are actually working. Many of the detectives are heading into their twelfth hour, and the lot is full of squad cars and unmarked vehicles. Hall flips on the light and does his morning routine. Moving to his desk, he picks up the phone and dials. But before completing the first ring, he hangs up. Getting out of his chair he goes to his bag, turns on his office AM/FM radio, sets the volume, reaches inside his pocket, and gets out an unregistered prepaid cellphone. After dialing the number again, this time a woman answers. It's the county medical examiner, the person charged with performing autopsies and other postmortem examinations as part of death investigations.

They speak on a regular basis.

He asks her about the autopsy she performed on the HT?

She say she didn't perform one on him and is surprised he didn't know.

He says how was he supposed to know?

She goes on to say his body never saw the inside of her lab, saying the Feds took the body and they're the ones who performed the autopsy. She never saw the body.

He thanks her for the info and hangs up.

The office phone rings.

It's a call from Lacy, and he want him to report to the conference room on the double.

He has three things he's scheduled to do today, so what can Lacy possibly want? He doesn't recall having any meetings, especially not there? His heart flutters when he thinks of the possible scenarios, not because he's fearful of Lacy, but because he's worried there's word of some new bulletin, another terrorist attack, or some new murder. Thinking it's probably has something to do with the proposed merging of the two south zones, or something regarding his upcoming meeting with

councilman Lewis; he opens his desk drawer, picks up a case
file sitting atop, puts it inside and closes it; spending another
eighty one seconds on his computer. He finally he gets up and
heads out.

Along the way he sees the smile of Detective Caroline Mason
passing on his right. He sees the chief's office too, but the door
is closed and the lights are off. Three dozen meters later he's
standing at the conference room door. He can't hear anything.
He opens it and enters.

Low and behold, he's taken completely aback by the amount of
suits!!!!!!

"Welcome major," said Lacy, sitting at the head of the table.
"Please take a seat."

He's flabbergasted!

The only available seat is the one at the opposite end. He
sees the head of the police union, he sees his assistant, he sees
investigator Shields, he sees the Internal Affairs head. But never
the two men before, and wonders who the *men in black* are?
He sees Walt Guericke, the public affairs director also. But he
doesn't see the chief.

"It's a pleasure to see you again major....Unfortunately, it's
not in the same light as our last meeting...It has come to my
attention a full investigation into the death of the HT has been
completed, and your name has come up in connection."
He pauses for effect.

BULLSHIT!

SETUP!

I KNOW THEY'RE NOT ABOUT TO DO THIS!

Every man at the table is staring at him. It reminds him of
the ugly way envy expresses itself. He's fuming that Lacy put
him on display like this when he could've done it in private!
It burns him that there's people in the department who want
nothing more than to see him fall!

"The purpose of you being here Hall is not to destroy you, like you probably assume. This is a chance for the department to regain some of the public's trust. Now major, I'm not here to determine the outcome. I'm here to give you an opportunity to get ahead of the curve. This report concludes, among other things, that your assault on the HT was a contributing factor in his death. It contends that after you shot him, you and a group of unnamed officers retaliated violently against him during the arrest. There are witnesses saying they saw you and another officers stomping on his head and striking him with batons. It cites your history of sometimes being too overzealous, and too eager to perform. It also cites the comment you made regarding gay adoption which got the department in hot water. It cites a lot of unfavorable things about not only you, but the entire force. But mainly you, because you were the commanding officer on the scene when the HT was taken into custody."

Lacy pauses to clear his throat.

"As you know major, we as a department are up to are neck in shit right now. Yeah, we know this report is BS, but the public will take it and run. They'll use it to justify more protests and more violence against police officers. The fact you've made yourself into a celebrity has put extra light on yourself and the entire APD. By no means am I saying it's a bad thing that you're such an outstanding officer. Nor is it bad that you're a charismatic individual. It's not bad you're good with the other agencies. It's not bad the officers admire you. But when your name comes up connected to the death of a suspect, it's *bad*... Here, have a look for yourself," and slides the report to the other end.

Hall picks it up and flips through it. Someone has already highlighted the most damaging findings.

They all remain silent while he reviews it.

He tosses it back to Lacy but it stops halfway.

"That's bullshit! And every one of you know it! You're going to sit here and-.."

"*Hall!-Hall!* No one's trying to do anything. Now just hold on before you go ape shit. We've come up with a way to get ahead of this...We've prepared this statement. It doesn't admit guilt or wrong doing, just something to pacify the masses."

He takes a document from one of the stacks, and passes it down.

Hall reads it.

"Nothing will ever come from it, and by Christmas it'll all be forgotten. Where going to release that to the media showing our contrition, showing we can admit when we're wrong. Hopefully, the fact he was a gangbanging murderer will work in our favor and this just goes away. Nobody really gives a shit about these kinds of cocksuckers. They're not the ones sniffing up our back. It's these goddamn reporters with their make-believe stories and dumb theories. They're the ones stirring the kettle. They just want something to sell and they'll use us, or whoever....Think about it major. Think about what you, the great Russell "Tusk" Hall, a.k.a. "The Big Man", admitting to the city he's a man who makes mistakes like everyone else."

"I already have. You want me to be the department's crash dummy. You want me to be the goddamn pariah! Yeah, take one for the team huh? I did not assault HT in anyway, and I *will not* get on camera and admit to a character assassination *just* so the department can save face! *Fuck that!*"

"Hall! This is not just about you! This is not something we're are just making up! There has been an investigation that is about to go live on the six o'clock news that has your name on it!"

Hall leaps to his feet!

"That report can kiss my ass! I don't know who you paid to drum up this garbage, but I'm gonna find out!" he shouted, pointing at Lacy. "You little weasel! You think I can't see what's going on! You think I can't see how you're poisoning the force with the same corrupt mess you pulled in Detroit!"

And starts towards him with his teeth clenched and fist balled. Director Guericke leaps from the table and grabs him!!

"Come on Hall, not here. Not here big man…..Not here," he whispered calmly, hugging him from getting to Lacy.

"Well I have no choice but to place you on suspension. It's a shame you would rather drag the entire force down with you, than do what's right as a man."

"You motherfucker!!"

Hall pushes hard against Guericke, who is using all his might to hold him back!

"You think you're gonna come here and destroy what I've spent thirty years building! You're wrong *jack!* Over my dead body! This ain't Michigan jerk, and my name's not Kwame," he scorned.

Pushes the director aside, and storms for the exit!

WHAM!

Punching a hole in the wall so hard it sends dust falling from the ceiling!

"You better be glad that ain't your face rat!"

And walks out, slamming the door!

The rain showers spoil Friday night's outdoor activities, sapping the highways of their normal thunder. There will be minimal showing off and bling-blinging in Hotlanta tonight—the weather is taking all the shine. Atlanta consistently racks in the top ten of rainiest U.S. cities. When there isn't rain there's humidity, high pressure, and elevated dew points. There's the pollen too, it blankets the city with green dust every spring.

Quoting Ray Charles: *It's just another rainy night in Georgia.*

To Viltié it looks like it's raining all over the world.
His mother used to tell him monsters aren't real, saying they're
only in his imagination. He would always rebut, that just because she doesn't believe something, doesn't mean it's not real.
The last time he saw the sky was when he was transported
from the other vehicle into this one. All he's eaten are packs
of dehydrated food their captors feed them. Empty bottles of
funny tasting water are everywhere, and the eight other boys
crammed into the cage with him are just as afraid as he. They're
in the back of a truck locked in cages with other people. Even
while sitting on his buttocks, he's still in pain. There's only the
floor for cushion, and the 7x7 cage he's in is tangled with the
bodies of other captive boys. There's others grouped in similarly
sized cages ranging in ages and nationalities. But they're prohibited from speaking, and if caught doing so will get severely
beaten.
He got lucky and was able to speak to a little girl that looks like
him. She ended up being from Croatia, not from Lithuania
as he; but they were still able to communicate. She explained
her family was so poor and dying from starvation because of
the war, that her father sold her to these men so the rest of
the family can eat, because girls are considered unfavorable in
her village since they aren't strong and productive like boys.
She said she's nine, and these strange men keep touching her
private area. She says she thinks they're getting sent off to do
"nasty stuff", or to be servants in the homes of "rich czars".
That's all they were able to say, and haven't spoken since. Some
of the people have soiled themselves, and others are crying and
grief stricken. There's a bright light bolted to the ceiling, and
a vent is blowing cold air from the roof. Earlier, this doctor
lady came and injected him with something, and ever since
he's been feeling sick. There are boys in there with him who've
been "messed with" and abused. He looks at all the people

around him and knows he won't make it. All he remembers is his mother sending him to the market, a van pulling up, and a group of men jumping out and putting him inside.

The first chance young Viltié gets, he promises to kill himself.
In the raining night of Georgia, a tractor trailer packed with a load of humans travels down I-75. The sooner the new hub is ready, the sooner they won't have to keep using the current location for "classification".

For the past three years, politicians and businessmen have been trying to convince the public to accept the fact that forty-million of their tax dollars is necessary to help a private company build a 450,000sq.ft plant so the company can bring 2,000 pharmaceutical jobs to Atlanta. They've been pushing the residents of Monroe to accept the noise and influx of traffic, assuring them it won't affect the Charlie Elliot Wildlife Preserve. The county laid down the law of eminent domain when residents fought to keep them from slicing their front yards in half so they can widen the street in preparation of the forecasted economic growth. The battle over funding is a raging one that crossed party lines and strained alliances.

The story of Eldrin Denmark and all the things that go with him is still good for ratings. But the story about "Tusk" Hall being a dirty cop, is the new heat. The media greatly embellished the story with the hopes garnering maximum interest. In retaliation to the lightning rod story, buildings were set ablaze, officer's cars are being fired on, classes are turning on each other. The media fast to the scene of these crimes as well, making sure the pubic gets every incendiary detail.

Hall is back in the office after spending the past two and a half hours driving around I-285. At 8:34 p.m. there's lots of people in the building. Lots of people who look up to him, and lots of people who hate what they're witnessing. Those who've worked through the night are still here, and as he heads to his office, they look at him. They don't speak, just look. And judging by them, he's not the only one who's hurting. Keeping his head high, he goes to his office and gathers his things in preparation of his suspension.

News travels fast in the police department the same way it does in any other workplace.

Hall knows he's here, he saw his car parked in his space. Now he's walking to his office and looking through the door. It's dark. And quiet. And all he sees is raindrops cascading down the window pane.

"Come inside Russell."

He pushes the door.

The chief is standing at the corner window with his back turned.

"Close the door please."

He does.

Looking around the dark office, the light from under the door , and the illumination of the moonlight is the only luminescent sources in the room. He was about to take a seat at one of the chairs before his desk. All the chief's medals, awards, and honors hanging on the wall behind his chair are reflecting the glare.

"Please don't sit down...I don't want this to seem like a father talking to a son...But a man talking to a man," the chief spoke softly.

Hall sees the bottle on his desk and knows he's probably holding a drink in his hand. But has never known him to drink on the job.

"....I remember the first day you came in this building. You and your spit shined shoes....Your pants were crisp....You were the first man I'd ever met who had a power so magnetic. It's like you radiated an inner-strength that others can feel...You had a gift like no other man I'd ever encountered."

The chief takes a long pause. He doesn't move.

"...I just knew one day you would rule this department and start this epic rise to greatness. I said to myself: This guy has the potential to be great..."
And pauses again.
Hall sees him raise his arm to his face, and lower it after a moment.
"...But you didn't know how to harness your brilliance. Your natural shine burned those around you, which caused them to close ranks against you. They knew you would supersede them if given the opportunity...You revealed yourself to be a formidable opponent in the face of cowards. That was your biggest mistake."

He takes another pause.

"The things you brush off as being just another of your many talents, cut lesser men to the depths of their soul..........And you're oblivious. You don't see what others see. You think you do, but you don't. If you did, you wouldn't be standing behind that chair...I was once a P.O.W Russell.........Seven months after enlisting I get sent overseers. A week after my twenty third birthday my platoon gets ambushed. All who survived were taken hostage. For sixty six days they tortured us for information. They hated us for being given things they died trying to get...The things we took as insignificant trinkets of freedom, they shedded blood just to have a piece. All but one man ended up surviving to make it home. The fact that I'm alive today is a testament to my very point."

Another.

"They had us in these bamboo shacks. In the day it would get so hot that some of the men would fall dead. To further torment us, our captors would let us out only after agreeing to accept the grim task of burying our dead brethren they'd killed in the day's battle.......Day after day they'd let us out and offer us freedom. But only if we joined them. Many of those men were just like me; young, fresh out of college. They had wives and families they loved.........Many whom they would never see again."

He turns his head slightly.

Hall sees the tears running down his face.

"All but one person agreed to be a traitor....All but one man refused to accept the deal....When they couldn't break him, they killed him by firing squad. They shot him down like a dog just as he was about to see freedom....All us traitors got rescued."

Another pause, and another raise of his hand.

"Every day of my life I think about that man. And every day I hate myself for not being able to do what he did…I always told myself, that if I could go back and do it again. I would've stood on that wall with him and took my bullets just like he did….It's hard living the life of a traitor,.......a coward."

He runs his hand over his head.

"They came at me hard Hall…They had something on everyone in my family…They told me they'll destroy me and everything I hold dear…But I held strong Hall! *This time I was strong!* I didn't wanna feel like a coward anymore!….I tried Hall, I did! I know you're a good officer. I know you're a good man, and told them I wasn't doing it! Even if they kill me."

Hall feels a tear roll down his face and fall to his lap.
He wipes it off and straightens his back.

"They came up with all this. They came up with all these *witnesses* and all these *statements…My god Hall, what did you do to these people?*"

Another pause.

"It's gonna be hard brother. It may even cost you your life. But you fight these bastards you hear me! *You fight 'em!!!*"

The room is silent. The chorus of rain blesses the interlude.

Hall takes a moment to gather his emotions, relieved to know he still has one friend. He's already made the decision that he can't fight the good fight from inside the belly of the beast. He knows what he has to do.
"I tender my resignation. Effective immediately. Thank you sir…..*Thank you!*"
Russell gets up and walks out with a tennis ball sized lump of emotion in his throat.

Neuf.

The average high for Queens, New York in October is 59°. When you factor in the Arctic trough coming down from Canada bringing low pressure and unfriendly winds, with the presence of scantily clad women on every corner; the temperature on Roosevelt Ave. is colder than a thermometer can register. The unsympathetic displays of the female anatomy, and the gangs behind them, are like ice in his veins. Roosevelt Avenue in Jackson Heights is "the heart of human trafficking in New York". Women from across America, and countries including Mexico, the Dominican Republic, Venezuela, and Asia are being sexually exploited right around the corner from the United Nations Headquarters. There are brothels from here to Corona, all the way to Elmhurst.

For the past month, he's been up here searching. For the better part of thirty days he's been pretending to be homeless, while he hunts for Troy Merciless and his white 300. Spending as many as twenty hours a day on foot, he trudges through the streets searching for any sign, of him, or his beloved Bailey Red. With all he's been able to gather, Merciless somehow got her out of the hospital. The fact the other girl died, and his name came up as the main suspect, he took off to Queens. He doesn't know if she's dead or alive, but he knows he won't stop until he finds the answer. The longer his search goes, the more he thinks Merciless is long gone, and he's wasting his time. He uses savvy schemes honed in Atlanta to pick up info about the local prostitution industry. He found that sixty percent of all the city's prostitution takes place right here. All the evidence points to this being the most likely place for him to see the white 300, or run into Bailey.

She mentioned there's dozens of brothels in New York owned by "Mr. Ruppell"—the guy Merciless works for; worked in one, but can't tell him where because she was blindfolded when they moved her. But does remember the clients were usually middle age white men, and this particular brothel was relatively clean and well ran; the men gentler, and less likely to desire S&M, urination, rough sex, or lewd performances. The majority of the clients only wanted to have oral sex with her, or have her perform oral sex on them. The best thing was they weren't dirty, and they didn't stink when they got on top of her.

Using an internet café and a prepaid gift card, he was able to search the city's bevy of bawdy online escort services. On site after site women posed as housemaids, schoolgirls, therapists, teachers, and animals; charging as much as eighteen hundred an-hour. Even on a computer screen, it wasn't hard to notice the bruises and scars. Many of the girls were visibly unhappy, but pretended to smile and look seductive for the camera—times and locations are listed. He's learned to decipher the acronyms, and abbreviations, such as "F/S" and "GFE". Bailey told him 'F/S' means 'full service' sex - i.e., sexual intercourse, and 'GFE' means 'the girlfriend experience,' which means the woman will pretend to be the customer's affectionate girlfriend, and is willing to engage in unprotected sex for an additional fee. But he saw no Bailey Red. Pain thought he'd seen it all while sleeping on the streets of Atlanta, but he hadn't. Homelessness and poverty are on a scale bigger than any he could've ever imagined up here. Then there's the rats, they're a whole other population. In Atlanta, a person can sleep on the street without having to worry much about rats—dogs roaches and robbers, yes. The rats in NY are of the wharf type, big as cats, bite, and known to carry rabies. The cockroaches are the size of 9V batteries, and hiss and fly. In his time homeless, he's never found it impossible to find an abandoned house, or a dilapidated building. But up here, everything from the burnt out skeleton of a car, to an old piece of sheet metal is already claimed.

With his new found wealth it was easy for him to obtain fake documents. He used them to get a room at a rooming house in the next borough. It's safe enough for him to rest there, and secure enough for him to stash his guns and cash. The only time he's there, is to sleep. The rest of his waking moments are spent walking and riding. He met a guy who claimed to be a former Navy Seal, who gave him a few pointers on how to stay out of the cop's way. Outside of him, that's the only person he's met. The borough's most plentiful commodities however, are drugs and prostitution. There isn't a day that goes by where he isn't approached by someone looking to sell or buy one or the other. He heard about this annual book convention that draws thousands of people. The last day of the annual awards ceremony is tomorrow. The hotels are benefiting and so is the local economy; which also means the criminals. Earlier this evening he ventured out and came to a corner where a man wearing a horse mask was holding a sign with a megaphone in his hand. Beside him a man was sitting in a replica electric chair with a hood over his face and straps over his body. Behind them a woman in a grim reaper costume held a staff atop five foot stilts. They were across the street from a famous bookstore, drawing loads of attention to their cause. All he kept saying was:

"End capital punishment in America!"
"Free the thousands of wrongly accused!"
"Gripping thriller examines America's improper collection of society's debts!"

He stakes out the same brothels over and over. He's played like a john to get info about where he can find the girls. Day after day he thinks of every angle he can. But what he finds most amazing, is how it goes on right under the guise of the police, they seem oblivious to all the traffic and women. It's not like they don't care, but more so of being overwhelmed and underpowered. There short term answer seems to be incarceration, but studies have shown, these girls are not criminals, but victims. Therapy is necessary. Not punishment.

Within walking distance of the popular, *Jackson Diner*, girls approach cars parked at curbs. The fact it's fifteen degrees from freezing doesn't matter.

He turns on 74ᵗʰ St. and heads towards the next light. Up ahead quick, movements between a woman and a man catch his eye. He hears her yelling something and can see the man handling her roughly. Another woman is yelling at him to stop. By the time he makes it over, the man is dragging the scantily dressed woman away, while this other woman is trying to follow. He's warning her to stop coming around here, but she keeps saying flying off at the mouth. There looks to be a stack of brochures in her hand, and carries a backpack. When she realizes it's best she not try to follow any more, she stops and reluctantly turns away. The look in her eyes tells the entire story.

"Excuse me miss," before she could continue.
She turns to him with water in her eyes.
"I'm sorry to bother you, but I was standing over there and saw what just happened. If you have a moment, I'd like to ask you a few questions if I can?"
"What do you need?" she asked skeptically.
He produces a photo of Bailey and shows it to her.
"This is my niece. I came all the way from Atlanta to find her. I saw what happened and wondered if I can ask you a few questions?"
In seconds her mood brightened. She lay her hand on his shoulder and hands him back the picture.
"I'm really sorry to hear about your niece. How can I help you sir?"
"Is there some place we can talk? Maybe buy you a cup of coffee? I've been trying to find her for a month now and you're the only person I've seen do what I just saw. Are you with a community group or something?"
"Yes..........Uhmn, there's a place right around the corner."
Intuition tells her he's okay, and offers him her hand.
"Victoria. I'm a counselor with Sanctuary for Families."
"Pain Bogart, nice to meet you Victoria."

In minutes they're heading inside. Two men were paying the parking meter after chaining their bikes to the pole. A purple sign with 'Indian Cuisine' in white letters are bolted to the sunshade overhanging the entrance. The sign in the window to the right of the door states: 'Buffet Lunch - $8.99'.

There's 2-person tables, and 4-person ones. The order counter and the kitchen are in the rear.

He purchases two coffees and sits down. Many of the patrons are put off by his appearance but she seems not to notice.

"So you say you're with a community group?"

Sipping her coffee she says: "Yes. We're a non-profit organization dedicated to empowering survivors of prostitution to move from fear and abuse, to safety and stability. We try to transform lives through a comprehensive range of free services, and deal with victims of domestic violence too—DV and prostitution go hand in hand."

"Don't call me crazy, but when I woke up this morning I had a feeling something good was going to happen today. I've been going undercover as a homeless guy to see if I can find my niece. She came here with this guy and now we can't get in contact with her. We got word she's here, so this is where I came. I haven't had any luck though. These are some rough streets."

"Again, I'm really-really sorry to hear about your niece. What you just said is the same story I hear from many of the women I encounter. It's always some guy that tells them he loves them and wants to marry them, only to push them into the sex trade. I assume the girl on the photo is who you're referring to?"

"Yes. You wouldn't by chance have seen her would you?"
 She hangs her head.

"No. I'm sorry. I wish I had've."

"No worries. It's not your fault?"

"If I may ask? What brought you to Queens? Did you have information she's here?"

"Well, all we have is info about her being *here*, we didn't get exactly where. Through research we stumbled upon this place. It's kind of like where I started."

She nods her head.

"This place has brothels and back alley massage parlors

everywhere. Soon as one gets busted another opens. It's sad because, in the few years I've been out here, I've met other relatives like yourself in search of their loved ones."

"I saw how passionate you were back there. I'd already told myself that if things got ugly, I wasn't going to stand by and watch. I'm no tough guy, but I would've intervened," Bogart admitted.

"*Aww*. Thanks, you're so kind."

She reaches and touches his arm.

"But the thing is, she was in our program, but she left and went back to her trafficker. When I saw her I tried to convince her to come back, that's when her trafficker came and stepped in. We try so hard to save as many as we can, but the gangs make it very difficult. The traffickers know we're out here, and they don't like it. Between us and several others, we're actually making an impact. Now with the mayor's new initiative to combat human trafficking, and these new Victims Justice Centers; change is being made. But we need tons more help. If the American people begin demanding the government put an end to human trafficking, it can end *easily*. I'm taking total eradication. There's just not enough public pressure to force lawmakers to act. But until that day comes, we're out here doing our part."

"How did you get into this fight? What moment spurred you into action?" while simultaneously visualizing the moment that changed him.

"*Wow*. That was scary," she stated, amazement on her face. "What?"

"I got chill bumps when you asked me what moment spurred me into action.......I remember like it was yesterday. I used to work in marketing and advertising, that was until my younger sister got killed by a john. They found her in a park raped and strangled. From that day I dedicated my life to ending human trafficking. This is a disgusting world that very few people know about."

"I'm so sorry to hear that miss. It rips my heart when I hear stuff like that."

"It's okay. I can't say it doesn't still hurt. But I *can* say that I'm healing. I'm way better than before."

She pull up her sleeves revealing the scars on her wrist.

"But at first I wanted to die too."

There's that warming feeling coming over him again! It's now becoming a normal occurrence. It communicates there's no greater accomplishment and sense of pride, than that which comes from performing acts of nobility. He pictures himself as a brave knight out to free the people from the clutches of a wicked monarch.

"Looking into your eyes, I can see the hurt losing her has caused you," she said.

"I want to find her so bad. I keep thinking I must find her soon or something bad is going to happen. She's only my niece, but I helped raise her. She's like a daughter to me."

"You'll find her, you will."

"I just keep feeling like I'm looking in the wrong area. Something's telling me I'm close, but not quite there yet."

"I'm going to ask you something. It may be hard to take, but it may help you. In the world of sex trafficking, looks and features have everything to do with value. The traffickers tend to force girls they deem less desirable to work the seedier sections of town where customers have less money. If the girl is deemed attractive enough, she's usually used to service the high rolling johns, and big-spending tricks who demand a higher quality, if you may."

He thought about that for a moment. The gears in his head start spinning.

"She would probably be deemed valuable. She's always been a very beautiful young lady."

"Well if that's the case, she's probably not going to be around here. The majority of these girls are considered on the cheaper

end, unfortunately..*God* I hate saying that...But yeah, the fat cat-johns don't come to Roosevelt Avenue. They go to the Upper East Side, Midtown, and Downtown. Maybe you can visit the local precincts over there and see if they have any information. Sometimes the girls get arrested. If she has, at least that'll give you an idea as to her possible whereabouts."
"I'll give it a try. Thank you for your help. I'll guess I'll let you alone now. I know you need to get back to the fight."
"It's no problem. You gave me my fuel for today. I needed it."
She finished her coffee, and checked her phone. After texting something, she reaches into her backpack.
"This is the pamphlet we hand to the girls. It has my number on the back. If you need any help, I'll be happy to assist."
And stands to extend her hand.
"Just stay committed. You can't ever give up trying. Sometimes help comes from places we never imagine."

"Thank you for your time again Victoria. Thank you."
"Anytime Mr. Payne. Hope to hear to from you soon. Bye now."

It's another cold day in New York City. The snow is a month or two out, but it's still chilly and the wind still a factor. Running into Victoria was a good thing. Her knowledge of the Queens sex trafficking industry led her to hypothesize that Bailey probably is in another area. Later that day he ran into another lady who claimed to have information where "all" the high rollers "trick off". For two hundred dollar bills, she told him of a place off 3$^{rd.}$ Ave. After surveilling the address, he verified there's definitely prostitution going on, but not the kind of place he believes he'll find Bailey. After staking out the place for half the evening, he saw these girls were strictly Asian. The men entering the building acted as if they're out with willing participants who probably didn't know they're actually dealing with victims kidnapped from the Far East. In this type of sex trafficking, the girl services the client on-site. At others, the girls leaves and role-plays to the tricks fantasy of being on a date with a flirtatious party girl. After that phase is over, they go to a predetermined location, usually a bar that's close to their apartment. This is where the money changes hands. The client pays in-full for the hours he requested online. There, a member of the trafficker's gang observes from afar, to protect both the trick from running off with the girl, and the girl from running away from them. Once payment is secured, the client usually becomes eager to have sex. The bar experience ends shortly thereafter. Once the date is over, he leaves the building and the date ends; only to begin again with the next client. The operation goes on like this day after day, but is so low key that neighbors are ignorant to the illicit activities happening around them.

A group of men with several girls come walking down the street. One of the guys is flinging his arms with his chest sticking out—his sportcoat is flapping with his strut, and his mouth is loud and boisterous. He's wearing a gold watch, and painfully flashy necklace. And keeps swearing at the one girl, snatching her by the jaw. The other girl seems to have a slight limp, causing the second male to push her to keep up. Up until now, he's seen nothing convincing him to stay. He's looking for Bailey, and as much as he would've liked to, he can't save them all.

When the men emerge thirty three point three minutes later, there's only one. Watching from across the street, his heart drops when he recognizes his face!! It's not Merciless, but he's certain he knows him from somewhere! He's never been to New York in his life, so it has to be someone from Atlanta!

He has his first clue!

Knowing the homeless look isn't good for the Manhattan, he switched back to his parishioner ensemble. He's carrying a case, and if anyone asks, he's "Pastor Cain".

When the man left, he tallied him from a distance. On the next block he's parked.

The reverend hails a cab, and has the driver follow the sedan. They traveled several minutes to another apartment building and disappear down the alley beside it.

Cain pays the cab driver and gets out.

Beside a short fence in the outdoor patio area of a quaint neighborhood coffee shop on the 400 block of W. 50th in Manhattan, nestled between the Church of Assumption and Hell's Kitchen; sits a pastor. Being a man of the cloth, it's easy to sip tea while he reads his scriptures and watches the building across the street. He'd yet to see where the sedan went because it vanished somewhere around back and hasn't reemerged.

So he sits.

The place isn't crowded, so to permit his extended stay, he keeps ordering knickknacks from the menu. The booty from the robberies is being put to good use. The food is tasty and the cold weather is keeping anyone else from joining him. People walking down the street nod, wave, and grin as they pass. He even sees policemen. But since he's a "bishop", it's all good. They would never suspect him of carrying a small arsenal with thousands of dollars in blood money and murderous intentions. Cain is becoming a master of his new persona. He doesn't know how he survived so long without them. He even had time to purchase a new watch. The Casio® ProTrek PRG240T-7, offers such options as, atomically synced sunrise and sunset times, a digital compass, barometer and thermometer for weather prediction, various alarms, a full calendar, a flashlight, etc.

A burdened nomad lost in an unforgiving wilderness, he sits

and pretends to be reading. His thirst for Merciless or any sign of Bailey is exhausting. Bouts with rounds of continuous migraines beating his head have him binge eating Goody's® headache powder. The paranoia of him getting exposed is causing him to see things that aren't there. With every rest of his eye lids, he sees Bailey. With every gaze at the side of the building, he sees her little girl. He remembers how the blood around the card table was on the bottom of his shoes. The stain of seeing those people locked in the cage has permanently scarred his memory.

He begins having grave inclinations that the end of his road could be right here in NY.

The sound of a jovial voice thanking someone one inside the café takes his attention of the disturbing images.

He turns his neck slightly, and cut his eyes.

When he sees the back of the coat, the hat, and the boots, the time he sits down, he didn't need to see any more.

New York's finest has taken a seat.

As he sips his coffee, he can feel him looking his direction, the chatter of his radio crackling from his hip.

He situates his glasses and focuses on the words in his lap. Some are in red print and some are in black:

For I know the plans I have for you," declares the LORD. "Plans to prosper you and not to harm you, plans to give you hope and a future!"

The officer coughs twice and wipes his mouth.

He can tell he's restless, just itching for something to do. The cop pulls a cell phone from his pocket and fumbles with the screen.

He sees the name and numbers 'Jeremiah 29:11' at top center of the translucent page. A ray of light shines across the pavement, and cuts across the table he's seated at. The fact that a streak of sunlight managed to break through the canopy of tall buildings could be considered a miracle.

"Cold today huh bishop?"
The blue finally let it out.

He thought for a moment. *How would a pastor respond?*
He doesn't.
He just looks up and gives him an agreeing nod and smile.
The officer tries to get a look at his eyes but he only gave him a second before looking back down. He has on the same skufia, the same cassock, and the same scarf embroidered with gold crosses.
"You must be from the church around the block?" he asked.

He didn't know there's a church around the block?
What's he going to say?
"Along those lines," their eyes momentarily locked.

The officer nods and looks back at his phone.
"I used to go to that church. My mother taught at the school. I remember it being catholic. You don't look catholic?"
His get-up is more Eastern Orthodox united with Jehovah's Witnesses', and a pair of Goodwill® slacks—he found all the stuff used. It isn't exactly the right combination, but it looks official.
"I'm visiting from another state. Spreading the gospels across all denominations is the theme."
Out the corner of his right eye he sees a tow truck coming down the street pulling a gray Dodge Charger.
He turns in his seat just in time to see the front blinker come on and it turn down the alley. Pulling about sixty feet down, it stops in the same proximity of where the sedan disappeared earlier. The message '*Not for Hire*' is stenciled on the side.
He hears Barney Fife's radio, but keenly watches the alley. He has to be discreet because the officer is acting a little shifty. He

keeps looking at the case beside his foot.

The driver hasn't got out of the truck yet.

The sound of screeching tires and the blare of a car horn causes the officer to stretch his neck and look down the street!!

The door to the truck opens, a man gets out and goes to the side to begin doing something. Seconds later, the car begins lowering.

Like a punishing wind cresting over the sharp peak of a sandy dune, a panicked numbness induced by molten rage pours from his head, and down to his feet!!!

Merciless emerges and shakes the driver's hand.

The holy ghost almost sends him to his feet, Pastor Cain is ready to get sanctified!!!

But the police is sitting right there!

FUCK!!!..........LEAVE YOU COCKSUCKER!!!.......GET THE FUCK OUTTA HERE!!!!

Hooooooooooooooonk!!!!..............CRASH!!!

The officer stands to his feet! Pacing forward he looks down the block!

At the light there's been a collision. He radio's something and steps over the short fence onto the sidewalk, and heads towards the accident.

The tow truck driver is the first to investigate? He walks to the end of the alley and peeks around the corner?

He doesn't see the pastor watching from the café.

He says something to the man he suspects to be Merciless, who comes to take a look?

That's when Cain goes in his pocket for the mini 5x20 Tasco® single scope, and put it to his eye. A risky move, but he has to do it!

It *is* Merciless all right! He's cut his hair and grew a beard, but it's him!

He drops his hand and looks to his right. A person in a car is looking questioningly at him?

Merciless and the other guy walk back down the alley. The pace of the tow truck driver seems to have changed. His movements seems more urgent now! He lowers the plain Charger and wastes no time pulling it forward.

Merciless disappears back out of view. It's obviously one-way out, because he doesn't see any more alleys or side streets intersecting with it.

He sees the rear quarter panel of a white car!

The fender of the 300!

He's hit by an anxiety typhoon! His body involuntarily moves in the chair, his legs about to stand on their own! Feeling his upper lip quivering, sour acid is coming up his throat!

Where's Bailey!!!

The tow truck driver hooks the 300, raises the front, gives Merciless the keys, and gets inside the truck. Merciless emerges to park the Charger, before running back to hand him something. He put it in his pocket, shakes his hand, gets inside, and prepares to back out. Pulling into this same hidden area, he backs out and pulls onto the street facing forward. In seconds he's heading back into the sea of concrete, people and pollution.

Cain looks up. It's getting dark.

The real action happens once the sun goes down. He rises to his feet, tosses a few singles on the table, picks up his case and Bible and leaves.

Shielded under the canopy of a news stand, he puts the scope back to his eye. Beginning on the ground floor, he studies the wrought iron gate wrapping the front and counts.

"One"

"Two"

"Three"

"Four"

"Five"

Six floors, with three arched windows on each one. The first level is designed with white brick. Every floor above is done with bricks of a reddish brown hue. A maroon awing hangs over the entrance. There looks to be a sub-level, because he can see the top of a window at the street. The top of the building is done in a European styled molding.

He lowers the scope, and desperately wants to get inside. He imagines her and the little girl tied up and beaten. He sees Bailey crying for his help. He runs a hand across his face and tries to stay calm! He wants to walk down the alley to see what's back there, but knows he'll have to be patient—cunning and stealth is required for this hunt.

Now that he has proof of Merciless' whereabouts, he can decide how to face it. He can't believe he actually found him, especially in a city this large. How has a country boy from South Georgia—while being on the lam, found Merciless *all* by himself? He doesn't have time to give it much thought. All he knows is he's grateful. For now, his most pressing concern is getting inside; which seems like a death wish. He can burst in and shoot people like he did at the house, but this is a six story apartment building with the potential to contain armed men.

A passage from the *Hit Man* handbook materializes in his mind. He sees where the advice in the technical manual can aid him in a real-life situation.

He looks at his watch. He needs to get some more intel if he's going to attempt something as daring as what he's thinking. Cain starts walking, hailing a cab anywhere near here may draw more attention than he already has. He sees the things in his path, but he's really perceiving how he's going to get inside the building.

Heading down 50th. street, a woman pushing a toddler in a stroller is coming on his left; Bailey and her daughter deserve the same opportunity. As they pass, the mother looks and smiles.

"God bless you Father."

"Thank you my child."

Passing a pawn shop, something hanging inside causes him to do a double take. Peering through the window he stops and looks again. From the street it sure looks like.........Aren't those are illegal?
He goes in for a second look.
A man wearing a yamaka stands behind the counter with Dirty Harry's revolver holstered to his hip. He asks the "Father" how can he help?
Pastor Cain explains he was passing by in route to service, and couldn't help but notice what's hanging behind the counter.
The man complemented him on his keen vision, and explains it's genuine, *and* for sale.
He responds by saying, as a man of God, he has no need for such a thing.
The bearded man with twisted locks rebuts, everyone should protect themselves, especially religious figures. He assures him it's not illegal, as long as he files the appropriate documents with the state.
By the end of the act both men are playing is over, the shop owner has made a thousand dollars, and Pastor Cain has a much needed bulletproof vest.

Second Synergy Corporation, Lima, OH. October 30th 2015.
A 3,500 megawatt surge of current powers towards Ontario, affecting the transmission grid at 10:31 p.m. EST.
New York's Independent System Operator, the service provider responsible for managing the state's power grid, sends a message to Lima notifying them they've detected a spike. They return, they too detected the anomaly and have taken the ap-

propriate action. Early analysis have the cause being
unpruned foliage overhanging a transmission station.

By the time he gets back to his room, it's well past nightfall.
The weather is even colder and midnight is just over the horizon. Being a weekday doesn't offer the same benefits as it does
down south. This is the city that never sleeps, so there's always
someone out and about. The ride took almost forty minutes.
Riding down FDR gave him a chance to think. It was during
this drive that he realized his bad judgment had almost caused
him to get apprehended. There's no telling how the exchange
with the cop would've transpired had that accident not
changed the mood. Being too comfortable in his new identify
and disguise had lulled him into a false sense of security. The
fact he was so comfortable in public could've been his downfall.

He must remember this isn't for him, there's something
bigger he's trying to achieve.

If he wants to stay free long enough to do it, he better remember he's a wanted man. In the back of his mind he's reminding
himself any moment can be his last. If he wants his life to have
any sort of significance, he better keep a low profile. There's an
old saying that mistakes happen when confidence runs amuck.
He promised himself never again to lose sight of who he is, and
why he's out here. If he gets captured or killed, there's no hope
for Bailey and her child. It's the belief he's doing something
righteous that's keeping him sane. He has nothing else to live
for.

Standing at the door, he double checks his gear. Another case is leaned in the corner. Not the one with the guns inside, a different one. Since a boy, he's loved the sound of the violin. While watching the stars over a cozy lit fire, his grandmother would play to him. With his new influx of cash, he purchased a used one. The strings are good and the craftsmanship is excellent. The French made bow produces a warm, smooth sound. The set-up is professional. Though he hasn't played in years, he knows he still has skill. He thought about what will happen if he doesn't return. What will become of it and the other items? That's why he prepared a note and left it in a special location. If the wrong person finds it, they'll believe what it says. If they aren't, it'll be a blessing. He badly wants to play a chord before leaving. It could be the last opportunity he has. But he tosses the idea from his mind, gathers his tools, flips the light, and slips into the night.

The air in Manhattan is heavy. The low temperature hangs from the sky like a great drape of discomfort, encumbering the masses below. The words of Charles Manson echo in his mind, the ones where Manson believes that during *Helter Skelter,* there will be a civil war between the blacks and whites. As a result, the black man will win this war, but later, due to the black man's lack of experience with holding the reins of power, will simply give up this power to the elite whites who survived the apocalyptic uprising.

But he doesn't consider himself an evil villain like Manson.

He's *Pastor Cain,* and he's a demon slayer!

The coat he's wearing goes perfectly with his righteous attire. He doesn't have a full plan yet, but he'll start by seeing if he can get in a position to where he can get down the alley and see what's back there. He has a stack of pamphlets in case he decided to pass out church fliers.

As the cab pulls away from the curb, he crosses the street and begins walking. Beneath his costume he wears tactical boots and the bullet proof vest. Using the proper surveillance techniques, he was able to gauge the men who come to this building are mainly white. The two women he got a glimpse of were African-American and Latin. Everything inside him screams that Bailey is inside this apartment building. The more he chews on it the more it becomes clear that this is Merciless' hideout. He just wishes something would hit him on how to get inside. There's nothing he can do if he can't get in. He can't think about the prospect of getting caught right now, he has to ignore these warnings.

The second he rounds the corner and his right foot sits on 50th., he begins feeling as if he's walking through his own valley of death. He's always struggled with believing in God, but for some inexplicable reason he believes he's been with him these past few months. Unexplainable things are happening. Like how he found these weapons, how he keeps avoiding capture, how he's became a one man wrecking crew, and how Bailey, a woman form his past has given him new life; a reason to live again. He finds none of this to be coincidence, he's never believed in luck.

The case in his left hand comforts him. Earlier this evening, he passed the waters of FDR. But they weren't still. The pastures he saw weren't green. He feels as if he's being led by an unseen force down this path of rectitude and principle. The desire to save this mother and child has ignited his soul. Before him lies a table. Prepared are a selection of enemies. Sweat anoints his head with perspiration, down his forehead it overflows. From the depths of his soul, his cup runneth over with emotion. But there are no assurances goodness and mercy will follow him in the forthcoming verses of his life. Whether they be Satanic, or whether they be mercies from the heavens, there's a good possibility that once he finds a way to enter this building, it could be the house he dwells in forever.

He reaches in his pocket to put the scope to his eye.
He can't see? He can't see his hand in front of his face?
He hears screams!!!
He hears panic!!!
The area is becoming an uproar!!!
Cars are slamming brakes!!!
Screeching tires own the night!!!
Doors are slamming!!!
Profanity is flying from the mouths of sailors!!!
Chaos is beginning to boil!!!

"What!..... The!..... Hell?"
He stops in his tracks? He can barely see?????????
....He begins figuring it out?
Inside some of the stores and buildings, the faint glow of backup lighting can be seen powering up!
In the void, skyscrapers stand idle like decommissioned cell phone towers.
"I'll be goddamn!" astounded.
"I'll be goooood-damned," he repeated with a smile.
For as far as he can see, the power is out!!!! In every direction he pans, there's darkness!!!!!
Headlights, flashlights, lights of smartphones, and Maglites® come to life!!! He begins hearing sirens and distress calls! A flare rockets into the air, turning the sky orange with its tail of burning phosphorous!
Cain wants to drop to his knees and thank the Creator! Who else could've caused this? Who else but the Almighty has the power to induce a blackout in New York City!
"HA-HA-HA-HA-HAAAAAAA," he laughed.
"I will execute great vengeance on them with *wrathful* rebukes!!

Then they will know that I am God when I lay my vengeance
upon them!"
The electric pulses of protection and purpose come over him in
an effervescent torrent!! He becomes baptized with divine protection!! He's honored to be pimped out for a righteous cause!
"Call me a hitman for angelic hire!"
The will to slaughter these sex traffickers becomes spiritually
encouraged! He thinks about David versus the Philistines! He
envisions all the stories his grandmother told him about war
in the bible, and how he has to decide which side he's going
to fight on! She taught him that just like he's a God of forgiveness, he's also a God of wrath!

"Well it's eye for an eye time! Y'all done fucked up now," he
declared, running towards the building.

While everyone panics around him, he's an arch angel of pay-
back marching towards his worst defaulter! As best as he can,
in partial darkness and partial light, he slows up and pushes
against the corner. Standing the right of the alleyway, it's pitch
black down there! He can't see a thing! At the other end he sees
the dim radiance of E. 49th. St. Overhead he sees air condition-
ers hanging out of windows. The fire escape stairwells glisten in
the darkness. Looking over his shoulder, he takes a deep breath.
The loss of power has sent people into a stupor. He can see the
traces of backup generators, candles, flashlights, and people,
and voices.
But no one's paying attention to him. He slips behind a stinky
trash dumpster. He can't see them but he can hear the rats scurrying around as he intrudes upon their space. Kneeling to one
knee he sits the case on the ground. Concealed by his trench
coat is the hi-tech optics. Being they give him options like the
ability to see in night, and thermal imaging; he can see things
normal eyes can't.
He put them on, tightens the strap, and with a press of the

power button, everything goes green. The dark alcoves are now exposed. A turn of a knob increases the intensity. Pressing the zoom button and the perspective increases 6x. Like parasites fleeing a toxic host, the door bursts opens and men of various dress exit the building. He wants to pick them off but he keeps his mind on his business. Pervert after pervert spill out like vomit. Two get in cars, others use the lights on smartphones to scamper off. Others simply walk out of the alley and disappear into the Manhattan darkness. Once the stream ceases, he readies his next move. The place Merciless and the other car disappeared behind turns out to be a delivery dock/parking area for about ten cars, or five SUV's. A large canopy prevents the sun rain and surrounding residents from looking down on their illicit activities. He sees the Charger delivered earlier. It's parked near the set of stairs closest to the door, a second set of stairs are at the other end, and a pair of luxury vehicles and a white Sprinter® van are still left.

He turns to the right and presses zoom, increasing it until he can see to the other end of the alley, which the binoculars calculate to be a distance of 243ft.

Looking around, he delves over the fact he doesn't know how long the power outage would last, but isn't about to let that stop him. Looking to the 5th floor of the building his back is against, he sees a woman looking out of her window shining a flashlight. Luckily she's too far to see him.

He shuffles his feet to a more comfortable position. Zoomed to the max, he scans the building from top to bottom. All the windows are closed, and all the curtains drawn. Above the rectangular cut-out that is the parking area, there's no windows. But over the door is a camera, and to the door's right is a button. Midway up, and to the right of the door's frame is a call box equipped with a speaker.

His heart pounds! His mind body and soul tells him this is his chance, and not to waist it on indecision! If he believes he's on a divine mission, he must walk in faith—trust and understand the signs, and realize the aids bestowed on him aren't of his doing!

He raises his hand and presses another button. The view transforms from glowing green, to dark with rainbow colors. The thermodynamic capability gives him a detailed perspective of red, lime, orange, yellow, and, purple, and blue. He scans the cars sitting in the lot. There's no heat signatures in any of them. He scans up and down the alley. Rats and a dog can be seen, but no humans. At the end of the alley he can see the frantic on 49th. St. The tactical gloves he's wearing are made from Kevlar®. He feels the weight of the silenced pistol clipped to his waist and the yearning in his chest! Switched back to night vision he picks up the case and makes for the building!

Tucked in the space between the Charger and the 6 series BMW, luckily there's a dumpster here too; but it's on the other side. He looks inside the Charger—it looks like a rental. Knelled to one knee, his back against the bricked building. Over his left shoulder is the Dodge, to his right is the Beamer, at the rear passenger tire he sits the case. Clicking it open he extracts the Calico and screws on the silencer. Next, he pulls up his robe and raises his pant leg. Strapped around his thigh is the *Becker® BK9*, an awesome weapon. The high-carbon, non-reflective, black steel is well over a foot long, and sharper than a surgeon's scalpel. Nearly indestructible, it's capable of cutting a man in half. Looking it over, he hears the faint sound of movement; sounds of human chatter coming from the other side of the door! He clutches the blade, slides the machine gun over his shoulder, and quickly closes the case.

Thinking he should put the knife up, he reaches for the silenced pistol!

The door opens! The beam of a flashlight is the first thing he sees, the intensity almost caused him to switch the mode to normal. The green perspective now includes the dark one of a man who's dragging a woman through the door.

How'd she get over here?
It looks like the woman he was pushing earlier at the other brothel. They're obviously brought here to work too; she's half dressed, and he's still wearing the cheap suit.
"Fuck did I tell you whore! You don't have no off days! Now I'm tired of hearing about your stomach cunt, and I don't give a fuck about your hurt leg either! You get back to fucking and sucking, or you can kiss any chance at getting that passport back goodbye…You knew the costs of coming to America. You knew you didn't have the money! Now you think you can just walk away without paying us back?" and strikes the woman in her face.
"You ready to get back to work, or do I have to put a bullet in your head and leave you out here with the rats bitch?"
"…I can't go any more," she sobbed. "I've been working for months, and you just keep telling me I owe you more money. My body's breaking down. I need time to rest," she cried.
"Please, I just want to go home," he teasingly imitated.
Slaps her first, and punches her in the stomach.
She doubles over.
But he snatches by the hair!
"That's what all you young runaway sluts say! Everybody wants the American dream, but don't nobody wanna pay for it!" and grabs her face, squeezing her jaws until saliva runs out of the corners.
"Look here….*BITCH!*…..You think this is a fuckin' game?"
The terrified and exhausted woman can take no more. She prays to her higher power asking for a miracle, and falls limp in his arms. She remembers her mother's words of how hanging with the wrong crowd can get her into trouble. Through the last glimmers of consciousness, she sees the blurry image of something………It's a man?……*A pastor!!!*
She knows she's dying, she has to be dead. There aren't any pastors around here…. But she can still feel tears in her eyes, she can still feel the pain in her body, she can still feel the

man's hand clawing into her side and striking her to get up. Now she's seeing pastor wearing a scuba mask holding something, and coming up behind her trafficker. She knows she's hallucinating. This must be what death is like....The trafficker raises his fist! She braces for the blow! A breeze of a sharp wind brushes across her cheek. The trafficker lets out a loud gasp! She feels his hand go limp, and shoot out like Frankenstein!.......He must be about to choke her! She feels herself falling sideways, and slides to the ground! The flashlight the trafficker was holding rolls of the edge of the dock and falls off! She sees the beam ricocheting off the walls........She catches a glimpses of the scene. A pastor is behind the man with one hand on his shoulder, one hand is holding something to his back. When she sees blood gurgling from his mouth running down his chest........She rolls over and faints!

Cain has sunk the knife into his back—tip protruding out of his solar plexus, sliced through his oblique, and sheared his Rectus sheath!
The man convulses and twitches as the final remnants of his existence flowed like water down the blades tang. After reading the 'Hit Man' manual several times, he learned the exact location to sink the blade so he won't severe the abdominal aorta and drench himself with blood. If done correctly, the severe won't take place until extraction, giving the assassin time to avoid the rush of red plasma.
The sounds the trafficker is making are similar to a person swallowing their tongue while having a seizure. He can feel the erratic thump of the man's heart reverberating against the steel embedded in his upper left abdominopelvic quadrant, before going lifeless on his feet, and falling backwards with the weight of finality. Using his shoulder, he leans into the heavy man, and in one swoon, snatches the knife while stepping back! The *"schling"* of the blade slicing flesh cuts the air, followed by a geyser of squirting red. His face smacks the ground! He's dead

as a doorknob!

With his chest heaving, Pastor switches the mode to thermal
and looks around!
No one sees a thing.
The woman lay on her back not moving. He switches back to
night vision and goes to her. Checking her wrist, she still has a
pulse, but barely. He begins softly tapping her face.
"Hey-Hey-Hey!!!"
But she's not coming to.
He looks towards the door, breathing so fast that he has to
take moment to steady himself! He's getting worked up for no
reason. He has to remember himself *he* has the upper hand, not
them. From the position he's in, if anyone comes through the
door, he can kill them before they know he's there.
Still holding the knife, he looks at the blood dripping off the
point, wipes it on his robe, and sheathes it back around his
thigh. The machine gun is at his side and the silenced pistol at
his waist. While calming his mind, he keeps trying to wake her.
When she collapsed, her shirt opened leaving her bare breast
exposed. Without looking, he covers her and continues trying
wake her. In a few moments she begins coming to.
He runs and hides!
As she opens her eyes he watches her. She blinks a few times
and looks around.
"I'm here to help you. You're safe now," he whispered.

She searches the darkness for the source. Slowly it comes back
to her.
He sees the look of terror come over her face!
"You're safe miss! The angels have saved you! You're safe now!....
Can you hear me! Nod if you hear me!"
The disoriented woman looks in shock!!! He realizes he'll have
to physically move her. She's too afraid and in bad shape.
"I'm a pastor! I'm coming out! God has sent me to save you!

Don't scream!" and comes from around the car.

It's good she can't see him. The sight would've sent her into cardiac arrest.

"You're safe. No more pain. I got you sweetheart. No one's going to hurt you anymore."

He sees the woman looking into the darkness at him—the bruises, the cuts.

"Come on, try to get up. We've got to get you out of here before the others come," and pulls her to her feet.

She winces as he carries her out of the parking area and sits her in the alley beside the dumpster, runs to pull the body off the dock, drags it beside the SUV, and rushes back to her.

"You okay?"

She shakes her head.

"I'm going to get you outta here okay. But I need you to tell me who's in that building. I need you to tell me anything you can about it? Do you know Bailey Red, Cailida Floriano?"

"*They're kidnapping girls and forcing us to be sex workers. They have places everywhere,*" she whispers. "*There's girls on every floor....*" Her head slumps.

Pastor is no expert, but the woman seems to be under the influence of something.

Sex traffickers routinely dope the women up.

Looking at her condition, he knows she needs medical attention. But he's a wanted fugitive, and still has to find Bailey.

"Can you tell me anything you know miss? *Please? Anything!* How do I get inside? Are there guns? How many guards are there?"

She's slipping in and out of consciousness. He's not going to get much from her. He digs some bills out of his pocket and balled them up in her hand.

"Take this money, and you get away from here! You get far away from this place! I have to go! I have to get to the others!"

Her lips are moving but no words are coming forth.

"What? *What!*" putting his ear to her mouth.

"...........*The code is two........two eight one.........one three.......
They stay on the top floor.*"

Pauses and swallows hard.

"Who? Who stays on the top floor?"

But she doesn't explain.

"*You can only enter on the third floor and,*" she panted. "*..... The
code is different for every service......School yard, means you want
underage.......Central Park mean you want rape,.........S&M,...
Greek means sod-....*"

She stops because she's having a difficult time getting the words
out, and he's growing anxious to get inside! She leans back
against the wall and breathes. It looks like she's done talking.
He leans forward and kisses her forehead.
She can't see him, but she can feel his compassion.

"I'll get you out of here okay."

But he doesn't expect an answer.

He focuses his attention back on the entrance.

"*God sent me an angel...,*" she whispered.

"*God sent me an angel...*"

He hears the woman say again.

"*....I knew you weren't going to forsake me. I knew you would
send me an angel....An angel of the night.*"

And that's all he heard. Because he's gone!

Back to where he was before, with his case in his hand, his
mind works to devise a plan. Nervous with fervor, he searches
for a way to initiate his assault. Moments turn into seconds,
wasted time becomes the by-product of his stagnation.

"Fuck it!"

Moving to the dumpster nearest the SUV, he opens the case
takes out the sniper rifle, assembles it, and straps it over his
shoulder. Now the other items, concealing them in various
places on his person. The case goes behind the dump.
Standing, he pushes his skufia down snugly and makes sure his

binoculars are secure.

Ready for war, the submachine gun leads the way as he dashes up the stairs! With the back of his skufia touching the brick, he listens for movement! Based on what she said about the 3[rd.] floor entry, he knows there's some type of stairwell. The red light on the call box is on but the door is making a buzzing sound.

A gust of wind blows through the alleyway. The instantaneous change of pressure creates a vacuum in the small area, causing the door to rustle and expose its vulnerability.

If that isn't convincing enough, the atmosphere sends a thunderous burst through the sky, followed by a flash of blinding white light! The rustling door is beckoning him to enter. He takes a deep breath pulls it open!

Under the faint light of backup flood lights, he pokes his head through and snatches it back out. Seeing nothing but a set of stairwells, he takes another deep breath, leaps from behind the wall, shoots inside!

Standing at the base of a stairwell looking up, he sees landings. Fire extinguishers in breakable cases are situated at each floor. As well as battery powered floodlights and closed circuit cameras. He sees the door to level 1 and the bottom half of what's most likely the door to level 3. He ducks down and crawls under the backside of the stairwell. It doesn't smell like urine like a lot of the others around the city. Surprisingly it's clean. The controlled access must be the reason, and the fact this is Manhattan is probably the other. Thankfully there's no one lying in wait, or he would've been toast.

Using this cut to his advantage, he takes a minute to process the scene. Faint sounds of voices and people are coming from inside the building. Males seem tense and agitated, females sound afraid. The stairs are concrete with railings of painted metal, the walls are cinder blocks painted beige. No graffiti.

A door opens above him!

He hears the voices of two males and can see the beam of a

flashlight! One's giving orders, and the other's listening!
"…Tell him I said enough with her and get back inside. Then find a way to secure that door until the power comes back on."
The other man responds yes sir.
He has but a split second to decide his move!
He makes it!
Back out the door!

The thug in the suit comes through the door swearing he heard movement? His phone begins warbling just as he was about to call and see where he is.

Pastor hears the man talking on the phone holding the flashlight. The person on the other end sounds to be updating him on the power outage. Judging from his responses, the outage is a result of a transmission failure at some power station and is only affecting Manhattan. The thug hangs up and begins pacing toward the SUV; the area where the body is.
He dials another number.
The muffled ring of a cell phone starts sounding! In the next building people are walking with candles and flashlights. Noise and commotion come from the surface streets. Emergency vehicles wail in the distance. A car alarm blares.
An odd look comes over him? There's blood on the ground? Lots of it!!!!!
"One of you tramps out here on your rag! Ha-haaa! Bitches!"
A gloved hand clutches his face and jerk his neck to the side!!!
He feels the cold steel against his Adam's apple, the smell coming off the person behind him holds the stench of death!!!
"Tramps huh?"
He tries to reach for his gun! But the pain from Pain's blade to his neck speaks a different truth!
"Do it motherfucker! Give me a reason to decapitate your weak ass!" and bites a plug out of his face, spitting it on the ground!!
"AAAAAAA-aaaaaah!! FUCK!!!!"

"Shut the fuck up!!" blood spittle flying from his mouth.
As if they were filled with helium, his arms rise in the air.
"Turn it off and drop it!" his scowling red lips millimeters from his ear.
The Maglite falls to the pavement.
Like a tarantula dragging his kill back to his lair, he leads the man up the stairs and back in the stairwell. Feeling the firearm holstered under his suit coat, he doesn't bother disarming him. One false move and it's off with his head.
"Where's Merciless!"
The thug plays stupid.
"Who?"
He cut him!
 "AaaaaahhhhhGGGGG!!!!!!!" The slice is deep—too deep for him to live much longer.
"Any last words!"
"Sixth floor!"
"Listen at you! Just a second ago you were a tough guy," and knees him in the balls. "How many are with him?"
"Eight….Maybe seven," wincing from the blow.
"Who's the first person on the other side of the door?"
"Receptionist,…………and……….a guy or two," he answered, losing blood fast.
"What they using to see?"
"Flashlights…Backup lights," wheezing, acting as if he's about to fall.
He buries a boot in ass!
"Stand up asshole! How many girls are you shitheads keeping in there!"
"…Maybe thirty!…..Sorry man, fuck……Man, shit!!!!!!"
"How many clients are there?"
"They left…slow night! Man I'm bleeding to death!!!"
He socked him in the stomach!
"That's the aim! Now I'm gonna ask you one time! Where's Bailey Red?"

"…I don't now!!! I swear!!! I don't who that is!!!"
His right hand wants to make him a martyr, but his brain says
use him first, then kill him!!!
"There's so many victims it's impossible to know them all huh?"
He stabs him in the thigh!
"AAAAAAAAAAAAAH!!!!!"
"Didn't I say shut the fuck up!!!"
Blood is coming through his fingers trying to stop the blood
loss! He presses harder, he's not ready to die—*he's afraid of
death!!!* A pistol meets the side of his face, sending his tooth
across the floor; swelling his temples with pain! *He sees darkness!*
WHAM!
A vicious strike brings him back!!
Now bleeding out of his mouth too, his molar lays on the
ground with a lump of meat stuck to the back.
A hand goes around his waist and removes his weapon; takes
his wallet phone and keys. All he horrible things he's done in
his life are making themselves known—his bladder and intes-
tines fighting against his will to empty.
"You know where we're going…Move!"
The thug does, barely. He's on his last leg.
With one hand in the air, and the other around his throat,
blood flows as he heads up the stairs, big splotches staining
each stair they climb. Cain doesn't think he's going to live long
enough for him to use him, but he doesn't care; he's gonna kill
him anyway.
But he makes it.
Now on the 3rd. floor landing, he stands in the shadows and
stands him at the door. A tall wooden one with designs made
into the face. From under the backup light he tells him what to
do.
"Open the door!"
With his left hand around his throat and stumbling to stay
upright, he uses the other to open the door, which is
usually secured by an electric lock. The thug opens it.

Like a hog hanging from a barn rafter, he raises the knife, and just as he's about to go through, a single swing slices him from the center of his back, and down his lower lumbar; opening him up like a can of Kipper Snacks!
The pain detonates through his nervous system like an atom bomb!!!!!!Shocking him to his tippy toes like he's walking on fire, he falls to the ground in a floorboard shaking heap, fucks the floor two times, and let out his final breath!!!

Pastor clutches his machine gun.

The beam of a flashlight is coming!
He pulls beside the dead thug and moves to the corner of the archway. Whoever comes through will be butterflied like a shrimp.
This must be the lobby. There's a reception desk and a table with magazines atop surrounded by leather chairs.
The beam of light gets closer, vibration of the floor increases! Heavy footsteps, light illuminates the room! A figure comes through the archway!
He pulls the trigger!
The suppressed submachine gun sending two quick, three round bursts into the man's neck and face! The sound of the body falling to the floor is louder than the gun's report. The Swiss-chessed headpiece is filled with hot projectiles!
He sees the glow of another light!

It's officially killing season!

He ducks and listens for his prey's movements! He can hear the vermin communicating; completely oblivious death is just around the corner.
Since his victim is coming from the other direction, he doesn't give him the chance to come inside the room. He lines him up with the green laser beam, and pulls the trigger. In .890 of a

second, his upper body is seeded with six lead rounds!!
With the tip of the barrel still smoking, he listens! He doesn't
hear any movement or see any more flashlights.
Sllluuump!!!
Goes the trash sliding down the wall to the floor.
He looks around the corner and sees a hallway straight ahead,
and another to his left and right. A door at the end of the
walkway is to his front. In the comfort of almost total dark-
ness, he goes left!
A man says something in the distance?

Arriving at the end, he peeks around and proceeds right!
The thug's standing in a doorway yelling inside. When he gets
finished instructing them, he shuts the door making sure it's
locked, and continues strolling.
Cain follows!
Ahead is the door he saw earlier. The man turns left and goes
through it. Before it has the chance to hit the jamb, Cain runs
and grabs it, the barrel of his sniper rifle just missing tapping
the frame.
Peeking through the crack he watches the man descend to a
lower floor and pass through another door.
He tiptoes down! After opening the door to check for the light
beam, he creeps down!
Exiting through the door he sees more doors down here. The
floor looks to be made in the pattern of a rectangle with an
outer hallway, a hallway crossing at the center, and one running
down the spine of the floor.
While he does his rounds, he can hear the cries and voices of
women coming from behind the doors. The distress emanating
from inside their depths surges his rage!!! It's like he can feel
their soul's cries for help. He now understands why the woman
said he can only enter from the 3rd floor. From the stairwell
it resembles a normal apartment building. But the other five
doors which seem to be real, aren't. They're just false doors with

walls behind them.

He hears a different male voice in the distance and can see light inching across the floor!

He falls back and watches from a distance!

Now comes a suit holding a long Maglite conversing on a cell, stopping in front of the man he was just following. He signals for the man to wait! From his body language it seems like he has something to tell him.

Seconds later the call ends, and the look on his face isn't good; his disposition tense!

Hiding at the other end, he wonders why they not speaking English? But after closer examination, he notices they aren't Latino or African-American like the majority of the woman he's seen, nor are they white, and they aren't Asian like the girls he saw in that cage. Their hair is black hair and straight, and they look Russian.

He grips the Calico® M960 with the 100-round drum, and with 82 bullets to go, plus another full one in his pocket; he eases his hand around his waist and grabs the 9-milly (mm). But before he gets it completely out, he notices a change in the goons' demeanor. He doesn't have to speak their language to figure it out. The one goon extracts a firearm from his holster and looks his way. The other says something and pulls his weapon.

The hairs on the back of his neck aren't on end when he sees the man spin and come his direction, but calm.

He's gotten used to extermination!

Missing getting caught by his flashlight, he leans at the blind side of the corner and focuses on the wall! It's getting brighter as the light creeps forward!!!! He can't keep going around because the other suit is likely coming from the other end!! It's either his life or there's!!! He's backed into a corner and has no choice but to do shoot it out!!! The man with the quickest draw will live!!

He likes the odds!

In the span of a millisecond, is able to surge around the corner— blinded by light, and squeeze the trigger!
The goon squeezes his too!

Cain hears the shot!

BOOM!!!!!!!!!

He sees the muzzle flash!

He feels the blow to his chest from the point blank round!

The shot reverberates through the tight hallway!

He feels his body blown into the wall!

BOOM!!!!!!!!!!!!!!!!!

The goon gets off another one, striking him in the chest again!

He's in the void of dead air!!!!! He thinks he's about to die!

The light hits the floor!

He braces for another one!

The wind is knocked out of him, he can't move!!!!!! His abdomen is deflated, his solar plexus locked in a hideous spasm!!!!!
He begs for it to be over!
His diaphragm opens! He gasps in a glutinous amount of oxygen!
The goon has dropped to the floor, the load of dying weight hitting the door caused the lock to give, cracking the door open a foot!

The other goon is coming fast, calling for his partner!

He's still trying to regain his equilibrium, he feels the rifle is on his back, and so is the pistol. Amazingly he hasn't dropped the Calico!

He pats his chest feeling the quarter-sized holes in his vest!!!!

The pain is almost unbearable, but he has to ignore it and get ready for the next wave of whoever heard those shots!!!!!

The acrid smell of gunpowder owns the air like a ruthless slum lord!!!! The quake of terrified people locked behind the doors provokes him to push himself up! He falls around the corner and stumbles off just as the goon runs up!!!

Moving quickly, he slings the Calico back around his shoulder and pulls the L42A1!

"AAAAAAAAAAAAAAAA!!!" the goon yelling bloody murder at the sight of his dead brethren.

Readying himself, he takes a deep breath and is almost back to where he's thinking clearly! Using his left hand to resituate his night vision goggles, he peers around the corner!

The man shouting in their language while coming down the hall in a defensive stance with a gun in one hand, and the other aiming the light!!

He doubles around to the other end!!

Like a mouse in a maze he doesn't see any one trying to sneak up from the rear, so he goes down the hall and looks around!!

Women are banging on the doors which causes the goon to yell at them!!!!

"SHUT UP WHORES!!!!!!!! SHUT YOUR FILTHY MOUTHS BEFORE YOU ALL DIE!!!" he screamed enraged.

Cain suspects it's because he just saw the bullet riddled body of his countrymen sprawled on the floor.

He starts firing the pistol indiscriminatingly, screaming to the top of his voice!!!!

With his arm in a stiff position, Cain moves quickly so he can get to him before he shoots the women! In the thick darkness behind the muffled worries of the hostages, the agent of retribution stalks his prey.

He stops shooting.

Cain doesn't know if he's run out of bullets or what, but he knows he's about to perform his "signature move" on him! After seeing how well it worked at the restaurant, he decided to make it part of his modus operandi. Watching from a standoff distance, the man creeps down one hall and around the other, every so often spinning around to check his rear. Cain follows, stops, and peeks until he rounds the next corner. He can see the prey sweating, and knows he doesn't want to be here. At every backup light he comes upon, he hesitates to continue; his reluctance to keep going becomes greater by the second. He watches him check the doors, and come back to the room where his dead cohort lay. He shines the light inside the room and kicks the door in!

A woman screams!!

"Where is he!"

But she keeps screaming!!!!!

"Shut up!"

He strikes the woman with the gun!

Now all is quiet, as she lay crouched in the corner bleeding from the head.

He slams the door and moves on!

Just as end of the rifle's suppressor is propelled into the back of his skull, causing him to drop the flashlight *and* the gun!

Cain blows a crater out of his leg!!

The man falls to the floor yelling in pain!!

"AaaaaaaaaAAAAAA!!!"

A booted foot smashes down on the side of his cranium bashing his head into the door's brass hinge, causing more damage than the shot! He picks up the gun he dropped, and crashes it into his nose; spins it around, and sends the butt into his jaw, shattering it like a stained a glass window!!!!

"Fucking filth!" and spit on him.

Staring at him in disgust, he swings the rifle around and unzips his pants.

"Noooaaaaahhh---," the goon whined. As he empties his bladder all over his face and hair; shake it off, and put it up. Wreathing in pain, and drenched from the golden shower, he catches glimpses of what looks like a nightmare, one worse than he can fathom! A man dressed like a pope is about to kill him!!!!!! His face is replaced with some sort of robot eye, and he's covered in blood holding a superweapon! He knows he's witnessing the opening of the gates, as he's about to burn in Hell!

But not yet.

Pastor clears the chamber and sends the round falling to the floor! Looking at the turd on the ground he feels no sympathy! He's a gratified sanitation worker getting rid of the trash! The atrocities they're committing are utterly unforgiveable—horrors of the worst type.

I'm going to make them pay!..DEARLY!

"Take me to Merciless," he said calmly.

The man fights to get to his feet, but cries out in pain and falls back to the floor.

"I assure you the next fall will be your last."

The trafficker fights to his feet, clawing himself up by the door knob and the wall, almost falling again. His face is fatter than a Mr. Potato head doll.

"How many are there?"

"….. Guss……ee…….Va ress-uh top…....Vour," he can't even talk his face is so destroyed.

"Get the light! Take me there!"

The heavily wounded thug pushes off the wall, wincing and slobbering from the mouth as he gets the light.

Cain switched to normal view causing the scene to change from green to clear. The red numbers and graphs to the right of his eye still showing a virtual display of distance temperature and angle. While pressing the gun to his spine the man drags his broken leg away, while using his left hand to hold onto the wall with blood dripping from the hideous grow-knot on his forehead, and all kind of mess dripping from his mouth.

It's obvious the thug is concussed.

Heading down and entering through the door leading to the stairwell, the walls are covered with embossed wall paper, the ceiling is trimmed in wood, and the lighting sconces are made of white tinted glass. Slowly, they come to the next floor. At each new level he stops, listens, and proceed with caution. The suit is losing a lot of blood, and isn't going to take many more steps; that hinge to the head, and that pistol whipping did him justice.

Once on the top of the flight, he makes him stop.

And listens!

The odor of burning cigarettes is apparent. He clicks the binoculars back to night vision.

"Kill the light!"

He did.

"Go through," and jams him with the barrel.

The man limps through the open door and steps into the darkness. They're in a short hallway with another door at the end.

The goon pushes the door open and goes through.

With the gun in his right hand he grabs the man by the shoulder and whispers in his ear.

"I want you to turn on the light and walk forward. If someone comes, you blind 'em! I'm already fighting the urge; give me a reason…..Move!"

He does.

Dragging his broken leg down the hall, he holds onto the wall while losing blood in liters.

They are now in the main corridor of the penthouse. A very nice one, not small and basic like the workers' quarters. A keypad is beside the door but the loss of power has it inoperable.

"Tell 'em you're back. Everything's okay."

"Vey awrey no yu her……Vey wayin vor yu."

"Well you better say something!"

He hobbles without moving. Standing in one place is agonizingly difficult.

He knocks on the door.

Nothing.

Cain jams him with the gun again.

Where they're standing is open on the right. He can see the living room and eating areas. The binoculars calculate the point on the ceiling he's focused on to be 14ft. - 3in. from his position. He can see the lounge area, the apartment takes up the entire floor and is quite expansive. It's hard to believe no one thought to install backup lighting. Their primary concern seemed to be lavish décor.

"I'm about to blow your head off!"

The man takes that to mean he better start moving.

On passing a door he catches a glimpse of a candle burning on a table.

Voices in the distance!

The sound of someone moving quickly!

Pain can't see them but can feel their footsteps. They're somewhere within forty feet of him! The hallway has two ends that go around the corner, with rooms and walkways breaking off of it. Even in darkness he feels exposed.

Using the man as a human shield, the tip of the silencer rests beside his ear on his shoulder. Cain slings him to where he can best protect him.

A light beam comes from inside the room with the open door! He massages the trigger in preparation for the kill! Whoever comes through the door, he's going to, without prejudice or bias, void of any empathy or compassion; ruthlessly lay down the law on this malignant spore which does the earth no good. The human shield breathes harder, his body is trembling extremely! He begins making cowardly sounds as the coming moment approaches! The intensity is sending him into shock!!!!

"Shine it right in they face!!!"

He clicks to thermodynamic. Before the person comes through the doorway, he sees their heat signature!

A shower of rain begins bathing the building with echoes of noise canceling hydration.

The wounded thug gasps when he hears his comrade call out his name! He wants to respond but is muted by fear!!!!!!

The man calls again?

Now he tries to say something!!!!!!! The glare from the Maglite is cast at the door!!!! The 7.62mm round awaits detonation!!!!

The upper body of a man leans sideways through the door!!!!

Cain pulls the trigger!

The thug screams!!!! The power residue that comes from the end of the barrel burns the side of his face with hot bits of saltpeter, sulfur, and metal! The fully jacketed projectile bores into the man's cheek, through his cerebellum, and explodes out the back of his skull!

The entry hole and spatter creates a portrait of wet flesh on the wall, sending the cancer collapsing the ground. Locked in his death grip, the flashlight shines against the baseboard—eyes open, he never saw his executioner.

Like a shadow puppet, the tip of his shoe's shadow casts against the wall.

Cock-Cock! Chambering another round, ejecting the spent shell.

"Move!"

The man steps pass his dead peer, and continues to the house-man's suite. At the end of the 'U' shaped hallway there's another door.

"..... dere," shining the beam at the door.

This is where Cain will perform his signature move. He whispers something, and backs away pointing the rifle. The binoculars' thermal imaging mode is not able to see through walls, but what it can do is detect the temperature *of* the wall; which in turn gives the person using them an idea to whether a person is standing on the other side. The area to both sides are giving off heat levels too elevated for drywall and wood.

Over the left shoulder goes the rifle, from the right comes the machine gun. From the small of his back, the pistol is front and center. Trained on the man's back, it's just like a typical track and field event; the start of competition is signaled by a shot. His is just the same. The only difference is, he shoots the runner when it's time to start.

"GO!" and pops him.

Believing the pastor's promise to let him live if he's able to break down the door on his first try, the terrified thug ignores excruciating pain, and moving as fast as he can, crashes through the door!

Whoever's on the other side, opens up on him, peppering him with friendly fire!

Playing right into the pastor's hand, he angles to the side and "one shot Charlie" the first man!! And spins into the room; spraying the other man from his back to his calf as he tries to run with the rest of scattering figures!!

Holding the 9mm in his left, as they lay on the ground he shoots them again, the Calico's lethal effectiveness on full display! One man has let go of his light allowing it to roll to the floor, the other guy falls face forward on his, completely smothering it out.

There's movement in a corner! He zooms in on the figure! A woman is balled in the floor with a gun in her hand shaking with panic!!!!

"Where's Merciless cunt!!!"

But she raises the gun, and to her detriment proceeds to fire in the direction of the voice. She only got of one before he stilled her too. Olga was notorious for forcing abortions and flushing fetuses down the toilet.

He walks over and gives her the same treatment as the others, right between the eyes; and rapes her for valuables.

In the expanse of the room there's another room breaking off of it.

He hears movement!

Walking as light as a ghost, he takes one cautious step after the next. Every so often the floor creaks, adding to the suspense.

He stops at the entrance to a restroom and can hear the person breathing behind the shower curtain.

He raises the weapon!

"They call him Merciless! Where is he?"

He starts begging.

"Get out and take me to him!"

The curtain opens and a man stands inside with his hands up. The white T-shirt is wet with sweat. A gold Gucci-link chain hangs around his neck, his wrist sports a gold Rolex, his other wrist showcases his love for diamond bezel bracelets.

"He's hiding in the closet! Don't shoot! I'll show you where he is!"

He falls over the tub as he tries to get out. Pushing himself upright, he uses his hands to guide him. Circling from a distance, he gives no indication of his position. Though the man can't see his hand in front of his face, he expects him to find his way to Merciless.

He's doing a good job so far.

Using the wall, he makes it out of the bathroom, patting his way down the hall, he keeps trying to see where the killer is.

HE SEES HIM!

Figuring the man has given him up, he's trying to escape but the darkness makes his efforts a waste.

He aims the weapon, and shoot his hostage nine times about the hip, kidney, shoulder and head. Before the man has slumped to the floor, he's already set his sights on Merciless!!!!!

Perspiring like crazy, enthusiasm surges! He retires his rifle and selects his blade! Clutched in his right hand, he moves like a tiger in the bush!

"I've been looking for you Terry. I've traveled *many, many* mi-lessssssss in search of you," his words seductive with revenge.

He swings the pistol and fires three shots with reckless abandon!!!!

"*Tonight!* Will be the last for the man who calls himself.... *The realest nigga to ever do it*...Isn't that your mantra," singing to him like a deranged baritone.

He fires more shots at the voice!!!!!

"After tonight....You will no longer be able to *harm*. You will no longer be able to *steal*. This building will be your final resting place. There will be nothing for your funeral, not even your ashes. You will be *eulogized* as an illustration, a *case in point!* A statement to your organization, and others alike. After tonight, the world will know...That to fight evil..You must embrace *death!*"

Bostic fires, screaming in rage until the clip is empty!!!!!
"Now it's my turn."
He tries to run!!! But all he does is crash over a chair!!!!!
"I want you to think of all the lives you've destroyed. I want you to think of what you've done to become who you are. I want you to think of your birth. I want you to imagine your slaughter."
"*FUCK YOUUUUU!!!!!!!!!!*" Merciless shouted.
"*Ah-ah-ahhhhh!*......Your days of fucking are over. But the penetration *is* about to begin."
Cain is frigid with brutality. He wants to repay him for each and every woman he ever hurt. He wants him to see the face of every girl he's raped. He wants him to regret every penny he profited from trafficking humans.

Terry moves in the labyrinth of stillness and sightlessness; the empty pistol is all the protection he has! Disoriented by the

pouring rain, and off balance by the killer, he can't see; he falls over thing after thing!!!!
"All of you rodents act just the same when it's time to die."

The murderous madman tracking him has him drenched in confusion!
The votary of death watches him run into walls and fall over tables! He watches as he bumps and collides clumsily with obstacles!
 Maneuvering himself closer, he waits at a corner for him to pass. He raises the knife, and sends a raucous slice to his leg!
"AAAAAAAAAAAAAAAAAHHH!!!"
Merciless screams and pulls the trigger! But it only clicks.

"Would you like to say a prayer? Okay. I'll lead..........The adversaries of God shall be broken to pieces; against them he will thunder in heaven!"
With force, he swings the one-pound knife down on his hand!
The razor sharp 0.365 thick blade cuts his index and middle fingers clean at the knuckle.
"AAAAAAAAAAAAAAAAAAAAH!!!!.- AAAAH!!!
His ring finger is also partially severed, and the back of his hand is hanging from the bone.
"The Creator is coming out from his place to punish the inhabitants of the earth for their iniquity, and the earth will disclose blood shed on them!!!.....What have you done with Bailey!.......*WHERE! IS! SHEEEEEE!"*
But he's screaming hysterically!!!! Blood is getting all over him!
Frantically, he rips off the shirt he's wearing and uses it to try to stop the blood! He can't believe part of his hand is holding on by a string!
Cain kicks him into the table!!!! It shatters like thin ice as he crashes through it, lacerating and goring his body on the jagged glass!
 "Where is she!"

Tired of hearing his mouth, he extracts the 9mm from his waist, moves on him with speed, and power-punches him in the mouth, knocking out his front row!!!
Grabbing him by the neck, he jams the silencer down his throat until the hammer is smashed against his upper lip!
Merciless gags on the long, hard silencer, before defecating on himself.
"Familiar?.....The women!!! Remember them!!!"
 Merciless can see the little red light and a faint glare of the strange contraption on the killer's face!
"Where! Is! She!"
And yanks it out, smelling the irony scent of Merciless' blood! He mumbles he doesn't know!!!!! He mumbles she's gone!!!!!
"She a ---ere!!! I ain't seen...t..t...he hospital!!!!!! She r-- off.......some lady----don't have......her!!!!!!!!"
"How can I contact her!"
"I.....don't.....e.....van-...ished!!!"

Before he sent him to hell, Cain made him tell him where each and every woman was locked. He made him produce every cent that was stashed. He made him tell everything he knows about Ed Denmark.

With the black Maglite under his chin, Cain pulls off the binoculars and shows Merciless his face.
It only takes seconds for the fear to show in his eyes, and him to become speechless!!!
"In life....It is often those we least expect who are the most dangerous."

And clicks off the light.

When Bostic finally expired, he was disrobed, dismembered, disfigured, disemboweled; dropped off the top of the building, and left in a congealing pool of blood and flesh spattered on the concrete sidewalk in front of the white apartment building burning on 458 W 50th. St.

Dix.

To an average man, a million dollars is an astounding amount of money. If obtained, he'll undoubtedly consider himself rich, believing all of his worries are over. There's usually impulsive purchases like the exotic sports car, a new watch. The monotonous relationship with the previous woman is usually shunned in exchange for the fresh influx of gorgeous young vixens. The address is updated to a sought-after location. For the average Joe, a million dollars is *stupid* dough.

But when you're Ed Denmark, the paltry sum of a million dollars is almost irrelevant. Insignificant things like supercars, flashy jewelry, or sailing the French Rivera on a hundred foot yacht with ten models doesn't interest his highly advanced mind. He invests his profits into things like, human embryo replication, and 21st century style thralldom. He, as well as the four fathers of America knew the secret reason why it's a integral part of society.

The Constitution's Thirteenth Amendment, Section 1 states:

'Neither slavery nor involuntary servitude, except as a punishment for crime whereof the party shall have been duly convicted'.

Yes. In America. Slavery is still *legal*.

Denmark believes it's a necessary part of not only American society, but the entire world. Eldrin Denmark is an evil genius, and far too superior of an intellect to be a racist. And far too intelligent to believe that one race of man is inherently smarter than the other. However, he does believe some races as a whole exhibit higher IQ levels than others. To him, there's a distinct reason why slavery has been practiced since the infancy of human existence, and holds firm to his belief that void of servitude, there is no advancement. In his opinion, the evolution of man hinges on suppression; one man lording over another man and using him as a mechanism to achieve his objective is absolutely necessary.
He believes Chairman Mao was justified when he made the decision to force slave labor on his subjects, starving forty million people to death while trying to bring China out of the dark ages and to the stance of modern super power.

In the last few years, Denmark and his cohorts have invested nearly two-hundred million dollars into the science of genetically modified organisms, known as (GMO) research. He has no interest in notifying the public about the introduction of modified foods into their diet, or making a profit from selling "roided up" chicken, and sixteen ounce apples. He's interested in the secret business of modifying food at is source, altering the genetic code to produce genes which can be used for mind control. Seeds which grow into plants which bear fruit packed with doses of natural chemicals and extracts that encourage subservience and docility. And the way he plans to achieve this is by purchasing seeds of all types by the metric ton.

In one of the world's most remote locations, on the coast of the Barents Sea near the Arctic Ocean, some eleven hundred kilometers from the North Pole; lays Svalbard. A barren stretch of rock claimed by Norway, and ceded in 1925 by international treaty. On this uninhabitable island, many of the world's wealthiest people are investing hundreds of millions of into what is called the "*Doomsday Seed Bank*." But officially the project is named the 'Svalbard Global Seed Vault'. From the seeds in the depths of this facility, Denmark hopes to realize his dream of global domination.

But the masses are too caught up in reality television, who has the nicest car, when's the new smartphone coming out, and who won the Super Bowl, to know.
It's quite easy to deceive millions of "educated" people.

When thinking of guns, the first manufactures which come to mind are names like, Heckler & Koch, Glock Ges.m.b.H, Smith and Wesson, and Browning Arms Company.
The average Joe may be able to break down his rifle and put it back together without looking, or thinks he knows all there is about firearms because he has a large collection. But in the little understood world of gun production, there's an even more surreptitious industry. One involving the black-market creation and selling of many of the exact same guns produced by legal manufactures. The only difference is these guns use the same

metals, same templates, and same design features, but lack serial numbers and identification marks.

While regular people get lost in the mirage of social media, pop culture, and celebrity gossip; billions in untraceable dollars are being made from the illegal gun production trade. Mercenaries, despots, and dictators are often unable to obtain the weapons they require to commit their atrocities by purchasing them from reputable sources. They either buy them used and in bad shape, or they go to Danno, Philippines. In the hills of these juggles, young men with no other way to feed their family, hand make weapons by the thousands. Not junk, but top quality ordinance.

After years of diplomatic efforts and millions in foreign investment, a deal was made with the country's corrupt leaders to allow Denmark and his affiliates to monopolize the market. What has historically been a way for drug cartels, shady world leaders, and tyrants for hire to obtain untraceable and unlimited amounts of arms, has now become controlled by one faction. By achieving this, Denmark and his group became the top players in the illegal gun game.

To lesser thinkers, they would assume this was done for financial gain. Though the profits generated from the move are immense, his sole purpose of achieving this is so he'd have a direct way to arm his global projects. Running an international crime syndicate requires large stores of weapons. Since he doesn't have to deal with the eye of the ATF, and the Homeland Security Department monitoring all large purchases of gun and ammunition in the U.S. and abroad, he can now buy and sell completely unregulated. Cut out are all the under the table purchases from "legit" manufacturers.

Denmark and his associates hope to achieve their collective goal of one world currency, one food source, and one class that dominates all others.

Also a connoisseur of history, he studies in great detail the past and present of civilizations and their cultures. He devours everything he can on emperors, presidents, prime ministers, and kings.

He determined long ago that religion is the "most powerful" tool of control. People kill for money, but millions die over religion.

But he's only interested in secular means of achieving his vision.

The underlying pattern he sees, the consistent ploy which surpasses almost all others: Fear.
If there is not the establishment of terror, there's a chance for loss of control. Those who ruled with the harshest hand are the ones who reigned supreme.
The second thing he learned from his studies, is those in power have to possess the ability to detect where their hidden enemies lay, and move swiftly to eliminate them.

Richford Chuld, once a loyal supporter, had become his enemy. He'd known him for years and was always grateful for the things he did. He was in an irreplaceable position, and valued his services greatly. There is no force more decisive in the physical world than the animalistic desire lust incites in man when he desires intimacy with a woman. In the world's loftiest seats of power, somewhere a woman is affecting the agenda.

Denmark's wife was that beautiful woman. Just like any other boy who became a man, he's taken his share of bumps and bruises along the way; he made his share of decisions he wish he could take back—there was a time when he was gullible enough to think humans can actually be trusted. He had to learn the hard way that it's dangerous to allow a wife to be privy to all of a husbands affairs. He wished Chuld wouldn't have allowed himself to fall victim to the draw of a wet pussy. The decision Chuld and his wife made, was be the very reason their elimination became imperative. Denmark had known for some time Chuld was sleeping with her. But didn't care. He let them have their fun.

Denmark isn't a homosexual, but he's past sex, and often goes long stretches without intercourse.

The fact she was telling Chuld his secrets was the reason she was rubbed-out. He had so much dirt on Chuld, that he black-mailed him with public humiliation, career death, *and* literal death. Knowing there's nowhere he could hide from Denmark, Chuld agreed to have Denmark's wife, the mother of his off-spring, killed. But he got tricky and tried to double cross Denmark, which led to the HT getting involved, which let to KT-36 getting in the mix, which led to the bomb strike, which led to all the misinformation in the media, which led the public to think they really know what's going on.

Which led to Chuld being assassinated.

Soon, all the attention will blow over and Denmark will continue with conquest.

In every municipality in America there is a courthouse. If it's large enough, it may be called a "justice center". These places of county government business hold many of the
localities main operation divisions. There's usually a traffic or municipal court, as well as criminal and civil ones. Usually in this same building, or within walking distance, is the licensing office where citizens apply for things like, marriage certificates, gun permits, and professional licenses, like those for plumbing and electrical trades.

The one overlooked more than any other, the one where the biggest cookie jar is shelved, is the zoning office. Arguably the most important branch in all of county government. This office is run by a zoning commission. The city manager, or CEO is often the person who chairs this board. This person works in close contact with the city mayor on all the city's building projects.

If a developer makes a private deal with the owner of a thirty acre ranch, and wants to use the land to build a housing subdivision, it must first be approved by the zoning board. The decision to zone, or not to zone is the key determination between breaking ground on a new venture, or not breaking ground at all.

After spending millions dollars trying to get the deal approved, his crowning achievement as a land acquisitor is finally complete. For the second week, his six hundred acre, quarter billion dollars plant is operational. Paying politicians to sell the people on the huge plant being built in their back yard was pivotal. The people were wary of the gargantuan "pharmaceutical" facility being built in the rural area they called home. But the sell was sold on the pretense of bringing thousands of new jobs, and heavy investment in the local economy. The voters passed the measure when the investment group pacified the East Georgia communities neighboring Conyers, Covington, and Madison, with a six screen drive-in theater complex, a new aquatic center, and a massive beautification initiative. But behind all the smoke and mirrors of goodwill, are sinister intentions. The people will eventually realize they've been taken. Not one of these positions will be filled by any of them. They're already assigned to people handpicked, many of which are scientists from abroad who have no interest in American culture. GMO research, genetic mutations, sonic wave experimentation, weapons testing, animal cloning, stem cell growth, sterilization by tubal ligation, pregnancy termination, and all sorts of unthinkable things is where their minds are. He now has an "intake facility" for all the humans he traffics from around the globe. This one benefit in itself will pay dividends far exceeding the cost of investment. Fifty miles from Governor Yates' mansion, a hop-skip and a jump from Hartsfield-Jackson, the world busiest airport, hours away from Savannah, a world serving port on the coast of the Atlantic, and located in Atlanta, GA, the world's preeminent destination for human trafficking; Ed Denmark has the perfect chamber of horrors. He's the world's leading pioneer to reinvent the age old slave trade, turning it from frowned upon blight on history, to well-oiled profit machine of the internet era; nourished in the bosom of 21st. century technology. When a teenaged girl can fetch as much as $125,000 on the world exchange, and when a being like White Man Ed controls an endless flow of top-shelf stock; he's about to reach a new plateau of debauchery.

But even at the top, looking down from his Ruppell's Nest, the vulture who's Ed Denmark is keenly watching one man. It isn't because he has wealth and power. But because he has a wealth of influence. Having seen him from afar many times, and meeting him in person twice, he sees the authority he commands. He's a force in his own right, and formidable he is.

The fact he's unable to be bought is a problem.

The look in his eye is threatening to Denmark. When oil and water meet, they immediately expel. He knows the major will eventually come after him. Whether he has the potential to be a thorn in his side, or a fatal stabbing; he isn't going to take him lightly. He knows all about the heroic name of Russell Hall.
If he ever gets off his righteous horse, he could run for senator and probably win, but he's too caught up in going against the grain to maximize his wherewithal. With all the new information that's been complied, now knowing Hall has somehow gotten his hands on information extremely detrimental to him, he has to die. The major's zeal, integrity, and unrelenting tenacity has become his downfall—he's left him no option but to terminate.
But he's a patient man.
He hasn't given the final order yet. He has to wait for the optimal time if he's going to kill a legend like Tusk Hall.

□□□□□□□□□□□

But for today he's very much alive, and breathing just fine. At the moment his eyes aren't permanently shut. Over the last slew of days Hall's been busting balls and shaking trees. His vast network of snitches, associates, and contacts have been tapped and exploited. With the help of his loyal officers, he's been able to gain valuable knowledge on Denmark, and is one step closer to unmasking the unknown. The fact that he's on administrative suspension doesn't mean the work stops. It just means the work had to be redefined. It means taking his duty subterranean. The underground arm of the law is often stouter than the one on the surface. In a world of don't ask, don't tell, it's the APD's secret protectorate. In this dominion, Hall gives orders aren't ratified by the chief. He's the sole authority. The loyal and brave Captain John Henry Peavey is by his side; Loop and Nguyen still believe in his direction. The brave men and women who see him as their guiding light aren't foolish enough to believe Big Man Hall is anything less than stellar. They do however believe the rumor about Denmark having a mole inside the departments ranking body.

The media's still churning out incendiary reports of officer involved shootings, police corruption, gang violence, and Ed Denmark; stories guaranteed to keep the public in a tizzy. Propping up Ed Denmark with propaganda paid for by him is used to buttress his public persona, with the spin: He's a victim of a smear campaign fueled by financial gain. But Tusk and his band of warriors know it's all a hoax. Early morning raids on establishments rumored to belong to Denmark are being executed by armed men who resembled SWAT officers but have no badges; just guns, demands, and violent interrogations. Hall is hell-bent on not allowing Denmark to crush him under his money and power. The fact someone broke into his residence and stole sensitive information is an act of war. They aren't as smart as he thought they were, thinking he wouldn't going to find the bug in his modem. He found each and every device they planted. He even has the chief under secret surveillance, not because he's worried he's corrupt, but because he could be in danger too. Meanwhile, contacts at the DMV are digging up everything they can on anyone ever affiliated with anything Denmark. His contact at the Georgia Archives is busy mining historical records for anything useful. The court clerk he's known since she first started, is going through property records in search of any real estate he's acquired. Major is good friends with many people, and they're all more than willing to help.

Sitting with him in the lair of his new hideout, are seven unmarked phones. The old Nokia® one begins playing music, and twerking across the table. Unlike smartphones, with their gyroscopes and information sharing, these relicts from the past are harder to track, and difficult to tap. He stops what he's doing and looks at the number. It's District Attorney Yuen.
"Are you on a secure line?" he asked immediately.
Hall says "Yes."
Kam gives him an address—one he recognizes as being in the city of Chamblee, and asks how long will it take for him to get there?
"Twenty minutes."
Kam says he'll be there!
"It's a date," and hangs up.
In minutes he's in his vehicle.

In sixteen minutes he's there.
Kam too.
Hall enters the building and sees him sitting.
"Glad you could make it. Sorry about the sudden call. How've you been?" Yuen asked.
"Couldn't be better. So what do you have," cutting to point.
Kam opens the briefcase, sits it on the table, and pulls out a

paper sack with the number '34' on it.

"I don't know how it was missed before, but it was."

Removing the gem clip clamping it shut, he pours a portion on the table. The vacuum sealed bag of something has already been opened. The substance inside comes out a displeasing grayish-brown, the size and shape of granola, but with the feel and powder-like consistency of dehydrated baked beans. No labeling.

"This was found at the scene of the restaurant robbery? It's the only thing the Feds missed when they confiscated the evidence. It may be nothing, but I thought you should have a look at it. This morning the evidence clerk contacted me and asked how should she catalog it. Until then, I had no clue it existed. I asked what it was, and she said this. So that's when I decided to go pick it up. When I got there it was already open. I don't know who else looked at it, but whoever it was, they obviously didn't deem it important. Here, take a look."

He slides it across the table.

Hall picks it up and takes a look.

"Weird."

"Tell me about."

And rubs it between his fingers. It's brittle but not overly dry. Being dehydrated, it's still rather moist. Spongy, but doesn't rebound like one; flattens and gums like dough.

"What do you think it is?" asked the DA.

"I don't know," and smells it. "But I know who will."

"Well you can take it. If it's something good let me know. That scum bag ruined me. I can't even sleep I wanna get that jerk so bad."

"You're only as ruined as you allow yourself to believe. Lighten up on yourself. It's not a fair fight."

"Isn't that the truth," he seconded. "So how've you been holding up? I hate to see how the media's dragging on you and the department through the mud."

"They can't drag me if I haven't fallen."

Kam shakes his head in agreement.

"Well I've gotta go." Shuts his briefcase and stands up.

Behind him is the seafood section. If customers don't want to wait till they get home to steam their Alaskan crab legs, or grill their Mahi-Mahi; for a fee they can have it prepared at the market.

Serving. Number. Fifty. Seven.

Alerts the computer generated female over the intercom.

"That's me. Let me know what you find. The wife is already pissed. I don't want to make it worse," the lawyer joked.

Hall stands and shakes his hand.

"Thanks for your courage. It won't be forgotten."

"You're welcome. You just get me something so I can bust this twerp!"

"Will do!"

And with that the meeting concludes.

Tusk knows just where he's going.

The menacing building at 901 Rice St. continues to be filled to capacity. The sixth and seventh floors are where the most violent inmates are housed. The tri-towered facility with skinny windows is known as, Fulton Co. Jail, the small sister on the same property is called "Bellwood", the tissue paper inmates use to roll up tobacco is called "blue steel," there's still a "red zone" on 4SW-400, and the man running store has "2 for 1's". Officers encounter the most fighting on commissary day and after visitation; not allowing the dorm bully get something off your tray may result in you having to "strap up" or "run to the button". This is "the thunder dome", and it's no place for cowards and punks. The "booty bandits" rape men they deem "free picks,"

the medical ward is often lined with bruised and broken inmates, the food is processed by-product scrapped from the floor of a dog food factory. And that's exactly why Hall is here.

As if he's bringing a suspect in for booking, he pulls to the intake sally port and enters the code.
The twenty five foot high gate opens.
After parking beside a transport bus, he gets out and goes inside. An officer inside smiles and nods while holding a handcuffed man.
The next person Hall sees is the officer standing inside the booth controlling the sliding slabs of access doors. Going around the metal detector, Hall heads through another secured door. By the time he goes through the third door he's standing in the heart of the intake area. He doesn't spend much time waving and shaking hands. He moves quickly through the sludge and makes for the elevator. They all see the brown sack, but not one person inquires about it. After going through three more security perimeters he gets on the elevator, enters the code to make it run, hits the button, and awaits the conclusion of the decent.

The sublevel is where the kitchen's located—the food prepared by privileged members of the inmate population. A team of three male staffers, and one woman oversee the operation. No mouth-watering aromas here, just the steamy nauseating fume of cheap, lab created feedstock being heated and seasoned with generic ingredients.

The woman over this operation goes by "Ms. Bee", a sweet woman from an area west of Atlanta known as "The Flatland". She's been working this industrial complex for twenty six years. When she first started they served real food, albeit the same low quality assortment. An inmate pushing a cart stacked high with brown plastic trays heads towards him.
He inquires about her whereabouts?

The trustee says she's in her office doing a report on an inmate who'd been caught masturbating in the grits.

He thanked him and proceeds through the maze of stainless-steel and confined chefs. Continuing to the rear where the stock room, freezer, sharps cage, and her office are, he anticipates seeing his favorite lunch lady. When he gets to her door it's closed and she sitting at her desk writing.

He taps on the door.

The sixty eight year old woman looks up and smiles brightly, waving him in!

He opens the swinging 3'0 x 8'0 door and enters.

"Jesus can strike me down if I'm lying! When I say I was just thinking talking about you, I mean like just now!............*Oh, my lord!* How've you been baby?" glad to see the esteemed and embattled lawman.

"I couldn't be better," he smiles.

She pushes herself off the seat and envelopes him in her warm embrace.

Before working here, she was the lunch lady who fed him when he was a skinny, wet-behind-the-ear whippersnapper.

Upon letting him go she says: "Come on in and rest your feet! You hungry? Some fresh steaks just come in," returning her wide rump to the cushioned chair.

"Nah I'm good. I see you're still holding everything down though?"

"Oooo honey, it's probably the other way around. To tell you the truth, this kitchen is the only thing keeping me living. I'm scared if I retire I might die."

The sheriff, as well as the staff food is prepared by her, not by the inmates. This food consists of earthly ingredients, and is delicious.

"You don't look like you're going anywhere anytime soon to me."

"Chile, looks will tell a lie. So how've you been Russell? I'm really glad you stopped by."

The compassionate look in her stare reveals her concern. She's not deaf to all the things being said about him and the police department. The craving to inquire wets her mouth, but she won't dare bring up the gorilla in the room.

"The feeling is mutual Ms. Bee. The pleasure is truly all mines," he charmed.

She leans back laughing, and hit him on the leg.

"Awwwwwwe hush! You better stop!"

He laughs too.

"But in all honestly Ms. Bee. I need a favor."

Her smile slowly washes away.

"You know you don't even have to ask that. Just tell me what you need?"

He sits the sack on the table.

"I need you to take a look at something."

"Sure. Whatever I can do."

He takes out the package.

"We found this at a crime scene. Before I send it off for lab work I want to know what it is. I can't tell you much, but I think it's some type of food meal…….Just so you know, this is off record."

"Sure-sure," she replied without hesitation.

Hall slides it to her.

Ms. Bee put on her glasses, picks it up, and spins it around.

"The fact it has no markings makes me think it came out of a box with others," he stated.

"Uhm-hmm," she replied, putting it on her fingers and rubbing it between.

"We get a lot of things that come in blank packages. That isn't especially odd," she pointed. "But I know what this is."

"What?"

She gets up and says: "Follow me."

They exit the office and go into the kitchen area.

An inmate worker holds a broom.

"Smith. Go get a bag of paste for me?"

He responds: "Yes ma'am Ms. Bee," and lays the broom against a prep table to hurry to the back.

She grabs an aluminum pot and a pitcher off the rack, takes it to the sink, and fills them both halfway with water.

"Grab that and sit it over here," and grabs a pitcher.

Hall grabs the pot off the sink and sits it atop the 10 x 4 stainless-steel table.

By then the trustee is back with a bag, the same type of white plastic but with ink on it.

Smith sits it on the table.

Ms. Bee tells him to open it.

In one yank he rips it open, uselessly displaying his strength to her.

She shows it to Hall.

"We call this paste. But actually it has no name. It comes in by the truck loads...........Now step over here with me."

Hall moves to her side.

She sit the bag he brought down, takes the paste, and pours the bag into the pot of water. Though resembling pulverized bits of grains and nuts, it's nothing grainy or nutty about it.

Before his eyes, like the birth of an inflating turd, this unidentified concoction morphs into a brown, meat-like paste.

He's astonished by how it changed to *so* much, so quickly!

"The city saves millions of dollars by feeding the inmates this stuff. You can form it into a dough, form into patties; meatloaf. It can be baked or boiled like a chili. It can even be added with sugar, frozen and served as a dessert."

He's disgusted.

"Looks good huh," she kidded.

"Is this stuff safe?"

"Who knows? I won't eat it. The staff members don't even want to touch it. No one we know of has died from it, so it's at least not toxic?"

She moves to his bag, and pours it on the table. Using the picture of water, she pours some on the grainy mound. But instead of growing twenty times is original mass, this other substance doesn't have the same reaction. It does more of a soggy, wet oatmeal thing. After several moments of waiting for it to do more, it stabilizes into a macabre clump of something resembling apple crisp.

"This isn't the same. I don't know what this is Russell. I'd be careful with this stuff if I were you."

At the moment he only has three of his seven unmarked phones. One of them is vibrating in his pocket.

"I'd be careful with that too," he replied, nodding at the pot.

By the time he makes it to the recycling center it's well past six. The date's November 8th. Quintus Recycling has grown from part-time hobby, to the biggest purchaser of scrap metal in the Southeast. In April 1994, fourteen years before the 'BeltLine Project' was adopted, with its promises to add forty percent to the city's green space; there was a deadly workplace shooting. It wasn't by a disgruntled worker, but the branch manager. He killed the drunken boyfriend of a female employee who commenced assaulting her with his fist and feet. The manger intervened, the man drew a knife, the manger drew his piece. Story over. One less woman beater.

The woman who was being beaten would go on to become the wife of Ed Denmark, and mother of his child. Figuring to glean information which will hopefully lead to Denmark's demise, Hall does what any other clever inquisitor will do, he begins digging into the past of the slain wife; maybe he'll find some clues as to why she was murdered.

He gets out of his vehicle and looks around. Up ahead past the scales are enormous piles of metal. Men on heavy equipment move about loading separating and cutting. In the far distance he can see trains with cars of open-top dumpsters being loaded with the valuable scrap. The yard isn't stinky like a trash dump, or putrid like a landfill, but sizzling with the sound of cold hard cash. During the day there would be cars, trucks, and semis teaming with residential, commercial, and industrial scraps of copper, brass, nickel, stainless-steel, aluminum, and even gold. The business is based on purchasing things like old furnaces, air-conditioner coils, engine blocks, aluminum awnings, brass water meters, industrial electric cable, old highway guardrails, metal building frames, iron I-Beams, and junk cars. It's cleaned of debris and crushed, where finally the material is sold to metal processing plants for a profit.

Hall crosses the parking lot and goes inside. The office closed at six and many of the staff are already gone. But he goes inside and hits the silver bell anyway.

A few seconds later a man appears. It's just the person he's looking for.

"How can I help you?" asked the middle-aged white man with graying hair.

"Yes. I'm looking for Harper Vardan."

".....Speaking," he returns, suspicious and watchful.

Hall extends his hand.

He doesn't take it.

"Well. Good evening Mr. Vardan. I'm Major Russell Hall with the Atlanta Police Department. Is there somewhere we can talk?"

"Regarding?" not moving a muscle.

"This is not an investigation into yourself. I'm trying to get some insight surrounding the death of Farah Denmark."

"I wouldn't know anything about that."

"Mr. Vardan, Is there somewhere we can talk? Everything will be explained. I just need to get your opinion on a few things. This has nothing to do with you."

Finally he says okay, and leads him to his office where they close the door and sit down. There's still a few people in the building and he doesn't want them hearing whatever it is Hall may say.

Vardan sips something out of a mug emblazoned with the company logo.

"So how can I help you major?" sitting the mug back on the table.

"I'd like to begin by saying you're in no way a focus of this matter. And next I'd like apologize for disturbing you in your place of business," and shows him his badge. "I elected not to come in uniform because I didn't want to make a scene."

"Thanks. But I know who you are. You're the cop caught up in the brutality thing….Aren't you on suspension or something?"

He doesn't honor that with a response.

"I need to ask you a few questions about Farah Denmark?"

"Do I need a lawyer?"

"….I prefer not?"

The man stares at him.

"I'm surprised. You're the first cop to show up asking about her. Shouldn't you be asking her husband?"

Hall sits silent before responding.

"I think you already know the answer to that Mr. Vardan."

More protracted staring. Two alpha males, each dominant in their own way.

Vardan speaks first.

"You come across like a man of principle major, but you still haven't answered my question. Why are they saying these things about you?"

"Again Mr., Vardan, my des-"

"So a man of principle should understand there's is a proper way to approach other men of principle."

Hall studies him.

For a man who's taken a life, he doesn't wear it like a badge of honor. Behind the tight hard line of his mouth, Tusk sees the same inner defiance he possesses.

"The worth of man in search of divine truth is in his work, not his words."

More staring duels.

Finally Vardan says: "What do you want to know Mr. Hall?"

"Everything you know about Ed Denmark."

Hall doesn't have a note pad, and he's not holding a pen.

Vardan laughs and shrugs.

"So that's how you see it? You come in here and flash your badge, toss around a few quotes, and throw out a name like Ed Denmark; asking me about an event that altered my life. You think it's that simple? You probably wanna be careful who you go around asking about?"

"Well if you have any advice on how I shall prepare for the onslaught, I'd gladly accept it," he witted.

Vardan shakes his head.

"In this day and time that badge has become irrelevant."

Whether Hall likes it or not, he can't keep denying the fact there's a grip Denmark has on people's psyche. If he fails to take this factor into account and continue minimizing its effect, it may one day come back to haunt him.

"I read the statement you gave that night," Hall begins. "I may not know it all, but I know from statements you made during the investigation, you claimed to not know much about Mr. Denmark. But somehow knew enough to consider him a man of high regard. Before I came, I tried to gauge what side of the fence you're on. The only way of me knowing was to meet you face to face. Now that I'm here, I see you hold too much resentment in the twitch of your lip to be a cheerleader. When I mentioned him the angle of your brow changed too much for you to be a sympathizer. I don't take you for a coward either Mr. Vardan."

"Your greater concern should be taking me for a fool."

"Well since it's not that simple, let's start with you."

"How about yo?" he rebuffed.

Now continues. "What gives you the idea you set the rules? He who holds the gold sets the rules....Since you fancy quotes," Vardan remarked. "I have nothing to gain and everything to lose by speaking to you. The longer I let you sit here, the more the odds work against me."

"You ask why they say those things about me? You just said I'm the only officer who's come. Well there's your answer. That's why! Because I'm always on my game. I'm always on duty! People with agendas don't like that....Don't be so sure to think you're protecting yourself by dicking me around, I may be the only person crazy enough to go after him. You'd do well by aligning yourself with like-minded people, if you get my drift. I'm going to hit him like a Scud missile, and anyone in his radius will be devastated. So if you're one of his puppets, I'm informing you of your doom. If you not, and are just another person he's trampled, and despite this, sit there and withhold information that could help me nail him, I'm wasting my time."

Behind his desk is a cabinet. Vardan rolls to it and gets his flask. Returning to the table, he takes the top off the mug and pours away. After topping it off, he rolls back, puts it back inside, and rolls again.

"…You don't want to get into a war with him."

"That seems to be the consensus opinion. It's amazing how one man can hold such a sway over people's imagination."

"What I'm talking about isn't fantasy. I'm talking pure evil, far worse than what you *think* you know."

He takes a drink.

"Well if you recognize evil, you better know how to recognize its nemesis."

The room goes quiet.

The micro-sized radio on his desk whispers.

Vardan sighs.

"…..Whatever I tell you is off record. If anyone asks me I'll deny it. I'll swear on my father's grave that I've never seen you," adding. "I won't ask if you're wearing a wire."

"I'm not."

"I've got an appointment at seven. I'll see if I know anything, then I've gotta run," and takes another swallow.

"I appreciate your wiliness," thanked Hall.

"Yeah…..But I'm not doing this for you. It's something I've wanted to get off my chest for a long time. You just happen to be the person in the chair."

Hall absorbs the significance of what he said.

"I appreciate your candor Mr. Vardan. I won't take too much of your time."

Pause.

"We've already spoken to the mother. She was able to give us a wealth of information regarding her daughter, including private details of her union with Denmark. Outside of you and her, there's really no one else we can find who knows much about him. Even she could only give us minimal information. She did however claim to know you, and was adamant in her conviction that if anyone knew anything about him, you would. She stated your grandfather and Denmark where childhood friends."

Vardan is well aware of the consequences. But he's tired. He doesn't care anymore. Such a simple question is a closely guarded secret and a blatant violation of trust. Questions of any kind are not to be answered. This has been a long held belief way before ethnic cleansing forced his grandfather and family to seek refuge in the U.S.

"The mayhem of his organization is a painful reminder of the lawlessness my grandfather sought to leave behind."

Pauses.

Another swallow.

"It is very likely no one outside of maybe, four people in the world know what I'm about to tell you."

Varden feels the thump in his chest. He feels the weight of what he's about to say. His better judgment is warning him to think things through.

"I had to be about nine at the time. My father hadn't come home yet. I was having trouble understanding why all of my classmates would thank this man named God or Jesus before they ate. Seeing this every day I thought it was something I should practice....So for some odd reason, this evening at the dinner table I decided I wanted to give it a try. Never before had my family engaged in this ritual, but my mother thought nothing of it and gave me permission...So here I am, sitting at the head of the table, about to close my eyes and put my hands together while I thank these people for my food. The last thing I saw before I shut my eyes was my mother laughing...So I laughed back and started thanking."

He pauses to clear his throat, takes a sip from the cup, and gazes into the distance as if some invisible guide is telling him not to do it.

He continues.

"...Suddenly my father comes through the door. And through my nine year old mind, I stick my chest out expecting him to be proud of me; his only son."

Long pause.

Hall can see the difficulty he's having telling the story.

"...Instead, he sees me and goes into a rage. The first thing I hear is him yell. Instead of the congratulatory hug I expected, I get knocked to the floor. Then he goes for my mother, grabs her by the hair, and starts beating her with his fist. While I lay on the floor in a state of confusion by what I was seeing,...he drags her to the bedroom."

He pauses another moment. The emotion is getting to him. He can see it just as he could when he was a boy.

"I laid there listening to my father beat her for hours. When he came out his fists were bloody.....Then he beat me to the point where I couldn't walk.....Afterwards he told me if he ever saw me doing that again he would kill me.......My mother later died from brain hemorrhaging......My grandfather knew him from being in an orphanage with him......"

Pause.

Drink.

"Kojori Orphanage, right outside of Tbilisi....He'd just started. He wasn't as big as he is now. Just a local guy. He got him to represent my father. It was one of the first cases he won...He didn't have money to pay him, I don't know if he ever did. He never told me what they worked out…My grandfather was a dirt poor Hungarian immigrant. It was Denmark and the connections he had that got us bumped to the top of the UN's transitional list…For the rest of my life that night became my endless hell. One that never stops giving……I never got much in religion, but I remember Deuteronomy 24:16 saying something about a father shouldn't be put to death because of their children, and a son shouldn't be punished for the sins of his father. It clearly states each man shall be put to death for his own sin.…I find it amazing that people still force one man to bear all their burdens…Pay for all of their sins……Whether I liked it or not, he was from the same homeland as him, they all were. In their tight-knit mentality that meant you broke from the same bread, you drank from the same well. He kept his end of the deal…… When he got on his feet, he reached down and pulled my grandfather up.…At the time, he was buying chemicals from Siberia, and paying a fortune to have them shipped to the U.S. That's how he first got into scrapping metal.…He used them to dissolve used circuit boards and old electronics so he could recover the bits of gold and platinum inside."

He stops talking and stares at Hall with this expressionless gaze.

"What made you shoot the guy?" Hall asked.
"…From how it was told to me, Farah used to be *something*……
She wasn't the prettiest woman you ever saw but she could have any man she wanted. Her family was pretty well off too. At the time, I think her father owned land in three states; something like sixty seven-hundred acres. He was also part Indian, he descended from some kind of high chief.……This was a few years after he made something like eighteen million from selling part of it the state.…Instead of going for a rich man, she went for a meth addicted truck driver…The father hated him. He was the guy who leased my grandfather the land to build the recy-

cling yard. Farah was his daughter....She had only been working there for a few months. I'd heard the stories of him beating
her and what-have-you....One morning she comes to work two
hours early with her two children in the backseat. She has this
hideous black eye and she looked like she'd been worked over
pretty good. I was the only one there....She runs inside and
tells me he's trying to kill her....Before I had a chance to think
he was on me. He was so geeked out of his mind on crank that
he went right through me and started throwing her around the
office....I can still hear him telling her to give him the money
before the demons return...."
He stops again. The look on his face tells it all.

Russell knows he's getting close to his limit.

"...It was so surreal," he continues. "At the time, it was like he
saved the day. He was the go-to man for anything my grandfather needed. He always offered to help...But this time he asked
for something in exchange, but didn't immediately tell grandfather what it was....A week after I get news the police have decided not to pursue charges, determining I acted in self-defense...
My father shows up at our house one night driving this car,
run's inside the house and disappears. At the time I didn't know
my grandfather had opened the scrap yard in the middle of the
night and was waiting for my father to arrive with this car.... A
week later Farah had to go to her father's funeral....Being she
was an only child, the will left her and her mother to divide everything ....Nineteen months later they got married."

The room goes silent again. The load of what he's shared is
laying on Hall like a woolly mammoth. Using his vast library of
information, and his high level of commonsense, Hall is able to
fill in the blanks, and is even able to draw new likelihoods he'd
previously been unable to.
"Though I am not a black man as you Mr. Hall, I do

consider myself part of an oppressed people.…That being said, I've learned it is easier to be a slave, than it is to be free."
And downs the rest of whatever's in the cup.

Russell watches him drink until the burn melts away the pain. Coming here and experiencing this isn't what he expected. Vardan has deep seeded issues which are far too embedded for him to understand. Being something he wanted to get out for a long time, he was right when he said he just happened to be the one he decided to release it on.
Vardan gets up and goes to the same cabinet that holds the flask. Inside is a men's leather jacket hangs on a brass hook. He takes his time opening it and slides his hand inside. He's in no rush to get whatever it is. Vardan extracts a wallet, and patiently unfolds it. The pace at which he fingers through is as if he's
unfolding an ancient terry cloth and doesn't want it to rip.
After coming out with something the size of a business card, he puts the billfold back inside the jacket, shuts the cabinet, and returns to his seat.
"….I often wonder was it God, Allah, Jehovah, Jesus or maybe Muhammad? Or Buddha it could've even been? Confucius or Zoroaster or Ezra with his six-point star. Maybe Shiva, Brahma, or Vishnu? Mother Mary could've been there when he prepared to stab Farah to death?…..I wonder did the Bible, the Quran, the Talmud, or the Upanishads play into the cop's decision not the charge me……..I wonder who sent the man who came up behind him, and shot him in the back of the head before I had a chance to pull my pistol?" pausing to allow the sound of a bull-dozer moving through the lot behind the office to pass.
"When my grandfather was on his deathbed, he told me he's going to give me something more valuable than gold.…Something only given to a select few. He said I was to never tell any-one about it, not even my father. He told me outside of me and him, it doesn't exist……He made me swear to never leave home without it.…He told me only in

circumstances of dire need was I to use it.…He told me to hold on to it as if my life depends on it."

He raises his hand from his lap and places it on the table.

When he moves it, there's what looks like a business card sitting face down.

He stands from the table.

"I give it to you with the same advice. Good day Mr. Hall."

Fresh off work from flipping burgers, he'd successfully made it to the mall before it closes; wanting to cash his check and get the shoes before meeting her at the movie theater. This is the first time he's meeting her outside of work and he's excited. He can never get anything done when she's there. All that ends up happening is him spending the shift with his hand in his pocket trying to keep his boner from poking out. She's *soooo* beautiful, and he's *sooooo* a virgin. He's had enough of jacking off to his dad's roommate's porn collection. Last time he got so overheated from squeezing his leg muscles together, while trying to keep one eye on '*Cherokee D-Ass*' take it from the back, he ended up spending ten minutes with his head in the deep freezer trying to keep from falling out. After the movie, his brother said he's going to let them ride with him to the dragstrip and catch some races. Hopefully, this is where he can make his move and try for some backseat action.

Standing at the corner waiting for the light to change, he thinks about how much he loves race cars, and dreams of owning one. Hearing the unmistakable sound of a revving engine, he spins around!

A car comes around the corner fishtailing hard, and burns rubber over the hill!!!

"*Ooooooooooooh, shit!* They gettin' it!!!"

Smiling from ear to ear.
"I can't wait till it's my turn!!!. Ahma show 'em how it's supposed to be done!" Looking at the twin drag marks on the street.

❑❑❑❑❑❑❑❑❑❑❑

Hall saw the young man at the corner, he wasn't going to hit him. He's a professional behind the wheel.
Pushing the potent V-8 to the max, he comes over the top of MacAfee Dr. doing 63 in a 35. He's just left the GBI headquarters and wants to get to Nguyen before she leaves for the evening! She hasn't returned his call and he needs her to run these samples!
In sixteen more speed-induced miles, he's slinging the sedan into the parking lot. It must be his lucky day, because she's getting in her car as he pulls up! Skidding to a stop beside her, he jumps out before the car stops rocking; startling her by his sudden appearance!
His excitement tells her it's big.
"I'm sure glad it's you! You scared the crap out of me Hall!"
Remnants of her Korean heritage lingering in her speech.
"Joy! I'm sorry to pop up like this! But I've got something!"
Running with something in his hand.
"Thirty more seconds and you would've missed me."
Revealing the old Samsung she's holding. "It finally died on me."
And turns towards the door.
"Well let's get inside and see what you have."

Minutes later they're passing through the three doors, getting off the elevator, and are now standing at the examination table.
"You've got me all worked up now. I'm excited to see what it is you have. Let's see if it's something good."
"Better than good. It's worth more than gold!"

Hall unrolls the paper sack and sits it down.

"I'll save the best for last."

And pours some of it out.

"I need your expert opinion on what this is? You're the second person I've shown it to. Loop and Peavey don't know yet. It came from the restaurant massacre but doesn't show on the inventory log."

Nguyen grabs her glasses from her jacket and put them on, turns on the magnifier task lamp, and pulls it to her. Popping a on pair of latex gloves, she adjusts the pivoting arm to where the magnifier sits just above it.

"The first thing that comes to mind is some type of desiccated protein substance," pointing to the right quarter of the glass.

"What you have here are ground Chia seeds—a cheap source of protein. These here are ground seeds of Irvingia gabonensis, or *Ogbono*. They're a popular ingredient in diet scams because its composition allows the person eating them to experience a false sense of fullness. I also see there is little actual useful protein here, especially with the way it's been drum baked. I can tell this by the way at which the grains are cut in almost the exact same diameter. In large scale desiccation processes, drum-drying is a low cost way to dry raw ingredients at low temperatures over rotating, high-capacity drums which produce sheets of the milled product. What's left over is void of nearly all its nutritional value. The sheen you see here on what looks to be a Pueraria lobate, also known as *Kudzu*—one of the world's oldest forms of edible plants. Though all the water's been removed, the fat acids remain. Hence, the reason for film. Saponification of the fats is the result of the sodium hydroxide used to inhibit bacteria growth…But this here looks to be an actual animal protein!… Rare with this type of mixture!"

"You said that like there's more?"

Nguyen takes a chemical spoon, scoops a few grams out, and places it on a Petri dish. Sitting in her chair, she pulls up to microscope. Next, out comes a glass thing the size of a television remote, with four bowls perfectly fit for golf balls. They each have one of the letters 'N', 'A', 'C', 'T' over each bowl.

"What's that do?"

"In food analysis, properties like composition, structure, physicochemical elements, and sensory attributes are based on the foods nitrogen, amino acid, carbohydrates, and triglyceride content. These can be measured and compared to other know substances."

And takes a battery of four chemicals, using a dropper to saturate each bowl with one of each.

After two hundred and fifty one seconds of quiet calculation and examination, she divulges her initial findings. A sample is placed between two glass slides and placed under a microscope. An American Standard clock ticks on the wall behind them. By the time the second hand went from 11 to 5, she says: "Just like I suspected...How come I didn't see it before?"

She pushes away from the table and heads for a cabinet.

"This might be big Hall!" she yells from across the room.

"I'm going to save my excitement until you figure out the might."

She passes the cabinet and disappears down a hall.

A minute later she returns with a box smoking with liquid nitrogen, sits it on the table, and opens it.

"I got this from Dr. Mort (county medical examiner). She said it's from a suicide victim and wanted my opinion on it!" Eager.

"When she gave it to me, I had so many things coming in that I took a quick look and put it up. I totally forgot about it until you came with this!"

"So what is it Joy?" getting impatient.

She takes out the translucent FDA compliant container with the green HDPE lid.

He can see the dark material inside of it.

She pulls back the smoking lid.

"This was inside the victim's stomach. A fifteen year old runaway who'd been missing since she was eleven. They found under an overpass by a man fishing the Chattahoochee."

"I remember that case."

"Mort couldn't figure out where it came from. She was baffled by it."

Using her chemical spoon, she scoops the substance out.

"This is what *that* looks like after it's been digested. Just from my early findings, it has the exact same properties as yours. I'm almost ninety-nine percent sure it's the same thing, but maybe an earlier production. It's less refined. The dominant ingredient is fish. I don't mean the kind me and you eat, but the piles of dead fish waste which comes from the commercial processing industry; leftover parts. Heads, tails, internal organs, scales, and all that. It's dirt cheap, and many times free. It's like rice and corn in dog food, filling but has zero dietary benefit."

And grabs his bag.

"But this stuff here is *far* worse. This isn't even fit for animal consumption. Whoever made this invested a great deal of time into development and research. The propensity it has to increase that many times its original mass is extraordinary."

Hall reaches in his pocket and gets the other item.

"I told you I was saving the best for last. If you think that's something, wait till you see this."

And lays it on the table.

Nguyen grabs a pair of tongs and picks it up. Looking at it she becomes just as awe struck.

"I've never seen anything like this! It feels like some type of hide that's been chemically hardened!"

So captivated is she by the material, she doesn't even concern herself with the lettering, or the ten digits under it.

Moving quickly to her magnifying glass, she removes the slide and places it between two others! Increasing the magnification 100X, she zoomed in!

Her jaw drops!

"It's the skin of a human being! The script has traces of plasma, erythrocytes, hemoglobin, and leukocytes!!!!...............The four main components of blood!!!!"
Hall can't find the words to convey his disbelief!!!!
The card itself is a homicide investigation!

Nguyen asks: *"Who is Orben Krolov?"*

Onze.

U.S. stocks plummeted on Monday, following a renewed rout in global markets under severe pressure from continued fears of slowing growth in China spilling over internationally. Vardan reads how stock index futures forced several major indices to fall several percentage points. Even before the opening bell, they had already hit limit down levels. He's never invested any of his millions into the stock market. They're too many vultures on Wall St.

"Fear has taken over. The market peaked last week", said one CEO of a major capital management firm. "We saw important technical levels break this past week, huge shifts in investor psychology."

There are undeniable similarities in the article, and what's going on with the dilemma he's facing.

The New York Stock Exchange invoked Rule 48 for the Monday stock market open, the paper reports.

He doesn't care to read the internet version. He feels something is lost when literature is digitized. Trying to do anything to keep his mind off the terrifying thoughts he's having, this is the normal way he starts his day. He's going to continue with his regular schedule and act like nothing's happened.
It's impossible for him to know the information came from me, Vardan assumed.
As powerful as Denmark is, he isn't God. He can't hear across continents and see through black holes. It's mainly his head getting to him, because he's the last person he'd suspect of becoming a traitor. But he's tired of everything that comes with this life, he doesn't want to keep living like this. All the money in the world can't make him forget the things his family has done to get the things they have, not including the unpayable amount of debt it was brought upon them. Not the financial kind, but the soul selling kind. On the verge of suicide, Vardan is doped to hell with Fluoxetine. His best chance is to try to make it to the end of each day. In his present mental state, tomorrow isn't guaranteed.
The article goes on to explain how rule 48 allows NYSE to open stocks without indications.

"It was set up for situations like this", said Bart Homer, chief market strategist at Wunderich Securities.
Last used in the financial crisis of 2007, the article closes with saying how European stocks plunged more than 4 percent, while the Shanghai Composite dropped 8.5 percent, its greatest one-day drop since 1987.

There are key phrases in the editorial which directly correlate with his present quandary.

The first two are: *"Under severe pressure"* and *"Fears of slowing growth spilling over internationally."*

For a man who does business like Ed Denmark, birth name, Orben Krolov; he also let his fears surrounding issues facing him in America spill over into his international interests.
He too is facing a tide of mounting pressure from all the un-wanted attention he's getting. All the publicity is exposing more of him than he wants revealed. Until this point, he's always been a ghost, a phantom of people's imagination. But now he's been transformed into some sort of enigmatic celebrity. It's definitely affecting the growth of his capital.

The second one that applies to him is the one stating:
"They hit limit down levels".

Like Wall St., Krolov has a point he won't allow things to cross. All people have their own forms of limit levels.

The next two are *very* important, perhaps the two most important of all: *"Fear has taken over"* and *"Huge shifts in psychology."*

After being a lifelong compatriot, and unwilling loyalist; fear has taken hold and disseminated panic in him. Huge shifts in Vardan's psychology has led him to make the insanely brave de-cision to turn against the powers of evil who've blessed him with the worldly powers of wealth and affluence. Krolov's initial investment of ill-gotten gains helped his families company reach the enormous height of becoming a multi-million dollar enter-prise. While human rights groups and environmentalists waste their time trying to shut them down, Orben Krolov and his den of dark forces showed his grandfather there's profits to be made from monopolizing Cambodian trash dumps. Places where famished children sift through tons of visibly burning garbage that emits carcinogenic fumes, methane gases; industrial waste. Paying them $2 a day, his family made millions off their misery. Who cares about them being children forced by desperation to work while suffering from exhaustion, malnutrition, and hunger, with little access to clean water; just so they can live. Denmark turned this into a cash cow for his family. They should be grateful.

The result of these circumstances culminates into the *"invoking of a rule"*.

Just like the New York Stock Exchange has interests to safeguard, so does Orben Krolov.

Vardan prepares his self just like he has every other morning. The only difference about this one is: It's not here yet. Today is Tuesday, and instead of being at the company he's heir to, he's at home siting at his bedroom balcony overlooking a picturesque lake, and a majestic 18-hole golf course. Amenities of the country club lifestyle and epitome of high society living. And he hates it. It plays a major role in his guilt. The sight of everything is the root of his torment. He has 6,500 square foot of living space and can't see his neighbors. He owns expensive automobiles, a yacht, a private jet, and a chef.

Yes, he *owns* the chef...................A gift from guess who?

He has Whole Foods® delivered to his estate. The wife has all the fine things: Swedish massages, exotic getaways, a Black Card, exclusive clothing. Everybody's happy. What's wrong with him? Why is he being such a party-pooper?

Sitting in his silk house robe, he sips coffee while the sun hovers above the tree tops. Lounging on his sofa with his arms hanging over the back, his hairy chest is exposed with nothing on his feet but the furry feel of an alpaca rug. He's chillin' like a villain.

The master bedroom was built with a huge glass partition which can be opened. The therapeutic way the fresh oxygen blows off the trees and wafts into the room, is nothing short of paradise. Over the years, he's reached many conclusions in this spot.

The first shot hit him in the bull's-eye of his kneecap!!!!! The second one hit him in the other knee, shattering it also!!!

"AAAAAAAAAAAAAAAHHHH-GOOOOOD!!!" he screamed, instantly knowing the reaper has come to roost!

Faster than he can comprehend, two whistling breezes cut through the air sending hot excruciating pain ripping through his hand!!!! *Shhwrruup!!-Shhwrruup!!*

Goes two more to his other hand, and chin!

"AAAAAAAAAAAAAAAAHHHH!!!

With the shot through his right shoulder being the most decisive, he 's slammed backwards into the sofa. The start of the red party has begun!

Blood spatter is everywhere! He's incapacitated by terror!

Through the blur of the sun and his waning consciousness, he sees a shadow step before him, completely blocking out the light! He doesn't have to see him to know who it is!!! He prays for death so he won't have to hear his voice! The eerie silence surprises him! The pain of the hot projectiles in his body isn't as intense as a few seconds ago!!!!! He feels his mouth hanging open and can tell his penis is hanging out of his boxers while blood runs on it!!!! The sticky wetness on his back is thick and cold!!!!

The voice speaks something but he can't decipher it!

They're the words of the dragon, the one he has feared his entire life!!! On the fringes of death, he takes solace in the fact he can't hear or see him!!!!! He hurries towards the white light.................................

His eyes shoot open! His heart's beating twice its normal rate! Intense heat is all over, and blood urine and excrement gang tackles his senses! He feels like a zombie who can only see blurs while his heart is over-revved to the point of explosion!!! But he can hear normally!!!!!

Krolov is a proficient killer. He's resorted to murder many times during his ascension to prominence, and well too versed in this art to vouchsafe Vardan with the privilege of an expedited death. He takes great pride in how he engineers a kill.

One of his assistants inject him with 2mg of the neurotransmitter, Epinephrine, followed by a hypercoagulant to slow the blood loss.

"In the year seventeen, seventy-seven, there lived a patriot. A ship merchant from Connecticut, who in time of war spent his own money to defend his country; the one he loved so dearly. Despite the way the misinformationists have skewed the truth, Benedict Arnold was an honorable man. A gentlemen who should've been given his due recognition. He fought with guts and glory to capture Fort Ticonderoga. He fought valiantly in the Battle of Valcour Island. He served with pride while coordinating the relief effort during the Siege of Fort Stanwix. He even gave part of his leg because he believed in defending this New World they'd colonized from the natives."

Krolov pauses his speech.

Vardan can hear him clearly but can't see what he's holding. He also can't see who's standing behind him, but knows someone's there. His mouth feels like a barren desert! The saliva in his mouth seems thick as bread pudding. He's never in his life been so thirsty.

"Good old America. Good old U-S of A...Instead of rewarding him for his stunning displays of allegiance, courage, and valor; the 2nd Continental Congress repeatedly passed him over for promotion. Men who'd made none of the sacrifices he had were given the recognition he rightfully deserved.....His adversaries, jealous he was willing to make concessions with Britain in an effort to end the bloodshed, fabricated charges of corruption and other claims of malfeasance......*Then*, as an ultimate sign of their gratitude, Congress claimed it was *he. HE!!!*.....Who was indebted to them!!!.....I find it amazing how disloyal and ungrateful humans can be…..You on the other hand are a true traitor, the epitome of a turncoat."

Vardan sees the blurry shadow coming closer!!!

"Your grandfather was a great man. He shared my love of history. He too put great significance on the concept of trust, the concept of gratitude, the concept of honoring one's allegiance.… He gave me this. As a sign of his gratitude, he wanted me to have it so that I may understand he appreciated my friendly gestures, and everlasting commitment to trustworthiness…The '1836 Colt Revolver', the first repeating pistol in history. Called the gun that won the West...A band of outlaws who went by the name of 'The James Gang' were the first to unleash its potential. ……But before the dawn of the frontier gun fighter, there was this little contraption. It's the 1830's version of the Colt……… They called it the 'Pepper Box gun'. It's so volatile that it's just as likely to blow up in the shooter's hand, as it is to kill the person they're aiming at…..I have no idea where your grandfather got it, but I've enjoyed it very much throughout my life. Your grandfather was my *dearest* ally, and *true* friend."

Wobbling on the brink of death, he watches the shadow move away from him, and reappear before him in the distance.

"In all fairness to him, the fact that you're his grandson, I decide to use this……The way to achieve enlightenment is to accept the unknown…Perhaps, it will be fate that takes my life as I attempt to take yours."

That was the last thing Vardan heard before his heart burst.

By the time Krolov pulls the trigger, he's already dead.

After he turns and walks out, a long-range shot from the assassin's rifle strikes the center of his forehead, putting the final nail in the coffin.

A caravan of dark colored vehicles with tented windows arrive at a remote location. One specially chosen due to its close proximity to the state crime lab in Trion.

Cloudland is a 3,485 acre park owned by the state of Georgia. Sitting on the back of the Cloudland Canyon River, it features a host of attractions like: Fishing, climbing, zip-lining, hiking, and camping. But its main attractions is the breathtaking waterfall cascading over a six hundred foot rock face.

In this location is where the group is parked. Krolov won't get out until it's time. When he sees what he needs, he'll give the signal, and the door will be opened.

A rubber bag lays on the ground with a body zipped inside.

For years this has been a premier destination for those looking to end their existence. But tonight it's a dump site, a statement move; a play of showmanship. The edge of the cliff is only feet away. With the vehicle's headlights illuminating the scene, one careless step will result in death.

The door opens, and Krolov steps into the cold night to watch the maneuver.

Zeus tells the men to step back. Being the ranking security official in the organization, and one of the few men Krolov trusts; no one had to be told twice.

The 6' 8" 400lb. behemoth grabs the body by the feet. Taking his time, he establishes a sound grip. Like the great hammer thrower Yuriy Sedykh, he lifts the body through the bag, and begins spinning! Grunting like a human centrifuge, he builds up steam! Hay, bits of turkey feed, twigs, duck droppings, pebbles of granite, empty potato chip bags, and dust begins whirling like an F-5 cyclone around his size 23 shoes!

On the fifth rotation he lets go, sending the body airborne over the cliff!

Sedykh's longest throw was slinging a 7.257 kg. ball connected to a chain a distance of 86.74 feet.

Zeus just threw a 234 pound corpse 49 feet.
The event is over.

Krolov smiles. He's glad he purchased this awesome specimen from the Arab sheik back when he was just an orphan from war torn Uganda.

My, how he's grown….

The universe gives us matter, the essence life, the absolute form of being. At the heart of its structure is the need for balance. The right amount of positively (+) charged protons, and the proper amount of negatively (-) charged electrons. Without the neutral (N) charge of the neutron, existence would not be possible. From the all the positively charged electrons of joyous celebrations bubbling in the atmosphere during miracle of birth, submicroscopic energy is also created from this fissioning. A new life-form is generated and welcomed into the world, predestined with its own atomic weight, and own atomic number.
But death is often a negative result of the delicate creation process of life. The minus of the passed mother completes the balance.
Within all off matter there is energy, this energy is called electricity. With the right equipment it can be harnessed, controlled, and tapped. It is the gel which hold atoms together, including humans. Including you. Like the positively charged blast of and pride and admiration created after a lifetime dedicated to hard work and perseverance result in scientists like, Dr. Glenn T. Seaborg, and Joseph W. Kennedy, who used the energy of neutron bombardment to isolate and discover the never before seen elements, plutonium and uranium.

Three weeks later, the negative charges which resulted fell down on Hiroshima, leaving one hundred and forty six-thousand innocent civilians dead.

The magnetic field which encompasses everything around us, the same field that keeps Pluto and Uranus out of our reach, is possible to be controlled and used. In scientific terms this marvel of creation is called: The Law of Attraction. A proven and universally accepted phenomenon that occurs throughout the universe. When conditions are favorable, it is possible to manipulate the magnetic field around you.

This is an old secret to those in the know.

But for every positive advantage which results from this alteration, there is an equal disadvantage. The neutral outcome of the discovery of these new elements, the electron which is equally charged with both *negative* and *positive*, was the fact that Hitler and his campaign of destruction was stopped by the Manhattan Project, and its advent of the nuclear bomb.

Life is filled with periodic tables of elements. One does not have to be a brilliant physicist to use them to create the atmosphere one desires.

Together, a man and a woman have dedicated their lives to the tutelage of this science. The fact it took almost fifteen years to be taught the skills he will need on his future journeys, has only recently been understood. For so long he teetered on a dead man's plank of confusion and anger, trying in earnest to decipher truth from falsehood. During this rebuilding phase he was close to defeat, close to death; he couldn't understand why this was happening. The pain of the molding process was indescribably excruciating.

She too had gotten lost in translation, suspended between two intersecting worlds of forgetting who she was, and becoming who she's meant to be. One realm emitting the last glimmers of its existence, and the other just expanding with the potential to hold infinite amounts of new discoveries. In the short time since its inception, new elements have become universally recognized reliable sources of light. Instead of casting darkness, he warms inhabitants with the heartfelt radiance of his star.

But just like anywhere in creation, there has to be a counter action, a force which pushes with all its weight, and all its might against his efforts. In an attempt to fortify his structure, he works with other like-minded elements in an attempt to solidify, and become one united body against this contrasting negative energy. Being he now has wealth, knowledge, an inherent affinity towards positive energy, a soul mate, and the potency of his charge towards opposing the forces of darkness; he's now a new element! One which has increased in both weight, and value!
He can now do things he never could before. He can affect (+) change on a global scale. No longer does he feel like his life is a waste. He now understands the power of the divine, and fears it more than he ever! Like kernels of hot popping corn, he steams with new ideas and new voracity. Greed for more understanding and more increase has become an indulgence.

But today his magnetic pull has led him back to his
"light working" table. The woman, the love of his life is here at his side. Without her, he would've never become this new element. She had to bombard him with her electrons of encouragement, intimacy, compassion, and commitment. She infused with him purpose, and through this fissioning he's able to realize a new plateau in his evolution as a man.
The golden flower, and its secrets are now his and hers.
As a couple they sit at their table, and with the power their union generates, they resume work. They know what piey're engineering is not a quick design. It may take years of commitment; plus the assistance of others to fend of the hordes of dark matter engorging the planet. The more they can teach

the power of this "light saber", the sooner they can bring down the guillotine on the negative forces, splitting their atoms in two! The sooner they can end this war of metals, the sooner they can bring the hammer down. And the quicker they'll be able to smash the whole of their universe.

Major Hall is hot on Orben Krolov, a.k.a. Ed Denmark, a.k.a White Man Ed, a.k.a The Grey Russian, a.k.a. The Denmark Jew's trail. With all the new info he has, he's moving at Mach 20 towards a major breakthrough. He and the rest of the force are working overtime to get back their good name. But in the heat of battle, he still has the presence of mind to be Russell Hall the father. His baby is now twenty two, but still his baby nonetheless. She's grown from little energetic bundle of joy, to young woman ready to claim her place in the world. Rest assured, where ever she is, he'll be there to protect and guide her.

Damn what they say about being overprotective!

Though an adult, she still enjoys the company of those she came to know as a child. Visiting with relatives and friends in Lakeview Estates, a town fifty miles east of Atlanta, he's somewhere lurking like a stalking dad. The nearest movie theater is the one at Stone Crest Mall. They enjoyed a movie, and ate at Arizona's Steak House, and closed their wonderful evening with ice cream. Being early winter, the franchisees of Brewster's ice cream parlor are still trying to get paid. They've invested a hundred and twenty nine-thousand dollars into the business, and after five years they're just starting to see a profit. No snow's on the ground, it's not raining, and plus it's only ten o'clock.

The fact someone came into his home was not only an invasion of his privacy, but her's as well; he can tell they went through her things too. It isn't her primary residence, but it's still her home. Until things are sorted out, she'll stay at her mothers and he'll come to her. This is the third time in seven days he's seen her; still not enough in his book. The wonderful time they had today will roll around his mind until the next time they kick it.

She's just finished her single scoop of black cheery and wants some water. Plus the gas meter sits at a quarter tank. Doing 74 MPH down I-20, traffic slows and creeps to a crawl; vehicles are going around something up ahead. When he gets there, he sees someone has struck a deer, a 10-point trophy buck to be exact. The animal is deceased and in bad shape. Men in 'H.E.R.O.' trucks hurry to get it off the expressway.
"Aaaaaaah," she winced. "I hate to see that. I wished they weren't so plentiful here."
"Yeah I know......Hopefully, it didn't die in vain."

Pulling off the interstate into a gas station, the temperature on the dash says 43°. Having the bad habit of pumping gas with the car running, he makes sure to turn it off before getting out.
"You want something lil mama?" (The nickname he gave her.)
"Yes, water please."
"What kind?"
"I like Viji."
"That's the worst water ever! The water in the public system tested cleaner than Viji. They dilute it with recycled tap water anyway, plus their government is corrupt and doesn't let the people draw from the springs. The company who owns the springs rations the water out to the natives at something like, two gallons a week. I stopped drinking Viji a long time ago. I don't want to support a company like that—you know I'm a good guy."
"Well why didn't you tell be *Daaaaaaad!* I would've like to have known that," she kidded.

"I thought you already knew. It's all over the internet. All you have to do is look it up. You know we talk about stuff like this all the time. We've had many conversations about how bottled water is a scam."

"Yeah. But you never told me about Viji. They've got the entire world thinking they're water's the best."

"Deception is a powerful tool," and opens the door.

With his wallet, three phones, and other items are in his jacket, he decides whether to do everything inside, or pay at the pump, before going inside to get the water while the tank fills.

She gets out with her arms crossed.

"On second thought, I think I'll run in and get it. Can I use your jacket?"

But she didn't have ask. He's already taking it off, and gives her the Big Man's jacket.

Zipped up and swallowed up, his heart warms at how much she's grown; gushing with love for her. In his eyes, there's no man good enough. But he knows he'll eventually have to let go.

❑❑❑❑❑❑❑❑❑❑

As of 10:11 p.m., Pain Bogart is back to himself. Pastor Cain is put away for today, but will have more work in the coming days. Without out knowing it, Pain has become one of the most prolific serial killers in history. As of now, the number of people he's killed sits at seventy two. But being a psychopath he doesn't view them as people. But as pests in need of extermination.

His body count increased exponentially when he located three other brothels in Queens. While the blackout wore on for three days, he attacked; earned another $277,721 in cash and "came up" on more weapons. Their very profits are being used to destroy them. He finds it fascinating that he's continuing to rack up kills and not be apprehended. It's like the police pressure evaporated, and he's been given a hall pass to kill freely. Each day he sees signs of things appearing to assist him. In the most psychotic of ways, by eliminating them he feels like he's getting closer to God. He feels like he's the cancer that's going to eat them from the inside until they are completely consumed. He doesn't feel like a madman but he knows he is. The fact that even after annihilating ninety four percent of their rank, he couldn't let the remaining six percent get away in the two vans they fled in, is proof of his obsession with radiating them with the chemotherapy of death. This is his form of ethnic cleansing.

Once they split up in Baltimore, he picked the first one off unabated. Now the second one's in his sights, and has just pulled off the highway into a gas station. He pulls into the space three down from it and watches.
After shooting the drivers of the first van at point blank range, he used the binoculars thermodynamic imaging capability on the to detect a large heat signature coming off the rear of the van. He didn't have time to wait, but he opened the doors and shot the locks off so when the cops come they'll find the hold of human cargo.
Now he's about to get the last one!
The driver has gotten out, and is inserting a card into the pumps reader. The passenger gets out and heads towards the entrance.

Wearing a red plaid shirt, black pants, and red sneakers, he gets out of his vehicle with a red bandana on his head. The oversized shirt and baggy pants hold a secret, the silenced 9milly is strapped around his leg, the Becker® is under his shirt sheathed to his side. Though it's night out, he still has on shades, which is perfectly fine. He looks just like every other gangbanger. The disguise is perfect for the hit.

He's the quintessential "fake gangster".

He enters the store.

Hall saw the reckless way the vehicle swerved into the space. Initially, he was looking straight ahead; daydreaming about how he's going to bring down Krolov, when he sees a dark colored Sprinter® van with two men inside, but doesn't pay it much attention. Realizing he's not on duty, though technically he is; his thoughts return to the unknown. He can't shake his belief he associated with Denmark, and this was all planned. But he really becomes interested when the person gets out the car draped in red and black, immediately thinking KT-36!
But catches himself. He's on an outing with his daughter, plus the man isn't breaking the law. Probably some suburban kid trying to act tough.
He watches the man disappear inside the store, he sees his daughter heading to the check-out.
The collapsed fender and sunk in bumper? The crushed headlight, the mangled mirror. The side of the van has a dent in it. Animal hair, streaks of blood.
Now he's bothered—this is the van that hit the deer they saw on the expressway.
An overwhelming urge to question them erects his desire.
Unfortunately, he's well outside his jurisdiction, and has no authority in Rockdale County. He's an APD officer, and these rednecks out here don't like city slickers; especially black ones.
No matter how much it burns him this is likely the van that killed the deer, there's no law stating it's illegal to strike a wild animal and keep going.
He turns his head so he won't have to see it.

Taking his thoughts back to the unknown, back to Vardan, back to the food paste, and back to and how it'll be a miracle if they can lift some prints off the "card". The number on it doesn't go to a phone. They called it, and even had it traced. They're still trying to figure out what the nine digit sequence is for. Vardan seems to have went to a vacation, so he hasn't been able to get info more info about it.

The peripheral view of his daughter coming out the store causes him to look. A man standing outside with a little boy gets her attention. He says something and points at the child.

The gangbanger is heading back to his vehicle without buying anything.

Now she's going inside her purse, and nodding in agreement to what he's saying.

Click!

The handle lock unlatched, signaling the tank is full! Atop the pump sits a television screen advertising various products which can be found in the store.

He glances at the Sprinter van. The driver has just gotten back inside after making sure the rear doors are secure.

Now the trailer of an up-coming movie is playing on the ad screen.

"Don't stick your nose where it doesn't belong! You have no idea what you're getting yourself into!"

What a mysterious warning, he thought. Now his antennas are up!

Screwing on the gas cap, it clicks three times; his spirit is telling him to be on guard!

Out of nowhere the gangbanger's car comes across the lot!

In the second it takes him to look at his daughter and yell, the gangbanger produces a gun, and opens fire on the van!!!!!

He freezes, panics! But only because of his daughter!!

He runs to protect her!!! But before he has a chance complete a second step, the gunman turns the gun on him.

He stops breathing.................................

Everything goes silent.....................................

It's like the earth stopped rotating...........................

He can't go like this....................

Not in front of his daughter....................

"This man deserved to die. You deserve to live. Inside you'll find your answer major."
And flees into the night!
His daughter comes running towards him! He leaps for the door and grabs his phone! Zooming to check on the driver, he informed 911 there's been a shooting! One deceased male, and the suspect fled in an early model Volvo station wagon!
The shattered windshield is riddled with bullet holes! The bleeding man slumped over the steering wheel still has his eyes open! Her hands fly over her mouth! A loud gasp! Tears begin rolling down her face!

That's the last she saw before he put her in the car.

The scene at the gas station became a mob. Once the media got wind that Russell Hall has been involved in another shooting, it became a circus. A Barnum and Bailey sized clusterfuck of epic proportion. The entire block had to be cordon off. Groups of angry protesters tried to incite a riot, but were quickly arrested. However, it didn't become a national news event until the human cargo was discovered. Now boom antennas stood everywhere, the area teamed with bright lights news anchors.

Twelve young women, and three school aged boys were found caged in four separate compartments. The van was equipped with a crude commode, and a shabby ventilation system. The occupants were dehydrated, hungry, and in need of medical attention.

One child was found deceased. Cause unknown.

The suspect is believed to be a member of the dangerous KT-36 street gang. Then reports came about there being a similar hit in Baltimore, MD—a van of identical type containing two dead men, and seventeen young people of various sex and ethnicity was recently found in the parking lot of a White Castle burger joint.

A connection developed.

News of another set of massacres at three New York brothels, and one in Atlanta start pouring in. They'd uncover the link and commence pushing their theories hard. Their notions have gained steam, and the authorities are using these new developments to calibrate their investigations accordingly. But what really turned this thing on its head, and caused the story to break the internet, is the fact a man dressed as a priest is supposedly committing these crimes; all alone, and armed with a stunning array of high tech weaponry and futuristic gadgetry. At all but one of the scenes, the message:

"Searching for Redemption"

Was spray-painted on the walls. Memes and caricatures are popping up all over social media. Three different FBI profilers are working to develop a suspect type. Names are being created to honor this man who's killing kidnappers and freeing victims. But the one the media has latched onto is: "The Archbishop

Assassin".
Now that he has a name, he's being thrust into the psyches of millions, riveting them to their televisions and smartphones with nonstop coverage of the bizarre drama.

Before the cops arrived, Hall had one of his trusted soldiers whisk his daughter away to safety. By the time the clock hit 2:13 a.m., he's done talking, done dealing with the media, and tired of his phone ringing.
Now he's finally alone and able to process the events of the evening. Sleep is nowhere on his mind. He's trapped in a cognitive whirlwind of phantasmagorias, assumptions, philosophies, and skepticism. Sucked down by the pit of agony's quick sands, he's going under and is losing breath fast.
He drops below the surface.

Douze.

Out of the past seventy two hours he's only gotten four hours of sleep. He's startled when he wakes up fourteen hours later wearing the same thing!
What's that irritating sound?
Once he realizes where he is, he runs a hand over his face and looks at his watch; shocked to see how long he's slept!
There it goes again: A call on his "special" line—Nguyen.
He still doesn't answer, the first time or second time.
She keeps calling and on the third try he does.
"Yeah."
She tells him there's something he needs to see, and to come down to the lab immediately!

At first he declines, saying he's not in the mood to deal with it right now. But she convinces him it's something important! He takes the bait when she tells him there's something on the backpack with the potential reveal the unknown's identity!

The fact Nguyen is still working hard for him fuels his engine of moral. It's only a spark, but enough to get his wheels back spinning.

Getting in his vehicle he notices how warm it is. It was just in the low 40's yesterday, now it feels like the high 60's. That's Atlanta weather for you, wildly unpredictable but consistently humid.

After meeting in the lobby, she escorts him to the back and buzzes the lock. It doesn't take him long to see the photos atop the table. Joy states she's been going over the test results of the items, and explained when she initially examined the backpack, she was so caught up in analyzing the DNA, that she paid no attention to what the plastic card said. On the zipper of the backpack is a key chain attachment. On the back an inspirational passage is printed on a cut of paper.

"No person was ever honored for what he received. Honor has been the reward for what he gave."

Something told her to run the passage through Goggle. The first result it returned is the mission statement of non-profit organization: "The Emma Jones Foundation". Upon visiting their website she saw pictures and videos of a recent clothing drive at a men's shelter. After including this new factor into the equation, she determined it's possible the unknown is a homeless person.

"I know who runs that shelter personally! Every person has to sign in to be given a bed number."

He hugs Nguyen and asked her to get with Hickenlooper, and brief him on the new development!

He contacts the shelter's director, but is informed she's on her way back from out of town business, and won't arrive in Atlanta until later this evening.

So after three dragging hours, he still hasn't heard back from her. Sitting at a table pouring over data, he massages his neck while looking out the window. The last remnants of sunshine were erased, and a full moon sits high in the clear sky; its white rays overwhelming the stars dimmer light.

The serenity is disturbed by the warble of his cell, but not on his overabundance of work phones, but his personal line. The same one his beloved daughter contacts him on.

He answers on the second ring.

"Hello."

"Hello Russell. I just got your message. Sorry I didn't get back with you sooner. This flight has been something," said the *sweet* voice of the shelter's director.

"Well good evening Simone," his voice deep and authoritative. Already he's feeling an erection grow.

"This is my first chance at a breather. I've been running non-stop. How've you been?"

"I've been well. I called to see if I could get a minute of your time?"

"*Sure.* What do you have in mind," she hints.

"I need to talk to you about a guy who may've come through the shelter. We found this book bag that maybe came from a recent donation drive. I need to see if this guy's been through there. It'll sure help me out a lot."

"Sure, but the office is closed. I won't be able to get to the logs until the morning."

"*Damn,*" he swore. "I was hoping you could get me in there tonight. It won't take but a second. You-"

"Russell I can't. There's staffers there at night, and security officers. It won't send the right message for me to bring you there this late. If you'll be patient, I'll happily let you inside in the morning, and you can take a look at whatever you like."

"Damn! I just was…Shhhh,..never mind," he said disappointingly.

"Hey," her voice soft and sultry. "I've spent my entire week doing for others. I already know what you've been through…… Let me go home, take a shower, and throw on something; how about we get some something to eat. I'd love to see you Russell. Why don't you take your favorite girl out and show her a nice time."

"I don't have time for that right now Simone. You just said you know what I'm going through. If you do, you should be able to understand. Any other time I'd love to, but right now I'm too wrapped up! I got crap coming at me from every angle! These bastards are trying to ruin me! I can't just sit back and let these cocksuckers go to town all over my career-.."

"Russell!" she spoke softly in his ear. "Russell listen at yourself. You're about to go crazy, you need to take a moment and breathe. You need to get to in calm state, *then* go back and attack it. You're not any good in the condition you're in now. Why do you have to make it so difficult to see you?……You make me think it's me or something. I shouldn't have to beg a man who says he loves me to spend time with me."

Russell sighs loudly.

There's nothing he can do at the moment. Either way he'll have to wait. He can go mope in his cave feeling sorry for himself, *or* he can spend the layover with a beautiful women who enjoys every second of his company.

His stomach growls.

"If you have to think that long about it, I'll just catch you another time. You can come by in the morning and look at the logs," she spat, preparing to hang up.

"What type of food do you have in mind?"

"We'll..Maybe something like 7th Heaven Oven. Far from the crowds and not too uptight."
He chuckles.
"That's actually the perfect spot for a night like this."
"Well why don't you come by and get me *innnn,…*let's say an hour? That work for you?"
"I'll make it work. Guess I'll see you soon."
"Goodbye Russell," she breathed.

When they arrive at the restaurant, they're both looking the part. They both choose the perfect arrangements to accompany such an unseasonal night. The temperature is comfortable and the breeze is a light.
They park and get out.
Walking inside, he's casually ensembled in a 2-button blazer and jeans. The pair full-grain calf leather lace-ups, dyed the color of wine accentuate his shirt well.
Seamless is her complement of casual elegance, her mustard yellow tunic and fitting denims meshes perfectly. The pearl necklace and sassy specs add pop; her curly hair is pulled back to display her high cheek bones and round eyes.
They aren't holding hands but can feel the energy between them.

7th Heaven Oven isn't your normal restaurant. It's an outdoor kitchen that serves Italian fare.

Walking under the low slung walkway covered with lush vines thriving with healthy leaves, Simone feels like the luckiest girl on the planet. The way he walks, the way his shoulders sit so strong and confident, the way he holds his head with such might and certainty; in no way is he haughty, or inflated with false swagger. The masculine way he swings his arms sends chills down her spine.

They reach the door, where he stands to the side and holds it; a whiff of his scent carried to her scenes by a tickling breeze.

He smells so good!

They approach the hostess and make their intentions known. Simone catches the women's glance—code speak women use to transmit messages.

Must be nice.

It said.

A server approaches and lays out to their options for the evening. Each day the menu changes based on what's available. It has to be organic, and it has to be fresh.

After making they're selections, she takes their orders, followed by offering them a seat there or at the bar, and promises a quick return with their items.

"You look good in a sport coat. I didn't know you had such style," she complimented.

"My father always told me: When you look good you feel good…………And you look pretty stunning yourself. Your skin is magnificent."

"Well you should come around and see it more."

Russell shakes his head in agreement.

He's trying hard to relax and enjoy the evening, but he keeps thinking about Krolov.

"So how was your trip?"

"It actually went pretty well. We're a lot closer to breaking ground on the new center."

"We'll that's good to hear."

"We finally have the instructors we need to teach the students. A lot of the investors had to be shown it's possible to turn a profit and change lives at the same time. The Panorama Women's House' will be a shining example of that. Even though we're a small foundation now, we eventually want to be become the next Emma Jones®. We're trying to obtain a global reach. I've learned so much from running the shelter. When I first took the job my friends thought I was nuts. They thought I was wasting my M.B.A. But what I've learned i-."

The attendant returns with their items.

"That *was* quick," Simone said with a smile.

"It doesn't take long," she laughed.

"Well if you'll follow me, I'll take you to your oven."

The trio follows the chipper waitresses through the door leading to the expanse of baking areas. In case of inclement weather, there is one indoor oven capable of accommodating eight to fifteen guests. But no one really comes when it's raining. The cold doesn't stop anything though. The winter chill mixed with the warmth of the ovens provides its own unique experience.

The owner spared no expense when creating this botanical dining experience. The plant life and artwork is native to Italy, with the décor distinctively reflecting this heritage.

They arrive at their area.

Hidden under a wooden canopy grown with just enough vines to allow sparkles of moonlight slice through, sits a quaint cozy section. The stone floor sits under a huge brick oven with a twenty three foot smokestack rising out of its dome. Nestled around it, this wide marble, half-circled table offers up to ten guests a place to prepare their dishes.

Situating them towards the opposite end of three other couples already there, the waitresses sits the wooden tray atop the thick slab of rock.

"Here we are."

Russell pulls her seat out, and seats himself on the plush wooden stool beside. Once they've settled, she gives them a brief but detailed overview about how to best prepare their dish. She starts by first explaining how extremely hot the oven is, the rules regarding safe preparation/emergency procedures, and closes by saying, if needed, they can notify her, and she'll assist them with the process. Shortly before the entrée is ready to be pulled from the oven, she'll bring the salad, bread, and or wine they select-ed earlier. She points to the sink where they can wash, and the lounge area where they can enjoy conversation over after dinner drinks.

"So is there anything else you need before I leave you to enjoy your experience?" her smile still bright.

"No. That'll do. Thank you," Russell responds.

"Enjoy your evening." Takes a bow, and walks away.

"I must say, she was very detailed," spoke Simone.

"Very," he agreed.

The tray sits stacked with the ingredients they'll need to make their own gourmet calzone. The dough is made fresh every hour, a sauce of their own proprietary blend of herbs and spices comes standard with every meal. A block of Parmesan and mozzarella cheeses cuddle beside a just-picked bouquet of basil, oregano, sage, thyme, rosemary, and parsley. A basket of ripe tomatoes, plump mushrooms, yellow onions, green and red peppers ignites the spread with color. A stable of aged Kobe beef chucks pose wonderfully marbled, and ripe with distinction. Beside them, the bloom of thinly sliced prosciutto, smoked to perfection is culinary shrewdness at its finest. A vase of imported olive oil, a bowl of coarse sea salt, an antique pepper grinder, a *mean* set of cooking utensils, two hand-knitted oven mitts, and a hickory cutting board jagged with bark complete the assemblage.

Moments later, another attendant shows and sits a baking sheet dusted with flower on the table; along with a wooden spatula—smiles and leaves.

"So Mr. Hall, how do you want to start?"

"I guess by grabbing the dough," replying with a smirk.

The lovely Simone grabs the ball and roller and sits it on the baking sheet. "Why don't you open the sauce."

"You know how I love the *sauce*." Mr. Debonair style.

"You better cut it out Russell before you get me saucy."

He winks, grabs the Mason jar, and opens the freshly made sauce—it smells heavenly.

"This is the only place I've visited where you can find an experience like this. Whoever thought of this is pure genius. I wonder if they'll franchise it."

"Probably not," he guessed.

"There's another one but it's in Italy. These are the only two," she stated.

"It's better this way. Too many will ruin it. The franchisees will go cheap and try to squeeze more money out of it. Greed sucks the joy out of everything."

The other couples are oblivious to their presence. Food, wine and smiles seems to be their only concerns. The large stone table and arid atmosphere gives everyone their own circumference of privacy.

The lawman and the lady engage in conversation while they preparing their dish. No talk of work is allowed, only stimulating topics and pleasing gestures. The occasional brush of skin, the occasional brush of her derriere across his sausage subtlety hints at what's later to come.

As the horde of ingredients become a united front, they notify the attendant they're ready to bake.

Arriving in an instant, she uses the big spatula to *slide the calzone in the oven.*

Without knowing it's even in there, they watch as she extracts a piping hot, golden roll of bread, and sits it on the table.

Like clockwork, another server shows with their dressing and salads of kale, spinach, almonds, croutons, persimmons fresh from Costa Rica, raisins, and Tuscan whey cheese made from water buffalo milk.

Moments later, he returns with two stone cups and places them beside the picture of well water—drawn and filtered on site.

The water alone is a sought-after commodity. Patrons repeatedly ask them to bottle it up and sell it, but they decline; having no desires to become water producers.

By this time, Russel is even more relaxed and receptive to her longings for his touch. He begins smiling more, his muscles aren't so tense, and he doesn't look to be lost in thought.

"Isn't it crazy how you can see the calzone in there cooking? Look at how the bricks are glowing orange," she stated.

"It's amazing how much heat they retain. Even from here I can feel it. I'm sure if we were on the other side we could feel it a lot more. I bet it's great here on a cold night."

"It probably is, but I can't do the cold," and takes another fork-full of her gourmet salad.

"Sure you can, you just have to come prepared."

"Well bring me, I don't have anyone one else to take me."

Though Simone Johnson is a mesmerizingly attractive female, he's never heard of a man bedding her. He's also seven years her senior.

"That's because you don't, *want* anyone else to take you."

"I see you're a smart man Russell Hall," she flirted.

"I'd like to thank you for this evening, I needed it. This fresh air has done wonders. But my mind keeps thinking about tomorrow and what awaits."

"We'll deal with tomorrow when it gets here. For now, let's just enjoy the evening. How often is it that two busy people like us get to enjoy something this magical. The last thing I want to think is tomorrow. Now and *you,* is *all* I want to focus on."

And lays her hand on his thigh.

Looking at the plate while chewing his salad, he enjoys her soft caress. He routinely pictures himself settling down with her, but tells himself his duty is to the people, and there's no time for love. But as the months march on, no matter how much he denies it, he'll have to confront the feelings he has for her. He's afraid to embrace the fact he's fallen in love again. But when he looks into her eyes, he feels her charge; she's meshed seamlessly with his molecular structure. He wants to tell her how much she means to him but can't yet let himself go. The carnage from his first shot at love still litters his psyche like bones across the Serengeti. He's not sure he wants to embark on another laborious expedition into the unpredictable wilderness of love.

Let go for a change. Learn to enjoy yourself sometimes. You miss out on so much. Why do you push away what feels right?

Russell turns to her.

She smiles and squeezes his hand.

He reaches over and pulls her closely, surprising her by his forwardness?

To thank him she kisses him on the cheek, and sighs. She feels that undeniable feeling too.

Before they know it, the lady is back, pulling their calzone from the oven; a steaming pie of reckless taste bud abandon. The mere sight of it makes their mouths water. The aroma torturous.

As if they're specially invited dignitaries visiting the Americas from a Mediterranean continent, they're shown the upmost in hospitality. A smartly dressed older gentlemen appears with a tray topped with a bottle of wine sitting on chill. Sided by a stunning blown glass decanter, and two wine glasses on tuck.

After teasing them with the prelude, he places the glasses down and prepares the show.

The opening act begins with him selecting the hammered copper ice bucket. But there's no ice, only a bed of orchard grass, and a bottle of vintage Italian wine—damp with dew, cooled to 58°, the perfect temperature to ensure maximum palate stimulation.

Expertly, he sits the tray down and removes the decanter; clear and curvaceous it is.

Pop!

"*Yaaaaaaaaaay!!*" claps a smiling couple, celebrating the uncorking.

Gently, the leading man administers a portion of the potion, and sits it down.

In the defining event, he raises the decanter and begins swirling. Like a seasoned veteran portraying an experienced chemist, he mixes the solvents, aerating the wine to allow any sentiments that may exist to settle to the bottom.

For the interlude, he allows the attendant to slice the fat calzone and set up their meal.

Once the plates are portioned, he presents them with two crystal drinking glasses, filling them to half.

Applause abound!

Finally, he sits the bottle down, bows, and excuses himself.

"Wow! What a way to dispense wine," Simone said.

"Is there anything else I can get you all?"

"No. Everything looks absolutely wonderful."

"Enjoy!"

And is gone.

"This looks amazing," said Simone. "How come I couldn't have thought of this?"

"See if their looking for investors?"

"Funny. I'm sure they get that a dozen times a day."

"Maybe they're not in it for the money."

The exquisite night culminates into a spectacular early morning. From the heavens blow the heat of love. As they drive, sexy sounds croon from the speakers. This is no radio play, but from Russell's CD collection; purposely selected for the occasion. At this point he's done playing games. Russell can feel his shaft elongating, as it crawled down his inner thigh. It's been a while since he's caressed her body; the only woman he chooses to sleep with. The way she's holding his hand and tickling his palm with her finger, he knows the opening phase of foreplay has begun. Sneaky subtleties, nondescript insinuations, and explicit innuendos are the best plays for this stage.

Before they know it, the fantasy is over and reality is set to begin! Pulling into her driveway, she uses her remote to open the garage door. The space he always parks awaits his return. Once in she closes the door.

The night is young and they're two consenting adults.

Russell cuts the car off.

"You ready?" he asked.

".....Are you?"

Dripping wet with lust he replies: "That's a question you should be answering...Either we can *come*…Or I can *go.* "

She smiles and opens the door.

"Enough said."

Holding the doggy bag he exits the car, waits at the hood for her to come around, and follows her through the door.

The ring of the alarm was silenced by a four-digit code.

Following her into its depths, they stand in the space between the foyer and the kitchen. She flips on a light and tosses her things on the table, reaches down to pulls off her shoes— wiggling her painted toes as they touch the cold hard wood! She takes the bag and sits it on the island, grabs him by the hand, and leads him through the living room to the stairs.

But before she has a chance to step one pretty foot on the first carpeted stair, he bends down and *sweeps* her off her feet!

Carrying her up, she kisses his neck.

At the top, he does not put her down, he does not allow her to take the lead, he does not allow her to dictate the policy; he's a selfish bastard when it comes to setting his table of seduction.

Arriving at the master bath, a night light glows adjacent the light switch. He leaves it on and the light off, his free hand turns on the water. Like a smooth criminal, steals her body and faces it forward, like a ripe banana, he peels her clothing layer by layer.

Returning the gesture, she helps him out of his, and wraps her body around his waist—arresting him with passion.

The distinguished gentlemen he is, kisses her lips as she swings from him.

They slip inside.

The showing in the shower was followed by a reenactment in the bedroom. After more squeezing, panting, shivering, and sweating, they fell asleep naked and exhausted in each other's arms. So now, at 9:04 a.m., the sun is peeking through her blinds and she's already smiling. Simone inhales deeply and rolls over and views the sleeping man. Touching his chest she lays her head, she feeling the thump of his heart. He rustles and hangs his arm over her shoulder. Though it's technically winter, birds are chirping morning lullabies in the Georgia pines. They listen to them sing and belt, warbling coded tweets of information; the satin sheets keeps the two lovebirds suspended in a state of wishful remembrance.

"You're late."

"I know," she replied. "Let me get my butt up."

"Wait. I want to tell you something first," he begins. "First off, last night was amazing. Thank you. Secondly, I wanted to wait until now because I didn't want the moment to lessen the certainty of my statement. I love you Simone..........I want you to know that. You know I'm not the type of guy who's going to say it a lot, but I'm sure you can feel it. Before we leave this room, I want you to be certain that I cherish you."

A tear falls from her eye.

"I love you too Russell. If there is ever a man who meets my heart's every desire, it's you. You're the *only* man I see."

And kisses him.

"I'm the only man you should be looking for."

"You know a girl could get used to this."

"You know, that's something I should think about. You give my life a flavor that's been lacking for years," he said, in his rich weighty tone. "One of the things I love the most about you, is how you make me feel like a man."

She kisses him again.

"I just don't understand why you can't find more time for me Russell. Why do I feel your passion so intensely when we're together, but then you leave me for weeks at a time? And I wait like a love drunk puppy until you to come back."

"You shouldn't feel that I leave you. The connection we have surpasses distance and time. As much as I care for you, I have an obligation to the Creator. I promised to use the abilities he's given me to serve the people. What we have is so special that it's become bigger than you and me. The passion and zeal you possess to help and protect the people you serve is unmatched in any person I've met. It's like you're a female spitting image of me. The fire which burns inside us both to change the world for the better is neither chance, nor coincidence......The fact we are her today is not unplanned. This is where fate has brought us. Soon we will be able to enjoy what we have. But baby right now, I'm in a fight for my life. I'm facing the fiercest assault I've ever been confronted with. I'm being met with foes who yield weapons the likes of which I've never seen......It would be selfish and unrealistic for me to think I can give you the love you deserve at a time like this......What I need for you is to fight hard on your front, keep your foot to the pedal so when we are able to rest, it'll be magnificent."

For her there's nothing else for him to say.

"I can't wait for that day to come."

*"Part of being a professional is keeping your patience when the
pressure gets jacked up………"*

He hears the man on the television proclaim. Hall doesn't know
why it's even on; he's too giddy for television right now!
While CNN airs the latest developments, Loop is in the process of drawing up the warrant application. Kam's joyous the
unknown has finally been unmasked, Hall can't believe it either.
But again, he does. Possessing the heart of a champion, he expects to win; he knew this moment would come, because he
wouldn't quit until it did.
After the morning with Simone, he went over the shelter's
admission logs. Upon realizing how painstaking the process of
going through hundreds of names would be, he called Loop and
Peavey to assist. But it wasn't until they began going over the
hours of camera footage that the face jumped off the screen.
Once the face was recognized they searched for more images.
Using the video's time stamp they crossed referenced it with the
sign-in sheet. When they saw the name 'Timothy Zarbin' they
knew they had their man, even have him on camera with the
backpack.

The only thing left is for Loop to call with news the judge
signed the warrant, which is a minor formality. With all the
evidence, it's practically impossible for him to deny it. Assistant
DA Yuen has his intern compiling the media statements and
press releases. Tameka Parris is getting ready for her interview
with BBC®. People are already beginning to celebrate this small
victory. But they all know the big fish is still out there. It'll take
many more of these small triumphs to bring down Ed Den-
mark/Orben Krolov.
Hall's siting but he's about to stand because the phone in his
pocket is ringing.
It's her calling him back.

He smiles.
Not that her, but the other her; the love of his life in another context. He already knows why she's calling. She's been telling him for days about the lady across the street, and if he doesn't do it now, she'll continue asking until he does.

So before leaving, he grabs a few tools and brings them along. In the event football didn't pan out, in high school he took a course on heating and air conditioner repair. He's no pro but he knows a thing or two.
She informs him from inside her friend's house it'll be a tad longer before she's finished.
"All right, I'll take a look right quick. Did you call and tell her so she won't think I'm a burglar and shoot," he joked.
She assures him it's safe, explaining she already told the lady you're coming over tonight and would probably look at it then.
"I guess I should just hire you as my secretary."
She laughs and says she has to go so the girl can finish her hair.

Puffed with pride from the impending announcement, he looks at his watch. There's still light in the sky, and he's bound by universal law to help those in need—there's no days off when it comes to humanitarianism and philanthropy.
He sighs and gets out.
Even when he's worn he has to find the traction to push himself. He's made for this.

The six men are fixating on each movement Hall makes. They split into two teams. As a contingent of three and body of one, they are there for the same person, but for different reasons; fighting from opposite ranks who represent opposing factions.

The five man squad coordinate their efforts amongst themselves, and splinter. The armed pair dressed in black moves towards the target, one stays in the driver's seat, and two others perform surveillance. These are professionals who know maintaining the element of surprise is paramount.

It doesn't take him long to diagnose the problem with the unit. The start capacitor is bad and needs to be replaced. The filter dryer isn't clogged, and the compressor rings show no signs of refrigerant blow-by.

Putting his left hand atop the condenser, he leans over and unhooks his Yellow Jacket® brand compound gauges—even brought along tank of recovered R-22 in case she needs a few pounds of chlorodifluoromethane. His mind clock tells him his daughter should be finished by now, and will probably be calling any second.

He feels the hair on the back of his neck turn to lightning rods!
The needle enters his neck, the potent sedative taking immediate effect! He stands but he's already falling! Stumbling into the side of the house, he tries to balance himself on the patio's railing, but he's already a sinking ship! He hits the ground like a ton of bricks!
The phone starts vibrating!
It all goes black.

The decision's been made: Russell Hall is to be rubbed out—he was a small problem that ballooned into a major issue. The

only way to stop him is to bless him with eternal sleep. Five
kinsmen from Slovenia were given the contract. They work as
a team and are regarded for their stealth. Krolov has already
been made aware of his capture, and wants the entire process
videotaped so he can verify its authenticity after it's complete.
A special representative is on their way to retrieve fingerprints,
hair follicles, and tooth samples; which will later be used to
frame the soon-to-be-missing officer for several unsolved
homicides. A forgery specialist is already penning the suicide
note to explain why he did it. A cinematic production engineer
from California is flying in to do an exact replica of the major's
voice, which will be used for a profanity laced drunken tirade
to the nine-one-one dispatcher.

After tonight, all the good Russel Hall has spent decades building will be demolished in a matter of seconds. When the
Hollywood style set-up, and slanderous propaganda machine
are done churning, he'll be remembered as one of history's
most reviled dirty cops.

Tied to a chair in the center of an empty storage space, he can't
believe what he's seeing. Thinking this to be kind of nightmare
he keeps trying to wake up, his brain refusing to comprehend
the reality that he's being held hostage, and most likely getting
ready to die. He sees the floor under his feet is covered with
plastic sheeting, and knows the bright lights and cameras shining in his face aren't here for a photo shoot.
A DVD of death will be more appropriate.

He doesn't want to think about what the chain saw and
machete are for. His fears don't deceive him when his captors
inform him his dismembered corpse will be stuffed inside the
55 gallon drum of fluoroantimonic acid in the corner. They
laugh at the fact his daughter will never know what happened
to her father, assuring him the caustic chemical will leave noth-

ing; not even bones. Mad scientists, they explain the silvery-white, metal based antimony has a pH of -31.3, and 100,000 billion billion billion times more potent than stomach acid. If the drum wasn't lined with a special coating, it would eat right through it.

He keeps expecting to be beaten, but to this point no one has done more than talk and stare. In a language he can't understand they speak back and forth. He isn't blindfolded and neither are they; wondering where the other two guys are, because he knows there's at least four. With the air is hot and heavy, he's having a hard time breathing, his heart's racing, sweats coming down his face blurring his vision, and heat emanating from the lights is vexing him!

One of the men makes a startled move and says something to the man beside him, grabs a walk-talkie, and speaks something. Using some kind of gibberish dialect, he points at him, before disappearing down the hallway!
In the distance Hall hears a door slam.
Now it's just them.
He hears the door open again? But this time it's slow and deliberate, the squeak of the hinges are noticeably prolonged?
The man yells something in his language!
Russel watches in bewilderment as his captors stand perplexed in the direction of the sound?
Without warning, the kidnappers begin acting as if they're being stoned by a sortie of invisible ghosts, the hail of gunfire slamming them backwards into the wall!!!
By the time they hit the floor, the holes in their faces, throats, chests, abdomens, scrotums, and legs have them looking like they've been hit with a cluster bomb!!!
Hall hears the door slam again!
Followed by slow footsteps!
When the figure steps into the light, he doesn't know if he'll be able to speak!!!!!!! The man has no mask, and is dressed like a pastor!!!!!!

"UUUU-HHHH-aaaaahhh," he gasped, his diaphragm about to collapse!!!!!!

The unknown now stands before him with the same smoking gun he had at the gas station!!!!

It didn't take a judge or a warrant application to bring Alexander Timothy Zarbin to him, all it took was Hall putting his mind to it.

"Hello major," the tripod lights and cameras behind him, giving him the look of a supernatural life-form emitting shafts of light.

But he has no words.

Blood from the slain men has puddled onto the floor like a spilled mop bucket of runny ketchup!

"You have nothing to fear major....Again the universe has favored you."

He's surrounded by a dead pool of men!!! The man who did it is telling him with a straight face he's favored!!!

"You major are a blessing to many. As a homeless man I once heard a story about a food truck that drives around the city giving out free meals and fresh water. I'd even heard stories of this same food truck arriving at nursing homes delivering charitable goods......The man telling me the story said he saw the same van at a children's hospital, and how the driver was in a elephants suit pulling a helium tank with balloons tied around his arm...He said when the man took of elephant mask, he recognized his face as that of a popular police major..."
Pauses to take a step closer.

"There is a force larger than us both that predestined this. Destined these men to follow you with the intent of killing you. Destined you to visit a shelter I once resided so that you may witness the extent of the Creator's power. Your eagerness to confine me has become the very reason I have become the key to your freedom. The men I killed at the gas station were destined to die. When men followed your daughter, I followed too. When they made the choice to do the things they did, their demise was authorized…It's not for me or you to determine the ruling of things.....The more man thinks he's in control, the more he learns he controls nothing at all."

He stops talking and stares.

Producing a sealed envelope from his person, he sits it on his lap.

"Rest assured major. You're right where you're supposed to be."

And reaches down and unsheathes the Becker® BK9

When Hall sees the size of the blade, his eyes buck! He still isn't sure this man's isn't going to kill him!

The wanted fugitive steps behind him, cuts him free, and patently steps back before him—only his ankles are bound to the chair.

"Be sure when you lay down tonight you thank the Creator for what he has done for you."

And calmly turns and walks away.

When Hall hears the door squeak and slam, he still hasn't found his voice! The fright brought on by this awe inspiring display of grace is utterly bone-chilling! Tears flow down his face in water falls of gratitude! He falls to his knees with his forehead pressed to the plastic sobbing uncontrollably!

All he can do is cry and be thankful for his life!

Treize.

For the second consecutive day he's been holed up in this one room, and in a few hours it'll be a new day. But for him, there's no promise of a new life. His is already made. Void of clothing he sits on the edge of the same bed he's been on since first picking up his instrument. He's locked in a hallucinogenic trance he can't escape from. The drugs mixed, with the harmony he's established with it is spellbinding. With qualities a beginner won't recognize, the virtuoso of retribution unleashes the full sonic potential of the Anton Krutz violin. Using a perfectly balanced Brazilian pernambuco wood bow, he produces sounds that captivate the mind, causing him to see lucid images and scenes he believed were all but forgotten. The frequencies emitting from the strings are sending signals to his soul which aren't allowing him to move. The chinrest is oily and wet from him resting on it hour upon hour, the cut on his finger has caused the stings to become crimson with stain. A perfectly synchronized pendulum, his arms swing to and fro with bouncing stokes and measured rips. The tonal beauty, range of color, clarity, and projection of notes has forced him to surrender his mind body and soul. Encased deep within this cocoon of vivid melodies and semi-conscious meditation, he accepts the treble clef of his plight.

The plaque she gave him sits beside him. Her scent radiates form the cloth as if her presence is woven within its stitch. He's experiencing a meltdown of his inner-self.

...........*My mother called me a rose, now the seedling of me has taken root. Sometimes I walk in my own garden and get lost in the beauty that surrounds me. I am a rare flower that grows on mountains high in the sky. Beyond my field of red petals and green stems, the world is dark..........*

The thought of where she is, and her safety are the main reasons he can't sleep. The number to her phone is now coming back disconnected. The reason he went into that building was to find her, he slayed all those demons to save her.

...........*The cold wind blows like an angry storm over a prairie; I am strengthened by the push, I grow in this storm to become lovely. Charmed by my blossom a gardener steals me and wants to implant his seed. Blinded by beauty he doesn't notice my thorns are unable to be contained..............*

Visions of her and her child cut into pieces and tossed on the side of the road are nauseating his mental. The sound of the violin is the only thing keeping him connected to what little sanity he has left. The anger for not being able to torture Merciless more before killing him still boils inside him; he died too easily. For all the wrong he'd done, he wanted him to suffer, he wanted him to feel pain like he made those women feel, he wanted to make him pay for hurting Cailida.

Before her, his life had no purpose. Now she's gone and he's left trying to pick up the pieces. The East Coast is littered with bodies on the account of her. If she's dead, he's going to find it hard to live. Like the oxygen a fire needs to burn, she was the key element of his life that allowed his flame of combustion to destroy the evils it encountered. The zeal she breathed into him is waning fast, and without her molecules of octane fueling him to fight, he's now feeling the crash as the elixir wears off.

.....................*He cuts me down and takes me to a faraway land. Unable to grow my petals wither and darken. My red turns deep with the color of pain. Parts of me are washed away by the erosion of life. Falling to the ground an angel rescues me. Planted in a new plot I bring hopes of a new harvest! People from all around come to appreciate my bloom. They call me their sacred floret, a gift from grace with the power to bring light to gloom.*
He's in a land of darkness. The news about the nationwide manhunt for him is more of an inconvenience than a surprise. He knew the authorities would eventually find out who he is and come after him. But the shock of realizing Bailey may be dead, or even worse somewhere locked in a cage calling for him, is way worse than any weak ass manhunt.

But there's another being in the room with him.

He can feel it, but for some reason his head won't turn so he can see it. He's eaten so many mushrooms that he's in a psyche-delic phantasm. The wide arrays of untrustworthy colors, and Satanic verses have changed his makeup.
Whoever the being seems to be enjoying the music he's play-ing. Something about the angelic sound of the violin has them attracted. They're quite large, the entire corner of the room is filled with their presence, and aren't in the least bit fazed by the sight of his nakedness.
He's sees writings on the wall warning him of a coming event, a

coming hour, the dusk of something destined to end at a prescribed time; the dawn of a new beginning. He can hear the ticking clock chanting verbiage he can't understand. He sees the vivid video playing on the wall above the balcony.

A man dressed in a tailored suit with a silver face is holding a book he believes will change the world.
Some guy keeps asking him about this book, and where he came from.
His answer: I'm not here for fame and fortune.

The violin is magnificent, an exquisite piece of craftsmanship. His arms move by their own command, he can no longer feel the polished wood in his hand, and he doesn't have to think about the notes he wants to play.

In the outer reaches of this expanding space of perplexity, he sees a curtain closing on a scarecrow who's just realized he's actually a lion who wasted his entire performance playing the wrong part.

.... This flower of the heavens must not be misused. For like the birth of an angel, her display only has one bloom............

Inside the bag laying on the floor is almost six hundred-thousand dollars. While congealed blood sticks to the cut on his finger; the crimson on the strings is nothing compared to the blood pouring from the money in the red fountain of screams and cries he's envisioning.

Alone on a stage in Carnegie Hall, the white light of the spotlight's beam on him like a waves of heat. He can see the violin, but the audience consists of empty seats with voices.

"An experimental project," the conductor announced.

But the announcer corrects him by saying: "Prodigy!"

Others shout: "Fool's Gold!"

The pragmatists in the cheap seats call out: "He's pyrite!"

While playing this celestially mandated performance on a stage void of structure, he can feel their opinions of him, and what they think of this test trial. Like the positive, negative, and neutral legs of any basic electrical circuit, their sentiments are on the same scale. Some are angered by the fact that as a universal body, such destructive means were used to achieve an end. Citing the current atmosphere, others support the measure and are positive it was a good fusion. Believing in times of war such as this, to counteract a force as evil as the ones they're facing, they have no other alternative but to terminate the hazardous matter. The group sitting in the middle are neither pleased, nor displeased by the results.

However, all atoms are all in the same molecule when they agree the creation of this new element will lead to the eradication of the destructive organism.

Mesmeric and enthralled, Pain waits for the powers of the seven spheres to configure the environment so the negative elements which have mutated into an epidemic are receptive to being neutralize by the violet fire. For the remainder of the evening he doesn't move, he finishes out the remainder of his swan song until the time comes for the curtain to close on his riveting performance.

The alchemists who reside in the realm of the unseen, prepare the magnetic field that will alter the earth's gravitational pull, changing the tide, causing the wind pattern to initiate storms that will pound Tenancingo for forty days and forty nights.

In his final rendition, Pain Bogart, aka Pastor Cain, aka Alexander Zarbin, will attempt to cross the Mexican border before hopefully going overseas to one of several non-extradition "sanctuary countries" which offer asylum to United States fugitives.

The commission closes the book and rise from the table. The

precise balance that determines all things, grabs it; just as it has for eons, and takes it to be cataloged in the infinite shelf of universal law.

The ordainment is already taking affect. A brutal war between two rival drug gangs has caused a mass exodus of the people living in the region. The widespread bloodshed in their villages has forced them to abandon their homes and head north. A reporter at the U.S. border asks refugees why they're leaving their homes and possessions behind. A man pushing his mother in a wheel chair down a railroad track responds by saying: " All we want is to be free. Somewhere we can be safe without the fear of the gangs and cartels."
The male reporter holding the microphone to the man surrounded by his younger sister, his younger brother, and his wife informs them of the barrier up ahead, saying: "What if you have to climb over a fence to get into the country?
The refugee stanchly responds by saying: "We have no choice but to get over, there is no *what if*, there is no *anything else*. Either we get over, or we die!"

The result is a city void of women and children, void of the very people they used to feed the human trafficking machine. The only ones left in the city of Tenancingo are gangs, cartels, corrupt officials, and the remnants of whatever other spilth decides to stay and soil the grounds of this naturally beautiful city. If there is ever such a thing as a killing field, this is it. It holds the highest concentration of demonic forces and negative matter than any place he knows; a cesspool of unstable gases that remove oxygen from the air, and replaces it with carcinogenic emissions that deteriorate everything in its vicinity. Buy their own doing, they created this environment to benefit only themselves. The by-product of this is the negative and counteracting toll it places on the overall balance. Lacking the vital amount of positive charges to exist, it's become extremely volatile, and is now on a fixed course towards implosion.

Chief Justice Arthur Masterson being in the fray is big; by the far the biggest and most decisive stance anyone has taken against the Denmark brand. He's said to control which laws are passed, and which aren't; akin to saying who gets to cheat and who has to play fair.
Levels of privilege usually come with a certain price, but there are often instances where he dishes out free samples of how fast a person with the right connections can be skipped to the front of the line. The name Denmark, and what it represents has become so scorching, that it's made it all the way into politics. Hopeful candidates and hot-seated incumbents are using the premise of good vs. evil to win the votes of hapless voters hypnotized by the ongoing saga. The media has done a brilliant job creating a perpetually profitable topic that can be spun to the tune of millions. The more they broadcast, the more the public wants. It's now pop culture. White Man Ed has been placed in the in upper echelon of criminal lore with the likes of: Al Capone, John Gotti, Pablo Escobar, and Chapo Guzman. His name is heard in rap songs, his likeness is showing up in tattoo parlors. Anything with the name Denmark is a guaranteed sell. The buzz around such a malevolent individual is unbelievable. Video clips of children saying they want to be Ed Denmark when they grow up are tearing up social media. Professional athletes with huge muscles and small brains are being heard proclaiming their support of him. But tycoons and sheiks are

staying quiet because they don't want it getting out that they're in bed with him. Pastors, reverends, and bishops are making him the topic of their sermons/motivational speeches; depicting him as Satan is a top earner. Dashing holy water and bellowing the end is near is a top-selling delusion. Playing on the congregation's emotions in hopes of getting them to feed more money into the collection plate is the objective.

Stupid T-shirt's saying idiotic things like: *"Denmark for President"* and *"White Man Ed is my Baby Daddy"* are seen walking through shopping malls and college dorms.

The power of deception, and immensity of how easily deceived are the masses, is extraordinary.

Studies have shown, humans are often times easier to sucker than animals. An animal's instinct forces them to do what is natural. While a human's high intelligence forces them to abandon instinct, and become bamboozled by illusion.

Justice Masterson is not mystified by smoke and mirrors, and will use his judicial might to roll the tide of opposition. He's the one who brought this to the president's attention, he's the one who contacted trusted friends in the C.I.A. to find out where Denmark's hidden money lies. They in-turn used their vast network of KGB defectors to find his Hungarian affiliations. Moles in Zurich were used to find what his holdings, and sheiks in need of U.S. aid to find out about his hidden enterprises.

Now on the first official freeze of winter, at the CNN headquarters in Atlanta, on this blisteringly cold day, the news agency is springing leaks something big about to down. Reports of a major development in the Denmark saga has apparently tipped the scales in the authorities favor. Rumors of someone by the name of *"Orben Krolov"* is burning up the wire feeds, gossips of this mysterious Krolov character shimmer behind the scenes. Theorists are coming up with theories as to who it might be. Some are saying it's Denmark's long-lost love child who was believed to be dead, and has come out of hiding to turn state's witness against his deadbeat dad. Others are saying it's actually a *woman* who'd once been a maid of his, who's now ready to spill decades of family beans; for a hefty price. Others are saying Krolov is actually Denmark's real name, and he's actually a Russian spy who's about to receive diplomatic immunity in exchange for top-secret information about Russian and Chinese hacking operations of U.S. companies.

The web of misinformation that's been spun on these people should be considered a crime against humanity, all the news agencies are guilty, and all the wormy politicians have agenda's. Only the British Broadcast Company made an honest effort to tell both sides of the story, but even they're under pressure to blur the truth; the queen on their back making sure they don't say the wrong thing. The monarchy still hasn't fully recovered from the Princess Di disaster. They don't want the world finding out about their other misdeeds.

The pope is being his normal secular self.

Here we have the major, Hall that is—Russel is what they call him. He doesn't drink Texas tea, he doesn't have any black gold, and he's not a hillbilly who struck it big. He's just a "Big Man", and that's what they refer to him as. But he's also Major Hall, and he's their leader—no fabricated suspension will tell them otherwise. They're aware some foes are so formidable that to smite them, it requires a collective effort, a shared cooperative to defeat such a challenging adversary. They understand the saying: *Like minds think alike*. They understand the importance of frequency, and how they must all be attuned to the same one if they're going to be successful in their mission.

The evil known by his earthly name Krolov, and the disparaging lassitude he projects on the masses has become so entrenched into everyday society, that it's become it's own new element. This one man has turned the age old relict of human servitude, into a 21$^{st.}$ century slave trading corporation, which earns hundreds of millions in untraceable currency. It's human trafficking on a scale George Jetson never imagined, with the basic premise of powerful being lording over weaker being for the sake of profit.

To mount an army capable of facing down this enormous legion of doom, it took a Supreme Court Justice, a scorned district attorney, an embarrassed police force, a courageous major, a serial killer with a cause, and a victim driven by the love for her child. The fact they'd got over the enormous obstacle of raising an army, the long journey it took to get here, and all who died along the way; will not be forgotten.

But now they have to fight!

Now they have to overcome the larger obstacle of winning the war. In this theatre, only after a succession of bloody battles can a victor be named; the side that perseveres the longest will win. On this great battlefield is where history will chose its heroes, this is where it will remember the men who pushed through adversity to conquer all.

He's one of these such men, a rare breed, an evolutionary marvel, a miscalculation of Darwinian Theory. As a spiritual body in a human form, one who's feelings of empathy and love for his fellow man is unrivalled—a one-off of natural proportion who wants to promote good will on a universal scale. Today Major Hall is in his *best*, epitomizing what it means to be sharp. Precise in his cut-throat selection of decoration, medals of valor, and purple hearts of bravery are showcased. His uniform is without a speck of lint, or flaw of a wrinkle, his shoes shine and are buffed to a mirrored finish Windex® would envy. The creases in his slacks are so lethal that walking too close may result in laceration. Wearing his best watch, he smells wonderfully masculine. Pheromones of his other worldly level of confidence scent his air with extravagant tones of dominance. Like a 4-star general about to lead his army into the battle that'll decide the war, he stands poised, certain, and prepared for the moment. Seventy two percent recovered from what happened in the storage room the other night, it was never reported. No one beside he and Zarbin know what transpired. When the news reported the slaying, they had no idea he was the escaped hostage. The experience has forever changed him, and one he'll never get over.

News he's been exonerated of all attacks against him, and his suspension over was like a shot of HGH into the arm of the force. Even though he told the chief he quit, he's never been gone. Now their major is officially back! They're whole again. Now the strong arm of the law prepare their force of concentrated and cooperating agencies operating as one regiment of embolden soldiers, bolstered by the return of Major Tusk, Big Man Hall!

There is an unexplainable phenomenon referred to as: "Incorruptible Corpses". *Rita of Cascia* is the most famous of them all. For whatever reason her corpse was neither buried nor covered. It was left to be otherwise, "observed". Though, being well over 1,000 years old, when she is viewed she looks as if she's literally, just died. It has been reported *and* verified that her body actually moves from time to time. There are indisputable times where her face needs to be readjusted, usually it is her eyebrows and eyes, which have a habit of opening.

The 1912 *"Miracle of the Sun"* event. Over 100,000 Portuguesians witnessed an event that was preordained by three farm children. The event began with a dazzling display of solar explosions, before morphing into a spinning wheel, came towards the Earth, and began giving off vibrant colors that had never been seen, producing strange shadows and dark patches over the landscape of shocked onlookers. They feared it was the end of the world, but it was only a misunderstood operation of the universe that man does not cognize.

Man has a bad habit of dismissing things he doesn't understand.

The warrant has been signed, and they're in route to carry it out. It specifically details what they are to look for. Anything not named in the warrant will be deemed inadmissible. Their only purpose is to find evidence of human servitude. Things like cells, cages, torture devices, shackles, dorms, live humans or human remains; incinerators can be checked for DNA. Computers, hard drives, servers, and anything related to GMO research, genetic mutations, sonic wave experimentation, weapons testing, animal cloning, stems cell growth, sterilization by tubal ligation, pregnancy termination, and all sorts of unthinkable things, are off limits, because they're considered legal fields of study. Though located in a rural East Georgia, officials from all over the state are on hand to witness this historic take down. The same plant politicians sold the people on, the same pharmaceutical company promising to bring thousands jobs to the community, the same six hundred acre, two hundred and fifty million dollar hunk of non-biodegradable junk which destroyed the natural habit, sterilizing the surrounding wildlife population for generations; *Zoxter Labs* in Covington, GA., is about to be raided by three hundred law enforcement officers.

The second this hit the air waves, it took off like a Hindenburg destined to explode. When footage of the caravan of blue lights, tactical vehicles, armored SWAT trucks, and an 18-wheeled command center hit the televisions, it was like a fireball of sarin gas, burning the eyes of all who watch; making the O.J. Simpson car chase look like mincemeat. More than one hundred million Americans watch thunderstruck, as helicopters track this bizarre motorcade rolling along the freeway. It's the *"only"* thing to be watching, and has completely taken over the environment. The negative pull emanating from this corpus of bad energy has attracted the minds of millions to such a point, they're completely *stuck* to it. Two opposing forces on a crash course towards one another, the cannon of good vs evil is on exhibition to the world. The drama is so riveting that commercials companies paid millions for, are being placed on hold. The networks can't afford to move the cameras for a second. Behind the stampede of sirens and lights, a caboose of media vans and press vehicles chase like hungry scavengers. By the time the throng of lawmen and law-women get to the property, an astonishing and unheard of, *seven hundred-million* people are watching. The amount of energy being directed towards one man, and one event has altered the earth's gravitational pull. Like the laser beams *HAARP* sends into the skies above Alaska, attempting to change the earth's weather patterns; this event too has changed the climate.

To get to this remote location visitors have to drive down a two lane road, which shrinks the rolling tide into an endless stream of flashing blue which goes for almost three miles. This enormous complex is separated into four heavily gated entrances. The force separates into four teams, stationing themselves at each one. Once everyone's in position, they're going in. But before they just burst inside, they give the property managers the choice to willing open the gates. They aren't dealing with some run-of-the-mill crack house ran by a shit-mass of dumb thugs. This is a publicly traded conglomerate with multi-national locations.

Like a rank of Roman centurions, from inside the plant pours lines of men with security uniforms and hats; booted and armed. Like soldier ants they come out in droves to protect their mound.

The helicopters capture the moment!
Caught by this unexpected surprise, officers below can be seen scrambling for cover!!! Cars and vehicles are repositioning!!! People are yelling at each other to seek cover!!!! They had no intention of encountering a squad of plant security personal! Almost immediately, news anchors begin drawing parallels to the last hostage standoff, and ready themselves for the unthinkable!!
News comes of a vehicle sighting!
A dark colored vehicle with tented windows is approaching from the far side of the compound!!!
The officers have no clue what to expect, but the gate is still closed offering them time to prepare a strategy!
But they don't have to.
A man dressed in a suit gets out and approaches the gate.
Men are yelling for the suit to put his hands in the air and get on the ground!
He disagrees, slides a yellow folder though the gate, and defiantly gets back inside the vehicle, and goes back inside the compound.
Cameras zoom in on the item. From high over the action, the best they could get is verification it's a folder.
From the ranks of officers, a robot clad in a bomb-proof shell retrieves the item, and returns to the rank.

Seconds turn into minutes that feel like eons. Obviously, something has happened, the march has clearly been halted.

Each and every last one of them are sadly mistaken. They must be out of their minds to think a paper, or a judge is going to get them into that facility. They're wrong, and have absolutely no understanding of the magnitude of this operation, and just how many players there are. Fortune 500 companies, and democratically elected governments benefiting from this shit. This is nothing new to them, they're used to attacks, they're used to ridicule, they have billions allocated to fend off the assaults; buttressed by the fact that greed ruins the hearts of men. It's something that can always be used as a means of control. These valiant men and women, and the millions watching, only have a clue of what they're dealing with. If what they're seeing on the surface is enough to send them into rage, the iceberg below is the part that will rupture their hull of reality, separating what's imaginable from what's not.

The 19th century Supreme Court ruling stating it's unconstitutional to force them to leave, is still one the books. When land has been federally sanctioned as an Indian reserve, the residents of this land are not subject to the laws of the United States constitution, or required to abide by the common law ordinary citizens are expected to.
The land this $250,000,000 plant sits on, is Creek Indian land, a federally protected reservation, one that is outside of government jurisdiction, and one that is not bound by the laws of the United States Constitution.

Krolov wins again.

Quatorze.

The day has turned to early evening. A flock of Mallards are amongst the last species of birds to make the migration to warmer climates—the weather and the serenity of the land-scape too much for them to let go. The thriving pond is robust and lively with life; new beginnings flourish in the lush and healthy environment. Its remoteness is like a greenhouse of seclusion, protecting those inside so they can grow strong and independent. Seedlings and shoots wounded by the elements are brought here to heal and repair their damaged leafs, nour-ish their frayed roots back to life so they can be replanted in a new garden, a thicket rich with nutrients; one which will allow them to blossom into the beautiful blooms they were always meant to be. Here, horses run wild and free, eating grass on a range free of whips and stirrups. Sitting atop a hill is a red barn. They can milk cows and use the healing energy of the animals to help restore their souls.

Some find it offensive to step on a rose, so why had he used her for so long, especially when she's one as precious as a Bailey Red? Why had he worked so hard to take away her dignity? How are these people able to do that to so many families and no one not know? How are they able to ruin the lives of so many kids, so many adults, so many victims, so much rape, and so much abuse?

Is it because the world doesn't care?????

Sitting in a rocking chair smelling the fragrance of country air rolling across the hills, this is where she can try to find understanding and forgiveness, allow the natural antidotes of this therapeutic habitat to help her find the peace and strength to move forward. She thinks about how she finally made it to the address, and remembers her mother describing a place with a beautiful arch rising high above the land. She said it's like walking through the gateway of heaven. From all she's been through, through all the nights of tears, through all the days of sorrow, through all the mornings of waking up and wishing she was dead; somehow through it all she was able to hold onto the piece of fabric her mother ripped from her dress. After all these years, all the disgusting men, she was still able to make it to her destination. It took sixteen years, but *finally* she made it. She and her daughter can at last begin a normal life, one free of sex traffickers, sex peddlers, sex addicts, and Afghan mullahs who keep little boys chained to their beds believing:
"Women are made for children, and little boys are made for pleasure."
Her child will have to be neither house servant, nor sex slave.

She won't be treated as a young Devadasi girl in India's wicked and sick caste system, born into life a sex work. She won't be sold off because she's considered inferior to males, and thus a liability; considered an unfavorable form of life. She can begin her introduction to education and bedtime stories, her mother comforted by people who actually care.

This is an extended-living retreat sponsored by the Emma Jones foundation, whose aim is rebuilding the lives human trafficking victims. Here they can live, heal, learn, and rebuild; one of several facilities created by this privately funded "positive energy" organization.

Sitting on a tractor wearing sandals and a sun dress, Cailida Floriano is amazed at how fun it was to roast marshmallows. She's never experienced laughter and smiles, and good food around a warm fire. She enjoys the fact she's with dozens of other women from around the world who share experiences similar to hers. Together, they and the staff dedicate their lives to spreading goodwill, and supporting this community of once forgotten women and children.
There's also facilities for boys and young men. People forget boys as young as 13 months old are being sold on the black market for the sole purpose of causing the child misery.

They too are victims who need our help.

Using the funds of wealthy donors, these sanctuaries and others alike serve as beacons of light, sources of positive energy. Neutral elements too can plug in and become overwhelmed with the good energy, and themselves become a positive element.

Cailida Bailey Floriano is not dead. Her fate was not to die in the parking lot that night, but be the spark which ignites a

blaze of change.
Her beautiful petals are what dazzled a misguided soul and
gave him a purpose. Her thorns are what pierced those who
tried to confine her. The environment punished them for exploiting her resources, attempting to reconstitute her as
fertilizer, and use her seedling to continue the vicious cycle.
Her mother always said she was a beautiful flower.
In Bailey's own words did she foresee that she'll one day be…..
Planted in a new plot, I bring hopes of a new harvest!

Quinze.

Major Hall sits in his car looking out the windshield.
A spider web of frozen sleet and icy rain has turned his
windshield into an opaque pane of fogged glass, sweating
condensation, and frost; the wipers frozen stiff by the weight of
the snow. The traffic on I-285 is also stiff, stiff as a cold brick.
National Weather Center forecasters predicted ice, snow, and
sub-freezing temperatures for the Southeast, and advised city
officials to prepare for a deep freeze with an expectation for one
to four inches of precipitation. Years prior, a similar ice storm
hit the city, shutting Atlanta down for three days. Lessons
learned from that state of emergency would hopefully prepare
them to defend the city in the event it happens again.

Well it did, today, and again they've been caught flat-footed.
The ice, snow, rain and 29° temperature mixed with high winds
has the highway looking like an infinite parking lot; black ice
is everywhere. Cars are slid off the road, and stranded tractor-
trailers are once again jack-knifed. One hundred and twenty
thousand Atlantans are stuck in the grips of another
"Snowmageddon".

Hall was on his way home when he made the mistake of
thinking he could make it before the storm hit. He and other
members of the department developed contingencies plans
in case the snow came. No one expected it to be as bad as last
time, but it is. His radios are buzzing with traffic. Though off,
he's still on. That's the life of a dedicated police officer. Their
oath to protect and to serve didn't say for eight hours a day.
The media's still creaming themselves over what happened in
Mexico, Hall's still thinking about the night at the gas station,
and what happen in the storage space. That night answered all
the questions he wanted to ask the Creator.
While the frigid wind blows relentless, he's in a quiet cocoon
of reflection, now understanding one of the splendors of life,
is that it gives us difficulty, and through the power of faith and
perseverance we become strong, coming closer to deciphering
the encryptions of universe.

Enabling us to see the majesty of the Creator.

Hall fully comprehends how becoming closer to his "true self"
has brought him closer to the environment around him. Yes,
he's still furious Krolov is free and hasn't faced one jury, going
on with his life as if all this was just a bump in the road. His legal offices are still open and still billing millions in fees, money
still rolls into his Swiss account, and he's still trading humans
for gold. Not much has changed in his life. The only thing he
didn't have before which he does now, is a household name.

He's the ultimate street god living legend, one that'll undoubt-edly go down as one of the most notorious figures in world history. His place in the hall of diabolical monsters is secure, his name will truly live on forever.

But Hall hasn't given up the fight. He, Justice Masterson, the DA, the Atlanta Police department, and everyone else are still committed to bringing down this tyrant; now even more than ever. Hall is no quitter. The mentality he holds regarding him is simple: Bring down Krolov or die.

He knows he's the one who sent the men to kidnap him. But he also knows he'll need help. Maybe he's not strong enough at the moment, but when he is, he's coming! He's a wounded dog, and isn't going to stop until he gets his bite!

But like famous samurai, Hattori Hanzō stated: Revenge is never a straight line. It's a forest, and like a forest it's easy to lose your way, to get lost and to forget where you came in.

Hall isn't pleased about Alexander Zarbin, the wanted mass-murderer, being killed either. He isn't excited the international manhunt tracked him to Mexico. He won't tell anyone, but he wished he would've escaped to some far off land and lived a long happy life—unconvinced killing those traf-fickers was a bad thing. He's not so sure he believes the details surrounding it either.

Apparently, while attempting to evade capture, Zarbin crossed into Mexico. It's said he went on a rampage in the small town of Tenancingo, and was somehow able to terminate the forty six man police force that ran the town, including all the top brass. As many as two hundred men were found dead and dismembered throughout the city, and as many as thirty nine houses believed to be brothels and gang hideouts of sex traf-fickers, were burned to the ground. The governor of the town, along with his two sons were murdered in their homes, and their heads left on stakes on the fence surrounding the proper-ty. Hundreds and hundreds of women and girls of all ages were

running the streets after apparently being freed from captivity. A town which has historically been the #1 source for girls trafficked to America, was destroyed in the span of a week.
The report goes on to say, he used the exodus of citizens fleeing the on-going turf war between rival gangs factions, to bring these very same gang members and corrupt officials to their death. While they thought they were killing each other, apparently he was killing them. The report ends with, after slaughtered the gangs and set fire to the city; tries to make it out, but was caught by the Mexican military.

This is where Hall feels things get even stranger.

The details go on to say he somehow made it all the way back to the city and vanished into the ruins. Supposedly, while searching for him, the military encounters the last remaining pockets of gang members and had no choice but to kill each and every last one of them. They said once they'd finished attacking the city with a full scale air assault, they went through the rubble and found the body of Alexander Zarbin. There was also apparently a note containing his last words found with him.

"Let my sacrifice be a blessing for all".

In a closed room located in the back portion of a nearby city, a man sits at his bench. Beside him is the woman he's chosen to share his life with. Together they work at this table of bright light, and as a team they continue to develop mechanisms they hope will promote positive energy. Each day they learn new strategies and try new combinations in hopes of creating the most positive products they can.

He has physical name, and he's a genesis. With an IQ far north of 250, he's now mastered the art of war. After being wrongly accused and forced to spend a decade and a half of his life imprisoned for a crime he didn't commit, he's been forged in the fire. The nature and extreme brutality of the killing has given him national notoriety. When he was found to be innocent and awarded millions from lawsuit settlements, it made him a national celebrity. Using this boost, he fashioned himself into an even wealthier man, and more formidable warrior. Having dedicated his life to goodwill, he's now ready to enter the arena of good vs evil, and hopefully become one of the fiercest fighters in the universe; the positive energy he creates in his lifetime will hopefully last for eons. He and his fellow warriors will use every means possible to become the most ferocious combatants they can.

By any means necessary, will they defend.

Epilogue

To celebrate his new found status in the billionaires club, the freshly minted member decided to do it in a style all his own. Packed with his normal fare of endangered species and vintage blood, Krolov invited a den of his closest demons to his Norwegian castle, where they'll collectively celebrate this momentous occasion. As a clan of negative energies, they enjoy the company of grotesquely mutated animals and underage youth. The sights of a three legged dog with a horse's head and the tail of a snake, engages in acts of bestiality with a well-endowed hermaphrodite minor. Experiments with drugs and serums which produce thirty second orgasms, Hors d'oeuvres of human brain sprinkled with the mummified remains of an

Egyptian cat flavored with sea salt, truffle petals, and toasted frankincense seeds, are being eaten. These are just a few of the things they're entertaining themselves with. Some of the goers brought along their purchased humans. It's chic to own multiple slaves, only the best that money can buy. One of them has a Cameroonian woman who stands 5' 9" with a flawless figure, and looks any world renowned model would envy. Bought for the sum of $2.9 million, she'll only be modeling for one man. While the peaks and valleys of the surrounding mountains and jagged cliffs lay frozen under tons of snow, the temperature inside this remote retreat burns with dragons. Only accessible by helicopter, this bastion sizzles with the fire of destructive forces. The more they can destroy, the hotter their flames burn—they feed off the positive energy they consume.

But for some strange reason, Krolov can't enjoy himself. Despite the plethora of revulsion to choose from, he's overwhelmed with anxiety and feelings of impending doom. He's one of the few members who passed on the hallucinogens, so he knows he isn't having a bad trip. This is real pressure not something imagined. While those around him really enjoy the occasion, he pretends. On a day he achieves the goal he set out for, he's not filled with the joy he was expecting. He drank fine wine, he sipped warm blood, he injected intravenous solutions, but nothing will quell his mood; one that is sneakily turning into paranoia. At a party in a remote fortress like this, people aren't asked to leave. The night turns into day, and day turns back into night until the fun ends on its own.
At a similar past gala, a guest got so high on experimental serums, he decided to offer his dead mother his slave. He strangled the young woman in a room full of people and no one batted an eye. While she lay dead on the floor, the party went on around her.
Whatever's bothering him is starting to drive him mad, and causing him to see odd colors. The walls seem to blend and

convex; frequencies are emitting signals which are throwing his equilibrium off. Thinking it's some kind of omen in the castle, he signals Zeus to get him the hell out of here.

Fifteen minutes later, he and his entourage have slipped away. At the top of a nearby mountain pass is another property, unknown to anyone besides the people there now. This location can accommodate up to ten guests, and is equipped with all the amenities of a 4-star hotel. It sits on the face of a sheer 9,000 ft. cliff. The overlooking veranda can be accessed by both the master, and guest wings, with his suite having a direct route to the secondary, and more breathtaking view; specially fitted with its own private balcony and observation deck. Initially, an 18th century lighthouse used to guide ships into the Norwegian harbor, Krolov purchased it and made it into a vacation home.

So now, he lay quietly in his bed waiting to be whisked off to dreamland. On a heavy concoction of serums, alcohol, narcotics, and anesthesia gases, his eye have grown heavy. Taking this to be his one safe place on the planet, he banished his guards to other parts of the estate, and for the first time in a while is alone; only the resonances of wind howling through the peaks is with him. The blanket of sleep begins enveloping him. The bad mood is gone, and he welcomes the relief of relaxation; his wrinkled penis still erect from the testosterone injection.

The comfort of the polar bears fur is sprinkling him with fairy dust.

HE'S STRUCK BY A FORCE THAT CAUSES HIS EYES TO SHOOT OPEN!!!!!!

HIS HEART BEGINS RACING!!!!!!

Clamp!

His mouth, slammed shut like a catastrophic case of tetanus, shattering his thirty two teeth!!!!!!!!!

No longer able to control his body, every hair on him stands and, becomes molten rods of flesh-burning lasers!!!!!!!!
He tries to scream but is utterly muted and absolutely powerless!
THE ROOM BEGINS TO REVERBERATE AND CONTORT WITH PAINFUL BURSTS, RENDERING HIM DEAF, AND REMOVING HIS ABILITY TO BREATHE!!!!!!!!!
The weight of terror lays on him with the force of a million metric tons! A great tsunami of heat comes over him like a point break of fire and brimstone, sending him into a cold sweat of total destruction!!!!!!!!!
Held down by the merciless under toe of suffocation, he can feel himself dragged off the bed, and mercilessly jackhammered off the floor until the fluids in his body seep from every orifice!!!!!
Ominous shadows come out of the walls and floor!!!!!!!!
HIS EYES BECOME TO SIZE OF BLOODSHOT PING-PONG BALLS WHEN HE SEES A 25FT. TALL BEING WITH WINGS MATERIALIZE OUT THE CORNER!!!!!!!!
Everything goes black! His gift of sight taken! *Now all he can feel is the excruciation of something being pulled out of him!!!!!!!*
He can feel beings moving around him, and the gale force winds of their movement!!!!!! He feels himself stood to his feet!!!!!
HE BELTS OUT A MUTED SCREAM!!!!
INTERNAL FITS OF TORMENT BEAT HIM TO A PULP!!!! His ankles break into right and left angles pointing inward!!!!! Unable to open his mouth or make a sound, he feels the burn in his throat, and the pain in his abdomen, as he cries out in inner agony!!!!! Whatever's attacking him has taken away his ability to shed tears, leaving no floodgate for him to release the pain! With the force of a hydraulic piston, his legs are snapped at the knees and buckled, as the might of the great unseen power-slams him down, embedding his face into the floor, shattering every bone!!!!!!!!!

He thinks he's experiencing the worst nightmare of his life and fights to wake up!
As the weight of ten planets force him on his chest, separating his rib like a hideous rack of lamb!!!!!
HE CALLS FOR THE GOD HE NEVER BELIEVED IN!!!!
As his arms are bent backwards, broken at the elbows, and impaled into his back!!!!!!!!
HE BEGS THE CREATOR HE THOUGHT HE COULD COMPETE WITH, TO HAVE MERCY ON HIS SOUL!!!!!
But is only blessed with the trauma of something ripping threw his shoulder, and grabbing his spinal cord!!!!!!!
As if they were blown away by the might of 20 hurricanes, the doors leading to the private Terrace disintegrate, and suck him into an infinite void of energy moving around him at speed!!!!! A blood moon rises from the sea, while the coast roars with tidal waves!!!!!
Not dead in the least, paralyzed, but very much aware, the armed guards down the hall hear nothing but silence.
Feeling himself turned into the form of a disfigured folding chair, rolled into a gruesome shape, and dragged across the rough asphalt!!!!!! He feels his eyes, cheeks, and jaws sandpapered to the bone!!!!!
The being holding him by the spine lets him go!!!!!!!!
HE CAN SEE AGAIN, HOVERING OVER THE 9,000FT. CLIFF WITH HIS ARMS STICKING OUT OF HIS CHEST!!!!!!
The angel from before appears, but this time all-encompassing, and so enormous, the being blocks out the moon and entire Norwegian coast!!!!!!! Behind it Krolov can hear the crashing of the tsunamis, the roars of earthquakes, and the melting radiation of intergalactic shifts—the sky is filled with red dwarfs, entire constellations of stars are moving around him!!!!!
His skin begins bearing witness against him, telling this being all the things he's done in his time on earth: those positive,

those neutral, and those negative!
In the seconds it takes for his 74 years of deeds to be reeled off, his skin removes itself from his body, and dissociates itself with him!!!!!!
His muscles separate from his bones, reform as a complete body, and denounce his entire existence!!!!
His organs looking to regain some sense of positive energy, fall out of his body pleading this being to spare them, and melt into the valley below!!!!!

As only a pulverized skeleton, he's dropped to the ground left to be calcified by the elements; reconstituted into a usable carbon gas—redistributed, and used by cells to birth new life.

The End...

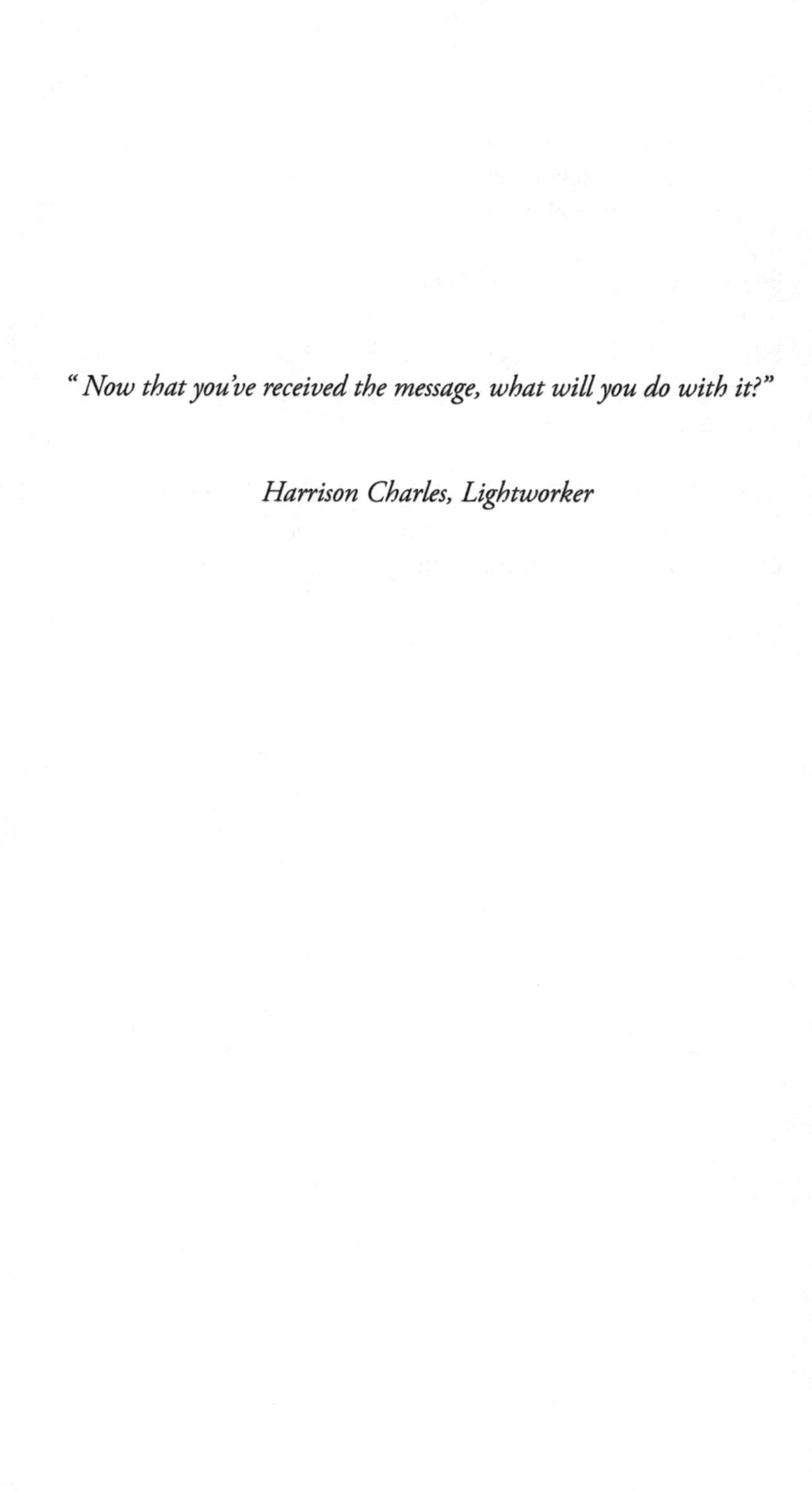

" Now that you've received the message, what will you do with it?"

Harrison Charles, Lightworker

COMING

OF

THE

HOUR

Harrison Charles

Second Edition

Prologue

"You think they knew he was doing this all along?"
"They always know, he was insulated by the cloth. The ranks of evil have swollen exponentially until the world is now rife with their kind—eradication is the only means of establishing an equilibrium."
A misty sheen agglutinates the air with dense condensation, meandering trials of dew trickle down the window's pane.
A cautious survey of the area reveals two playful youths engaged in a two-wheeled duel across the paved lot; obviously enjoying the muggy weather. Thus far, it's been the wettest month in Atlanta on record.
When will the time come when she'll be able to conceive? Maybe a

new baby will rekindle their happiness, reckons the co-conspirator. "The fucker uses all these degrees and scriptures to hide behind," staring at the many plaques and awards atop the fireplace's mantle.

In his free hand is a micro-cassette recorder. And despite being paused at the moment, the preceding lengthy session has just about drained the batteries.

"Telling from this photo, it looks like he used to be a coach or something as well. I'm ready to resume our work, I hate pigs like these. The only problem I have with Robin Hood is that he didn't have the guts to kill the sheriff. As the old adage goes: Never do minor damage to a major enemy."

And picking up the video camera says: "Always be conscious of our mission, focus on what you're doing. Take no mercy when enacting retribution."

"I won't. I'm quite ready to finish him off."

"Just follow my lead. Don't be so eager to attempt something, even if you have experience with it. Mistakes happen when confidence runs amuck. Now hold this while I look for something."

Passing his cohort the camcorder, he searches under the sink.

Exhausted whimpers are coming from somewhere in the sprawling loft.

After a final look out of the window, and another glance at his wristwatch, the two vigilantes are ready to continue.

"Let the defrocking resume."

SLAM!

Goes the cabinet.

Five short steps and the door opens with a creak. In the center of the floor sits a naked man bound to a chair; a ceramic sculpture of the Apostle Paul lay shattered on the floor. The bookcase of religious texts is turned on its side, and from his neck hangs a stained glass rosary—the congealing words: '*False Prophet*' etched into his chest. Although the room is in shambles and reeks of sweat, the windows are covered and tightly shut; the adjoining patio's blinds drawn and dusty.

He steps forward and glares at the wannabe evangelist; disgusted by what he did to that innocent boy's. Today he'll be recompensed for his repulsive transgressions.

"State your name for the audience," holding the vintage voice recorder to the man's lipless, herpetic mouth.

His companion powers on the camera's light, training it on his mug.

And he presses the play button: a robust concerto piece.

"J-Joseph," he managed to say. *"Joseph Tangier,"* lips trembling from the uncertainty of what's next to come.

"What do you do for a living Mr. Tangier?"

Sobbing.

"Say it!..All of it!"

"....I'm a placement advocate with family and children services," he admitted sadly.

"And?"

"….I pastor a church."

The captor extracts a picture and shows it to him.

"Now you know what this is for. How much have you profited from exploiting children you were supposed to help?"

Shame won't allow him to respond. All he can do is hang his head and cry.

"Remember them!"

He reaches for the electric iron and places it against his bare chest; the microphone vividly capturing his pain and agony—part of his velvet pulpit robe stuffed in his mouth.

Scattered around his feet like cigarette butts; charred wicks of twisted Bible were ignited and used to sear him.

The swath of cloth does little to dampen his screams, as his eyes roll backwards, and his teeth clenches the expensive fabric.

The captor removes the iron, and details his work into the device; wanting the authorities to have a clear picture into his suffering. In his quest not to omit the smallest detail, he places the machine to his mouth, and notifies the listeners:

"No one is exempt from accountability."

In the final act, a revolver ends the pedophile's life.
The recording session is over.

All that remains is Mozart's genius, the playing children's laughter, and the calm breathing of the murderous composer—what an exhilarating performance.
He ejects the cassette, and drops it on the floor.

Chapter 1

Stockton pounds on the slab of lumber!

"What took you so damn long?" is the greeting he gives her as she holds the door.

"Don't start Stow! I'm not in the mood for it today! Is there one day when you're not mad at the freaking world," she replied.

"Working at that prison is making you crazy."

"It's not the job that's making me crazy," he hinted.

Kathy decides against saying anything else, having experienced too many times what that leads to.

"One of those inmates stole my fucking keys, probably waiting till they make parole so they can come steal all our shit."

"I doubt it."

"You always think stuff can't happen to you."

The de-facto twosome live in a newly gentrified neighborhood in the historic Summer Hill section of Atlanta. The house is a small, three bedroom structure in a neighborhood occupied by other small three bedroom ones. The home's generous furnishings remains in top condition thanks to them both, but mainly Kathy. The kitchen is fitted with an array of high end appliances, as is the rest of the home.

Stockton goes straight to the living room, flops down on the recliner, and grabs the remote.

"You don't think you're overreacting Stow? There just some keys. You'll probably find them tomorrow, I bet someone's already found them."

He ignores her and flips to the evening news.

She gives up on conversation and returns to searching the pantry.

Stockton Billings, Kathy met him ten years ago, back when he was the missing ingredient. He was affectionate, hardworking, barrel chested and devilishly handsome. He was the perfect catch. But just not for her. He made every attempt at sweeping her off her feet just as she was healing from a nervous breakdown. He footed the $150 an hour bill for her countless therapy sessions, despite never knowing what happened. Whatever it was almost pushed her over the brink. During this time, he fell madly in love with her, but could always sense she never let go of the past. She repeatedly explained that she cared deeply about their friendship, but just wasn't ready for another shot at love. He insisted that he could *make* her better, and after enduring years of repeated proposals, she reluctantly accepted—well sort of. By doing so, she thought it would help her forget about the past. But the past traumatized her entire soul. So for almost the last decade, she's been playing house with a man she knows she'll never love. She doesn't love Stockton, and he knows it. Despite treating him kindly, deep down sits the stark reality that she's in love with something, or someone else. However, he's unwilling to move on, and continues living with the notion that, he and time can make her better.

"Anything you want from the store?" she asked.

"Nothing in particular."

"Okay, I'm gone."

"Bye."

She opens the door.

Bright sun ray stream in, warming the foyer with light.

Turning she says: "Cheer up. They're only keys."

Making for her modest Camry, Mr. Vickers waves from across the street, wishing he was eons younger so he could request her hand in marriage. It isn't hard to see why Stockton has such a hard time ungluing himself from Kathy. At thirty-two years of age, and 5'9" with brunette hair, the old war vet thinks she's the goddess of his dreams.

But what he's not aware of, is that she's gone to tremendous lengths to keep her past hidden from him, and anyone else wants to get to *know* her.

A selfish thing indeed she thought, situating her designer shades in the rear-view, and backing out the driveway.

Fair or not, no one can ever learn the truth about the enigmatic Kathy Billings.

News Flash

In an effort to stem the skyrocketing murder rate—including new legislation on violent crime, while in the face of wide spread criticism from human rights groups: The state of Georgia has ceased the use of death by lethal injection, in favor of death by electrocution.

The raucous effect of dozens of doors simultaneously opening, and the guard's voice echoing throughout the cell house, he's rescued him from his daze.

"Count tiiiiiiime!!" repeated the shouting behemoth, as if the inmates don't already know the annoyingly repetitive procedure; they've been performing the exercise four times a day for years. Many welcome the thought of it all coming to an end. This is Georgia's infamous death row unit, where the condemned rot before being strapped in "Old Sparky's" lap. The fog of hopelessness and despair hangs so thick, that one would think it's being pumped through the ventilation system.

"Parson!" said officer Harry Fawell, standing outside of his cell holding a clipboard.

Dressed in the traditional sky blue button down, and gray polyester slacks that all Department of Corrections officers wear, his face is tanned and weathered with deep stress lines, permanent bags are under his eyes, and an unkempt gray nest perches atop his head—effects of working death row for twenty eight long years.

"Still here, same as yesterday," replied Parson.

Harry's a good guy among the seventy one men awaiting their turn to repay society for their crimes. But he's violated the cardinal rule: Never become friends with the inmates.

Having lost his only son to malevolent prosecutors in Texas, he doesn't think they're all scum.

Douglas Parson, EF#-8071613, returns to his thoughts as the rusty bars slide shut. He's played the tape in his head thousands of times, even has transcripts of it. First hearing it eleven years ago when the district attorney played it, he'll never forget how it brought the jury to tears, and made him the most hated man in the state—convicting him of the murder of highly esteemed bishop, Joseph Tangier.

"Fuck it," and rises from his mattress.

Only to be greeted with a look of contempt from the person staring back in the mirror.

He scans the cell.

His heart rate quickens!

"Talking to yourself again," came a husky voice from next door.

"I look like hell."

Visitation is in two minutes.

"And you smell like it too," joked his neighbor.

"Parson! Visitation!"

A reverberating call over the PA system.

Avoiding eye contact with the mirror, he hurriedly combs his hair, grabs his prison I.D. card, and waits at the bars.

The old pulley system slowly turns the sprockets, and the dusty chains pull the door back.

Clank.

Clank.

Clank.

Until it's halfway open.

He squeezes through the remaining space, and exits the cell.

Walking down the tier, he looks into eyes similar to the ones he encountered moments ago. Not wanting to look so many hopeless faces, he lowers his gaze and focuses on the often-buffed floor.
SPLASH!
The warm mixture collides with his skin!
Considering the empty cup rolling around on the floor, and the wetness seeping down his face; the unmistakable stench of urine and feces is evident.
Gus "Sheephead" Beasley, the man who raped and killed eight women in one day, doused him as he passed his cell.
"Awwww shit! You motherfucker!!"
"BwaaaaaaHahahahaaaa!Hahahah! Wooooooooooweeee!!" he bellowed. "Yo ole' lady gone luvta see yo' perdy lil' shit covered face!" Displaying his badly decayed, and missing teeth.
Parson spits in his face, and tries to punch him through the bars.
Harry yanks him around the corner.
Sheephead shouts obscenities, as he ushers him away.
"Bring dat bitch back! I wanna fuckeem!"
"Let it go. There's nothing you can do," Harry advised. "Just wash it off, and go see your people."
Breathing angrily, he goes into the supply room and refreshes.

Stockton hasn't moved muscle, not as much as batted an eye since Kathy has made the thirty minute trek to her favorite store. "I hope they have the nerve to use those keys," speaking through clenched teeth.

"Be my guest," and strokes the .44 Magnum®.

He retrieves the remote from the hidden compartment and starts flipping. Coming upon a documentary about a dead musician, he presses a button in the vicinity of the cup holder.

The chair hums to life, adjusting to a reclined position.

Now with his feet elevated, he unbuckles his leather belt.

Thunk!

His pride and joy meets the carpet.

The program's narrator speaks mightily from the surround sound system. Mixed with this, and the comfort of his $1,100 chair, he succumbs to a much needed nap.

Stockton Billings, a Georgia native, born thirty five years ago to Lewis and Ibsen Billings—the only child they managed to produce throughout their on again-off again marriage. His mother was a sweet and caring woman by nature. But repeated blows from Lewis' right hand had hardened her heart; placing a strain on their relationship. In her pursuit of a better life, Ibsen would frequently leave, taking little Stockton with her. But as luck would have it, she never found it. Each time she left, she'd shortly return. And each time Lewis would greet her with open arms and false promises; each time becoming increasingly violent.

Dependent, depressed, trapped and abused was part of her plight —discernment wasn't. She knew exactly what she wanted. Problem was, she didn't know how to get it: love. Unadulterated, unequivocal, and everlasting, a never ending cascade of bliss and companionship; not emotional carnage. Her soul had been massacred, her heart trampled upon like dirt at a horse racing track. Nevertheless, she continued to patiently wait for fate to release the valve on her stream of tranquility. Sadly for Ibsen that never happened. She never discovered the happiness she yearned for, only sank deeper into despair. That was up until a debilitating disease took her life at forty three, five months after being diagnosed with ovarian cancer. Stockton was left with only fond memories from the twelve years he'd known his her, and the uncertain future he now faced with his father. It didn't take long for him to see just how worthless and sorry he really was—the kind of person that made you wonder what purpose they served. He would've been more useful as manure dropping from a donkey's ass; at least that way he would've helped grass grow. The only effort his good for nothing father put forth was cash the monthly check he received from his wife's annuity.

On the other hand, Stockton worked all sorts of menial jobs—when there were no laws to limit the time, or scope of labor a minor could perform.

Until the winds of change blew the ominous cloud hovering over his life away, he busted his tail. Every pair of pants he wore, every shirt he'd washed, and every pair of sneakers he muddied, he bought. Four and a half years after his mother's death, he was adopted by the proprietor of the farm he worked on; his boss was now his father—a better situation for everyone. Sharing chores with his new brother Alex was nothing strenuous, basic stuff, normal things kids do. Despite having things better than he ever had, he felt out of place. Waking up to breakfast was foreign to him; he shied away from things like that. Taking hot baths, being hugged, and playing baseball was odd. He had a hard time adjusting to coming home from school and not having to toil till nightfall.

But in time, he transformed back into a regular boy, and started enjoying life. Unfortunately, his heart never changed towards his father, but became as hard as a billiard ball.

One evening, after his seventeenth birthday, and exactly one day before the anniversary of his mother's death, Lewis Billings was found stabbed to death in the parking lot of a bar. According to legend, he smarted off to a patron earlier that day, and the guy supposedly came back and ambushed him. However, none of this was ever proven, and the culprit was never caught. The case was marginally investigated and quickly forgotten—fine by

Stockton and everyone else who regrettably knew Lewis Billings. Someone had done the town of Rex a great service. Whoever it was will always be remembered as the unsung hero of that town.

Moving away and joining the Atlanta Police Department proved to be a step in the right direction. At twenty one, he was the youngest person to be accepted to the academy. After eighteen weeks of training he graduated at the top of his class, and quickly climbed the ladder. Without the usual antics employed by others in their quest for advancement, he accomplished his by being good at what he did; a natural, he had a knack for leadership. This caught the attention of his superiors, and he was quickly promoted, much to the dismay of everyone else. Long gone were the days of being just another uniform. He now had a title: Sergeant Billings—a force to be reckoned with.

The department erupted; many resigned, refusing to work under someone so inexperienced. His twenty five years of age too much for them to handle. They'd been brown nosing their entire careers, and yet to be rewarded.

They eventually they got their wish. Internal Affairs tarnished him with allegations of police brutality, and prostitute rapes. His demise drew rave reviews from his peers, and left him with no choice but to resign. Whispers of a frame job ensued, but there was no evidence to support it.

Unable to land a job with a different department, he was forced into the penal system. Reluctantly, he accepted a position at the Atlanta Federal Penitentiary, badly wanting revenge on the A.P.D., especially that conniving bitch who spearheaded the investigation. He'd done none of the things they'd accused him of. He was indeed the victim of a strategic set-up.

Along came Kathy Easterbrook, and she changed everything.

Stockton awakens to the mating rituals of the African Elephant, the camera man thorough in capturing every intimate detail.

He rubs his eyes to be sure he's seeing clearly.

There seems to be a fifth leg hanging from the mammal's underbelly. Then he sees it's the animal's gigantic member.

A glance at his wrist tells him it's 5:45 in the afternoon, prompting him to lift off the chair, yawning as he walks to the kitchen.

After grabbing a beer from the fridge, he stands at the sink gulping while watching kids play basketball in the street.

How many times did he get that opportunity.

However, he finds it easy to recall how many times his father was sober.

He takes another gulp, but pours it out when he pictures his sperm donor doing the same thing.

"Dipshit."

Now it's about her, about how distraught she was during their early years. If it wasn't for him, she'd be a basket case by now. She swears the reason she can never tell him what transpired is because the ordeal caused her to lose parts of her memory, and what she can remember is much too painful to speak on. Her psychiatrist recommended that he not try to jar her memory, fearing it may cause further damage. Whatever happened, her brain removed recollection of it.

But Stockton has secrets too, a past he's also gone to great lengths to conceal.

His heart flutters at the sight of his reflection on the glass.

The death row visitation area is a ghost town. Not many people care to once labeled a diabolical monster; the occasional letter is a miracle. Once found guilty of having committed some heinous act, erasure from memory is the usual result. Somehow Parson has beaten the odds, even staff members are perplexed.

In the third seat on the opposite side of a three inch slab of Plexiglas®, sits a striking blonde. Her eyes glisten like blue sapphires in a kaleidoscope, she possesses perfectly symmetrical features, and impeccable skin. Wearing a hound's-tooth pantsuit and crimson heels, she makes his heart sink; truly a sight for sore eyes. Much too gorgeous to be wasting her time visiting a condemned man.

"Hi baby."

"It's a pleasure to see you again," he speaks into the black phone.

"The pleasure's all mine. Stand up and let me see you."

He stands up.

The 4 ½ ft. wall below the glass makes it impossible to see anything below the chest while sitting down.

Two years ago, a man received a visit from a pastor who brought along his elderly wife. While they engaged in prayer, the prisoner decided to partake in a quick masturbation session. The misses opens her eyes to see veins popping out of his head, and him geyser all over himself.

She fainted.

Determined to thwart future occurrences, the warden had the wall installed the following day.

"You just saw me last week," his teeth as white as hers.

"I know."

Getting right to business, she grabs the briefcase and removes a thick folder, which produces dozens of photos of different people. None of them knew they were being photographed. She takes one labeled *#1*, and places it against the glass—fingers along and elegant, nails freshly manicured.

"This is her."

Using an index card, she shorthands the name, address, and occupation of the woman.

Knowing their every word is being recorded, they say as little as possible into the phones, and instead employ code words, and advanced sign language. At even this very moment they're being eavesdropped on. The four correctional officers stationed at opposite ends of the long room are supposed to be there to ensure no prohibited acts are performed. But the real reason are as spies for Warden Stuckey; he's highly suspicious of their activities. The fact that she's been coming to see a condemned man every week for the past decade isn't normal. Each time she comes, she always has some kind of information, and always carries that briefcase—never coming empty handed. Stuckey has yet to discover what all the hushed meetings are about, but vows to find out what. Douglas Parson is very peculiar, doesn't talk much, always reading something, and always studying. He's not interested in what's going on inside the prison, but is good friends with inmate Matthew Grainger. Maybe it's because they're part of death row's elite. Both have been convicted of brutal crimes, and both deemed psychopaths by the same noted psychologist. From day one the investigators adamantly believed Parson had an accomplice when he tortured and killed Joseph Tangier. They also said it's quite possible that it could've been a female. Blonde hair follicles not matching his, or the victims were recovered from the scene, including other tell-tell signs of feminine involvement.

"How'd you come up with her?"

She smiles.

"I think she can be a great asset to our cause. I spoke with her and she's willing, in direct accordance with all of our ideas," her manicured hand shooting off fluent sign at blazing speed.

With a crooked brow he studies the photo.

"I don't know. Are you sure?" his sign equally fast.

"Positive."

"Who's the others?" he asked, nodding at the stack face down on the cold steel table.

On one photo is a man wearing an expensive suit standing between a man and a woman with his arms draped over their shoulders. The man on the left looks to be in his mid-forties, and wears blue overalls and a straw hat. The woman about the same age wears a yellow paisley sun dress and brown moccasins. All three are smiling.

"This is the couple I told you about. The man in the middle is…"

She picks up an index card and shorthands the name.

"How much does he want? I'm sure he's not doing it out the kindness of his heart."

"Nothing, as long as I come up with something new, stuff he can use."

"What do we have that's new?"

"Not much at the moment, but I'm working on it. Have I ever let you down?"

He shakes his head no.

Parson knows she loves him immensely; would even go through hell and back for him—even climb Kilimanjaro barefoot if she had to.

But….

The question is for how long? How long will it be before she wakes up and realizes what she's doing? The situation would've already crushed him had it not been for her steadfast devotion.

The puzzle slowly seems to be coming together.

But will it be too late?

It can happen as long as he keeps her on his team.

"Just believe in me like I believe in you. I know this is going to happen for us. No one, or no *thing* will compromise our mission," sounding very sure of herself.

She stares into Parson's piercing eyes, thinking of how much she loves him, how much she's infatuated with him, and how much she lusts for him. How long has been since she's made love? How long will she wait?

Forever.

What had they done wrong? What could they had done different? If only they could get a second chance. Someone's going to pay dearly for what they've done to them, even if it means paying with their life. She taken a vow to avenge the demise of Douglas Parson and Christine Chase.

A lone tear falls from her eye.

"I hate this happened to us," her glossed lips beginning to quiver.

"You gotta stay strong.….How are you doing out there?"

"I'm doing all right I guess, just concentrating on doing my part, trying to make sure everything goes to plan," while shuffling through the folder to remove a document.

He reads it while she holds it against the glass, nodding his approval; they don't care who sees this.

"Make sure she doesn't change her mind."

"She won't, I'm very persuasive," replying with a mischievous grin.

"You become more beautiful with time."

"And still all yours....Last photo," she said. "I know this isn't exactly what you wanted me to get," holding it up. "But I feel a bit more comfortable with this one."

Parson examines what he sees, confident she'll be able to handle it.

"The rest of these are just these are just shots of the same things. I took different angles so you can get the full view."

She lets him see them all, closes the manila folder, and places it back inside her briefcase, locking it with a click.

With her elbows resting on the counter, and her face cradled in her hands, she smiles with those sensuous lips.

"So, how did I do?"

"Splendid. We'll shock the world."

They spend the reminder of the time in idle conversation, all of which they speak through the phones, until one of the guards signals the two minute warning. They say their goodbyes, and she stands to leave.

"You think I should've gone with the semi-auto?"

"No. What you're comfortable with is always the right choice."

Waving goodbye she blows him a kiss, and vanishes as quickly as she appeared.

"She'll do fine."

The spies shackle him for the long walk back to death row.